It's Only a Movie... Isn't It?

The Fact & Fiction Behind 'True Stories' On The Big Screen

It's Only a Movie...
Isn't It?

The Fact & Fiction Behind 'True Stories'
On The Big Screen

Jason Day

Copyright © 2009 by Jason Day

The right of Jason Day to be identified as the Author of the Work has been asserted by them in accordance with the Copyright, Designs and Patents Act 1988.

ISBN: 978-1-4457-5737-7

First Published in 2010 By:
Phantom Encounters Publishing.
3 Shortridge Court
Witham, Essex CM8 1ET
United Kingdom

All rights reserved. No part of this publication may be reproduced, stored in a retrieval system or transmitted, in any form or by any means without the prior written permission of the publisher, nor be otherwise circulated in any form of binding or cover other than that in which it is published and without a similar condition being imposed on the subsequent purchaser.

Dedication

This book is dedicated to Kelly Day, the love of my life. You are a true friend of the paranormal who asks for nothing and gives so much. You ask for no fame or fortune and I am all the richer for having you by my side. You are very much appreciated and loved by all who know you.

This book is also dedicated to:

All the believers & sceptics - keep searching for the truth!
All the movie goers out there – keep putting your butts on seats!

Acknowledgements

There are a great many people I would like to thank for making this book possible.

To my family: Kelly, Tanzie, Steve, Kristina, Declan, Leonne-Jay, Simon, Alison, Tomas, Sophie, Jack, Tony, Sharon, Aaron, Sean Jnr, Gary, Sarah, Sonya, Martin, Kyle, Nene and Bob - thanks guys, the belief you had in me has seen me through.

Mum, Dad, Sean and Matty - thanks for watching over me, the inspiration you have given from up above has kept me going.

This one's for all of you!

To my friends in the Paranormal: James Randi, Neil Arnold, Alexandra Holzer, Jason Karl, Mike Hallowell, Lara Wells, Darren Ritson, Mark Webb, Phil Whyman, Barrie John, Bill Bean, John Zaffis, Brad Steiger, Nick Redfern, Jeff Wamsley, Phil Mantle, Dan Shephard, Mela Giorgio, Ray Jorden, Matthew Coles, The Dibbers lot (including 'Lazy Student' and 'Stick Head'), Tara Edge & Millicent Tirk.

You guys helped keep me going and had the belief in me when I needed your support. You gave me the gift of your time and shared your knowledge and expertise in the field of the paranormal too.
I really cannot thank you enough.

Special thanks to:
- Allison Jordan (Former Editor of Paranormal Magazine): Thank you for having the belief in my ability and the grace to use the platform you created to share my work on the Paranormal with the world.

- Lee and Chrissy Hamman (Pulse Paranormal Radio): Thank you for giving me the opportunity to put a voice to the name behind my written work and to share my views, both good and bad, with the listeners. I wish you both, and indeed Pulse, all the very best in the future.

- Steve Younis and Dr Malcolm Gaskill: Thank you for sharing your expert opinions. I am eternally grateful to you both for sharing your vast knowledge in the history of your chosen fields of work with me.

I would also like to thank Peter Underwood, Hans Holzer, Maurice Grosse, Guy Lyon Playfair, James Randi, Tony Cornell, John and Anne Spencer, Jenny Randles, Colin Wilson, Ed and Lorraine Warren, Harry Price, Houdini, Sir Arthur Conan Doyle, The Society for Psychical Research and The Ghost Club. You are the real forefathers of paranormal research and my inspiration for entering the field itself. If one day I can look back and have made even a fifth of the contribution to the Paranormal that you have I will be happy. Thank you all for your tireless work both past and present, you truly are heroes.

Of course a huge thank you to my publisher, I hope your faith in me has been rewarded.

Contents

Introduction	11
The Experts	13
Curse Or Coincidence?	15
The Curse Of Superman (1948-2006) - Super Curse	16
Rebel Without A Cause (1955) - Rebel Without a Curse?	23
The Exorcist (1973) – The Devil's Retribution	38
The Omen (1976) – The Mark Of The Beast	47
The Curse Of The Poltergeist (1982 – 1986) - 'They're Still He-eere!'	54
Out Of This World?	61
The Bermuda Triangle (1979) - From All Angles	62
The Philadelphia Experiment (1984) – The Vanishing Ship	79
Fire In The Sky (1993) – The Travis Walton Abduction	95
Alien Autopsy (2006) - Is There Any Body Out There?	104
Hauntings Or Hoaxes?	121
The Amityville Horror (1979) – The Defeo Murders And The Lutz Haunting	122
The Entity (1982) – The Carla Moran Case	136
The Haunted (1991) – The Smurl Haunting	144
Exorcism Of Emily Rose (2005) – The Possession Of Annelise Michel	154

An American Haunting (2006) – The Bell Witch Haunting	163
1408 (2007) – The Haunting Of The Hotel Del Coranado	173

History or Legend? **184**

Witchfinder General (1968) – Matthew Hopkins	185
Countess Dracula (1970) – Elizabeth Bathory	193
The Curse Of King Tut's Tomb (2006) - King Tutankhamun	201

Reality Or Myth? **216**

Fairy Tale: A True Story (1997) – The Cottingley Fairies	217
The Brotherhood Of The Wolf (2001) – The Beast Of Gevaudan	227
The Mothman Prophecies (2002) – The Legend Of The Mothman	239
The Untold (2002) – The Search For Bigfoot	251
Mee-Shee: The Water Giant (2005) - The Quest For The Ogopogo	270

Sources	**285**
About The Author	**289**

Introduction

There is nothing like a good old fashioned horror movie to get you biting your nails and sat on the edge of your seat…or behind it.
As an avid fan of this genre I have spent many an hour in front of both the big screen, and the small one, watching just about anything and everything horror related. I grew up on a staple diet of 'Hammer' and 'Amicus' studio movies and I still believe they were the greatest horror movies ever made to this day.

However, the movies that always intrigued me most were the ones that began with 'Based on a true story' in their opening credits. I would always come away from those films even more scared than usual. I'd come away thinking, if these things could really happen to somebody else then they could happen to anybody… even me!

As I reached adulthood my enthusiasm for horror movies had taken me even further into the paranormal realm. I became a paranormal researcher, investigator, broadcaster and writer specialising in the subject. Then, one day an event occurred that inspired me to combine all of my skills and passions, those being; research, writing, movies and the paranormal.

I had just finished watching 'The Amityville Horror' (for the 'millionth' time), the original version that is. To me you can't beat the original version of any movie, (to remake something like 'The Omen' or 'The Amityville Horror' is tantamount to sacrilege in my eyes, but I digress). Anyway, as I ejected the DVD from the player and put it back into its case, a thought occurred to me. I began to wonder just how close to the 'true story' the movie had been. Sure, it claimed to be based on the real story, but I had just watched the 'Hollywood' version. How much of what I had seen really happened and how much was 'embellished'?

I decided to find out.

As I researched the subject I found that the 'true' story behind the movie was in question itself. I discovered that there were people that believed that the events the film was based on may not have happened as they had been reported. Even more interesting was the fact that some people believe that the events may not have even happened at all. Who knows? The 'true story' may not have even been 'true' in the first place!

Once I had looked into this case I began researching even more of them. My original aim had been to compare the movies to the stories they were based on. Now I found that I had inadvertently taken this one step further. I had gone on to research the stories to the extent that I could now compare all the evidence/theories from them and try to get to the bottom of what really happened.

So it was with this in mind that that I enlisted the help of several experts in their fields and wrote this book. I didn't want the 'Hollywood' versions of these 'true' stories to become the historical reference for the viewer. I suppose I just wanted to present them with all the facts, so they could take a balanced view on what they have seen and make up their own minds as to what really happened, and how close the movies come to portraying this.

Whatever you decide to believe just remember one thing.

The next time you turn on the television, put on a DVD, or even feel brave enough to venture out to the cinema to see a scary movie. Just tell yourself:

"It's only a movie... isn't it?"

The Experts

Neil Arnold — Cryptozoologist, Paranormal Researcher and Author

Bill Bean — Author, Survivor of a Haunting, Lecturer

Dr Malcolm Gaskill — Reader in Early Modern History at the University of East Anglia, Historian and Author.

Alexandra Holzer — Paranormalist, Columnist, Broadcaster and Author

Mike Hallowell — Cryptozoologist, Paranormal Investigator and Author.

Barrie John — International Medium and Paranormal Investigator.

Jason Karl — Paranormal Investigator, Presenter, Actor and Author.

Philip Mantle — Author, lecturer, broadcaster & UFO researcher

James Randi — Investigator of Paranormal and Pseudoscientific claims, Magician, Escape Artist, Founder of the James Randi Educational Foundation and Author.

Nick Redfern — Journalist, Ufologist, Cryptozoologist and Author

Darren W Ritson — Ghost Hunter, Paranormal Investigator and Author.

Brad Steiger　　　　Author and Paranormal Researcher.

Jeff Wamsley　　　　Director of the Mothman Museum and author.

Lara Wells　　　　　Medium, Columnist and Lecturer

Mark Webb　　　　　Paranormal Investigator

Phil Whyman　　　　Paranormal Investigator, Researcher and Author

Steve Younis　　　　Superman Historian and Owner/Editor-In-Chief of the Superman Homepage

John Zaffis　　　　　Paranormal Researcher, Demonologist and Author.

Curse Or Coincidence?

Over the years, many a movie has been said to be the victim of a 'curse'. The events surrounding these films were often more bizarre then the plots of the actual movies themselves. Film sets plagued by freak accidents, unexplained occurrences, and even cast, crew, and those indirectly involved with the movie, meeting mysterious and sometimes tragic ends.

The 'cursed' movie has been the subject of many a discussion. There are those that believe something or somebody was responsible for the incidents surrounding these productions. There are others who believe that the movies weren't cursed at all, and that the incidents were in fact 'stories' leaked to the press and public to engineer maximum publicity. The debates continue, as does the making of movies and every so often, another 'cursed' movie comes along.

What were the tragedies surrounding these movies?

What may have provoked these incidents?

Were they really cursed or was it all just coincidence?

The Curse of Superman (1948-2006)

Super Curse

It is not unknown for tragedy to strike a production in the world of film and television. It has even been known, on occasion, for a production to be beset by so many mishaps, accidents and tragedies that it has been said to have been 'cursed'. So surely when a whole franchise has been plagued by bad luck since the moment of its conception this could be deemed as a 'Super Curse'. So it would seem most apt that the comic book, television and movie superhero 'Superman' should be the franchise that appears to have befallen this fate.

From his first appearance on screen in 1948 to the latest blockbuster movie release in 2006 it would appear that the 'Man of Steel' has been dogged by a 58 year curse that even the mighty superhero himself cannot vanquish.

The curse itself seems originate almost immediately after the conception of the character, even before his screen debut.

Superman was dreamt up in 1938 by two comic book 'nerds', Jerry Siegel and Joe Shuster. The concept involved a child with superpowers who was sent from the heavens to save all mankind and uphold the values of truth, justice and of course, the American way. Their creation should have earned them a fortune but instead they have lived their lives in poverty, constantly fighting and losing court battles to regain ownership of Superman. This is because back in 1938 they sold the rights to the character to DC comics for just £75 and were paid only £5 a page for drawing the cartoon strip. When they demanded a pay rise they were promptly fired by the publisher. Although the popularity of their creation caught on straight away and within a year Superman comics were selling around a million copies a month, the pair never saw a penny from them.

The first actor to play Clark Kent/Superman on the small screen was Kirk Alyn, who donned the cape in 1948 for 15 episodes. Although no tragedies occurred during Alyn's reign as the Man of Steel, it could be said that the seeds of the curse would appear to have been growing during his time. For whilst filming a flying scene Alyn's stunt double broke his leg 'jumping off a building' and was taken off production. Alyn had to do the rest of the stunts himself. Kirk Alyn's career stalled after becoming the first ever Superman and work soon dried up for him.

Next to follow in Kirk's footsteps was one of the more well known actors to play the character. George Reeves also portrayed Superman on the small screen. He starred as Clark Kent/ Superman between 1952 and 1958 clocking up 104 episodes on televisions all over America. The entire nation would find themselves in front of the television every Monday night at 7pm to watch Reeves portray the ultimate superhero. Though the man who had beat the likes of Bogart and Gable in a poll as the man most women would like to be rescued by soon found himself shunned once the series came to an end. He found himself rejected for role after role and often on the cutting room floor for the scenes he did manage to land in movies. He was reduced to wrestling in his Superman costume as this was the only character the public could recognise him as. He was dejected, depressed and by now heavily reliant on alcohol. In 1959 Reeves, once the hero of a nation put a gun to his head, pulled the trigger and ended it all at his Beverly Hills home.

By 1975 the curse of Superman was about to take even more of a hold. Siegel and Shuster, the original creators of Superman, heard that Warner Bros were planning on making the first major motion picture of their creation. They were infuriated to learn that they would receive nothing from this venture. Realising they were going to be 'cheated' yet again Siegel took public revenge. He wrote a letter that was published in newspapers across America declaring that Jack Liebowitz, the original publisher of their creation and at the time on the board of directors at Warner Bros, had 'strangled his career'. Siegel declared:

'I, Jerry Siegel, the co-originator of Superman, put a curse on the Superman movie'.

Christopher Reeve was to play Superman in the movie and both he and co-star Margot Kidder scoffed at the idea of the curse when questioned about it. Just as those before him though, Reeve's life was about to be touched by the curse.

The movie itself was a huge success on its release in 1978 and spawned three more sequels. For those associated with the movie things were about to take a downward spiral though. Christopher Reeve, who played Clark Kent/Superman, is a case in point. Outside of playing the Man of Steel in the four films Reeve never had another hit movie. He turned down roles that became huge successes for the actors that took them and the roles he did take became box office flops. Reeve eventually ended up in obscure theatre productions until 1995 when he was thrown from a horse and paralysed. He spent the rest of his life with a broken neck in a wheelchair until his death in 2004 from heart failure. Reeve's wife died of lung cancer two years later in 2006. She had never smoked a cigarette in her life. Margot Kidder, who played opposite Christopher Reeve as Lois Lane in the Superman movies, was also hit by a bizarre series of misfortunes. Kidder had a car crash in 1990 and the medical bills from the accident lead to her declaring herself bankrupt in 1995. Kidder fell into depression and a year later she was found sleeping on the streets in Los Angeles. She suffered a mental breakdown, believing the CIA was chasing her. She had cut off her hair with a razor blade and was found in bushes, just outside the studios where the original Superman movie was made, confused and accusing strangers of trying to kill her. Like Reeves, outside of the Superman franchise Kidder never had another big movie. Though Kidder still denies the curse of Superman exists:

> *'I think the curse is nonsense...The reality is if you get any group of people, x number are going to have some sort of calamity in their life because that's what life is'.*

The ever increasing list of victims of the curse might suggest otherwise to some less sceptical people. Marlon Brando was paid £500,000 a minute for his appearance as Jor-El, Superman's father in the 1977 movie. The appearance, which lasted 9 minutes, seems to have been enough to seal his fate. In 1990

Brando's son Christian, was convicted of murder after shooting his sister's boyfriend dead. His sister, Cheyenne, Brando's daughter, committed suicide five years later in 1995. She hung herself after suffering from schizophrenia. Lee Quigley, the 10 month old baby who played Superman as an infant in the same movie as Brando tragically died aged only 14 as a result of solvent abuse.

As the sequels were produced the curse continued. In 1983 Richard Pryor was paid the highest fee ever for a black Hollywood actor for his portrayal of Gus Gorman in Superman III. He was paid £2 million and spent the next 20 years battling multiple sclerosis. By his final years Pryor was unable to wash, dress or even feed himself and confined to a wheelchair. The legendary comedian died in December 2005.

Pierre Spengler, despite having produced four Superman movies that earned £300 million, ended up bankrupt. Perhaps Siegel's curse had worked after all?

Transferring the Man of Steel back to the small screen appears to have transferred the curse back with it. John Haymes Newton-Clark played Superboy for 26 episodes between 1988-1989, in the US television series of the same name. After which he was reduced to obscurity and bit parts on the small screen. Gerard Christopher, who took over the role between 1989 and 1992, faired no better after his 71 episodes as the 'Boy' of Steel. He too made no more of an impact in the world of film and television then to struggle for work afterwards.

The curse seemed to be abating by 1993 as Lois and Clark; the New Adventures of Superman hit the small screen. Dean Cain played Clark Kent/Superman for 87 episodes between 1993 and 1997. Cain, like George Reeves 41 years earlier, was a national celebrity in America. Cain must have been weary of the curse though, as he had insisted the studio took out a £12 million policy to cover him in case he too became a victim of it when he signed to the role. Inevitably Cain did fall victim to the curse. He sank back into obscurity once the series had come to an end, like so many before him who have donned the cape. Teri Hatcher, who played Lois Lane to Cain's Superman in the same show, was also hit by the curse. Hatcher has been through two divorces and spent a 10 year spell in which she landed only one film role since the series ended. Unlike many before her though, Hatcher seems to have escaped the clutches of the curse before it became the end of her. She once again found success in the American television show 'Desperate Housewives'.

In 2006 Superman took the leap from the small screen back to the silver screen. This time little known actor Brandon Routh picked up the famous red cape to play the title role. Many established Hollywood actors such as Nicolas Cage, Brendan Fraser and Keanu Reeves turned down the chance to play Superman. Actor Ashton Kutcher openly admitted he'd been put off the part because of the curse. Brandon Routh however is not a believer in such things:

'What curse? I don't think curses exist…I don't live my life in fear and I'm not scared'.

The curse may have struck the 2006 movie, even if not directly through its lead actor.

A crew member filming extras for the DVD version of the movie was badly mugged by teenagers whilst another member of the crew fell down a flight of stairs. A third crew member crashed through a plate glass window whilst filming and punctured a lung. Brandon Routh has pledged to go on playing Superman in more sequels, only time will tell if the curse will eventually catch him up and strike again.

Is the curse of Superman just a bizarre series of unfortunate coincidences?

Or is the curse of Superman the very real result of the bitterness of two men who dreamt up a superhero only to have it cheated away from them?

What The Experts Say
The Curse of Superman (1948-2006)

Steve Younis - Superman fan, Historian and Owner/Editor-In-Chief of the Superman Homepage (www.supermanhomepage.com). Superman Homepage has been a respected and definitive Superman online resource since 1994.

"In my opinion, the Superman curse is nonsense. For every example given to prove the curse exists, there's equally as many examples that go against this so-called evidence.

Clayton "Bud" Collyer is most famous for voicing Superman for over 20 years, both on radio in the 1940s, through to cartoons in the 1940s and 1960s.

Kirk Alyn, while limited in his career choices after Superman, went on to appreciate the legacy he'd left behind, appearing in a cameo appearance in the 1978 "Superman: The Movie" as Lois Lane's father. Noel Neill, who starred as Lois Lane in both Kirk Alyn "Superman" serials, also went on to play Lois in Seasons 2-6 of the "Adventures of Superman" TV series with George Reeves, made cameo appearances in other incarnations of the Man of Steel (both in the movies and on TV), including her appearance as Gertrude Vanderworth in "Superman Returns" in 2006. In 2007 Noel celebrates 60 years of being involved in the Superman mythos. A fact this woman, now in her mid-80s, cherishes and embraces. She's an annual visitor to the Superman Celebration in Metropolis, Illinois. And is in fact known as the "First Lady of Metropolis".

Noel's co-star in the 1950s Superman TV series, Jack Larson (who played Jimmy Olsen), while typecast in the role, went on to become a highly successful writer of operettas. In his mid-70s, Mr Larson also appeared in "Superman Returns" as Bo the bartender.

George Reeve's death by suicide is highly debated, with many suspecting he was murdered. While a tragedy either way, to attribute George's death to a "curse" is, in my opinion, disrespectful to a man who by all accounts was loved by all who knew him.

The role of Superman shot Christopher Reeve to stardom. Before his horse riding accident (many years later) he lived a full life. He flew planes, sailed boats, and lived life to the fullest. He had 3 loving children, was married to a wonderful woman in Dana. We should all be so lucky to live such a "cursed" life. Chris suffered an accident, nothing more sinister. He made the most of this accident, becoming the source of hope and inspiration for many afflicted by paralysis. He brought spinal cord injury awareness to a new level, helping thousands of people, and projecting SCI research leaps and bounds from where it once was.

Dean Cain was an injured football player before the role of Superman made him a household name. He's since gone on to star in a number of movies and host TV shows. Dean Cain's success in life is because of Superman.

Over the years Superman has helped create and boost careers for countless writers and artists working on his comic books. Names like Curt Swan, Wayne Boring, Julius Schwartz, Murphy Anderson, Win Mortimer, Elliott S! Maggin, to modern day names such as Geoff Johns, Ed McGuinness, Jeph Loeb, Greg Rucka and many others.

Jerry Siegel's family was photographed with director Bryan Singer during his time working on "Superman Returns". In the contact I have had with Jerry's wife Joanne and his daughter Laura, I'm certain they would be mortified by people thinking that Jerry or the character he helped create would be the source of pain and suffering for anybody, anywhere.

There's no such thing as the Superman curse. The character has endured so long (70 years and counting) because he's an inspiration to so many people. That's the legacy left to us thanks to Jerry and Joe."

Rebel Without A Cause (1955)

Rebel Without A Curse?

Like the script of a movie, there seems to be a standard format to the movie 'curse'. The odd happenings on the set, inexplicable accidents behind the scenes, the tragic loss of one or more of the cast, all of which are often reported and all of which are always attributed to the 'curse' that has been cast over all those involved with the production. In 1955 however, it would seem that a variation on the 'typical' movie curse had occurred, for a movie was released where the star of the film appears to have brought the curse with him. A curse that would affect his co-stars cost him his life and continue to claim victims. Even after his death.

Rebel Without A Cause was released by Warner Bros on 27th October 1955 and had cost an estimated $1,500,000 to make. The movie tells the story of Jim Stark, a rebellious teenager who moves to a new town. Stark has been in trouble before and that's why his middle class family has had to relocate. Jim meets a girl, defies his parents, faces the local High School bullies and befriends a troubled younger boy. Stark becomes involved in switchblade fights and car races in a bid to prove himself to his peers and find the respect and love he doesn't get from his parents.

Rebel without a Cause became one of the most talked about movies of its generation. The tempestuous view the film portrayed flew in the face of every other Hollywood teen movie made up until then. The reality of 1950's teen life it depicted, as oppose to the 'perfected' version shown in the movies of the time, caused a sensation and guaranteed the success of the film at the box office. Natalie Wood, Sal Mineo and Nick Adams were the stars of the movie, but none of them were bigger than the man who played the lead character, Jim Stark. That role was taken by an actor that would become a Hollywood icon and whom the curse of the movie would centre around. The man in question of course was none other than the legendary James

Dean. Little did Dean know that before the release of the movie that gave him his legendary status he would be dead.

Around 7:45 am, on the morning of 30th September 1955, James Dean and his mechanic Rolf Wutherich met up at Competition Motors on Vine Street, Hollywood, California to pick up a Porsche 550 Spyder. The car had been prepared for a sports car race in Salinas, California in which Dean was going to race it. Dean and Wutherlich then picked up Sanford Roth and Bill Hickman, who were accompanying them on the trip. The original plan was for Dean to tow the Spyder behind his station wagon, but he decided that he needed more time to familiarise himself with the vehicle before the race. So, at 1:30pm, followed by Roth and Hickman in the station wagon, James Dean and Wutherlich began their journey to Salinas in the Porsche Spyder.

At 3:30pm Dean was stopped by police in Kern County, California for speeding. He was given a ticket for doing 65mph in a 55 mph zone. The driver of the station wagon was also given a speeding ticket for being over the speed limit. Having left the other car far behind Dean and Wutherich stopped at Blackwell's Corner for fuel where they met up with fellow racer Lance Reventlow, after their brief stop off the pair continued their journey. Around an hour later Dean and Wutherich were travelling west on Route 466 (which would later become Route 46) near Cholomone, California. At the same time 23 year old student Donald Turnupseed was driving his Ford Tudor Coupe in the opposite direction. Turnupseed attempted to take the fork onto Route 41 and crossed into Dean's path without seeing him. Dean was said to have said:

"That guy's gotta stop…He'll see us."

The Ford and Dean's Porsche Spyder collided virtually head on. Turnupseed suffered a gashed forehead and a bruised nose in the accident. Rolf Wutherlich was thrown from the Porsche Spyder in the impact and survived with a broken jaw and other minor injuries. California Highway Patrol Officer Ron Nelson and his partner were finishing a coffee break when they were called to the scene of the accident. Nelson said:

> *"The wreckage and the position of Dean's body indicated his speed was more like 55 mph."*

This would appear to contradict reports that followed the accident alleging that Dean was speeding at the time of the collision. Nelson watched dean being placed into an ambulance bound for Paso Robles War Memorial Hospital. On arrival at 5:59 pm on 30th September 1955, James Dean was pronounced dead. His neck had been broken by the steering wheel of the Porsche Spyder and he had been killed instantly in the crash. Donald Turnupseed was not cited by police for the accident. Dean's funeral was held eight days later at Park Cemetery in Fairmount, Illinois. Nineteen days after his burial *Rebel Without A Cause* was released in cinemas in the USA.

James Dean's flamboyant lifestyle and penchant for drink, drugs and fast cars had been a constant concern for both insurance companies and studio executives. Dean was an intense actor and suffered from depression, which he was medicated for by the film studio doctors. Dean himself once said:

> *"A neurotic person has the necessity to express himself and my neuroticism manifests itself in the dramatic..."*

At the age of 24 it would seem that the studio's worries were justified. The fast cars Dean loved to race to escape his depression had cut short his movie career and cost him his life. The tragic end of James Dean's life would only be the beginning of the curse that would envelope the cast of *Rebel Without a Cause* and affect almost everything and everyone Dean had touched in life, even the car that had claimed his.

George Barris was a legendary hot rod racer and friend of James Dean's:

> *"Jimmy and I got together when we did Rebel Without A Cause and we did the chicken scene where we did all the chases..."*

Following Dean's death Barris bought the wreckage of the 550 Porsche Spyder for $2,500 for spare parts. After buying the car it slipped off its trailer and broke a mechanic's leg. This was only the beginning of a bizarre series of accidents that would later give rise to the legend that the car that killed James Dean was also cursed.

Barris sold the engine of the car to Doctor troy McHenry and the drive-train to Doctor William Eschrid. Whilst racing against each other McHenry was killed instantly when his vehicle spun out of control and crashed into a tree. Eschrid was seriously injured in the same race when his car rolled over whilst going into a curve. Barris later sold two tires that were unharmed in Dean's accident. The tires blew up simultaneously causing the buyer's car to veer off the road.

Similar misfortune would befall would be 'souvenir seekers' who tried to steal parts of the vehicle. One thief tried to steal the steering wheel from the Porsche and his arm was ripped open on a piece of jagged metal. Another man was injured whilst trying to take the bloodstained front seat. George Barris himself recounts the tale of another victim of the car:

"One guy stole some of the metal from the original car as it was parked and he called in and he says take this away from me. I lost my wife, I lost my house, I lost my business and I dying of cancer."

Barris decided to store the car away but the California Highway Patrol persuaded him to loan 'Little Bastard' (the name James Dean had given to the Porsche) to them as a part of a highway safety exhibition. The first exhibition featuring the car was a disaster. The garage storing the Porsche went up in flames in a mysterious disaster. Everything was completely destroyed, everything that is apart from the car itself which suffered almost no damage at all. The second exhibition took place at a High School in Sacramento. The event ended when the car fell and broke a students hip.

There were also problems when transporting the car. On two occasions the Porsche fell off trucks whilst being transported. On the first occasion the car fell off a truck on a freeway, luckily no injuries were reported. The second instance happened in Oregon. Whilst nobody was hurt, another vehicle's windscreen was shattered. The most severe accident happened whilst the car was being transported to Salinas. The truck containing the Porsche lost control and the driver fell out of the vehicle. Tragically he was crushed by the car after it fell off the back of the truck.

The car was last used by the California Highway Patrol as an exhibit in 1959. The following year the Porsche was being returned to George Barris in Los Angeles, California when it mysteriously vanished. The car has never been seen since. George Barris remarked:

"They loaded it on a truck and trailer and eight days later it came out here, we opened up the trailer...and the car was gone. Just a trail of unusual things that happen (around the car) and that's how we got the name the curse of the James Dean death car."

The disappearance of the car seemed to focus the curse back upon the movie.

Nick Adams played 'Chick' alongside Dean in *Rebel Without A Cause*, gaining a reputation as a prankster and scene-stealer on the set of the production. In 1968 Adams had just completed some filming in Mexico and had bought a plane ticket to Rome. Adams was about to co-star in a sci-fi horror movie called *Murder In The third Dimension* alongside actor Aldo Ray. Upon arrival in Italy Adams discovered that the project had been dropped. Susan Strasberg, who had worked with Adams on a movie some time before, was living in Rome at the time. Strasberg remembered encountering a thoroughly demoralised and somewhat upset Adams in a bar around the same time. He returned home to the USA still smarting from the blow of the project having fallen through.

On the night of 7th February 1968, Adams missed a dinner appointment he was due to attend. His friend and lawyer, Erwin Roeder, drove to the actor's home to check on him and find out why he had failed to keep his appointment. Roeder arrived at 2126 El Roble Lane, Beverley Hills and saw a light on in the house. He also noticed that Adams' car was still in the garage. After several attempts to get an answer, ex-LAPD Officer Roeder became concerned about his friend's well being and broke in through a window to gain entrance into the property. Following a search of the ground floor Roeder went upstairs, where he was to make a startling discovery. In one of the bedrooms Roeder found Adams wearing a shirt, blue jeans and boots. He was slumped against a wall with his eyes fixed in a blank stare. At the age of 36, Nick Adams was dead.

The autopsy carried out on Adams by Dr Thomas Noguchi concluded that there were enough sedatives, paraldehyde and other drugs in the body to cause 'instant unconsciousness'. Adams' death certificate attributes the immediate cause of death to 'Paraldehyde and promazine intoxication'. There is also a note on the document stating 'accident; suicide; undetermined'.

There has been a large amount of speculation as to what happened to Nick Adams on the night of his death. There have been claims that there was no evidence of any paraldehyde ever found at his home and even claims that he was murdered. Through the years Adams' own children have even added to the mystery, offering various explanations ranging from accidental death to murder.

The fact is that in 1968 the awareness, and subsequent warnings, of the dangers of the interaction and 'mixing' of drugs was not as prominent as it is nowadays. The American Medical Association currently warns that paraldehyde and promazine should never be taken together. It is also known that Adams' brother was a medical doctor and had prescribed sedatives to him. This would point to the conclusion that Nick Adams' death was indeed accidental, a stance that his best friend actor Robert Conrad has constantly maintained. Following his death movie reviewer Dan Palvides would write of Adams:

> 'Plagued by personal excesses, he will be remembered just as much for what he could have done as for what he left behind.'

After a 20 year career consisting of over 150 television series episodes and several feature films the evidence would suggest that accidental death had claimed the life of Nick Adams. Those that believe in such things would say that the curse had claimed its second victim. Worse still, more were to follow.

Five months later another accident occurred. In July of 1968, the building on Blackwell's Corner where James Dean had stopped for fuel in 1955 was destroyed in a mysterious fire. The same building was also the last place that Dean ever visited during his life. Perhaps he had inadvertently left a little of the curse in the building during his visit.

Sal Mineo was another co-star of Dean's in *Rebel Without A Cause*. Mineo played 'Plato' in the movie, a role that would prove both a blessing and a curse to him. Two years after the film Mineo made a brief foray into the world of music. He recorded an album and had two songs that made the top 40 in the music charts. By the late 1950's Mineo had become a major celebrity, going on to star as legendary drummer Gene Krupa in the 1959 movie *The Gene Krupa Story*. Things seemed to be going exceptionally well for Mineo, then things suddenly took a turn for the worse.

By the early 1960's he was becoming typecast as a Native American or Jewish emigrant because of his exotic looks. Mineo wanted to break away from this situation and in doing so he began being rejected for leading roles, an example being that he auditioned for David Lean's epic *Lawrence of Arabia* but was not hired. Mineo was flummoxed by his sudden loss of popularity:

"One minute I had more offers than I could handle, the next, no one wanted me"

Mineo realised that perhaps he was getting too old to play the type of roles that had made him a household name so in 1965 he accepted a part unlike any he had had before. He took the lead role of stalker Lawrence Sherman in the movie *Who Killed Teddy Bear*, a performance that earned him praise from the critics and seemed to have put his acting career back on track. Unfortunately for Mineo the performance only served to lead him to be typecast once more, only this time as a deranged criminal.

Mineo returned to the theatre and in 1971 he produced *Fortune And Men's Eyes*, with Don Johnson taking the lead role. Although the production received positive reviews in Los Angeles it was panned by the critics during its run in New York. In the same year Mineo made his final appearance on the big screen. He played chimpanzee Dr Milo in *Escape From The Planet Of The Apes*.

Following a string of failed projects Mineo's career was about to take another turn for the better, albeit it a short lived one, literally.

In 1976 Mineo had been playing the role of a gay burglar in the stage comedy *P.S. Your Cat Is Dead*. During its run in San Francisco the production and Mineo had received substantial publicity and positive reviews. Both he and the play moved on to Los Angeles.

On 12th February 1976 Mineo was returning home from a rehearsal for the play in preparation of its opening night, a night which Sal Mineo would not live to see. As Gregg Davidson, a resident at the apartment block where Mineo lived explained:

"The story I know is that he (Mineo) was doing a play at the Westwood Playhouse. He came home at about nine thirty that night, he parked in the garage, he got out of his car and he was apparently attacked. During the struggle he was stabbed. His body was found right here (behind the apartment building) but he had lost so much blood that actually his body was taken away by the coroner. There wasn't even time to get paramedics or take him to a hospital."

Sal Mineo had been stabbed to death in an alley behind the West Hollywood apartment building he lived in. Ironically in the early years of his movie career he had been known as 'The Switchblade Kid' for his depictions of juvenile delinquents. He had not been repeatedly stabbed as was first reported; a single knife wound had struck his heart leading to immediate and massive internal bleeding.

Mineo had revealed himself to be bisexual in a 1972 interview, published after his death and his biography notes that he dated men in the last years of his life. Following the crime investigators reportedly found gay pornography in Mineo's home and there was suggestion that the circumstances of his murder suggested a 'homosexual motive'.

A career criminal named Lionel Ray Williams was later sentenced to life in prison for the murder and released on parole after 12 years. Williams claimed that he had had no idea who Mineo was and that the murder had been a mugging that had gone wrong.

To add even more mystery to Sal Mineo's tragic death at the age of 37, his family and friends have maintained that the police caught the wrong person and that his killer may still be at large.

The fact that Sal Mineo was murdered is not in question. Who murdered him or why he was murdered may be open to question. A similarly intriguing question may be was Sal Mineo another victim of the curse of *Rebel Without A Cause*?

The final co-star of the movie had been destined for stardom from an early age. Natalie Wood landed the role of 'Judy' in *Rebel without a Cause* at the age of 17. Starring alongside James Dean she earned an Oscar nomination for best supporting actress for her performance. Wood married actor Robert Wagner two years later and with her movie career going well she was once again nominated for an Academy award in 1961 for best actress in the film *Splendour In The Grass*.

Wood's marriage to Wagner ended in 1962. Wood would later say that they were both scared, insecure and listened to others who said their marriage wouldn't work. Whilst her personal life had hit a setback, Wood still continued to enjoy success in her career and earned a third Oscar nomination in the form of a best actress nomination for her role as Angie Rossini in the 1963 movie *Love With The Proper Stranger*.

Unfortunately, as with her two previous nominations, she failed to win the award.

In 1969 Wood married producer Richard Gregson and had a daughter, Natasha. She later discovered her husband was having an affair and Wood was divorced for a second time.

By 1972 Wood's 'roller coaster' personal life of ups and downs seemed to be on the up again when she remarried Robert Wagner on 16th June that year. The couple had a daughter, Courtney Brooke, and they lived happily as husband and wife. Despite Wood's bouts of depression and inferiority complex their second attempt at marriage seemed to be going well.

During September and October of 1981 Wood and Wagner were staying in Raleigh, North Carolina. Wood was doing location work on a science-fiction film called *Brainstorm* which she was starring in alongside Christopher Walken. She spent most of the following month, November, filming in the studio with Walken and the rest of the cast members on the MGM lot in Culver City. Following the Thanksgiving holiday Wood, Wagner and Walken went onto Catalina Island. They were sailing on Wood and Wagner's yacht *Splendour* along with the boat's skipper Dennis Davem.

On 29th December 1981 the boat was anchored at Isthmus Cove with all five people onboard. It is unclear whether Wood was trying to board the dingy belonging to the yacht, or whether she was trying to secure it from banging against the hull. What is known is that she lost her footing and accidentally fell overboard.

A witness on a nearby yacht claimed that she heard calls for help at around midnight that lasted for about fifteen minutes. She also said that she heard somebody else answer by saying 'take it easy, we'll be over to get you'. The witness also recalled:

"It was laid back…there was no urgency or immediacy in their shouts.'

By the time Natalie Wood was recovered from the water it was too late. She had drowned.

Following his investigation, Los Angeles County Coroner Thomas Noguchi returned a verdict of accidental drowning. He concluded that Wood had drank seven or eight glasses of wine and was intoxicated when she died. Noguchi added that had Wood not been intoxicated she would have realised that her heavy coat and wool sweater were pulling her underwater and would have removed them. Noguchi had also found her fingernails embedded in the side of the dingy. At the time of her death, aged 43, Natalie Wood had made fifty six films for cinema and television. *Brainstorm* (the movie she had been filming when she died) was released in 1983 to neither commercial nor critical success.

Twenty eight years after the release of *Rebel Without A Cause* four of the cast were dead, including all three stars of the film. There were rumours that a curse was responsible and that the curse was not only centered around the movie but on James Dean himself. The car he had died in had claimed victims of its own, the last place he had ever visited had burned to the ground and all of the co-stars of the final film he had starred in were dead. The evidence to support the rumours continued to grow.

Following James Dean's fatal car crash Rolf Wutherlich, who was in the car with him at the time of the accident, received huge amounts of hate mail from Dean's fans who blamed him for the actor's death. He moved back to Germany and became a car mechanic and salesperson in Stuttgart. Shortly afterwards he had a nervous breakdown and flew back to California, USA where he underwent electro shock therapy in a psychiatric ward. In 1959 he returned to Germany where he started work with a psychotherapist and made progress and regained sanity. Although he was mentally ill, homicidal and suicidal for the rest of his life, he felt stable enough to go back to work for Porsche where he was in charge of racing. In 1965 he joined Bohringer in the Rally Monte Carlo and he also won the Vice-Europe Championship as a rally driver. Wutherlich also opened a Go-Kart race track in Stuttgart for a while.

Over time his depression and suicidal tendencies exasperated again and in 1966 he was hospitalised after a failed suicide attempt. The following year he stabbed his wife fourteen times with a kitchen knife in an attempt to kill both of them in a double suicide. After this incident he moved to the small town of Kupferzell where he worked in a motorcycle shop. Wutherlich continually received hate mail from Dean fans who insisted that he was responsible for dean's death, and never recovered from the guilt he felt about it.

In 1981 Rolf Wutherlich died in a car crash in Kupferzell town centre. He was driving whilst intoxicated and ran his Honda into a building. Was Wutherlich's association with Dean the cause of his tragic death?

The other man involved in the accident was Donald Turnupseed, the student whose car hit James Dean's Porsche. After the accident Turnupseed spoke with the Tulare Advance Register a few hours after the crash, but then apparently refused any further interviews or public comment on the accident for the remainder of his life. His son David claimed a published interview with his father, supposedly conducted by crime writer Maria Moretti is not genuine.

Following the accident Turnupseed, along with his parents, went on to establish a successful electrical contracting business, Turnupseed Electrical Service in California's San Joaquin Valley. In July 1995 Donald Turnupseed died of lung cancer aged 63. Advocates of the curse would say that Turnupseed's illness and death was the result of the curse taking its toll on the man who was most directly involved with the cause of the death of James Dean.

So what are the arguments for and against a curse?

The believers would say that the curse of *Rebel Without A Cause* was very real. They would say that the death of four of the principal actors at such early ages was more than just a coincidence. That perhaps the curse was brought on by the graphic portrayal of 1950's youth, combined with the undertones of homosexuality and blatant incestuous content within the movie.

Some would go on to take things even further, suggesting that the curse was in fact brought to the production by James Dean himself. The proof of this being the string of misfortunes that surrounded those involved with him, the last place he visited and the car he died in. Accidents, tragedy, illness and death had seemed to follow where Dean went and there are those that believe it was a curse that he carried until his death and beyond.

Sceptics would say there is no such thing as a curse and all of the occurrences can be easily explained. James Dean was known for his love of fast cars. It would seem far more likely that his death was caused by bad luck and an out of control supercharged vehicle than a curse.

Accidental drowning, suicide, murder, racing car accidents, terminal illness unfortunately all of these things happen in everyday life. Spread over a forty year period then maybe, as the sceptics believe, you would get instances of all these occurrences that have some kind of tie to one individual or movie.

There are also instances of individuals that were connected to both James Dean and *Rebel Without A Cause* that remained pretty much untouched by misfortune, Dennis Hopper being one example. Hopper played the role of 'Goon' in *Rebel Without A*

Cause and also appeared with James Dean in the movie *Giant*. Following the filming of the movies he became good friends with Dean and was devastated when he heard of his death. Given his association with the movie and Dean himself Hopper should have been affected by the curse?

Dennis Hopper went on to lead an amazing cinematic career for more then five decades. He appeared in such box office smashes as *True Grit* (1969), *Easy Rider* (1969), *Apocalypse Now* (1979) and *Blue Velvet* (1986) to name but a few. Hopper then went on to direct *Colors* (1988) which was warmly received by both critics and audiences alike. He continued to act throughout the nineties in movies such as *True Romance* (1993), *Speed* (1994) and continued acting into the new millennium. At the time of this book going to press he currently has two films in production (2008). Sceptics would say this is hardly the career of a cursed man.

The believers cannot provide the proof that curses really exist and the sceptics cannot provide definitive evidence that there are no such things as curses. Both parties can only present the facts as they see them. It is an age old problem; it is all a question of the individual's interpretation.

Could James Dean really have been a cursed man? Could he have carried the curse around with him throughout his life, inadvertently spreading the curse to the individuals he met, the places he visited, the movies he worked on and even the car he died in?

Or was *Rebel Without a Cause* at the root of the curse and James Dean was simply carrying the curse that he inherited through being a part of the production?

Was there a curse at all or just an unfortunate serious of unusual events?

The answer is simple. You just have to decide whether you believe in curses or not.

What The Experts Say
Rebel Without A Cause (1955)

Barrie John – International Clairvoyant Medium and Paranormal Investigator. Barrie is well known for his work within the UK Radio, Media and Television circuit. He has also appeared on the *Living TV*'s top rating paranormal television program *Most Haunted*, as the Guest Medium for Series 10 and was voted Most Popular National Male Medium at the UK's Spiritual ConneXtions Awards 2008.

On reviewing the piece 'Rebel without a Curse', I found both the subject matter interesting and curious, as this is a film I haven't seen or had a personal fascination with the deaths surrounding it. Other than knowing that James Dean had died tragically and of a young age, all the other information gathered and written in the piece are new to me as is the belief that there is a curse associated with James Dean personally and/ or the film Rebel without a Cause. My opinions therefore can only be surmised from reading this chapter and on the understanding that the facts were and are as written.

he Curse appears to have been a discussion which has been carried over many years. Was it really a curse or just a 'bad hand of luck' which was attributed to the actors and actresses lifestyles and subsequent deaths?

The world of media and TV, seems to add so much pressure and stress onto individuals, and forces them to be the characters which they chose to play. Maybe the media were actually at the core of there deaths and not the 'curse of James Dean himself'.

"How can a car carry the curse when a vehicle has no physical spirit?"

In the case of Dean and his apparent accident, why did a man previously ticketed for speeding continue to drive recklessly, even to the point of his own death? If this was a curse, why did his co-partner in the 'car of death' survive, surely the curse would have killed them both at the same time simultaneously. We all know that Dean was a young man in his time and 'enjoyed' life to the full; he was known for his love of life and high risk pursuits. Maybe his 'demise' was caused purely by his way of living, fast cars, drugs and alcohol?

The other associates of this film whose deaths are connected by the film and the so called curse of James Dean seem to me, to be circumstantial and no different than any other connections of lives should you choose to link them up by one centre point, i.e. the making of a film. I am sure that if you took another film and connected key people over a 40 year span you would find a lot of similarities in there live and their deaths.

Other than in the case of Natalie Wood this has previously been both documented and suggested as suicide and murder, and if neither of these and you should choose to believe it was a curse then do you not find it strange that 1, her death occurred almost 20 years after the film and 2, that she had a very emotional unstable life, which obviously caused her major distress.

I feel that if the curse theory was to be believable that the deaths associated with James Dean and this film, would all have happened a lot closer in time to each other and not been over a prolonged period when you include the co-stars.

I would suggest that the film of Rebel without a Cause, just had a very 'unlucky' group of actors, whom just fell into there own path of death.

In terms of Curses, I believe that curses can be created by individuals to cause harm. Many films have been portrayed, in which people have been cursed. I believe that this can happen to an individual and that we can all create harm by our own living thoughts. I suppose within this area we could also consider Karma as being a 'sort of curse' i.e. what we give out we get back in terms of good and bad.

Finally, if the curse was of James Dean himself, why had this not happened on previous high profile films and to other close associates and co-stars whom he must have worked as intimately with?

The Exorcist (1973)

The Devil's Retribution

Peter Batty was struggling to find a topic for his latest novel. The field in which he had been writing, comedy, was a well which was quickly running dry.

His thoughts took him back to a report he had heard about in a 1949 edition of the Washington Post. A boy had allegedly been the victim of demonic possession. After a large amount of poltergeist activity in the home his family had sought help from the church, in the form of an exorcism.

The original article appeared in the Washington Post on August 10th 1949 and was titled 'Pastor Tells Eerie Tale Of 'Haunted Boy'. The story was also picked up by The Times-Herald (Washington D.C.), the Evening Herald (Washington D.C.) and continued to run in the Washington Post. Between the three publications over the next ten days the story of the boys' ordeal was told.

On January 18th 1949 a family from Mount Rainier, Maryland, USA began experiencing strange occurrences. Scratching noises were emanating from the walls of their house with most of the activity centering on the families 13-year-old son. The boys' bed would shake violently as he slept in it and objects would fall to the floor in his presence. These included pictures jumping from the wall and fruit jumping from bowls. The family also reported witnessing demonic messages written on the boy in the form of a red rash. Although when this was brought to the attention of a minister involved with the case he detected nothing more then a rash.

The same sceptical priest arranged for the boy to spend the evening of 17th February 1949 at his home. During his stay a heavy armchair the boy was sitting in tilted and tipped over. Later that night as the boy dozed off on a pallet of blankets they started moving around the room. Eventually the minister and the boy retired for the evening. As the boy slept in a nearby bed, the minister heard scratching noises on the wall and vibrating sounds coming from the boys' bed.

After his affliction was studied at both Georgetown University Hospital and St Louis University, the boy was given the ritual of an exorcism.

The exorcism itself was said to have been carried out by a priest from St Louis who was in his late fifties. The ritual was conducted in St Louis, continued in D.C. and completed back in St Louis in a Catholic Church. The exorcism took between twenty and thirty forty-five minute performances of the rite. During the rituals the boy recited a string of blasphemous curses. He screamed and broke into violent outbursts, began having seizures and uncontrolled urinating. During the final ritual the boy became quiet and calmed and reported witnessing a vision of St Michael. It would seem the boy was finally free and the devil had been cast out from within him.

After changing his lead character from the young boy that the original report had centered upon, to a twelve-year-old girl named Regan, Blatty now had his inspiration and a novel. After every studio passed on the chance to make the story into a movie, fearing the subject matter, Warner Brothers grudgingly agreed to make the film. So in 1973 the movie and the legend of The Exorcist were born.

Though it seems that in the fifteen months or so of filming the cast and crew were not the only ones at work on the set. There was a growing feeling amongst them that they were playing with something they maybe shouldn't be.

They weren't the only people who thought that either.

Jason Miller, who played Father Karras in The Exorcist, frequented a local restaurant during breaks in filming. On one visit to the restaurant an old priest gave him a medal.

The priest asked Jason if he knew why he had given him the medal and Jason replied no.

The priest explained to him the concept of intervention.

He told him the concept dated back to the 15th century. That being, if you do anything to reveal the devil for the 'trickster' he is, the devil would seek retribution against you and would stop you doing what you were doing to unmask him. The priest regarded the movie to be an attempt to 'unmask the devil' and said the medal would protect Jason while he was working on the project. He also said he should be careful and take care of himself.

Around three days later Jason was on another visit to the same restaurant. Again during a break in filming. He was walking along a hall when, from the corner of his eye he thought he saw a casket in one of the rooms. He walked back to enter the room to make sure he wasn't imagining things. When he entered the room he could indeed confirm that he had indeed seen a casket.

Laid to rest inside it was the same old priest who had given him the medal.

Further into filming The Exorcist there was an unscheduled shut down in production, for around six weeks. There had been a fire on the set where burning silk had fallen onto the walls and carpet causing substantial damage. The fire, which had happened on a weekend when there was no one there, has yet to be explained. There was no substantial evidence of an electrical fault, arson attack or any other 'earthly' explanation for the accident.

A priest was asked to exorcise the set but refused, not wanting to add to the feelings of unease surrounding the production.

Actress Ellen Burnstyn, who played Chris Macneil in the movie, said there were nine deaths directly or indirectly associated to the movie. Whilst none of these deaths happened 'on set' or as a direct result of the filming process, there were certainly ties to The Exorcist movie. Amongst those she mentioned are:

- Actor Jack McGowan who 'died' in the film, died in real life shortly after filming had ended.

- Actor Max Von Sydow, also a victim in the film, had a death in the family. His brother died.

- The man who refrigerated the set for the 'breathing' effects in the movie also passed on.
- There was a young night watchman who died during production.
- Unfortunately the assistant cameraman's child, who was born during shooting, also sadly died during this period.

Now you could just say that during the time span of over a year, with such a large crew, there are bound to be some tragedies. Maybe nine deaths isn't such a large number in that context.

You could say that there are bound to be fires on film sets. Whether or not they can be explained, these things happen. Don't they?

You could also say that maybe, for the old priest that had given Jason Miller the medal, it was just his time to 'pass on to the other side'. He was elderly after all. Wasn't he?

Maybe this was just all coincidence or hype surrounding a film that was so shocking; it literally had audiences fainting in the aisles. All publicity is good publicity. Isn't it?

Or maybe, just maybe the priest had been right, Maybe the devil was seeking retribution on those who were trying to unmask him.

Maybe this was intervention.

What The Experts Say
The Exorcist (1973)

Darren W Ritson – Ghost Hunter, Paranormal Investigator and author. Darren is the founder of The North East Ghost Research Team and co-founder of WraithScape (Paranormal with a Passion). He has authored eleven books on the paranormal including The South Shields Poltergeist, One Family's Fight Against An Invisible Intruder, (with Michael J Hallowell), Ghost Hunter, True Life Encounters from the North East, and In Search of Ghosts, Real Hauntings from Around Britain.

He has had an interest in the paranormal for most of his life due to unexplained goings-on he experienced as a child growing up. Ever since he was a small boy he was fascinated with the thought of ghosts existing and after experiencing poltergeist activity at the age of thirteen in France in 1986, his path was set and he decided to try to learn more. Over the next 20 years he built up a library of books, magazines and literature on the paranormal including the works of the late Harry Price (1881-1948) Peter Underwood FRSA, and Guy Lyon Playfair to name a few.

His team - The North East Ghost Research Team - was founded in May 2003 and over the years he has worked with who he considers to be some of the finest paranormal investigators in the country.

After becoming a member of The Incorporated Society for Psychical Research (SPR) in May 2006, he hopes to continue his ghost hunting and paranormal research in addition to meeting new people and working with them in order to try and make some sense of ghosts and hauntings.

Darren also regularly corresponds with veteran ghost hunter Peter Underwood FRSA - president of the Ghost Club Society, and Guy Lyon Playfair who co-investigated the famous Enfield poltergeist with the late Maurice Grosse. For years he has travelled across the UK in his search for ghosts and has carried out dozens of radio broadcasts (Metro FM, BBC Radio and

Howard Hughes talk show – The Unexplained) as well as carrying out countless talks and lectures based on his cases and his findings - most notably he has addressed the Society for Psychical Research, and The Ghost Club.

"As a young boy growing up I had heard of the movie that was once said to send viewers into frenzies and had its audience literally vomiting and fainting due to its 'shocking and disturbing nature'. This intrigued me; I thought to myself how could a movie do those things? I need to see it for myself. I had a video recorder in my bedroom so I began to ask around for the film but to my dismay I had heard it was banned. Nevertheless I managed to acquire an old copy of the movie on VHS but it was so used, it played only in black and white, but that didn't bother me – I had my copy.

In all honesty the film scared me shitless and for weeks after I found it hard to sleep. The movie had affected me in the same way it had affected millions of others, no wonder it was banned! Then I found out it was based on a true-life possession. At that time in my life I had a little interest in the paranormal and the idea of demonic possession and poltergeist activity fascinated me but I was always "on the fence" when it came to making decisions about whether or not I thought they could be real. That opinion stayed with me until July 2006.

These days most horror films are said to have an element of truth involved and one wonders if the words 'based on a true story' is now more a cliché rather than a true statement. Of course movies are also grossly hyped up and exaggerated to the point where if they were true stories then the paying audiences would probably not believe it. The Exorcist – for me – now has a certain ring of truth to it and let me explain why.

Let me take you back to Jason's write up regarding the real family in question. They began to experience strange occurrences. Scratching noises were emanating from the walls of their house with most of the activity focusing around the family's 13-year-old son. His bed would shake violently as he slept in it and objects would fall to the floor in his presence. Pictures would fly off the wall and objects would fly around the house as if thrown by "unseen hands". Eventually the boy in question would suffer from cuts and scratches that would appear on his body and they seemingly materialised into 'messages'. When the boy was taken out of the household to spend a night elsewhere, it followed, resulting in a heavy armchair being hurled over along with other paranormal activity.

To me, this has "poltergeist" written all over it. They are all classic symptoms of poltergeist phenomena. The scratching, the displacement of objects, the cuts and welts on the victim – or the polt focus! I think knowing what I know now in regards to the poltergeist and such like I can safely say these things really do occur. Having personally investigated a vicious bastard of a poltergeist first hand for a protracted period in 2006, I experienced many of the above-mentioned phenomena, and more. Back in 1949 the concept of 'evil demons' were still commonplace and that is how many poltergeist cases were explained as. However, more modern theories suggest another explanation - the RSPK theory.

In short, psycho-kinesis (PK) and tele-kinesis (TK) is said to be the ability to move objects with the power of the mind. Recurring spontaneous psycho-kinesis (RSPK) - is said to be the ability to move objects and manipulate solid matter, again with the power of the mind, only RSPK is done on a subconscious level and the individual in question is not even aware they are doing it!

In extreme cases of stress, a latent power or energy is said to build up in an individual but for some reasons these individuals cannot expel their anger in the normal way. Eventually, something has to give and the result is an overspill of this pent up emotion in the form of RSPK. What they really want to do is punch a wall, or kick a door through, but the effects of the RSPK are far more destructive. I have coined the phrase and likened it to a "psychic temper tantrum" although the actual theory regarding it has been around for many years; it is not a new theory. For a full explanation consult the book *The South Shields Poltergeist, One Family's Fight Against An Invisible Intruder*. Of course the RSPK explanation is only a theory too, but one that is more accepted these days. The debating however, still goes on."

Paranormal or Paranoia?

"The poltergeist works in mysterious ways and all those that come into contact with them can be affected in certain ways, and in more ways than you could possibly think. Anyone that has studied poltergeist cases will know of a certain aspect of the polt known as contagion. Contagion is where an investigator becomes contaminated by the polt to a certain degree and experiences polt-like activity at his or her own home although the phenomena experienced is not as intense as it is as the primary infected location, or ground zero. It happened during the South Shields case to a large degree. It also happened at Enfield in 1978. It happens more than you could imagine and is a common polt aspect – although it is little understood.

No one yet knows for sure how the polt really operates, or the mechanics behind them. We do know however what they do and in most cases what pattern they employ. During poltergeist cases the investigators also seem to be hit with the most bizarre coincidences and one wonders if these coincidences are also somehow related. What we found during our research during the South Shields case is that sometimes the coincidences and the contagion of the poltergeist can be experienced by not only those personages that have a direct link to the principal experience, but to those with an indirect link with them too."

Contagion or Curse?

"During the making of the movie a string of harrowing coincidences and mishaps plagued the actors and the set, which resulted in major setbacks and loss of money. Strange occurrences took place during the film including mysterious fires on set, accidents, and even deaths, which led to the assumption that The Exorcist was cursed. Maybe it was, but by whom, or should I say what? Some suggest it was the Devil himself, others say it was nothing more than spooky coincidences, but what we have learned about spooky coincidences begs us to ask the question was there another dark force at work? One thing is certain, these things did happen.

I suggest a string of weird coincidences and poltergeist contagion may have occurred during the filming of the movie through a poltergeist that originally infested the house of that young boy back in 1949. It's a crazy notion I know, but there is an indication of indirect polt contagion. I guess with all that metaphorical water under the bridge and with the facts becoming mixed with fiction over the years I guess we will never know for sure. "

The Omen (1976)

The Mark Of The Beast

'Here is wisdom. Let Him that hath understanding count the number of the beast: for it is the number of a man; and his number is 666'
Book Of Revelation Chapter 13 Verse 10

In 1976 these words were amongst those in the opening titles of a controversial and shocking film that hit cinema screens around the world.

Every studio had turned down the movie. It was only at the second time of asking, after director Richard Donner managed to talk Alan Ladd into it, that Fox Studios gave the project the go ahead.

That movie was *The Omen*. The story of a politician who substitutes an orphaned infant for his stillborn baby to shield his wife from the devastating truth of their loss. The couple are both unaware of the child's satanic origins and that the boy is in fact the antichrist.

Surely the making of a film of such disturbing subject matter could not go without incident? According to those involved there were 'incidents' aplenty, many of which may have had a hand from the devil himself.

Robert Munger the religious adviser to *The Omen* was discussing the project with a famous theologian over dinner one evening. He mentioned during the chat that although he was himself a Christian, he did not believe in the devil. To which the theologian had a rather daunting reply:

"If you go ahead and make this movie, before you are done you will believe the devil exists".

Munger concedes that after all the bizarre incidents linked to the film, he can't help but believe there was some other force at work during production.

Filming mainly took place in London. This meant for stars such as Gregory Peck who played Robert Thorn in the movie, a flight from the USA was a necessity. On one such flight from Los Angeles Peck's plane was hit by lightening. Three days later David Seltzer who wrote *The Omen,* was also London bound from LA. That plane was also hit by lightening.

Who says lightening doesn't strike twice?

These are not the only aviation related incidents related to the movie. As if the first two did not serve as enough of a warning to the makers of the film to cease production, they were about to receive a more startling and tragic one. As Richard Donner the director of *The Omen* explained.

Money was running low and Donner needed an aeroplane for a scene to film at a small airport. So he chartered a Hawker Sibly. Shortly afterwards he received a call from the owners of the aircraft stating that they had a full charter that morning. If Donner allowed them to charter the plane out for a flight first then he could have it for practically nothing afterwards. Taking into consideration his cash flow, Donner told them to go ahead.

The flight took off and almost immediately hit a flock of birds. The engines cut out causing the plane to lose air speed and hit the runway. It then slid onto the nearby road and hit a car. Killing everybody in the vehicle. The people in the car were the wife and the two children of the pilot.

The pilot of the very plane that was to be used in the production of the movie.

Once in London things were no different. The *curse* of *The Omen* was just getting going it would see. The making of the movie was taking place during a period of heightened IRA bombing activities in London.

Mace Neufeld the executive producer of *The Omen* said some of the crew had made reservations for a restaurant whilst in the capital. Just an hour before they were due to eat a terrorist bomb destroyed it. Luckily for the crew, they hadn't arrived there yet. A bomb also went off in a subway station as Mace and some of the others were literally walking towards it. Again, luckily no one was harmed.

Another warning to cease production perhaps?

With filming now in full swing director Richard Donner went on location to Windsor Safari Park. He shot a sequence that never actually made the final cut of the movie that featured lions in a lion enclosure. The crew finished the scene and headed over to film the infamous baboon sequences in another enclosure.

The very same day the guard at the Safari Park was in his booth, where he had forgotten to close the door. Two lions wandered in and attacked him. Sadly he did not survive.

Donner himself had a brush with the *curse* that seemed to have taken a hold of the production, but he was more fortunate in the outcome.

Donner was being let out of producer Harvey Bernhard's car to go into his house when a car came hurtling towards him. The car crashed into his car door trapping Donner in-between the two vehicles. Miraculously he wasn't seriously hurt. Had he received a personal warning to halt filming?

It seemed that nobody involved before, during or even after the production was safe from the *curse* of *The Omen*.

This is no more evident then in arguably the most chilling and possibly the most tragic incident associated with the movie.

As Harvey Bernhard, producer of *The Omen* explained.

John Richardson who worked on the special effects for *The Omen* was working on the movie *A Bridge Too Far* in Belgium. John had been responsible for the scene in which Jennings, played by David Warner, was beheaded with a sheet of glass.

Whilst driving along a road in Belgium he and his girlfriend were unfortunately involved in a horrific accident. Sadly John's girlfriend was killed in the crash. She was beheaded.

Stranger still, as John gained consciousness he saw a sign at the side of the road.

The sign read *'LIEGE 66.6 KM'*.

The three sixes? The number of *The Beast*?

Opinion is mixed amongst the cast and crew of *The Omen* as to whether these bizarre and often tragic incidents were in reality curse or coincidence.

Producer Harvey Bernhard said that throughout filming there were strange things happening. He said:

"...There was an aura of not being welcome...I sincerely believe the devil didn't want the picture to be made".

Director Richard Donner however has an entirely different view of the incidents surrounding the movie. He said:

"...It's incredible coincidence."

In religion the three sixes are the unholy sign, seven is the perfect sign. Was the sign of the three sixes written all over the production of The Omen?

What The Experts Say
The Omen (1976)

Darren W Ritson – Ghost Hunter, Paranormal Investigator and author. Darren is the founder of The North East Ghost Research Team and co- founder of WraithScape (Paranormal with a Passion). He has authored eleven books on the paranormal including The South Shields Poltergeist, One Family's Fight Against An Invisible Intruder, (with Michael J Hallowell), Ghost Hunter, True Life Encounters from the North East, and In Search of Ghosts, Real Hauntings from Around Britain.

He has had an interest in the paranormal for most of his life due to unexplained goings-on he experienced as a child growing up. Ever since he was a small boy he was fascinated with the thought of ghosts existing and after experiencing poltergeist activity at the age of thirteen in France in 1986, his path was set and he decided to try to learn more. Over the next 20 years he built up a library of books, magazines and literature on the paranormal including the works of the late Harry Price (1881-1948) Peter Underwood FRSA, and Guy Lyon Playfair to name a few.

His team - The North East Ghost Research Team - was founded in May 2003 and over the years he has worked with who he considers to be some of the finest paranormal investigators in the country.

After becoming a member of The Incorporated Society for Psychical Research (SPR) in May 2006, he hopes to continue his ghost hunting and paranormal research in addition to meeting new people and working with them in order to try and make some sense of ghosts and hauntings.

Darren also regularly corresponds with veteran ghost hunter Peter Underwood FRSA - president of the Ghost Club Society, and Guy Lyon Playfair who co- investigated the famous Enfield poltergeist with the late Maurice Grosse. For years he has travelled across the UK in his search for ghosts and has carried out dozens of radio broadcasts (Metro FM, BBC Radio and

Howard Hughes talk show – The Unexplained) as well as carrying out countless talks and lectures based on his cases and his findings - most notably he has addressed the Society for Psychical Research, and The Ghost Club.

"I first saw *The Omen* when I was twelve years old. I shouldn't have done, I suppose, but there you have it. I've watched it many times since, and the fact that I keep going back to it shows that the movie must have something; but what?

The allure of *The Omen* has more to do with me and less to do with the film, I think. I've always liked films of that genre, and still do. The truth is that it scared me, and there's something in each of us that likes to be scared.

One question that's often asked about *The Omen* is whether it matches up to real life experience. It's impossible to give a simple answer to this; some parts are wildly exaggerated and have little to do with reality. Others, however, mirror events that allegedly occurred in real life. Separating the two only becomes necessary if you want to clinically take the movie apart and see it in its social context. I can't be bothered with all that stuff; I just like to watch it and enjoy the tension. There again, who can say that *anything* in the movie is impossible? Maybe it's our imaginations that need stretched and not the film's credibility.

But there's another way of looking at *The Omen*. Some might argue that films of this nature serve a greater good by heightening public awareness of the occult, the paranormal and the supernatural. Well, I think it depends on the movie. Some undoubtedly work in this way, but I suspect that others are simply too hyped up to be of any value when it comes to educating the public. Mind you, that doesn't mean that they can't be brilliant entertainment though, and *The Omen* is certainly that.

One disturbing feature of shock-movies like *The Omen* is the rather negative effect they can have on some members of the public. Those involved with the production of the film certainly knew how to rack up the tension, and consequently the heart rate of those watching it. Of course, that is what cinemagoers pay for, but more than one fan has actually committed suicide after watching a scary movie. There are legions of people out there who would argue that the movie-makers bear a great responsibility here, and there's probably some logic in their argument. Personally I feel that those who watch such films also bear a responsibility; they shouldn't go to see movies if they think it might scare the living daylights out of them.

The Omen has been re-made, but I haven't seen it yet. Most times re-makes don't have the same magic as the originals, but occasionally they rise to the challenge. Maybe the re-make of *The Omen* will, who knows? I'll have to reserve judgment till I see it.

After the release of *The Omen* in its first incarnation – if you'll excuse the pun - rumours abounded that there was a curse attached to the film. Spooky coincidences attached themselves to it that to some were as unnerving as the movie itself (as Jason has so eagerly enlightened us with) and to be honest, they make the flesh creep. My take on this is that there *may* actually be a "higher force" of some kind at work here, all of which serves to enhance *The Omen* and not detract from it.

The Omen will go down in history as one of the world's eeriest films. Its longer-term impact on the public consciousness may be harder to quantify, but at the end of the day it is – and will remain – a damn-good scary movie."

The Curse Of The Poltergeist (1982 – 1986)

'They're Still He-eere!'

The *Poltergeist* movies are a trilogy of horror films produced in the 1980's. Steven Spielberg, the man behind such other paranormal classics as *'Close Encounters Of The Third Kind'* and *'E.T.'*, co-wrote and co-produced the first *Poltergeist* movie.

Poltergeist, the first and most successful of the trilogy was released on 4th June 1982.

The movie tells the story of 5 year old Carol Anne Freeling, who has began communicating with seemingly benign spirits. The spirits use the static on the family's television to communicate with the child through a kind of 'white noise'. Eventually the spirits use the television as a portal into the house itself and kidnap Carol Anne, taking her back through the portal. The majority of the film involves the Freeling's efforts to rescue Carol Anne from the spirits, led by a demon known as The Beast.

It seems that one single decision made in relation to this first movie may have been responsible for bringing upon the 'curse' that seems to have beset the *'Poltergeist Trilogy'*. It is alleged that real human skeletal remains were used as props in a well known 'swimming pool' scene. In television interviews actress JoBeth Williams, who played Carol Anne's mother Diane Freeling in *Poltergeist* and the sequel *Poltergeist II: The Other Side*, has said that she was told by the people involved behind the scenes of *Poltergeist* that the skeletons used in the scene were indeed real. The fact that real skeletons were used is widely blamed for the tragedies that followed. Advocates of the curse claim that the angry spirits of the deceased whose remains were used, wanted their revenge.

'They're he-eere!" – Carol Anne Freeling (Poltergeist (1982)

One of the first and biggest tragedies to beset the trilogy involved one of the key actresses in the first movie. Dominique Dunne played Dana Freeling, Carol Anne's older sister, in the first movie, *Poltergeist*. Shortly after completing filming of the movie Dominique met a popular Los Angeles chef, John Thomas Sweeney. Sweeney was working at the restaurant Ma Maison. The couple had a short and volatile romance due to Sweeney's abusive nature toward Dominique and she ended their relationship. A few weeks later, Sweeney turned up at Dominique's house to try and reconcile things. After she refused Sweeney strangled her on the driveway. Dominique Dunne died a few days later on the 4th November 1982 at Cedars- Sinai Medical Centre in LA, California. The 22 year old actress had become the first victim of the curse it would seem. A mere 5 months after the film's release.

Sweeney incidentally, was convicted of manslaughter and sentenced to 6 and a half years in prison for his crime.

The second in the trilogy of movies *Poltergeist II: The Other Side* was released in May 1986. This second installment explains why Carol Anne was targeted by the spirits in the first movie. It appears the Freeling's house in the first movie was built above an underground cavern that was below a graveyard. This cavern was the final resting place of a cult that died in the 1800's. The cult was led by a Reverend Kane who wanted to control his followers in life and death. The second movie was not as successful as the first, as is the case with most sequels. The one thing that would have seemed to have followed on from the first movie though was the curse.

'They're Baa-aaack!' – Carol Anne Freeling (Poltergeist II: The Other Side (1986)

Julian Beck played the Reverend Kane in *Poltergeist II* and had been diagnosed with stomach cancer before accepting the role. Although it may have been expected, he died of his ailment on 14th September 1985, aged 60 at Mount Sinai Hospital in New York. The film was released 8 months later. Was it the curse or would Beck have sadly lost his battle with the disease anyway?

Ill health also beset another actor from the second movie, Will Sampson who played Taylor the Medicine Man in *Poltergeist II*. Sampson received a heart-lung transplant in 1987, it is said that he knew his chances of survival were small due to his weakened condition before surgery, yet the 53 year old had to undergo the surgery in a Houston hospital. Sampson died on 3rd June 1987. The cause of death was given as pre-operative malnutrition and post-operative kidney failure. Once again the question begs to be asked had Sampson sadly succumbed to illness or had the curse struck again?

The final installment of the *Poltergeist Trilogy* was to come with more aplomb then its predecessor, more for the apparent influence of the curse then the actual film itself.

Poltergeist III was released in 1988 and sees Carol Anne being sent to live with her Aunt Pat, Uncle Bruce and their daughter Donna in order to make a new start and escape the demon Revered Kane. Things seem to be going well until strange phenomena appears to be affecting the family…it appears Kane has managed to track her down.

During the making of *Poltergeist III*, whilst shooting a fire scene, a movie set of a parking garage was engulfed by flames. Luckily nobody was seriously hurt although only one crew member managed to escape the accident totally unscathed.

To add even more paranormal links to the movie, whilst shooting a photography session for *Poltergeist III* Zelda Rubenstein, who played a Clairvoyant in the film, had an unexplained light obscuring the view of her face. The light only became apparent once the photographs were developed. Rubenstein claimed that the photo shoot was done, and the photographs taken, at the exact time her real-life mother died.

The cruelest tragedy and perhaps most famous incident of the curse were just about to happen.

Child actress Heather O'Rourke, who played Carol Anne Freeling in the trilogy, had been ill for months when production of *Poltergeist III* began. She was eventually diagnosed with Crohn's Disease and subsequently underwent medical treatment during parts of filming in Chicago. Principal photography lasted between April and June of 1987 and Heather, by all accounts finished her work on the film which was due for a June 1988 release. She returned home after a family holiday with her illness apparently in remission.

Whilst at home Heather was taken ill and what was thought to be a bout of flu had turned into a cardiac arrest on the drive to the Children's Hospital in San Diego. Heather was discovered to have an acute bowel obstruction and bacterial toxins had made their way into her bloodstream. Her heart was successfully restarted and she was flown by helicopter to a larger Children's Hospital where she underwent an operation to remove the obstruction. The toxins had already done their damage though and sadly Heather died on 1st February 1988 on the operating table of the hospital. Heather O'Rourke was interred in the outer wall of the 'Sanctuary Of Tenderness' mausoleum at Pierce Brothers Westwood Village Memorial Park Cemetery in Los Angeles, California. Her tomb is close to the tomb of Dominique Dunne who played her on screen sister Dana in *Poltergeist*. Had the 12 year old star of the *Poltergeist Trilogy* tragically become the youngest victim of the curse?

Even stranger was what was to happen following Heather's death. *Poltergeist III* had yet to be released, leading to rumours that Heather had passed away during shooting and that a double was used to complete the movie. O'Rourke's family and agent said at the time of her death that her scenes had been completed in June 1987. Writer-director Gary Sherman has always maintained that filming of *Poltergeist III* had not been completed when Heather died and he had to make changes to the movie due to her death. Whether or not this is true remains a mystery to this day.

Even with the completion of the films it seems that the *Poltergeist Trilogy* curse, or coincidences depending on your point of view, continued.

In 1994 the 'Freeling' home in Southern California, where, the first *Poltergeist* movie was partially filmed in 1982, was badly damaged by the Northridge earthquake.

More was to follow as in 2001 Beatrice Straight who played Dr. Lesh in *Poltergeist* died aged 87. Three years later, Brian Gibson the director of *Poltergeist II: The Other Side*, died aged 59 of Ewing's Sarcoma in 2004.

As with any 'curse' or 'urban legend' there are detractors and believers. That's what makes the world go around. Is this just a series of unfortunate coincidences?

People whose illnesses and tragedies would have sadly befallen them regardless of their involvement with the *Poltergeist Trilogy*? Or is it really a curse?

Have the angry spirits conjured up by the movies reached out into the real world to claim the victims that disturbed them?

Whatever you decide, I will leave you with a thought that perhaps Carol Anne Freeling herself might have said on the subject of the curse of the Poltergeist:

'They're Still He-eeere!'

What The Experts Say
The Curse Of The Poltergeist (1982 – 1986

Alexandra Holzer – Paranormalist, Columnist and Author of 'Lady Ambrosia: Secret Past Revealed' (May 2007) and' Growing Up Haunted: A Ghostly Memoir' (Publish America, Schiffer Publishing Ltd, Feb 2008). Alexandra appeared in two documentaries on the extras section of Poltergeist 25th Anniversary DVD (2007). Her many radio appearances include being on shows such as 'Darkness Radio', 'Yvette's Fright Night on Kerrang Radio' and 'Beyond Reality Radio with Grant and Jason from 'TAPS'. Alexandra now hosts her own online radio show on the Para-X network. Alexandra is also the daughter of world renowned 'Ghost Hunter' Hans Holzer.

"Drama always seems to surround a film set whether the genre is comedy, horror, a biopic to the paranormal. So-and-so was in the trailer together for a long period of time and so the gossip train leaves the station filled with rumours beginning to surface as the list goes on. And with this drama, comes a certain stigma attached especially when it is pertaining to the subject matter of ghosts, demons and beyond. When I think of the word 'cursed,' I think of my own black clouds hovering over my head as I try to convince people of my own projects. Then there is the thought of Egypt, Indians and so forth that would cast a curse upon anyone who desecrated a grave, robbed or disrespected sacred hallowed ground. Is it possible that when one shoots a film and all the drama surrounding it, that it pulls in an unseen energy from the 'other side?'

The film 'Jumper', recently released starring Canadian Actor Hayden Christiansen had many accidents and a death on its set. Now, that is horrible and one never wants that to occur on the job anywhere. But, being that this film was a sci-fi adventure packed story, would end in the headlines with the tragedy itself without any connotations to a ghost or a spirit creating the havoc. The film and being cursed would not become a topic of conversation any time soon. Words like 'bad luck' would be more suited in a headline like this.

Having said that, I think that anything is possible, but to place a curse over the Poltergeist Trilogy due to the people involved in the films is maybe stretching it a bit. We all have a life path to live and at any given moment, stuff happens. Now, in the case of *Poltergeist III* Zelda Rubenstein, who played a Clairvoyant in the film where "an unexplained light obscuring the view of her face" occurred, I would say this could be a normal paranormal experience found anywhere and at anytime. "The light only became apparent once the photographs were developed. Rubenstein claimed that when the photo shoot was done and the photographs taken, at the exact time her real-life mother had died." Perhaps often times this does occur, where her mother came by her work to say goodbye or even a reassurance that she really isn't gone. Just in the physical sense and to give her a sign then and there knowing this photo would later surface. The 'other side' does indeed work in mysterious ways and who are we to judge and put down whether or not it exists? Many may go through their life and never have one experience to boast about. And how sad for them I say as then they are truly missing what life really is. Which for me is alive and in it's natural course of events leading all the way up to the Universe and its infinite wisdom. This includes things going 'bump in the night.'

In the fall of 2007, my father the original Ghost Hunter Dr. Hans Holzer, Ph.D and I appeared on both featurettes of the re-released DVD for the anniversary of the film. The film itself was based off of documented experiences and morphed into a great cult classic still capturing our imaginations, thoughts and feelings today. It was well done and had many truths wrapped up into their 'beast' and 'medium' along with probably adding to the drop of television sales that year.

In all seriousness folks, I think things can and do manifest around a lot of energy that we create and when doing a film, there's a lot of that going on. At a baseball game, at a crowed carnival and so forth, were never alone. Just because you can't always see them with your eyes, you can still feel and when it becomes dark better keep that light on for a while because you never know who's watching."

Out Of This World?

From Fritz Lang's Metropolis to George Lucas' Star Wars, science fiction movies have always been a staple diet of cinema audiences. With the release of Steven Spielberg's Close Encounters Of The Third Kind in 1977, a new kind of science fiction movie had arrived. The possibility of beings from another planet paying us a visit seemed more realistic. More importantly, it gave people who had a story to tell the confidence to tell it.

People who believed they had witnessed UFO phenomena began reporting their encounters. With the increase of UFO sightings in the 1980's and the new phenomena of alien abductions in the 1990's, it was inevitable that some of these 'real' encounters would make their way onto the silver screen.

How true are these movies in their portrayal of the cases they are based on?

Did the cases themselves even happen at all?

Are they science fiction or science fact?

The Bermuda Triangle (1979)

From All Angles

The 1970's saw a spate of disaster movies hitting the big screen. These included disasters at sea, disasters in the air, burning buildings and even an invasion of killer bees.

In 1979 an even more unusual 'disaster' movie was released. The film in question did not involve killer insects, but it did involve both air and sea disasters. It also involved one of the world's most debated mysteries, the mystery that shares its name with the movie, the mystery that is the Bermuda Triangle.

The movie opens with a 100 year old schooner being thrown around at sea during a hurricane. A little girl who seems to be the only person onboard the boat scrambles for safety, fearing for her life. The film then cuts to present day. The crew of the yacht the Black Whale and a team of underwater explorers are hoping to locate the legendary City of Atlantis. The family of the crew members are also onboard, including a little girl who spots a doll floating around in the sea. When the doll is retrieved it bears an eerie resemblance to both the girl on the schooner and the girl on the yacht who claims the doll as her own.

Interspersed with the 'goings on' onboard the Black Whale a squadron of U.S. Air Force planes are shown going off course. A last desperate SOS is radioed in:

"The magnetic gyroscopes have gone crazy! I can't see the water anymore! My God! What's this?"

The plane then disappears within the co-ordinates of Miami, Puerto-Rico and Bermuda, the area known as the Bermuda Triangle...the exact area where the Black Whale is headed. Will the crew find the lost City of Atlantis? Or will they become another victim of the Bermuda Triangle?

Just mention the Bermuda Triangle to anyone and almost everybody knows what you are talking about...or at least they think they do.

The Bermuda Triangle has become as much of a 'brand name' as 'Mars Bars' and 'Adidas' or the last 50 years or so, albeit for entirely different reasons. Despite there being several other areas around the globe where ships and aeroplanes have been mysteriously lost in equally alarming quantities, none of these places have enjoyed such notoriety as the 'Devil's Triangle'.

So what actually is the Bermuda Triangle and what sets apart from such areas as the Bass Straits off the coast of Australia and even the Great Lakes of the United States of America? Why is the 'Devil's Triangle' near Bermuda more infamous then the 'Devil's Sea' near Japan?

Firstly let's establish what and where the Bermuda Triangle is.

The Bermuda Triangle is an area off the East coast of America where several aircraft and boats have suffered unusual and unexplained effects. For instance aircraft that have been able to report difficulties before being lost in the area have often cited instrument failure or distortion. A 'yellow sky' is also an all too often reported phenomena in the area.

The location of the Bermuda Triangle is not a specifically defined geographic area… you won't find it in an atlas, but it is generally accepted as the area of the Atlantic Ocean off the Florida, Georgia and Carolina Coasts of America extending to the Islands of Bermuda and Puerto Rico whilst also taking in the Northern coasts of the Caribbean…thus forming a 'triangle'.

The first 'coining' of the phrase 'Bermuda Triangle' stemmed from a report by E.V.W Jones on the associated Press wire service in 1950. Jones voiced his concern regarding the volume of recent unexplained ship losses in the area and one of the world's greatest unsolved mysteries was born.

The first victim of the Bermuda Triangle by sea is believed to have been claimed some 170 years before Jones' report…long before the press even existed in fact.

In 1780 the vessel 'General Gates' went missing in the area of the triangle and was never seen again, despite the fact that no British warship laid claim to the sinking.

Thus began a long line of mysterious incidents and disappearances of sea vessels in the area.

One of the most well know of these is the loss of the USS Cyclops, a 500 foot ship weighing 19,600 tonnes. The Cyclops disappeared in March 1918 along with 300 crew members.

Less then two decades later the amount of unexplained incidents at sea in the area began to increase dramatically and people such as Jones began to take an interest.

In 1944 the vessel 'Wild Goose' was being towed in the 'triangle' by another ship, the 'Caicos Trader'. Joe Talley was onboard the 'Wild Goose' sleeping when suddenly he awoke to find himself underwater. Realising that the 'Wild Goose' was sinking Talley managed to get a life jacket and swim the 60 feet up to safety. The crew of the 'Caicos Trader' had to quickly sever the tow line to avoid being dragged under the sea themselves and Talley was rescued. There has never been a satisfactory explanation as to why the 'Wild Goose' sank within minutes, far faster then would have been expected or indeed for the fact that it sank at all.

In 1954 Ray Clarke witnessed a less life threatening incident in the area, but it was no less dramatic or mysterious. Whilst stood on the deck of the 'Queen Mary' Clarke saw two 45 foot columns of water suddenly shoot up from an area of the Ocean which had been, what he described as, 'unusually calm' just minutes before.

In February 1963 the Triangle claimed another victim; the 'Marine Sulphur Queen' along with her 39 crew and 15,000 tonne cargo were lost without a trace.

Three years later, in 1966, tugboat Captain Don Henry was taking the trip from Puerto Rico to Fort Lauderdale, A journey that took him through the heart of the Bermuda Triangle.

On what was a clear afternoon he became alarmed when suddenly the compass on his boat began to spin wildly and a strange darkness descended. This fog became so thick that Henry couldn't even see the horizon. Things began to become even more bizarre as water began coming in from all directions and the electrical power failed completely on the tugboat.

Luckily for Henry, as a dense fog now totally engulfed his boat, the engines did not fail and he was able to eventually sail out of the fog. Now clear of it, Henry looked back at the area. The fog was so densely concentrated that he said it looked like a solid block. Henry also described the water in the area covered by the fog as 'boiling' whilst outside of that area the sea was calm. Henry survived the incident and made it safely to his destination.

A similar incident of unexplained instrument failure occurred in 1971 when the ship the 'USS Richard E. Byrd' mysteriously lost all communication and navigational aids on a voyage to Bermuda. The vessel remained helpless for a staggering 10 days before suddenly regaining communication.

The most recent recorded case of a vessel lost at sea that is attributed to the Bermuda Triangle was in 1992. On 23rd December a 42 foot catamaran travelling from Rhode Island to Martinique disappeared. A five day search found nothing, despite there being no adverse weather conditions at the time. Was this vessel another unfortunate victim of the triangle?

With the advent of flight came another way to travel. This also gave people another way to cross the Bermuda Triangle. As you are about to read, it would seem that whatever was causing the unusual events in the waters of the area was not confined to the Ocean. It was also about to cause them in the skies above it, and at a more alarming rate.

In 1928 Charles Lindbenbergh reported both of his compasses failed whilst flying through the triangle to Florida. He also reported a 'heavy haze' which had obscured his vision. He reached his destination safely.

The first recorded incident of an aerial loss over the Bermuda Triangle came 14 years later when a TBF Avenger aircraft was lost in 1942. This signaled the start of an incredible amount of incidents in an alarmingly short period of time.

Two years later in December 1944 seven air force bombers encountered clear air turbulence in the area. Their planes were thrown backwards and dropped 600 feet. Five of the seven aircraft crashed and two managed to recover. No debris of the unfortunate aircraft that were lost was found.

The following year, 1945 the most 'famous' of all the Bermuda Triangle mysteries occurred. The Grumman TBM-3 Avenger Bomber was believed to be 'ahead of it's time' and one of the most powerful and efficient aircraft in the skies. The plane carried three men; a pilot, a radio operator and a gunner.

On 5th December 1945, five US Navy Avenger Bombers prepared for a training flight.

The aircraft were given sufficient fuel for approximately 1,100 miles, far more then what was needed for the anticipated 300 mile flight duration. In terms of time, Flight 19 would be able to stay airborne for around 6 hours with the fuel they had onboard, a full 4 hours more then what was needed for the expected 2 hour flight.

The mission would involve the bombers flying outwards to the Bahamas, making practice bombing runs, turning north to Great Sale Cay and then finally turning south-west back to Fort Lauderdale. In effect, Flight 19 would be flying a triangular course within the 'Bermuda Triangle' itself.

Although this was to be a 'training flight' most of the airmen were experienced aviators. Each man had around 350 hours experience including over 50 hours flying the Avenger aircraft itself. Sergeant Robert Galvin for example had seen active service over the Pacific throughout the war.

The man who was to lead and instruct Flight 19 on this exercise was Lieutenant Charles Taylor. Taylor was a pre-war veteran and had over 2,500 flying hours to his credit.

As final preparations were taking place for the flight Gunner Corporal Allen reported sick and pulled out of the training exercise. This meant that only four of the five planes would now have full crews. Kosnar would later go on to say he had had a premonition not to fly on that day.

On 5th December 1945, between 2pm and 2:10pm, Flight 19 (consisting of 5 aircraft and 14 men) took off from Fort

Lauderdale, Florida. The flight took to the air in clear skies and for the first hour and a half the exercise seemed to be going well.

Between 3:40 and 3:45 pm, the control tower at Fort Lauderdale received a call from Lieutenant Taylor. The mission was due to end shortly and they fully expected it to be just a routine communication. Little did they know the training exercise was about to become a mysterious and historic disaster.

Lt. Taylor called the tower reporting that Flight 19 was lost. He had become frantic and making rational contact with him had become a problem. A request was made from the tower for Taylor to assume a bearing due west. Taylor responded with:

'We don't even know which way is west…Even the ocean doesn't look right.'

Lieutenant Robert Cox, a flight instructor, was flying his own students near the Fort Lauderdale base and was encircling the airfield in preparation to make a landing. Cox heard the communication between Taylor and the tower on a radio frequency reserved for training flights. Lt. Taylor, the Flight 19 instructor was now overheard in conversation with Captain Powers, one of the Flight 19 pilots. Cox heard:

'I don't know where we are, we must have got lost after that last turn.'

Lt. Cox then intervened and asked Lt. Taylor what was causing the problem. Taylor answered:

'Both my compasses are out.'

Captain Powers was then asked for a compass reading strangely his compasses were not working either. The loss of both Lt. Taylor and Captain Powers' compasses may have been a coincidence, but it appears that none of the aircraft of Flight 19 were able to offer a compass reading at this point. Suggesting that perhaps some external force was causing equipment malfunctions.

Lt. Taylor regarded training exercises as 'so simple' that he rarely took a plotting board or even a flight plan with him. The experienced aviator was now lost and flying without a compass, clocks and possibly even without a watch. Clearly disorientated, Taylor asked Captain Powers which course he was taking and then, extraordinarily, Lt. Taylor, the flight instructor, handed over the leadership of the flight to Captain George Stivers.

Lt. Cox decided that Flight 19 was now in serious trouble and gave Lt. Taylor instructions for locating Fort Lauderdale. He told Taylor to 'put the sun over his port wing and fly up the coast'. Cox indicated he would fly south and meet Flight 19, believing he knew their whereabouts. He then flew out in an attempt to guide Flight 19 into port. As Cox flew what he believed to be 'towards' Flight 19 the transmissions he was receiving from them became fainter, although they should have been getting stronger as the aircraft approached each other. Cox had inadvertently led the flight into even more trouble. He had directed Taylor north, taking Taylor's estimate of his position as being over the Florida Keys, when in all probability Flight 19 was flying aimlessly over the Bahamas and away from Lt. Cox. Eventually Cox lost all communication with Flight 19 and bizarrely his own radio failed and he had no option other then to return to base. On returning to the Fort Lauderdale base Cox asked to take another aircraft to search for the doomed training flight but he was denied permission.

By this time (between 4:30pm and 5:30pm), a search party was sent out from the Banana River naval station. A Martin Mariner flying boat, with a crew of 12 was dispatched out to sea in a rescue operation. After reporting in twice to give their position the crew failed to report in a third time when they should have done. Flight 49, as the rescue plane was known, along with her crew of 12, had vanished.

Sometime between 5:50pm and 8pm (reports of the time vary dramatically), crew aboard the SS Gaines Mills, an oil tanker, reported seeing a ball of flames hitting the ocean. The explosion occurred approximately 50 miles out from the Banana River naval base, almost certainly the location of the Martin Mariner sea plane at the time.

The Martin Mariner aircraft is known to be an unstable plane and is often called the 'flying gas tank'. This is because they often carried an immense amount of fuel on rescue missions, some 2,000 gallons on most occasions. This made the aircraft highly susceptible to ignition from a spark or a careless smoking crew member.

Although we cannot be certain that it was Flight 49 that the crew of the SS Gaines Mills saw plunge into the ocean it is highly likely that this was the case. By the time the Gaines Mills reached the exact location of the event all that remained was an oil slick and neither wreckage nor the bodies of the crew were ever found. The captain of the Gaines Mills remained convinced it was an exploding aeroplane he had witnessed hitting the water that night.

Flight 19 was now hopelessly lost, rescue missions had either been aborted or ended in disaster. To make matters worse the training flight were heading even more off course and the weather had gone from being a clear day to a tropical storm.

Taylor and Flight 19 continued to fly under the misapprehension that they were on course. They continued changing direction from north to east and so on, believing they were heading for the Gulf of Mexico.

Taylor gave the order that all the aircraft were to close-up and fly in a tight formation so that when the first plane ran out of fuel they were in a position to ditch together.

Just after 7pm the final message from Flight 19 was transmitted. The barely audible radio message was part of Flight 19's call signal. It said:

'FT...FT'

After that there was complete silence.

The following day the largest air-sea search in history was underway. An area of 300,000 square miles was covered by hundreds of aircraft and 20 ships. They found precisely nothing. Flight 19 had vanished. Coupled with Flight 49, 6 aircraft and 27 men had disappeared.

If we account for Flight 49's fate with the sighting of a crash by the SS Gaines Mills that still leaves us with a question that remains unanswered. What happened to Flight 19?

On 8th December 1945, three days after the disappearance, a Captain Morrison reported a sighting of flares and human figures in the Banana River area. The sighting was confirmed but search parties found nothing. The area was west of the radio – fix position obtained on Flight 19 just before they were lost. With Taylor first flying north and then east as the squadron became more and more disorientated it seems highly unlikely that they would have had enough fuel to reach this location. If they had, their radio signal should have gained in strength instead of diminishing.

The most logical explanation is that Flight 19 crashed or voluntarily ditched into the ocean when it ran out of fuel somewhere in the Atlantic north of the Bahamas.

The radio transmission made by Lt. Taylor saying *'the ocean doesn't look right'* may refer to him expecting to see the lighter blue costal waters when he was in fact flying over the deeper blue water of the ocean.

In 1991 a team of explorers located 5 TBM Avengers in 750 feet of water 10 miles off the Florida coast. It seemed that Flight 19 had been found 46 years after its disappearance. However, an investigation discovered the bombers were five of the other 100 Avengers lost in the area as a result of military exercises. Wreckage thought to be that of the doomed flight had also been found in the 'Bermuda Triangle' in 1961 and 1987, and as with that found in 1991, upon examination, it was found not to be.

Even if Flight 19, or any part of it, is ever recovered it is unlikely that this will shed any light on the reasons for the disorientation responsible for their disappearance.

Perhaps the answer lies in the realms of the paranormal.

Bermuda Triangle researcher Richard Winter organised a flight through the area for a number of mediums in an attempt to solve the mystery. One of the psychics claimed to be 'channeling' a pilot by the name of Gallivan. Gallivant had been a member of Flight 19, he was a gunner who had flown with Captain Stivers. Through the medium, Gallivan described an approaching storm with an unusual cloud pattern, lack of visibility and malfunctioning equipment. He went on to say:

'I can't tell the water from the air. I have no control. Ahead there is an opening...a clearing...something like a crack of light under a door. It seems like an escape from the storm. The plane is flying toward it, but I have no control. It's sort of like a vacuum...Ahead is a long cylindrical object. The end is open and parts of the plane are being pulled inside...'

The medium went on to make reference to UFO's and obscure energy sources.

This was not the only proposed theory for the tragedy involving UFO's. A Florida radio ham had tuned into the transmissions between Flight 19 instructor Lt. Taylor and the flight tower during the training exercise. The last message he claimed to hear from Taylor were:

"Don't come after me. They look like they're from outer space.'

Although this alleged transmission from Lt. Taylor has never been confirmed by naval authorities.

Had Flight 19 had a close encounter with a UFO? Is this what had caused their equipment failure, disorientation and ultimately their disappearance? Had Flight 19 been abducted by a UFO?

Bermuda Triangle debunkers will say this is nonsense and that human error, fatigue and other more 'rational' or 'scientific' explanations are the real causes for the loss tragedy.

Surely Flight 19, with the combined experience of 14 personnel, was capable of overcoming any such 'lapse' or human error. Surely these men, some of whom had flown from the decks of aircraft carriers in the Pacific Ocean and found their way back, were capable of finding the east coast of the United States after a routine afternoon flight? Or was Flight 19, as the medium and the radio ham's evidence claim, not such a 'routine' flight after all?

The Board of Investigation issued a statement that suggested there was no explanation which could be offered for the loss of Flight 19. The loss would go down as one of the Bermuda Triangle's most famous enigmas.

Three years later, January 1948, South American Airways 'Star Tiger' along with 6 crew and 25 passengers vanished over the triangle. In December of the same year a DC-3 aircraft carrying 27 passengers was lost. In January 1949, only one month after this incident, South American Airways 'Star Aerial', with a crew of 6 and carrying 12 passengers was lost over the same area. Even more bizarrely, this aircraft was the sister plane to the 'Star Tiger' which had vanished over the triangle almost exactly a year before.

Along with the alarming losses being suffered by aircraft over the triangle there were also more reports of unusual occurrences. In 1963 captain R Shattenkurk reported seeing a huge white bubble of water forming on the Ocean whilst flying from New York to Puerto Rico. This phenomenon was reported again after being witnessed by the crew of another airliner a month later. In 1968 Jim Blocker reported navigational failure inside a bank of clouds whilst flying from Nassau to Palm Beach.

Another mysterious incident involving the skies above the triangle happened to the author Martin Caidin who was flying from Bermuda to Jacksonville Naval Air Station in Florida. Caidin took off in perfect flying conditions in clear, warm weather. Suddenly the blue sky turned to a creamy yellow colour and Caidin was unable to see the outer portion of the left wing of his plane. Later the right wing became obscured, even though satellite readouts on his navigational equipment told him he should not be obscured by mist. As the mist worsened Caidin's navigational instruments began acting erratically. As he put it:

'Two million dollars of avionics just up and died'

Caidin was able to make out a 'tunnel – like' hole in the mist through which he could see the blue sky. This hole was immediately above the plane and upon examination; Caidin noticed another one below the plane. The holes were pacing the plane exactly. As Caidin described:

'As if a long pipe extended from the surface (of the Ocean) to the sky above'

Caidin and the rest of his crew managed to remain calm during the incident and after enduring 4 hours of the phenomena…it suddenly ended. The navigational equipment sprung back to life and they were flying in perfect skies again. Caidin immediately swung the aircraft around to take a look at the area they had just left and the sky was clear as far as the eye could see. The 'mist' had just vanished. They continued their flight and safely landed without further incident.

The most recent recorded case of an aircraft lost in the skies above the Bermuda Triangle was in 1991, when a Grumman Cougar Jet vanished.

As is the case of incidents and losses in the water, the amount of incidents and losses in the skies above the Bermuda Triangle are too numerous to mention every single one. I have just tried to present to you a varied and representative selection of these cases and what allegedly happened.

So what did happen? Does the cause of the phenomena occurring in the Bermuda Triangle have a scientific explanation? …or a paranormal one?

In 1975 marine insurer Lloyds of London issued a statement indicating:

'Our intelligence service can find no evidence to support that the 'Bermuda Triangle' has more losses then anywhere else'

The United States Coastguard concurred, saying:

'There are genuine mysteries to be explained, but they are probably applicable across the world'

So what are the keys to solving these 'genuine mysteries'? Let's take a look at some of the theories and explanations put forward by various sources as to what is happening in the Bermuda Triangle.

- There is a large amount of air and sea traffic crossing the area. These include; inexperienced sailors, large amounts of illegal immigrants and drug trafficking by sea and air. So it

could just be a case of the 'laws of averages' due to the volume and nature of the traffic.
- Bad weather.
- Sea Piracy
- Live bombs still remaining under the water from previous conflicts that are caused to detonate for some reason.
- Tidal waves. Some rogue and freak waves can reach 100 feet, engulfing a vessel.
- Giant whirlpools, which could swallow a ship without trace.
- Meteorite. This theory is not as strange as it seems if you read my explanation. The Seasat satellite was launched in June 1978 to measure and map the contours of the Ocean's surface and map ridges and troughs in the water. The satellite uncovered evidence that in the area of the Bermuda Triangle there was a 25 mile across and 50 feet deep, almost perfectly circular depression. The meteor theory is that a meteorite has buried itself in this location and created a magnetic anomaly which in turn has caused gravitational effects. This theory suggests this may in some way be contributing to the losses of aircraft and ships in the area.
- Methane gas deposits. Dr Richard McIver suggests that under the Oceans, including the area of the Bermuda Triangle there are large deposits of frozen methane hydrate trapping large amounts of methane gas. If something such as a landslide would break up the methane hydrate it would in turn release the methane gas. This would account for sudden turbulence on the water's surface and could even affect aircraft as it moves up into the atmosphere. An aircraft finding itself flying into a cloud would then find its engines starved of oxygen and could very well explode if the gas was somehow ignited by heat or a spark. This could also account for some of the cases of 'clear air turbulence' reported in the Bermuda Triangle. According to McIver a large released methane gas deposit could affect a ship's buoyancy so drastically that it could swiftly sink it. In one case of methane gas release a drilling rig sank in minutes and survivors found that the water buoyancy was affected so drastically that they sank even though they were wearing

life jackets. The water turbulence that would be caused by the gas release would also cause huge clouds of ionised air that could affect compasses and other navigational equipment. This theory would also account for the disappearance of aircraft and vessel debris, as the water into which it would have sank is so lacking in buoyancy the debris would sink so quickly that it would allow disturbed sediments to settle over it thus covering the wreckage.

There are also of course the 'less scientific' theories.
- A time warp in an unknown location within the Bermuda Triangle.
- Sea Monsters. Supposedly in the area that are capable of sinking ships.
  - UFO's. Abduction of not only the pilots/sailors but of their aircraft/vessels too.

As surely as aircraft and ships will keep vanishing in the Bermuda Triangle, as it has done since the day E.V.W Jones sent his wire, the debate will rage on.

As with any good mystery there are plenty of paths to lead you the door of 'truth'. You just have to decide which one you wish to take.

What The Experts Say
The Bermuda Triangle (1979)

Mike Hallowell – Paranormal Investigator, Journalist and Author. Mike is a freelance writer and specialises in penning books, newspaper columns and articles about the paranormal. He also writes extensively about Native American culture and spirituality, and has Indian heritage in his family. His first book 'Herbal Healing' was published in 1985. Since then he has penned a number of other books including 'Ales & Spirits', 'Invizikids' and 'The South Shields Poltergeist' which he co-authored Darren W. Ritson.

Mike contributes regularly to a number of journals and newspapers. He has penned his 'WraithScape' column for The Shields Gazette for over a decade, and it is the longest-running paranormal column in a provincial newspaper in the UK. He is also a regular columnist with Vision magazine, and contributes to other periodicals such as 'Beyond', 'Paranormal' and 'Magnolia'.

Mike has starred in as number of documentaries about the paranormal, including The Ghost Detectives with Tom Baker, filmmaker Gary Wilkinson's Anatomy of a Haunting and G. P. Taylor's Uninvited Guests. He regularly appears on the BBC and other channels both in the UK and abroad.

During his decades of investigation into the paranormal and alternative spirituality, Mike has interviewed most of the main players in the field including Colin Fry, Uri Geller, Tony Stockwell, Cliff Crook, Larry Warren, Richard Freeman, Stephen Holbrook, Jonathan Downes, Derek Acorah, Billy Roberts and Nick Redfern.

Mike was the founder of the Twilight Worlds Paranormal Research Society, but left the organisation after a number of years due to disagreements regarding how it was being run. He is currently the patron of the North East Ghost Research Team and the Tyneside regional representative of the Centre For Fortean Zoology.

"The Bermuda Triangle is one of the most bewitching phenomena in recent history, and the development of the story is no less intriguing than the enigma itself.

For centuries reports have been made concerning ships going missing under mysterious circumstances and, from the 20th century onwards, aeroplanes started to vanish too. Of course, the crucial question is whether such disappearances can be explained rationally. Some researchers would say not, and that something truly paranormal is going on.

At the outset it has to be said that at least some of the disappearances undoubtedly have a prosaic explanation. Ships, planes and boats disappear every day due to inclement weather conditions and/or mechanical failures. However, not all such events can be dismissed so readily. In the Bermuda Triangle an unusually large number of disappearances take place – some of them are truly baffling and seem to defy any logical explanation.

When Charles Berlitz wrote his definitive book on the subject he drew the world's attention to the enigma, precipitating a large number of documentaries and movies. Some exaggerated the affair, whilst others gave a balanced overview of it.

In recent years a number of scientific explanations have been put forth to explain away the disappearances; everything from geomagnetic anomalies to gas eruptions from the sea bed. Some are pretty convincing whilst others are patently flawed. Personally I don't believe that any of them provide a comprehensive solution. Even if we dismiss 99% of cases, there is still a hard core that are truly enigmatic.

Over the last two decades the pendulum has swung towards finding a rational explanation, and the belief that "paranormal forces" are at work has taken something of a back seat. However, we need to be careful that we don't throw the baby out with the bathwater, as they say.

Human nature being what it is, its tempting to whip out Occam's Razor at every opportunity and look for neat, simple solutions. Alas, we're unlikely to find one – at least one which covers every strange disappearance. Life just isn't like that, I'm afraid.

Cynics who debunk all paranormal phenomena as either fraudulent or delusional – and they are the most pitiable of all creatures, believe me – will always look to the rational at the expense of the exotic. Its funny, but some of the most bizarre solutions to the Bermuda Triangle mystery have not spilt forth from the lips of believers, but from the throats of sceptics. A grizzled paranormalist once said to me, "Mike, when the rational explanations become wilder that the spooky ones, then you know you're on to something".

One of the problems with disappearances at sea, of course, is that locating evidence is so much harder than on land. Unless we are able to examine the wreckage of marine vessels we may never be able to determine the cause of their demise. In fact, we may not even be able to determine whether they are there at all. Perhaps they truly were sucked through some sort of vortex into another dimension. Oh, this is the stuff of science fiction, I know, but you'll have to indulge me. Once you get past fifty you can take liberties that are unavailable to you in your youth, and you'll just have to put up with it.

Seriously though, my gut instinct is that the greatest chapter in the history of the Bermuda Triangle saga is yet to be told. Are ships being attacked by giant sea monsters? It's not impossible. Are they being teleported elsewhere in the universe by creatures from another world? Well, strictly speaking that's not impossible either. Or, maybe, it really is all down to giant gas bubbles and geomagnetic anomalies after all. This would be boring, true, but one day the truth will out..."

The Philadelphia Experiment (1984)

The Vanishing Ship

Not every 'Out Of This World' movie involves a visitation from, or a close encounter with a being from another galaxy. There are the also the kinds of movies where an evil professor creates an ingenious machine or a groundbreaking experiment goes disastrously wrong. Most of these incredible stories have their origins firmly planted on mother earth and, even more shockingly, some of them even claim to have their origins based on fact. The following movie is a case in point.

On the 3rd August 1984, *The Philadelphia Experiment* was released in the USA. The Stewart Rafill movie was based on an 'actual event' that took place in the year the film was set, 1943. The movie tells the story of two sailors, David Herdeg and Jim Parker. The sailors are stationed on a ship that is to be a part of an experiment involving invisibility. The navy proceed with the experiment, which goes horribly wrong. Somehow the parameters of the experiment are unexpectedly exceeded and Herdeg and Parker find themselves in the future. Having 'jumped ship' the sailors, who are the only two survivors of the experiment, discover they are now in the Nevada desert in the year 1984. Having travelled 41 years into the future what will become of them? Will they be able to adapt to their new surroundings? Can they get back to their own time?

The supposed true story that the movie was based is a far more intriguing and complex case than is shown on the big screen.

During World War II, the United States Navy are alleged to have conducted an experiment on a small destroyer escort ship. The experiment became commonly known as The Philadelphia Experiment, but researchers and investigators believe that it was officially known as Project Rainbow. It is believed that by creating an incredibly intense magnetic field around the ship, that the refraction or bending of light and radar waves would make the vessel invisible to enemy radar. It may even achieve complete optical invisibility of the vessel.

In June of 1943 the USS Eldridge, DE 173 was fitted with tons of electronic equipment. This included two huge generators that were mounted where the forward gun turret would have been. These were to have their power distributed through four magnetic coils mounted on the deck. Also mounted on the deck were three RF transmitters, three thousand power amplifier tubes (used to drive the generators and the coils), and an array of other experimental equipment designed to enable the project to be a success.

The first experiment, allegedly carried out by Dr. Franklin Reno, was carried out sometime between July and August 1943. The power to the generators was turned on as the USS Eldridge sat in Philadelphia, Pennsylvania, USA. As the electromagnetic fields built up a green fog enveloped the ship, eventually making it entirely from view. As the fog completely disappeared, so did the Eldridge. All that remained was undisturbed water where the ship had been only moments before.

Observers including scientists and naval officers watched for a full fifteen minutes before ordering the generators to be shut down. The green fog slowly reappeared and as the fog subsided the ship came back into view. The feeling of achievement that the ship and crew had not only been made invisible to both radar and the human eye slowly turned to uneasiness. It became apparent that something had gone wrong.

The observers from the shore boarded the Eldridge to find that the crew who had remained on deck during the experiment were disorientated and nauseous. The crew was removed and the equipment was altered.

The 28th October 1943 saw the final and most startling test of this 'new technology'. At 17:15 the generators were turned on again. This time the electromagnetic field caused the Eldridge to become only a faint outline in the waters of the Philadelphia Naval Yard. With only the faint outline of the hull visible for a few seconds, suddenly there was a blinding blue flash and the Eldridge completely vanished. Within seconds of this happening the ship appeared miles away in Norfolk, Virginia. The Eldridge was seen for several minutes in its new location before disappearing again, as mysteriously as it had appeared. The Eldridge then reappeared in the Philadelphia Naval Yard where the experiment had originally begun.

As with the first experiment, the ship was boarded after the ship reappeared; although this time the findings were more horrific. Upon inspection it was found that many of the sailors were violently sick. Some of the men were 'missing' and never found, but most disturbing of all, it is claimed that five of the sailors were 'fused' into the ship's metal structure.

The men that survived the experiment were discharged as 'mentally unfit for duty' and were never the same again. Some of them went insane. As a result of these terrible side effects, the navy abandoned exploring this new technology they had discovered.

At least one of the experiments was said to have taken place in full view of the SS Andrew Furuseth (a Merchant Marine ship), along with other observation vessels.

It was in fact one of the crewmen of the SS Andrew Furseth that first brought these events to the public's attention twelve years later.

Morris Jessup was man who had written a dissertation in the field of astrophysics and had an interest in, amongst other things, 'fringe science'. The 55 year old astronomer never officially received a PhD, but in 1955 he had his book *The Case For The UFO* published. In the book Jessup speculated that anti-gravity and electromagnetism would be better then using rocket fuel to propel space vehicles

In October 1955 received some very interesting mail. Carl M. Allen, as he signed the letters, began sending strange letters to Jessup, describing several phases of the Philadelphia experiment. Allen claimed to have witnessed some of the events himself, as it would later come to light that 'Carl M. Allen' was in fact Carlos Allende, one of the crewmen on board the SS Andrew Furuseth.

The letters sent to Jessup by Allen were strange ramblings written with several different colours of pencils and pens. Allen described such strange events as some of the crew walking through walls and appearing to 'walk upon nothing'. He also explained that the ship had disappeared, reappeared in Virginia, and then returned to Philadelphia. Allen claimed that he had observed the experiment from a merchant ship that was nearby at the time and he also said that he had later read about the incident in a Philadelphia newspaper.

Jessup paid little attention to the letters until he was visited by the Office of Naval Research. Admiral Furth had been anonymously sent a paperback copy of Jessup's UFO book. Inside the book were various incoherent notes, handwritten in various different colours. Furth took little notice of the package he had been sent but Commander George Hoover, Major Darren Ritter and Captain Sidney Sherby of the ONR did. They visited Jessup to see if he could shed any light on the matter. Jessup recognised the writing to be the same style as the letters he had received and showed them to the ONR men. The ONR made copies of the book and the letters and distributed them amongst a small number of people they believed may help them identify 'Carl M. Allen'. Jessup also began investigating Allen's claims but both Jessup and the ONR were both unsuccessful in their searches to find the man and evidence for his claims. Jessup died in 1959 as the result of a suicide, but the story did not end with his death.

In 1969 Carlos Allende walked into the offices of UFO researchers APRO in Tucson, Arizona, USA. Allende confessed to being 'Carl M. Allen' and to being the person who wrote the letters to Jessup. He also confessed to sending a copy of Jessup's book to the ONR and writing the notes in it. Allende said that the section in Jessup's book regarding invisibility and force fields had scared him into making the whole story of the USS Eldridge experiments. He said the whole story had been a hoax he had concocted in order to scare Jessup into not writing anything else on the subject of UFOs. It would appear that that Project Rainbow never happened at all.

However, in 1979 William Moore and Charles Berlitz wrote a book entitled *'The Philadelphia Experiment'*. The book focused on the suicide of Jessup and the uncharacteristic interest of the ONR into the case. The authors also suggested that Allende's confession may have been false. Most interesting of all was the inclusion of what the authors say was a copy of a newspaper article from 1943. The book suggests that the sailors mentioned in the article were suffering from the after effects of being involved in the Philadelphia Experiment. The article of the headline read *'Strange Circumstances Surround Tavern Brawl'*. The article says that during an altercation at a Philadelphia bar two sailors disappeared into thin air. The article was sent to Moore and Berlitz in the form of an anonymous photocopy and had no date or headline on it. Strangely enough the newspaper article didn't seem to match the column size of any Philadelphia newspaper of that day. Unfortunately the circumstances in which the article was sent made it impossible to find out whether the article was genuine or a hoax. Later another 'witness' to the experiment would come forward.

In 1990, Alfred Bielek came forward. He claimed to be a physicist onboard the USS Eldridge in 1943 and was part of the team that conducted the Philadelphia Experiment. He also claimed to have time travelled in 1942 to 1983 during the experiment. Bielek supported the 1984 movie *'The Philadelphia Experiment'*, commenting on how accurate the first 15 minutes of the movie was to the events he had witnessed. Bielek continued to support the truth behind the Philadelphia Experiment and even added more 'facts' to the story that had been previously unknown.

In March 1999 fifteen members of the crew of the USS Eldridge held a reunion in Atlantic City. They all denied the Allende, Bielek and Moore/Berlitz versions of events in 1943. Many of the survivors were growing tired of being asked about The Philadelphia Experiment one of the crewmen went as far as to joke that the only accuracy in the accounts was that the sailors were 'a little crazy'.

In 2003, Bielek's version of his participation in the Philadelphia Experiment was debunked by a small team of investigators including American Marshall Barnes, Canadian Fred Houpt and German Gerold Schelm, and the general consensus now is that he was nowhere near the ship at the proposed time of the experiment. Bielek however, would continue to maintain his involvement in the project.

The US Navy of course denies that the Philadelphia Experiment (Project Rainbow) ever existed. A search of the archives failed to identify records of a Project Rainbow relating to making a ship disappear or any other teleportation experiments. The only records of any 'Rainbow related' names found in the records for the 1940's were:

- Codename Rainbow – The codename used to refer to the Rome-Berlin- Tokyo axis.
- The Rainbow plans – The war plans to defeat Italy, Germany and Japan.
- Rainbow V – This plan was in effect on the 7th December 1941 when Japan attacked Pearl Harbour. Rainbow V was the plan the US used to fight the axis powers.

The US Navy records for the USS Eldridge during it's commissioning on the 27th August 1943 at the New York Navy Yard through to December 1943 show that the vessel was never in Philadelphia. The USS Eldridge remained in New York and in Long Island Sound until the 16th September when it sailed to Bermuda. From the 18th September the ship remained in the Bermuda area for training purposes and sea trials until the 15th October. On the 15th October the Eldridge left in a convoy for New York and arrived on the 18th October. The Eldridge remained in New York harbour until the 1st November when it was a part of the escort for Convoy UGS-23 (New York Section). On the 2nd November the convoy entered the Naval Operating Base, Norfolk. On the 3rd November the Eldridge and Convoy UGS-23 left for Casablanca where it arrived on the 22nd November. On the 29th November the Eldridge left as one of the escorts for Convoy GUS-22 and arrived with the convoy on the 17th December at New York harbour. The USS Eldridge remained in New York on availability training and in Block

Island Sound until the 31st December when it went to Norfolk with four other ships.

The records for the movements of the civilian merchant ship the SS Andrew Furuseth are in the custody of the Modern Military Branch, National Archives and Records Administration. The movement report card shows that the Andrew Furuseth left Norfolk with Convoy UGS-15 on the 16th august 1943 and arrived at Casablanca on the 2nd September. The ship left Casablanca on the 19th September and arrived off Cape Henry on the 4th October. The Andrew Furuseth left Norfolk with Convoy UGS-22 on the 25th October and arrived at Oran on the 12th November. The ship remained in the Mediterranean until it returned with Convoy GUS-25 to Hampton Roads on the 17th January 1944. The archives also hold a letter from Lieutenant Junior Grade William S. Dodge, USNR, (now retired), the Master of SS Andrew Furuseth in 1943. In the letter he categorically denies that he or his crew observed any unusual events whilst in Norfolk. In fact the records for both ships show that the USS Eldridge and the SS Andrew Furuseth were not even in Norfolk at the same time, further lending weight to the sceptical argument that *The Philadelphia Experiment* never occurred.

To add to this the ONR stated that the use of force fields to make a ship and its crew invisible does not conform to known physical laws. The ONR claim that DR. Albert Einstein's Unified Field Theory was never completed, therefore it could not have been used to by them for experimentation on the USS Eldridge. Einstein was a part-time consultant with the Navy's Bureau of Ordnance between 1943 and 1944, but he worked on theoretical research on explosives and explosions. There is no indication that Einstein was involved in research relevant to invisibility or teleportation. Both independent researchers and the staff of Operational Archives have never located any official documents to support the claims that an invisibility or teleportation experiment involving a US Navy ship occurred in Philadelphia or any other location.

Denial by the Navy of any involvement of course only fuels the argument for conspiracy theorists, that the experiment really did take place. The US Navy does however; suggest that a misunderstanding of a practice undertaken by them may have been the origin of the *Philadelphia Experiment* legend.

During World War II ran a program to degauss ships. Deguassing involved running a system of electrical cables around the circumference of the ship's hull. A measured current is passed through the cables, which run from the bow to the stern on both sides, which results in the ship's magnetic field being cancelled out. This process made a ship undetectable to some types of mines and torpedoes, but would still be visible to radar, underwater listening devices and most importantly, the human eye.

This 'misinterpretation theory' was also backed by Edward Dudgeon, who claimed to be on the USS Engstrom which was harboured together with the USS Eldridge.

Dudgeon told UFO investigator Jaques Vallee:

'They sent the crew ashore and they wrapped the vessel in big cables, then they sent high voltages through these cables to scramble the ship's magnetic signature. This operation involved contract workers, and of course there were also merchant ships around, so civilian sailors could well have heard Navy personnel saying something like, "they're going to make us invisible," meaning undetectable by magnetic torpedoes...'

The degaussing of the USS Engstrom may have been confused with the USS Eldridge, which it was docked alongside, and the story may have become confused and embellished over time. Dudgeon also claimed that the crews from both ships would often spend time on shore together and he never heard anything 'unusual' regarding the Eldridge mentioned. Though they did witness some spectacular electrical storms, St. Elmo's fire is common in the area they were in at the time. Dudgeon may have been able to shed some light on the mysterious legend of the disappearance and reappearance of the ship too. As he told Jaques Vallee:

'I was in [a] bar that evening, we had two or three beers, and I was one of the two sailors who are said to have disappeared mysteriously...The fight started when some of the sailors bragged about the secret equipment [radar, sonar, special screws, a new compass, etc.] and were told to keep their mouths shut. Two of us were minors....The waitresses

scooted us out the back door as soon as trouble began and later denied knowing anything about us. We were leaving at two in the morning. The Eldridge had already left at 11 p.m. Someone looking at the harbour that night might have noticed that the Eldridge wasn't there any more and it did appear in Norfolk. It was back in Philadelphia harbour the next morning, which seems like an impossible feat: if you look at the map you'll see that merchant ships would have taken two days to make the trip. They would have required pilots to go around the submarine nets, the mines and so on at the harbour entrances to the Atlantic. But the Navy used a special inland channel, the Chesapeake-Delaware Canal, that bypassed all that. We made the trip in about six hours'

Although the overwhelming majority of the evidence appears to point at the fact that the Philadelphia experiment never took place, as with most of things in the paranormal world there will always be those who believe despite the odds, especially when there is a conspiracy theory 'angle' that can be taken.

So what became of the vessel that was the cause of all the controversy and still causes debate amongst believers and sceptics to this day?

On 15 January 1951 the USS Eldridge was transferred under the Mutual Defense Assistance program to Greece, with whom she served as with whom she served as destroyer escort Leon (D-54). The Leon was decommissioned by the Greek Navy in 1991 but she was retained as a training hulk. On September the 21st 2000 an announcement was made by a scrap metal trading company that the Leon (USS Eldridge), had been transferred to a demolition company for dismantle/destruction. It appears that the USS Eldridge, may have finally disappeared... but this time it would seem it will be forever.

What The Experts Say
The Philadelphia Experiment (1984)

Brad Steiger – Author and Paranormal Researcher. Brad has authored/co-authored 162 books with over 17 million copies in print, including the biography of Rudolf Valentino, later made into a feature film by British director Ken Russell. Brad's first published articles on the unexplained appeared in 1956, and he has now written more than 2,000 articles with paranormal themes. From 1970-'73, his weekly newspaper column, The Strange World of Brad Steiger, was carried in the USA in over 80 newspapers and overseas from Bombay to Tokyo.

Brad has also appeared on numerous television and radio shows and also given many talks on the paranormal.

"Even from the beginning of the mystery in 1956 when M.K. Jessup, author of *The Case for the UFO*, received the first of a series of letters from Carlos Allende detailing the effects of an experiment in invisibility and teleportation in which a ship disappeared from a Philadelphia dock and reappeared a few minutes later at its dock in the Norfolk-Newport News-Portsmouth area, most UFO researchers believed that Allende's claim was a hoax.

Not long after Jessup began receiving correspondence from Allende, the Office of Naval Research in Washington D.C. received an annotated copy of Jessup's The Case for the UFO. It appeared that three different people, each writing in a different colour of ink, had written notes suggesting awful things had happened the crew of the vessel involved in the experiment, such as dematerialization, bursting into flame, and becoming embedded in the steel of the ship. The ONR was unimpressed with the claims of the anonymous annotators.

Jessup died in 1959, whether by his own hand or as some UFO researchers insist, by murder made to look like suicide.

By the mid-1960s, the mystery of the Jessup-Allende letters and the annotated book was little more than a brain-teaser over beers for the inner-circle of UFO buffs. Vincent Gaddis briefly discussed the affair in his Invisible Horizons (1965), but most readers found the wide variety of maritime mysteries discussed in the book more interesting than the Philadelphia Experiment.

In August, 1966, I received a letter from a bright young college student named Steve Yankee who was one up on most individuals who were still intrigued by the Philadelphia Experiment in that he actually had in his possession of a microfilmed copy of the annotated edition of Jessup's Case for the UFO. Yankee described a number of strange occurrences which he had undergone as a result of his possessing the copy, and when he left for military service, he sent the microfilm to me.

As I read through the weird annotations and scribbling in the margins about an ancient race, UFOs, and crewmen undergoing dreadful transformations as a result of the experiment, I thought it all made for a good article for Saga magazine, a kind of review of a forgotten UFO mystery. Marty Singer, the editor, was keen on all things UFO-related, so he green lighted the article early in 1967.

I was astonished by the number of letters that I received from readers who claimed personal involvement in the Philadelphia Experiment. One letter writer said that he had participated in the experiment and scolded me by saying that I would not be able to write so objectively if I "were forced to live with this horror."

Numerous correspondents claimed to continue to be harassed by ominous "agents" who still kept them under surveillance these many years after the experiment. Others said that they were "controlled" by "forces" that would not allow them to tell the real truth of the Philadelphia Experiment. Some of these letters were many pages in length, and they all told of participating in the experiment or of witnessing phenomena which they believed to have been closely associated with the secret Navy experiment.

Baffled, but very intrigued, by such a response to the article, I decided to include a chapter on the Philadelphia Experiment in a book that I was writing with the late Ufologist Joan Whritenour entitled Strange Flying Saucer Mysteries. The book dealt with reports of UFO Silencers, alleged sightings of robots near UFO landing sites, the possibility of our genes and our gods having come from another world, the mystery of UFOs under the seas, and a chapter on the Jessup-Allende enigma. Then, in a most surprising turn of events, the publisher became so excited by the chapter on the Allende mystery that he instructed the editor to change the title of the book to The Allende Letters: New UFO Breakthrough and he commissioned me to assemble a one-shot magazine special for the newsstands on the Allende-Jessup-Philadelphia Experiment.

Both the book and the magazine were published in 1968. Immediately I came under fire from UFO researchers who understood from the title of the book and one-shot special that I was claiming that the Allende Letters comprised the key to the entire UFO mystery. Such, of course, was not the case. The Jessup Affair and the Philadelphia Experiment were, in my estimation, just another "strange flying saucer mystery," as the original title of the book had implied.

For a time, our book created a bit of a furor. I received six letters from men who claimed to be Carlos Miguel Allende, and a letter from a woman claiming to be his widow. In addition, one of the largest private UFO groups published an account in their newsletter that Allende had appeared in their office one day with a woe begotten tale of how he had learned that I was writing a book on his correspondence to Jessup and how he had begged me not to publish it. According to the newsletter, I had brushed him aside, and he had limped away a broken man, incapable of securing legal assistance to combat a New York publishing empire. Without a single letter or telephone call to myself or Award Books to determine the truth of such an allegation (which was totally without substance or credence), the UFO research group headlined the story across the front page of their members' newsletter.

One again, the Philadelphia Experiment had come alive. The ONR was bombarded with letters insisting that the cover-up be lifted and the truth be told. Some UFO researchers reconsidered their earlier dismissal of the event and began once again to look for clues in the tri-coloured scribbling in the margins of Jessup's book.

Shortly after The Allende Letters: New UFO Breakthrough was published, I met Alfred Bielek, a scientist-engineer, who took the Philadelphia Experiment quite seriously and considered as true the claims made by some researchers that the event had actually taken place and that a number of crewmen aboard the Eldridge had suffered greatly for their participation in the experiment in teleportation and invisibility.

Bielek would often be in attendance at conferences at which I spoke, so we continued to become better acquainted over the years. Al was usually in the company of other scientists interested in the paranormal, and I began to call them my favourite "Mad Scientists." Usually, we would go out to dinner and discuss their latest theories on a vast array of research, all of which may have been a bit far-out, but never dull.

From about 1970 to the end of the decade, all was basically quiet on the Philadelphia Experiment front until Charles Berlitz and William Moore published their book on the subject The Philadelphia Experiment: Project Invisibility in 1979. Once again the twice-told tales were revived, and accusations of government cover-up during World War II were raging anew, but only the diehard buffs were stirred by the old theories remixed by Berlitz and Moore.

In 1984, Stewart Rafill released the motion picture The Philadelphia Experiment, starring Michael Pare and Bobby Di Cicco, as two seamen who find themselves projected 41 years into the future during the 1943 experiment in invisibility. The film is quite well done for its genre, but there were no resultant waves of excitement over the possibility that the experiment may actually occurred. Some reviews, unfamiliar with the Philadelphia Experiment, considered Rafill's film a rip-off of The Final Countdown (1980), in which the USS Nimitz is thrown back in time to 1941, just prior to the Japanese attack on Pearl Harbour.

Sometime in the mid-to-late 1980s, Al Bielek moved to the Phoenix, Arizona, area where Sherry and I were also residing.

We often had Al over to the house during Holidays and for dinner. We also had occasional movie nights, and since none of us had even seen The Philadelphia Experiment, we rented the film one night in 1988.

And now we have a dramatic instance in which life imitates art. Sherry and I noticed that Al seemed particularly moved by the film. Sometimes he seemed very troubled; sometimes, close to tears. Since Al would generally fall asleep during our movie nights, we knew that there was something about this film that truly spoke to him.

Later, we would learn that after viewing the film, he called two friends in New York and told them that the motion picture had jogged his memory. He told them that he had been a part of the Philadelphia Experiment--and so were they. One of them, Al said, was his brother. The two friends replied that they had been aware of their role in the experiment. They had just been waiting for Al to remember his participation.

Early in 1989, our friend Timothy Green Beckley came to Phoenix to visit us. After a few days of relaxation, he said that he wanted to sponsor a UFO-New Age conference in Phoenix. Sherry and I thought that the city certainly had enough interest in such subjects to sustain such an event, and I suggested to Tim that he include Al Bielek on the Philadelphia Experiment as one of the speakers.

Tim was not excited about my suggestion; arguing that the Philly Experiment was old hat and that no one had anything new to say about the subject. I countered that there were always people in attendance at such events who were not familiar with the range of topics in the paranormal and UFO field and who may have heard only brief comments about the alleged event. Al, I argued, had followed the story since the early 1960s.

Tim, Al, and I met in a Denny's restaurant to discuss the program, and after speaking with him at considerable length, Tim decided that Al could give an excellent overview of the many mysteries surrounding the Philadelphia Experiment.

In September of 1989, Alfred Bielek provided a thorough presentation of the secret experiment--and then startled everyone by announcing that he had been a participant in the astonishing experiment, that he had survived time-warping, invisibility, and electromagnetic zapping to emerge from many years of brainwashing to tell his story. Although he began investigating the mystery back in the 1960s strictly as a research project, he had now awakened to the reality that he had experienced one life as Alfred Bielek and another as Edward A. Cameron.

To say that Sherry, Tim, and I were stunned is to express an extreme understatement.

Al Bielek has continued from that September afternoon in 1989 to the present day explaining details of what is was like to be aboard the Eldridge when it dematerialized in 1943 and ripped an enormous hole in Hyperspace, a rent 40 years wide. The entire experiment, he maintains, was set up by a group of extraterrestrials who met with Franklin D. Roosevelt in 1934.

In 1990, Sherry and I interviewed Al for the book The Philadelphia Experiment & Other UFO Conspiracies. Bielek is so convincing in his details that one seriously entertains thoughts of an alternate reality, of other dimensions of time and space overlapping. Maybe, on one level of reality, Bielek did participate in a kind of Philadelphia Experiment.

To make matters even more complex and weird, invariably there will be certain individuals who will approach Sherry and me after our lectures and swear that they or a close friend or relative either participated in or observed the Philadelphia Experiment. Some provide extensive details of the time that their father, uncle, or whomever spent in the hospital recovering from the effects of the experiments. Others insist that their friend or relative has been kept in a mental hospital since the event and ask our help in getting them released.

The controversial Allende letters, the mysterious annotated volume of Dr. M.K. Jessup's The Case for the UFO, and the military's famed Philadelphia Experiment has now been proven to have been a hoax due to the research of Robert A. Goerman, who tracked down the elusive Carlos Allende (Carl Allen) and made the astonishing discovery that the Allen family lived in his own home town in Pennsylvania. Carl was a former sailor who loved to read about strange mysteries and UFOs. Perhaps he wanted to create a myth that would survive his own physical death. In this regard, he most certainly succeeded.

Regardless of Goerman's squelching of the mystery, the Philadelphia Experiment is a legend that refuses to die."

Fire In The Sky (1993)

The Travis Walton Abduction

In 1993 a movie based on one of the most famous cases of alleged alien abduction was released.

The film recreates the strange events that occurred when a group of loggers were driving home after work. The men arrive back in town claiming they encountered a UFO during the journey home and more shockingly aliens abducted that one of their friends. Nobody believes them and despite a lack of motive or evidence of foul play, their friend's disappearance is treated as a murder. Five days later their friend reappears. At first he has no recollection of his disappearance, in time the startling details of what took place over those five days begin to come back to him.

That man is Travis Walton and the movie is Fire In The Sky.

So what happened to Travis during those five days? What happened when he came back? What is the real story behind Fire In The Sky?

The case began on 5th November 1975. Travis Walton was working for Mike Rogers. Rogers had a contract to clear scrub bush for the United States Forest Service near Turkey Springs, Arizona. Along with five other members of their crew Walton and Rogers were working long shifts. They had fallen behind clearing the 1200 acres of scrub and would typically work from 6am until the sun set to try and get back on schedule.

Just after 6pm the crew finished work for the day and began their journey home. During the drive home they saw a bright light behind a hill. As they got closer to the light they saw a large silver disc, it was around eight feet high and twenty feet in diameter.

As Rogers brought the truck to a stop, Walton jumped out and ran towards the disc. Amidst the shouts of the other men telling him to come back the disc began making noises and moving from side to side. As Walton moved away from the disc a blue-green light emanated from the craft and struck him. Walton rose about a foot into the air with his arms and legs outstretched and shot back ten feet, still immersed in the light. Rogers, believing Walton to be dead, sped away fearing the disc may be in pursuit of the truck. After a quarter of a mile Rogers brought the truck to a halt, skidding off the road. The crew decided to go back and look for Walton. After returning to the site they discovered the disc was gone. After a twenty-minute search they also discovered there was no sign of Travis Walton either.

At 7:30pm the crew called the police to report Walton missing. Sheriff Ellison answered the call and arranged to meet them at a shopping centre. They told him the story and Ellison was sceptical. He notified his superior, Sheriff Gillespie, who told him to keep the men there until he arrived. Less then an hour later Gillespie arrived with officer Ken Coplan and heard the story from the crew. The officers and some of the crew returned to the site to search for Walton whilst the rest of the crew returned to Snowflake to relay the news to friends and family. Back at the scene the police became suspicious of the story due to the lack of evidence there. More police and volunteers arrived to search for Walton but to no avail. Rogers and officer Coplan went to inform Walton's mother of the bad news. Upon arriving Rogers told her the story. She asked him to repeat the story and asked calmly if anyone other then the police or the eyewitnesses had heard what had happened. Her calm manner created even more suspicion amongst the police. At 3am Kellet, Travis's mother, called Duane Walton. Travis's brother. He drove immediately to Snowflake.

By the following morning police suspicions were growing that the UFO story was concocted to cover up an accident or even a murder. On the morning of 8th November Rogers and Duane Walton arrived at Sheriff Gillespie's office, they were furious they had found no police at the scene that morning. That afternoon police had helicopters, jeeps and mounted-officers scouring the area.

By now word had spread worldwide of Travis Walton's disappearance. News reporters, curious members of the public and ufologists flocked to snowflake. One such UFO Investigator was Fred Sylvanus. He interviewed Rogers and Duane Walton on 8th November. They criticised the police search for Travis and expressed concern over his well-being. They also made other interesting comments. Rogers said that he would now be unable to complete the contract for the Forest Service and that Travis's disappearance would hopefully mitigate the situation. Duane Walton said he and Travis had a keen interest in UFO's and Travis had said if he ever got the chance he would get up as close to one as he possibly could. Travis Walton would later say he never had a 'keen interest' in the subject, even after his alleged abduction. Shortly after the interviews the Town Marshall of Snowflake announced the entire case was a prank. According to him Travis and Duane had lit a balloon, released it at an appropriate time and fooled the logging crew.

Meanwhile police made repeated visits to Kellet's home to question her, contributing to the feeling that she was hiding something or somebody amongst sceptics.

On 10th November Rogers' crew undertook lie detector tests. Cy Gilson conducted the tests. The questions he asked were if any of the men caused harm (or knew who had caused harm) to Travis Walton, if they knew where Travis's body was buried and if they told the truth about seeing a UFO. They all denied harming Travis, or knowing who had harmed him, they denied knowing where his body was and they insisted they had all seen the UFO. With the exception of one member, Allen Dallis, whose examination was incomplete, Gilson concluded all the results were conclusive. He said the results concluded the men saw a UFO, they had not injured or murdered Travis Walton and if it was a hoax none of them had prior knowledge of this.

Following the results Sheriff Gillespie announced he accepted the story. He said:

'There's no doubt they're telling the truth'

Around midnight on 10th November Travis's brother in law Grant Neff answered a phone call. The caller said he was Travis Walton and he needed help. Neff thought the call was a hoax. The voice again claimed he was Travis and he was hurt and needed him to come and get him. The caller was hysterical. Neff reconsidered and accompanied by Duane Walton they drove to the gas station the caller said he was phoning from. When they arrived they found Travis Walton collapsed in a phone booth wearing the same clothes as he had been wearing the night he disappeared. On the journey home Travis mumbled about beings with terrifying eyes, he was also stunned when he found he had been missing for nearly a week. He thought he'd only been gone for a few hours. They went back to Travis's mother's house where his return was kept quiet, as Duane had concerns for his fragile condition. Travis bathed and tried to eat but he couldn't keep anything down.

At 2:30am a phone company tipped police off about the phone call to Neff. After dusting the booth for fingerprints the police could find none that were Travis's. By the afternoon of 9th November Travis's return had leaked out to the public. One of the many calls received by the household was from Carol Lorenzen of APRO, a civilian UFO Research Group. She said she could arrange a medical examination of Travis by two doctors at Duane's house. Duane agreed and the examination took place at 3:30pm on the Tuesday. The examination revealed Travis was in good health. It also revealed that he had a small red spot in the crease of his elbow, consistent with a hypodermic needle, although it wasn't near a vein. They also concluded Travis's urine sample revealed a lack of acetones. This was unusual if he had indeed gone without food or water for five days. These revelations gave sceptics even more ammunition with which to debunk Walton's claims.

Sheriff Gillespie was furious when he learned of Travis's return through the media. Duane had chosen not to tell him, as he was still bitter over the lacklustre police search during Travis's disappearance. Travis chose to now tell Gillespie what had happened to him during the time of his absence.

Travis Walton said after approaching the UFO the last thing he remembered was being struck by the beam of light. He woke on a reclined bed with a bright light shining over him thinking he was in hospital. As he came too a little more he realised three figures in orange jump suits surrounded him. He said they were less then five feet tall, had no hair and domed heads. Similar to the 'greys' often described in these cases. Travis got up, fearing for his safety he grabbed a glass-like cylinder from a nearby shelf. He tried to break the tip to create a makeshift weapon but the tip wouldn't break. So Walton just waved the cylinder at the creatures and shouted. They left. Travis crossed a hallway and entered another room. In here he saw only a high backed chair in the middle of the room. He sat in the chair and the room filled with lights, similar to the star display on the ceiling at a planetarium. He noticed a lever on the chair arm and as he moved it the lights moved. He decided to stop moving it and got up. As he did the lights disappeared. Travis heard a sound behind him and saw a tall human figure wearing blue overalls and a helmet. The man's eyes were gold in colour and larger then normal. He asked the man questions but the man just grinned and motioned to follow him. Travis followed the man down a hallway, through a door and down a steep ramp. He was now in what he described as being similar to an aircraft hangar. Here he saw other disc shaped craft as he was led into another room. There were three other human like beings in here. The woman and two men were not wearing helmets so Travis tried asking them questions, thinking they may answer. They just grinned and led him to a table. Once seated on the table the woman placed an oxygen-type mask on his face. Before he could put up a fight Travis had passed out. He woke up outside the gas station just in time to see the disc hovering above the highway before shooting off. Travis then scrambled to the phone booth to call for help, where he called Neff.

Sheriff Gillespie speculated Travis might have been hit on the head or drugged and woken up in a hospital. This may be the reason for his account being confused. Travis said he would be willing to undergo a lie detector test. Duane and Travis then headed off to meet an APRO consultant where Travis was hypnotised. He revealed no further details other then he had already recounted and expressed the view that if he continued with the regression he would 'die'.

Upon returning, Travis underwent a lie detector test conducted by John McCarthy of the Arizona Polygraph Laboratory. Walton believed McCarthy to have behaved unprofessionally during the test. Being aggressive in his manner. McCarthy insisted Walton both failed the test and tried to cheat. McCarthy concluded Travis Walton was lying:

> 'Based on his reaction on all charts…Walton, in concert with others, is attempting to perpetrate a UFO hoax…'

The results were kept secret due to the Walton and APRO's doubts about McCarthy's methods and objectivity. When word of the decision was made public eight months later the sceptics once again had more grounds to claim a deception. Travis Walton later took two more lie detector tests and passed both of them. They would always be overshadowed by the earlier suppressed results though.

There now seemed to be a growing campaign to debunk the whole case, claiming several motives for a hoax. There was a strong financial gain to be made, which being that Rogers was trying to invoke an 'Act Of God' clause. He could do this by claiming the UFO incident was the cause of his failure to complete the Forest Service contract. Even the fact that a television broadcast 'The UFO Incident', had recently been televised. The fictionalised account of the Hill Abduction might well have inspired Walton's 'hoax'.

There were also those who noted that Rodgers had in fact failed to complete two previous contracts for the Forest Service and had never tried such a thing before. There are those that also state Walton's alleged abduction bears hardly any similarity to the Hill Case or indeed any other case.

1978 saw two books published on the Walton case. 'The Ultimate Encounter' by Bill Barry and 'The Walton Experience' by Travis Walton himself. Following the 1993 release of Fire In The Sky, adapted from Travis Walton's book, there was more controversy to come. The portion of the film detailing Travis's time on the UFO bore no resemblance to the books narrative. So much were the inaccuracies that screenwriter Tracy Torme wrote letters of apology to Ufologists. Torme claimed studio officials forced the changes. Following the renewed interest caused by the movie Travis Walton, Mike Rogers and Allen Dallis all agreed to take lie detector tests again. Again Cy Gilson conducted the tests. Gilson concluded all three men were truthful regarding their responses about the events of 5th November 1975.

Was Travis Walton really an unwilling guest onboard an alien spacecraft? Or was he just the perpetrator of an elaborate hoax?

What The Experts Say
Fire In The Sky (1993

Nick Redfern - Journalist, Ufologist, Cryptozoologist and Author. Nick has authored several best-selling books on UFOs including: 'A Covert Agenda: The British Government's UFO Top Secrets Exposed' (Simon & Schuster, 1997), 'The FBI Files: The FBI's UFO Top Secrets Exposed' (Simon & Schuster, 1998) and 'Cosmic Crashes: The Incredible Story of the UFOs That Fell to Earth' (Simon & Schuster, 2000). He has appeared on a wide variety of television programs in the UK (including The Big Breakfast; Channel 5 News; and GMTV) and abroad. Nick is in constant demand on the lecture circuit both in his home country and overseas and has appeared in internationally televised shows regarding UFO's.

"When I first heard that a film was being made on the subject of Travis Walton's 1975 UFO encounter, I eagerly looked forward to seeing it. On doing so, one thing in particular struck me: namely that certain portions of the film (and particularly those on board the spacecraft) didn't exactly reflect what Walton had claimed to have experienced.

I understand that it's Hollywood's role (and goal) to entertain us; and so in that respect I know why the changes were made. And if you view the film for what it is, then you'll be entertained. At least, I was! I would hope, however, that people realize that in an effort to understand the truth of the affair, there's no better source than those involved. So, I would recommend a deep reading of Walton's own book on his experience.

Although the Walton case has been pounced on by the sceptics as nothing more than a gigantic hoax, I still find it an intriguing one, and for one prime reason: it doesn't fit the general theme that is presented in alien abduction lore.

For a start, the amount of time that Walton was reportedly abducted for - 5 days - is practically unparalleled in such accounts. Likewise, Walton's recollections of seeing what appeared to be distinctly alien-looking beings, but also a very human-looking one in the same setting, is (a) intriguing, (b) very rare, and (c) almost suggestive of a Contactee-like connection, too.

So for me at least, the Walton story is a highly interesting one that I think deserves our attention - chiefly because it doesn't follow the general 'rules' of abduction lore.
And I think anything that's a little bit out of the box should be studied seriously and at length - it may be within these rogue cases that we'll ultimately find some surprising answers."

Alien Autopsy (2006)

Is There Any Body Out There?

One of the most elusive answers to evade the paranormal world is whether or not intelligent life exists on other planets. Many people have claimed to have seen UFO's, some have even alleged to have encountered aliens themselves, yet not a single person has ever brought forward any definitive evidence of the existence of either.

In 2006 a movie addressing this subject was released in the UK. The film portrayed the story of a man who claimed to have proof that extra terrestrials had visited our planet. Oddly, the proof he had was in the form of 'actual footage' of an alien autopsy. Even stranger still, the movie professed to be based on a true story.

Alien Autopsy was released on the 7th April 2006 and starred British television personalities Anthony McPartlin and Declan Donnelly in the lead roles.

The movie tells the story of Ray Santilli, a man who owns a London market stall. Ray and his friend Gary go to America to find Elvis memorabilia to sell on the stall, when they meet Harvey, a former US Army cameraman. Harvey sells Ray a silent black and white movie of Elvis performing live and ray adds a soundtrack to the footage.

Later Harvey contacts Ray and Gary with a seemingly irresistible offer. The friends travel to Miami, Florida to see some interesting footage Harvey has to sell them. The film is allegedly footage of an autopsy carried out on an alien killed in a UFO crash at Roswell, New Mexico, USA in 1947. Unable to finance the purchase of the footage themselves, Gary and Ray find an investor. Hungarian art dealer Lazlo gives Ray the $30,000 they require to purchase the footage and the deal is done. Ray and Gary discover that the footage has degraded over the years and is now completely unwatchable. Fearing a reprisal from Lazlo, Ray and Gary decide to recreate the footage based on their memories of the original footage. They turn Gary's sister's living room into a movie set and remake the autopsy film. Ray gives a copy to Lazlo who is convinced of its genuineness. Lazlo hears that the footage is going to air worldwide and demands that the film is not shown or else they will be hurt. Luckily, for Ray and Gary, Lazlo is killed in an accident before he can carry his threat out against them.

With the media now alerted to the footage a news reporter begins trying to track down Harvey, the cameraman of the original footage. Ray and Gary help try to keep Harvey's identity a secret by producing an interview with a homeless man and convincing the news reporter she was onto the wrong man.

The film ends with Ray and Gary being given back the original 1947 footage, which they had left with film restoration experts in the hope that it could somehow be restored. Ironically some of the sections that were beyond repair had been remade. After viewing the film they decide to bury it, saying they couldn't go through something like this all over again.

The movie cost $10,000,000 and flopped dramatically on release. Warner Bros. took back less than half of the film's budget. Despite the subject matter of the movie it appeared that the conspiracy theorists and UFO investigators were not drawn to the cinema in their droves. Perhaps they did not appreciate the 'comedy take' the movie had adapted to the story. Maybe they wanted the true story, or perhaps as one of the film's taglines says *'The truth isn't out there'*.

Did real footage of an alien autopsy ever exist, or was it all a 'less then elaborate' hoax?

The term autopsy is used to refer to the procedure of a post-mortem and therefore an alien autopsy would mean a post-mortem carried out on an extraterrestrial being. This is what the real Ray Santilli claimed to have film footage of in the 1990's.

Ray Santilli's story begins in Cleveland, Ohio in the summer of 1993. Santilli was researching a music documentary in the USA when he came across a local freelance cameraman who had some early footage of Elvis Presley on stage. The man had shot the film for Universal News in 1955. Santilli purchased the footage from the man who then asked him if he would be interested in purchasing some more film from him. When Santilli asked the man what sort of film the man explained to him the details of the footage he had captured in 1947. Here Santilli describes in his own words what the footage was and how he came to purchase it:

"He (The Cameraman) explained that the footage he was offering to me came from the Roswell crash, that it included debris and recovery scenes and of most importance footage of an autopsy.
At the time I had no knowledge of the event, Roswell was not the household name it is today but when someone tells you they have real footage of an alien autopsy it is of course interesting.
The cameraman was in his eighties and seemed a genuine enough person, he explained that from 1942 to 1952 he worked as a cameraman for the Army Air force and special forces, that during his time with the services he filmed many events including the tests that were part of the Manhattan Project (Atomic bomb testing White Sands).
He explained that on June 2nd 1947 he received an order directly from General McMullan stating there had been a crash. He was to go immediately to White Sands and film everything. The cameraman had authority over and above the on-site commander and reported back only to McMullan.
The cameraman Flew to Roswell then was taken by road to the site he describes as being a dried up small lake bed.
After hearing the story I was taken to the cameraman's house and viewed the footage. The cameraman had one reel of film that he was able to show on an old projector. He moved the projector over to a wall and projected the image onto the wall itself. The footage was remarkable. From his house I telephoned Kodak to ask their advice in checking the film. I was told to look for an edge code which would indicate the year of the film. The code I saw matched the code for 1947.
I quickly confirmed a cash offer subject to further checks and the cameraman accepted. I said I would require a few days and a small sample of the film to take back. The cameraman gave me around two feet of leader from the film itself which I brought back to the UK. Unfortunately raising the money required became a problem and a few days turned into a few weeks, then a few months. This was made all the more difficult because the cameraman needed money for a family wedding. By now the cameraman was becoming very nervous and refused to take my calls. Each time I called, his wife would simply take a message. The story stops there until November of 1994 when with the

money in hand I flew over without warning to buy the film and succeeded.

I believed the cameraman was genuine; he had been married to the same woman for over 50 years and lived in humble surroundings. I had the opportunity of going through old photo albums, his film collection, and personal papers. I am certain that the cameraman was everything he claimed.

I came away with 22 reels of film, 21 safety prints and one negative."

Ray Santilli had indeed purchased some rather interesting footage for his $100,000.

The grainy black and white film shows what appear to be two masked and gloved surgeons carrying out an autopsy on an alien being. The creature is similar in form to a human being but with minor anatomical differences, one of which being the creature has 6 fingers. At points in the footage a third man can be seen watching the procedure from behind a window.

Santilli returned to London and took the footage to BUFORA (British UFO Research Association). The film was examined by the organisation and Philip Mantle, BUFORA's Press Officer, who saw the film in the early part of 1995, exclaimed:

"The footage is unique. It is the only known instance of aliens on film."

Santilli claimed the cameraman, who wished to remain anonymous, had filmed the clean up of the crashed UFO at Roswell in 1947 and later recorded the autopsies of several aliens. The man was able to keep some of these reels of film in his possession as he claimed there had been an administrative oversight and not all the footage had been collected from him. Santilli stated that he did not have the entire footage of the complete autopsy procedure as he had been unable to obtain all the reels of film from the cameraman.

To back up his claim of the footage's authenticity Philip Mantle of BUFORA made this statement in a press release on the 26th March 1995:

"We have had the film checked by Kodak who confirm it is 50 years old...we now plan to have it examined by film experts at Sheffield."

Intrigued by the find, Graham Birdsall the editor of UFO Magazine contacted Kodak and asked them about the Santilli footage. A representative from the company stated that they were not aware of any tests being done on the film at that time, at least not by anybody from their company.

On the 5th May 1995 Ray Santilli presented his film to an invited audience at the Museum of London. Media representatives, UFOlogists and other special guests were invited to the screening of the footage and many of them went away with more questions then answers. The debate as to the footage's authenticity had begun.

The alarm bells began ringing almost immediately for sceptics of the film. It was not until the 5th of July 1995 (40 day's after Philip Mantle's claim), that Kodak were contacted about the footage. A representative of Ray Santilli approached the company in Copenhagen, Denmark, regarding the dating of the film. A salesperson at Kodak was asked whether a square and triangle, found on the edge of the film indicated that the film was manufactured in 1947. After checking references the salesperson confirmed that these markings did in fact indicate that the film was manufactured in that year. Unfortunately the Kodak salesperson that was consulted did not realise that the same edge markings also applied to film manufactured in 1927 and 1967. Kodak did offer to confirm the film's date but they were not sent the two frames of footage they would need in order to do so.

Almost four months after the screening of the footage at the Museum of London, the alien autopsy footage was aired on national television in America. On the 28th August 1995 over ten million viewers tuned in to what has become one of the most controversial TV documentaries ever aired on prime time television.

Alien Autopsy: (Fact or Fiction?) included footage from the autopsy as a part of the 60 minute show. Along with the footage such noted UFO and Roswell experts such as Stanton Friedman, Philip Mantle and Kevin Randle all gave their opinion on the film's authenticity. Others that appeared on the program were Dr. Jesse Marcel, Chris Milroy (a senior lecturer in Forensic Pathology), Dr. Roderick Rock (a Navy Combat Cameraman) and Ray Santilli himself. Following the broadcast the film was shown in over thirty countries worldwide (including Channel 4 television in the UK) and later sold on video. With the footage exposed to the world, the debate over its legitimacy became more heated and the sceptics began to find good reason to doubt it.

The sceptics began to point out a long list of inconsistencies and errors in the footage.

One of the first things to come into question was the authenticity of the 'alien' itself. A case in point being the way the body lies on the table. It is claimed that the alien's body lies on the autopsy table unlike a body resting on its back. It is said to look more like a body standing in an upright position that has been laid on a table. The sceptic's, including those that work in movie special effects departments, suggest that this would support evidence that the body was cast from a real human being and then altered. The point being that the easiest way to accomplish a body casting is while the subject is stood up.

Some medical authorities argued that the autopsy procedure itself is very amateurishly done. The film is far from the usual systematic, careful study that an authentic autopsy would require. There are also the 'convenient' cuts in the film. The surgeon is seen making incisions into the chest area and then the film cuts to the chest flaps being opened. At no point is the skin seen being folded back. Another interesting camera cut involves the alien's head. The surgeon is seen sawing into the skull and then the film cuts to the removal of the brain. Sceptics argue that this cut is to allow the placement of the 'brain' into the skull. They also would argue that the alien is a 'dummy' and the reason the footage does not show any skin being folded back is because the skin is latex rubber which wrinkles when it is bent. The medical community also pointed out that an alien body would not be subjected to an autopsy. Given the unprecedented opportunity of studying an alien being a careful study that would have taken weeks would have to be done. This would include a careful dissection and microscopic analysis, which is not the procedure carried out in the footage. However, other members of the medical community such as Professor Cyril

Wecht and French surgeon Patrick Braun were less critical. They believed that the footage could have been of a genuine autopsy.

The greatest evidence the 'debunkers' gave against the film involved the film itself.

The military have standard procedures for recording events such as an autopsy and according to many sources the footage is unlike anything they would have carried out.

For an autopsy such as the one in the footage two cameras would have been used. One camera would have been mounted above the table; looking down on the subject. The other camera would have been located on a stationary tripod with a clear view of the proceedings. Experts also suggested that a 'still' photographer would have also been present during the autopsy, of which there is no record of in the footage. The experts also claimed that colour film (with sound would) have been used at the time and not black and white. An argument that counteracted this was that research carried out at the National Achieves in Maryland, USA showed that all the footage of medical procedures shot during the Second World War were filmed in black and white. Researcher Theresa Carlson could only find US military medical film footage that was shot in colour that was filmed after 1954. In fact in their own literature, Kodak themselves recommend the use of their Super XX film in medical photography including surgery.

There was however another sign that suggested the footage may not have been what it appeared. The film lacked a 'flash' that usually appears at the beginning of each segment when filmed on a spring wound camera; which was claimed at the time. The flash would occur because cameras of that type and that time would start up slowly and over expose the first few frames after pressing the trigger. The lack of flash would suggest that a more sophisticated motor driven camera was used or the film had been edited for some reason.

Some sceptics wondered if the cameraman's lack of professionalism during the filming (climbing over the medical staff, having his view blocked, etc.) would even suggest that he may have even been attempting to hide 'flaws' in the hoax. This led to the doubts that the unnamed cameraman was even a military cameraman at all. Qualified military cameramen with top-level security clearance were stationed all over the country at the time. This included New Mexico, so there would have been no need for the cameraman to have been flown from Washington DC as he claimed he had to Ray Santilli. Roswell Army Airfield could have dispatched their own cameraman. Sceptics also argued that it seemed incredible that a top-secret film like the autopsy footage could go missing and unnoticed.

With the weight of sceptical opinion adding up against his footage Santilli eventually submitted a few frames of the film for analysis. The frames were analysed by Bob Shell. Shell was a photographic consultant for the FBI and the US legal system. He also was the editor Shutterbug; a photography magazine. In August 1995 Bob Shell concluded:

"I have been hard at work on this film. I have now physically examined a section of the film, a section showing the "autopsy" room before the body was placed on the table, but clearly consistent with the later footage. The film on which this was shot is Cine Kodak Super XX, a film type which was discontinued in 1956-57. Since the edge code could be 1927, 1947 or 1967, and this film was not manufactured in 1927 or 1967, this clearly leaves us with only 1947 as an option."

The frames Santilli sent Shell did not show any actual footage of an alien, therefore they proved little as to the footage's authenticity. Confirmation of the date of the film's manufacture would also neither prove when the film was shot or processed.

Another flaw in the footage was the canister the film was stored in itself. This appears in the film briefly and shows the emblem of either the National Military establishment

(NME) or the Department of Defense (DoD), the NME emblem subsequently becoming that of the DoD on it. The stamp bears writing which is not legible.

In response to a query from researcher Robert Irving, Alfred Goldman, Historian at the Office of the Secretary of Defense, Pentagon, confirmed that:

"The original seal was for the National Military Establishment. It was changed to the Department of Defense in August 1949. The original

seal could not have come into existence until some time in October 1947 or later."

Interestingly, although the stamp may not be an official seal, it bears the emblem of an organisation which did not exist at the time of the claimed filming. Some say it would therefore seem it must have been applied some time afterwards. Others argued that as the emblem itself stayed the same (only the wording around the edge changed), and the wording around the emblem on the canister was unreadable, there is no way of knowing which organisation the seal was from. Even with some of the facts still being debatable, things were about to get worse was still for Ray Santilli.

On 20 April, 1996, Bob Shell commented publicly that:

"My 19th August statement was written when I still thought I had camera original film. It has been superseded by new information. Please disregard it."

Despite the ever growing evidence of a hoax and the increasing number of sceptics, Santilli and the footage still had their supporters. Members of the UFO community continued to support the alien autopsy footage. Philip Mantle in particular was very pro Ray Santilli and the authenticity of the footage in 'Beyond Roswell', the book he co-authored with Michael Hesemann. The debate raged on for a further ten years until another television 'special' brought what many thought would be an end to the speculation regarding the footage.

At 8pm on the 4th April 2006, Sky One, a British television station, aired the documentary *'Eamonn Investigates: Alien Autopsy'*. The program, presented by Eamonn Holmes included what has been considered by many the inevitable, a confession from Ray Santilli.

Santilli said that a set had been constructed in an empty flat in Rochester Square, Camden Town, London, England. Santilli and fellow producer Gary Shoefield, who also appeared in the documentary, then employed sculptor John Humphreys to construct the two alien bodies. The models were made from latex using clay sculptures and contained sheep's brains set in raspberry jam and chicken entrails. Knuckle joints from nearby

Smithfield Market were also used in creating the props. To enable him to be in control of how the special effects were filmed, Humphreys was also given the role of playing the chief scientist in the film. He also created the alien symbols and six-fingered control panels that can be seen in the footage. These items were supposedly recovered from the crash site in Roswell, New Mexico along with the alien bodies. In the Sky Television documentary Santilli admitted that these objects were artistic licence on his part.

The footage showing a man reading a statement 'verifying' him as the original cameraman who sold Santilli the Alien Autopsy footage was also debunked in the show. Santilli and Shoefield admitted that they persuaded a homeless man they met in Los Angeles to play the part of the cameraman and filmed him reading the statement in a hotel.

After filming the autopsy footage, which took two attempts, the men disposed of the alien 'bodies' by cutting them into small pieces and putting them in different rubbish bins around London. Whilst admitting that most of the footage was filmed in London, a 'few frames' were real. The rest, Santilli and Shoefield claimed, was a reconstruction of the twenty two rolls of film Santilli had viewed in 1992. They said that by the time they had raised the money to purchase the footage almost all of the film had degraded from humidity and heat. Santilli and Shoefield stated they had 'restored' the unusable footage by filming a simulated autopsy based upon what Santilli had seen on the original reels. They added the few remaining original frames into their footage but did not identify which frames were the original ones.

Twelve days after the Sky documentary broadcast, and ten days after the UK release of the *Alien Autopsy* movie, John Humpreys made his own confession to *The Sunday Times* newspaper. He admitted it was he who made the models for the autopsy footage. Humphreys also added:

"It was a very, very strange feeling to know that I played a part in it."

Philip Mantle, who had been one of Santilli and the footage's 'staunchest supporters', said Humphreys had been a prime suspect but had never before admitted involvement. It would appear that after ten years of investigating the alien autopsy footage, Mantle had had a complete turn around in his opinion on its authenticity:

"I didn't think it would take so long, but I am delighted this hoax has finally been exposed and the mystery has been solved."

This would appear to be the case…or is it?

Mantle was about to discover another man who claimed to be involved in the Alien Autopsy controversy.

On the 22nd June 2007 Philip Mantle travelled to London to meet up with Ray Santilli and Gary Shoefield. Within a couple of days of the meeting Mantle's friend, Russell Callaghan, editor of UFO DATA magazine, called Mantle. He told him he had had a call from a man by the name of Spyros Melaris who claimed to have headed the team that faked the whole alien autopsy. Melaris was a magician and filmmaker who owned his own TV studio in London making TV shows for major networks and independent companies in the UK. He was planning a book and thought a TV documentary might also be a good idea as he was considering going public with his story. After meeting Melaris for the first time at the UFO DATA annual conference Mantle arranged a second meeting with Melaris. He travelled to Melaris' home on the 16th November 2007. Melaris showed Mantle some of the documentary evidence he had to support his claims. This included a diary from 1995, hand drawn sketches of the alien, hand painted storyboards of the alien autopsy film, fax messages from Kodak and a portfolio of research material.

Melaris told Mantle that in January 1995 he attended the MIDEM music industry event in Cannes, France. Melaris had contacted some production companies asking them if they wanted to hire him and his crew while they were in Cannes, one of which was the Merlin Group, owned by Ray Santilli. Melaris had talked to Santilli on the phone but had not arranged to meet him. By pure chance they bumped into each other in a restaurant in Cannes and it was there that Santilli first told Melaris that he had obtained footage of an alien. Melaris asked Santilli if he was serious and he replied that he was. He then told Melaris that he wanted him to make a documentary from the footage. A few days later Melaris met up with Santilli in his office in London, Santilli was almost distraught as he told Melaris that the film he had bought had turned out to be of very poor quality. Melaris was shown what has become to be known as 'the tent footage' on a VHS format video tape. Melaris immediately recognised the footage had been shot on video which surprised Santilli. He was shocked that Melaris had recognised this so quickly and he realised that he had been found out.

Melaris met up with his friend John Humphreys who was a sculptor and who had worked with him in the past. Melaris told Humphreys of his meeting with Santilli and asked him if he fancied making an alien. The idea was to make the autopsy film, release it to the world and then later make a follow up program showing how they did it. Humphreys agreed and then Melaris pitched the idea to Santilli who also agreed. Melaris put a budget forward of £30,000 and Santilli's business partner Volker Spielberg put up the money. With the funding in place, contracts and confidentiality agreements signed the project was started. Melaris, his brother Peter and John Humphreys manufactured the wreckage. Melaris designed the lettering on the I-beams, basing it on Greek lettering, ancient Egyptian stylising and artistic licence.

Melaris claimed that Santilli was under a lot of pressure from various parties to arrange a meeting with the fictitious cameraman he claimed to have bought the footage from. Melaris flew to Los Angeles and met up with Santilli's partner Gary Shoefield. Melaris wanted to find an old tramp on the streets of L.A. pay him a few hundred dollars and put him in front of a camera reading a script. Santilli and Shoefield were nervous but Melaris was confident he could pull this off. Melaris found an old man living rough on the street and offered him $500 and a bed for the night in the hotel, to which the old man agreed. By a stroke of luck many years ago the old man had been an actor. They cleaned the man up, gave him a shave, added a prosthetic nose and chin and make up and the interview was filmed. The film was delivered in person by Gary Shoefield and a man claiming to be the cameraman's son to American TV producer

Bob Kiviat. The film was broadcast on television in Japan and was then copied and distributed to UFOlogists worldwide. With the film made the plan was to release the footage to a broadcaster, ask them to investigate it and then see what happened next. After a few months they would then expose their hoax to the world. The trouble was that Santilli told Melaris that he had invested a lot of money into the project and he needed to recoup that before they went public. Santilli reminded Melaris that he was bound by the confidentiality agreement he had signed and that he was not to say anything until Santilli said so. So apart from the £10,000 Melaris was paid (which he split with his team) he never received any royalties from the film. As time past Melaris carried on with his life and his work and all but forgot the alien autopsy film.

During his visit with Melaris Philip Mantle asked him why he had decided to go public with this information twelve years after the film was shown to the world. Melaris said that he had stuck to the confidentiality agreement as he would have been sued had he broken his silence. In 2005 Santilli and Shoefield approached Melaris to ask him if he would be involved in the movie version of the alien autopsy case. Melaris asked if they were going to now reveal the true story and they told him they were not. They said that they were going to maintain that they had the original footage. They also told Melaris that there was no money in this project for them and that they were just doing it for 'fun'. When pressed about this they admitted that Santilli and Shoefield would get a percentage of the profits from the film but Melaris was not offered the same deal so he declined. Melaris left this meeting under the impression that the film would not go ahead. When the movie did come out and the story was in the public domain Melaris felt he was now free to tell his story without fear of legal action.

Mantle also found out more evidence to back up Spyros Melaris's claims that he had been involved in the whole affair. After the UFO DATA Conference in October 2007 Mantle received an email from German researcher Michael Hesemann who had researched the alien autopsy footage between 1995 and 1997. Hesemann told mantle that in 1996 he had received an email telling him that a man called Spyros Melaris was the hoaxer. Hesemann had then phoned Ray Santilli and asked him if he knew Melaris to which he replied that he didn't. That was that as far as Hesemann was concerned. Melaris informed Mantle that in 1996 he had received a phone call from a man with a German accent asking him if he was the hoaxer which he of course denied. He only found out that the caller was Hesemann in 2007 when he met him at the UFO DATA Conference. Mantle asked Hesemann whether he had called Melaris in 1996 about the hoax and he admitted he had.

This new evidence would seem to indicate that in 1996 Spyros Melaris was outlined as the hoaxer to German researcher Michael Hesemann. In 2003 US television producer Bob Kiviat spoke to UK sculptor John Humphreys who confirmed that Spyros Melaris was the man in charge and that there was no original footage. Four years later, 2007, Melaris himself went on record for the first time and told the public of his involvement in the hoax, with a book 'ALIEN AUTOPSY: The Myth Exposed' being released the following year. As Melaris told Philip Mantle:

'The question isn't whether I made it (the film)...There's too much evidence. The question is did I make it from original film? And the simple answer to that is no.'

Will Spyros Melaris be the man to finally lay the unanswered questions of the Alien Autopsy footage to rest?

Were the frames Santilli claims are original really part of actual footage of an alien autopsy? Do they even exist at all?

Even if this mystery has been solved and the whole episode was an 'out and out' hoax it seems to have spawned another, equally intriguing, debate. For some conspiracy theorists are now claiming that the Santilli alien autopsy footage is in fact a Government cover up to hide real alien autopsy footage from us. That, as the saying goes, is another story...and probably another movie one day.

What The Experts Say
Alien Autopsy (2006)

Philip Mantle - Author / Co-author, publicist, lecturer, broadcaster and researcher of Unidentified Flying Objects. Philip Mantle's interest in UFO research began in 1979 when he joined the British UFO Research Association (BUFORA), and Yorkshire UFO Society (YUFOS). In 1985 he was nominated 'Investigator of the year' by YUFOS. By 1987 Philip was appointed to Council of management of BUFORA and subsequently acted as Press Officer, Conference Organiser, and Secretary to the National Investigations Committee. In 1988 he was appointed England's representative for the Mutual UFO Network's (MUFON). Four years later Philip was awarded an honorary membership of the Research Institute on Anomalous Phenomena (RIAP), a science based UFO-study group based in the Ukraine and in 1993 he was appointed Director of Investigations for BUFORA.

Philip has authored/ co-authored four books including Alien Autopsy Inquest (PublishAmerica 2007). He was also the editor of Quest and Beyond magazines and currently the features editor of UFO Data Magazine (www.ufodata.co.uk).

Philip has made numerous international newspaper, magazine, radio and television appearances and also lectured around the world on the subject of Ufology.

"There is a possibility that the alien autopsy film depicts exactly what Ray Santilli says it does: a dead alien from another world came to earth in 1947 in a crashed UFO. It was recovered by U.S. military authorities in the desert of New Mexico and the truth has been kept from the public ever since. The supporters of this idea poi8nt to various factors, for example the type of film, the camera and all the artifacts in the footage are all circa 1947. There is an unusual 'crash site' where the cameraman said it would be and some medical professionals are convinced it is a genuine medical procedure seen on the footage.

Some people think the film is nothing more than a hoax made to make money. Supporters of the hoax theory point out that almost every movie special effects artist who has viewed the footage is convinced it is a rubber man, a dummy. Some medical professionals also state that the procedure seen on film is not carried out by a professional, but by clumsy actors. Supporters of a hoax also claim that Ray Santilli, at times, has been somewhat liberal with the truth. They also site the fact that the main convincing factor is the failure of Ray Santilli to have the film scientifically tested for its age.

Another theory is that the film could be authentic but that it does not depict an alien. That the film does in fact show an unfortunate deformed human. Supporters of this idea have cited a number of possible genetic conditions that might account for the creature's appearance including progeria and Turners syndrome.

Finally, some people believe the footage is none of the above and is in fact a disinformation or propaganda film produced by the U.S intelligence services. This theory could also explain how others could have viewed the footage before Ray Santilli. This is an old trick, showing someone something and then saying 'but don't tell anyone'. This is what is known as a 'real fake'.

However, for me personally the mystery of the Alien Autopsy Film is now solved. In June 2007 a man by the name of Spyros Melaris contacted my colleague Russell Callaghan at the offices of UFO DATA Magazine. This man's name was Spyros Melaris. Russ passed him onto me as he had a fantastic tale to tell about the Alien Autopsy Film. Spyros Melaris was the man who led the team that faked the whole thing. Melaris is a film maker in his own right and he owns one of the UK's largest independent TV studios. He is also a magician and has many other strings to his bow. Over the next few months I met and interviewed Melaris on several occasions and have also been party to some of his documentary evidence. This includes original drawings, faxes and interviews with others that were involved. Having been privy to all of this there is no doubt in my mind that Spyros Melaris is the man who lead the team that faked the Alien Autopsy Film. He is bringing his own book out in 2008 to show everyone the evidence I have seen.

Ray Santilli still sticks to his story and he still does have a few supporters but for me the Alien Autopsy Film ended with the phone call from Spyros Melaris and it is one big fake".

Hauntings Or Hoaxes?

Everyone loves a good ghost story. Except perhaps for those people whose real life experiences are the bases for those stories.

Many a horror movie has carried the tag line 'based on a true story' over the years, and many a sceptic has questioned the authenticity of both the movie and the subject matter.

How much of what is portrayed on the screen actually happened behind the closed doors of these alleged 'haunted houses'?

What caused the disturbances?

Was it paranormal or pranks?

Hauntings or hoaxes?

The Amityville Horror (1979)

The Defeo Murders And The Lutz Haunting

'For God's Sake Get Out!'

This is the *'tag line'* that was used to entice moviegoers into theatres worldwide in 1979.

The movie was 'The Amityville Horror'. It starred James Brolin and Margot Kidder as George and Kathy Lutz. A couple move into their dream home unaware of the nightmare it is soon to become. The evil past of the house once again manifests itself and the Lutz's must flee their home…or fall prey to what resides within its walls.

Jay Anson first brought the Lutz's story to the world's attention in his book *'The Amityville Horror'*, published before the release of the 1979 movie. The story was also given a new lease of life to a new audience with the release of a remake of the same name in 2005.

The real story begins not with the Lutz's, but with the homes previous occupants…the Defeos. Ever since Ronald Defeo and his family had moved into the three storey Dutch colonial house strange things had happened.

Ronald's son, Ronald Defeo Jnr had run away from the house three times and three times he had been brought back. The third time he pleaded with his father to let him go. He just knew he was going to kill his family one-day but nobody would listen. With things such as unexplained noises now becoming a regular occurrence, Defeo's father had taken to placing statues of catholic saints all around the house. He even went as far as to place them in the garden. All the plants died.

The Defeo's residency of 112 Ocean Avenue Amityville came to an abrupt and tragic end in the early hours of November 13th 1974. At 3:15am Ronald Defeo Jnr went from room to room and methodically killed his entire family. Eight shots were fired from his .35 calibre marlin rifle. His father, mother, two brothers and two sisters were all found lying face down in their beds. Amazingly it seemed that none of them had heard the gunshots. Nor had any of the surrounding neighbours.

Forty hours after the tragedy Defeo confessed to the killings. He was convicted of second-degree murder and sentenced to six consecutive terms of 25 years each. A total of 150 years in prison. He remains in Greenhaven Correctional Facility where he is currently serving his sentence.

Although he knows he committed the murders Defeo still maintains he doesn't know why. The only explanation he could give at the time was he saw a pair of hands draped in black that reached out to him and passed him the rifle. He also heard a voice, which said to him *'kill'*.

It would seem whoever, or whatever had instructed Ronald Jnr to carry out the murders had decided to stay after the unfortunate departure of the Defeo's.

George and Kathy Lutz were newlyweds looking for a new home. They were living separately. Their plan was to sell both their houses and use the money to buy a home big enough for the both of them and Kathy's three children. Kathy's house sold first so she and the children moved in with George. That summer they saw over 50 potential properties with no luck. Then the estate agent told them about 112 Ocean Avenue in Amityville.

George Lutz would be the first to tell you that some of the events in the book and indeed the movie *'The Amityville Horror'* aren't factual. In October 2003 he appeared in front of a paranormal convention at Penn State University. Here George related what happened in and around the family's 28-day residency at 112 Ocean Avenue.

George says after telling them of the house's availability they were also made aware of its 'past history'

"The realtor eventually told us what had happened in the house... that six family members had been murdered there and asked us if that made a difference, if we were still interested in looking at the home. The kids

didn't seem to have any reservations about whether to at least look at the house, and so we went through it. Afterwards, we had quite a discussion as a family a couple of different times, about whether or not we should still consider buying the house".

The Lutzs agreed to at least look around the property.
"As soon As Kathy had walked into the house, she had a smile on her face that just beamed. That hadn't happened in all the previous homes we looked at... I knew from the look on her face, that this was to be our dream home."

 The $100,000 home included 4,000 square feet of property, a boathouse and a garage. It also had a heated swimming pool in the back garden and a full basement. The Lutzs made an $80,000 offer which was accepted. So they put down a $20,000 payment and arranged to move into their 'dream home'. In December 1975 the 'nightmare' began almost as soon as they moved in.

As George began unpacking Father Ralph Pecararo came up the driveway.

 "When I told a friend of mine what home we were buying, he made me promise that I would get the house blessed. I didn't know what that was at the time, I was a non-practicing Methodist". "I asked Kathy what a house blessing was... she was Catholic, and so she explained it to me. We agreed that we would do that, and the only priest I knew was Father Ralph Pecararo".

 Father Pecararo wasn't normally the type who would perform a house blessing for just anybody. Father Pecararo had handled George's first marriage annulment and had become a friend of the family. So as a favour for a friend he agreed to come over and bless the house. After exchanging pleasantries Pecararo left George and entered the house to perform the blessing.
"While performing the house blessing, a number of abnormal things occurred that he did not tell us about. Later, as he was leaving he told us simply that he was uncomfortable about one particular room, on the second floor. It was a room that we planned on using as a sewing room and not a bedroom".

Father Pecararo was happy the Lutzs were not going to use the room as a bedroom. He told the Lutzs he had *'felt something strange in there'*, although Father Pescararo never discussed the actual events of the blessing with them. The priest's testimony only later came to light after Jay Anson interviewed him for his book *'The Amityville Horror'*.

Some people insist the priest never experienced anything. That he never actually blessed the house. That he never even existed. Father Ralph Pescararo did exist. As their story broke the Lutzs did their utmost to protect his identity, but eventually his name was leaked to the public. Unfortunately causing him many problems in following his profession.

Also on the day of the move another incident occurred. George had tied 'Harry', the family dog, up in the backyard while he unpacked. George went to check on Harry and discovered he had tried to jump the fence and hung himself. Luckily the dog survived the ordeal.

The Lutzs began to settle into their new home and in keeping with its past history, strange things began to occur.

"If we hadn't had the house blessed, I don't know how things would have turned out - or what may have happened. Until there was a threat like that of some kind perceived by whatever was there... the events in the house were all very subtle. "The house was very patient... it was willing to wait"

Amongst the things the Lutzs experienced were:
- Swarms of houseflies in the sewing room.
- Toilet bowls turning black.
- Repulsive odours around the house.
- Strange jelly-like substances leaking from the walls.

There weren't only strange things happening with the building. The family were being personally affected too:
- George would wake suddenly at 3:15am each morning with an uncontrollable urge to check the boathouse. *The same time Ronald Defeo had set about the murder of his family when he had lived in the house.*

- George would go days without bathing. He was also getting sick and losing a lot of weight.
- Kathy began having nightmares.
- Even the children were changing. Constantly arguing and fighting with each other.

Footsteps and other noises were now being heard around the house. On one occasion George heard the front door slamming. When he went to check what it was he found Harry the dog sleeping on the front porch. He had been oblivious to the slamming or the cause of it.

"*In the middle of night, you would hear the front door slam... it was a very distinctive sound*". "*It was the only door in the house that made that type of sound, I knew what I had just heard* ".

George heard another noise that he could not explain. Upon reaching the first floor to investigate the noise, he found the rug rolled back and furniture moved around.

"*It sounded like a clock radio that was tuned slightly off station, or a marching band that was tuning up. An unorganised musical sound, coming from downstairs. At first I thought it was indeed a radio that may have gone off...* ".

The Lutzs weren't the only ones to hear such noises. Guests that came over would often hear them too. One such guest explained how he had lived in a house where he had experienced similar noises as a child. He remembered his parents had opened the windows and gone around the house saying the Lord's Prayer to try and stop the noises.

The Lutzs decided to give it a try. They opened one window in each room of the house and went from room to room together reciting the Lord's Prayer. From out of nowhere voices screamed at them 'will you please stop!' George searched the house for speakers, thinking it may have been someone playing a sick joke. He found nothing.

Apparitions were also manifesting in the house. Shadows were seen moving around. The Lutzs saw things peering thru the windows at them at night. Kathy would be in the kitchen and even feel a presence embrace her from behind.

It was around this time they also noticed their daughter Missy had begun interacting with an imaginary friend called Jodie.

"Our daughter came to Kathy one day and asked her if angels talked, and started talking about her imaginary friend. Missy had someone that she spoke of, and she called this... entity, or thing...person... 'Jodie'. At the time, we thought that it was just an imaginary friend". George continued, *"You know, it's a pretty funny thought to have kids with imaginary friends. It's not so funny when the 'imaginary friends' have things that they are trying to influence upon your children". "Missy had a friend, she called him 'Jodie'. Jodie had the ability to change form, and for Missy, she thought it was a good thing. We also did too, having an imaginary friend like that, until Jodie said, 'Your going to live here forever'. That was too strange a thing to come from a four or five year old kid".*

The incidents escalated in occurrence and became more unnerving. After seeing eyes staring in thru the living room window again George raced out to apprehend the culprit. All he found was hoof prints in the snow. Kathy also had an unsettling encounter with 'the eyes'. She saw them staring in at her thru Missy's bedroom window and hurled a chair towards them. As the chair broke the window Kathy heard what sounded like a pig squealing in the night air outside.

After a 28-day ordeal the Lutzs decided enough was enough and they fled 112 Ocean Avenue.

"The last night in the house, we knew that there was a terrible, terrific storm going on outside. Later, people checked the weather reports for the area, and say that there was no such storm. I don't really care what the weatherman said. For us...there was a storm raging that night".

As the family managed to grab a few things in their haste to get away that night the temperature in the house fluctuated from icy cold to extremely hot. The noises became more intense and the interior walls 'groaned' and seemed to shift around.
As George was leaving he encountered a hooded figure on the second floor landing. The figure stood motionless pointing directly at him.

On the night of the interview at Penn State University in October 2004 George Lutz refused to give specific details about the events surrounding their escape from the house. George's only comment was: "*There are stories about this that have never been told. They may never be told*".

In the autumn of 1976, following the Lutzs vacating the Amityville house, Ronald Defeo Jnr's attorneys approached parapsychologist Hans Holzer. They asked him to work with them as far as the supernatural aspects of the case were concerned. The Lutzs had moved away and their story had yet to break in either film or book form, 112 Ocean Avenue was now empty. The bank however, who were now in charge of the property were reluctant to allow a visit. William Weber and Bernard Burton, attorneys in charge of the Defeo case, finally persuaded them.

On January 13th 1977 the investigation took place. Weber and Burton accompanied Hans Holzer. Also with him were Laura Didio, a Channel 5 researcher and Ethel Johnson Meyer, his friend and trance medium.

They entered the building and Meyer and Holzer went from room to room getting acquainted with the house. It had been 15 months since the Defeo killings and the house was empty and devoid of furniture. Hans Holzer described it as 'curiously bland'. Whilst filming the proceedings his camera stopped for no apparent reason. Try as he might to get it working again the camera remained 'dead'.

Although unaware of the location she was to visit and its history Ethel Meyer was able to gather a lot of information during the investigation. As far as she knew it was just another routine investigation as Holzer and she had carried out many times before. She had no previous knowledge of the 'Amityville House' other then what her psychic senses told her.

According to her psychic senses the troubled history of the house and the land it was built on went even further back the Defeos occupancy. Meyer said the spirits of both an Indian Chief and what she described as a 'slung jaw' Indian were present in the house. The house was built on an ancient Indian burial ground. Both Indians are apparently from the Swanee tribe.

Indicating it is their burial ground the house was built on. The spirits of the Indians were apparently not happy.

Long before the present building was erected a farm stood on the land. A farmhouse was built close to the long forgotten burial ground. A young boy dug up a skull from the burial ground and made a 'toy' from it. The skull was that of the 'slung jaw' Indian. This incident seems to have been the trigger for the unrest amongst the Indian spirits. The 'slung jaw' Indian began to take over spirit sensitive people and cause them to commit 'foul deeds'. Indeed the young boy himself who discovered the skull seems to have succumbed to this according to Meyer.

'The boy was vulnerable too. He was chopped up.'

Meyer then sensed the tragic events that unfolded on the 13th November 1974 it would seem.

'I hear pistol shots'. 'Four people have been killed here. A family'.

Meyer said a young man had committed the murders and it was the 'slung jaw' Indian that had overtaken him. When asked by Holzer if the young man was doing the killing under the influence of anyone else Meyer answered.

'Yes, yes, yes…they think he's crazy the one who did it…he was taken over'.

Holzer then asked Meyer if the individual who committed the acts would realise that he was taken over. Meyer replied.

'I do not believe he would know this. No…the best we can do is simply say he was the right hand of the fury…of past fury'.

She concluded he killed his family *'Absolutely under the influence of a ghost'.*

Meyer then stated that the (Defeo) victims come back to the house in visitation, wandering around and sobbing. She also stated that after the first individual being taken over (Defeo), there was a second instance.

'…a second one but not like the first'.

Meyer said this involved a man and a woman.

'I would say they must have felt the depression and heard screams and sounds'.

It would seem that Meyer had also sensed the events during the Lutzs occupancy. The investigation concluded with Meyer stating the only way to save 112 Ocean Avenue and end the 'Amityville Horror' is to put the Indians to rest.

Following the success of both the book and the movie depicting the Lutz's story, many people have questioned the events that are said to have taken place in Amityville. One such 'debunker' is researcher Rick Moran. Moran compiled a list of over one hundred discrepancies and factual errors between Jay Anson's 'true story' and the truth itself. One such 'error' Moran noted was that the Indian tribe mentioned in the book was not from Amityville. In fact the tribe had inhabited the eastern tip of Long Island, which is 70 miles away from Amityville. Moran also claimed that during an interview he himself had conducted with Father Pecoraro, the priest said he never saw anything in the house.

Author Joe Nickell, who had personally visited Amityville and interviewed later owners also found inaccuracies in the story. Amongst these were:

- The book details extensive damage to the house's doors and fixtures, yet the original doorknobs, locks and hinges were all undamaged.
- There are claims that the Lutzs found a demonic 'hoof print' in the snow. On the day in question the weather records show there had been no snowfall to leave a print in.
- Both the book and the film depict police being called to the house. Nickell claims not once during their 28 day occupancy did the Lutzs call the police.

The most damaging hit to the story's credibility came when Ronald Defeo Jnr's lawyer, William Weber claimed the whole thing had been a hoax. Weber admitted that he and the Lutzs had created the 'horror story' over many bottles of wine. He said that 112 Ocean Avenue was never really haunted; the horrific experiences the Lutzs had said they had experienced were invented. Weber had planned to write a book about the Defeo murders and use the Lutz's 'haunting' experiences in the house at the end of it. Weber hoped this would gain a new trial for his client, while the Lutzs would profit handsomely from their story. Rick Moran also attested to Weber's claim in an interview with Rick Wood on Wood's 'Audio Martini' talk radio show in July 2007. Moran said:

'The Amityville Horror Hoax came from a meeting between George and Kathy Lutz, Ronnie Defeo's attorney at the time (William Weber) and Paul Hoffman…talking about the possibility of a book at which…they drank many many bottles of good red wine.'

Moran says that during the meeting the attorney showed the Lutzs crime scene evidence from the Defeo murder case. Kathy Lutz picked up a crime scene photo in which green slime could be seen on the walls of the house. Kathy commented on the 'green slime' to Paul Hoffman who replied that the 'green slime' was in fact graphite that scene of crimes officers used to detect finger prints. A light from a camera causes the substance to show up green in photographs. Kathy maintained that it still looked like 'green slime' to her. Moran says this photo is what inspired the Lutz's account of the 'green slime' on the walls of the house in their version of the Amityville haunting. Moran also says that another idea came from a crime scene photo during that meeting. Kathy Lutz was looking at another photo of one of the bedrooms in 112 Ocean Avenue where two red lights from a radar tower half a mile away could be seen through the window. Kathy mentioned that the lights looked like 'two red eyes'. This is where, according to Moran, the 'eyes at the window' sighting in the Amityville haunting case came from. Moran went on:

'Kathy Lutz wasn't afraid of that house, George Lutz was not afraid of that house and that conversation took place over (a) "shall we write a book about this" (conversation) after they had been in the house'

During the 'Audio Martini' radio show interview Moran told host Rick Wood that this meeting took place several months after the Lutzs had left 112 Ocean Avenue. Moran added that at the end of the meeting Weber and Hoffman decided the story was a 'no go' as they wanted to write about the possibility of paranormal activity going on in the house that had something to do with the Defeo murders. Without Hoffman, who had been brought in to write the book, the Lutzs decided to find another writer to tell their story before Weber and Hoffman had a chance to publish their book. Jay Anson was brought in to put the Lutzs story into book form and further embellished it whilst doing so.

By the time the film's screenwriters had adapted it, any ounce of truth there may have been at any point was long gone.

Despite all the claims of the Amityville Horror being a hoax, George Lutz maintained the events to have been true. Even after his wife Kathy's death in August 2004, George continued to profess the stories legitimacy.

At the Penn State University Convention in 2004 George Lutz himself showed some slides of photos taken from later investigations at the Amityville house.

Amongst the images were:

- Misty faces peering thru windows from both inside and outside the home.
- The ghostly figure of a young boy stood on the second floor landing.
- An entity manifesting out of a wall, peering down at investigators.

George Lutz passed away two years later, on the 8th May 2006 from heart disease.

Decades after the story first broke to the world the Amityville Horror still remains one of the world's most investigated and prominent hauntings. Believers and sceptics alike are determined to prove their argument for the case being the truth or a hoax.

With both George and Kathy Lutz no longer with us, and George having maintained there was some reality to the story until the day he died, the whole truth may never be known.

I feel it only fitting to give the final words on the Amityville case to the man who gave the paranormal world one of its most celebrated cases.

After the slide presentation at Penn State University was finished in 2004, George Lutz was asked why he felt it important to inform people of what had occurred at the Amityville house. He replied:

"You see... you may never go through this. But in your lifetime, as this kind of thing gets talked about more and more, and as we learn more... it's likely in one-way or another that you will hear of this kind of thing. This stuff happens... it happens everyday, there are people in this room tonight that can tell you all kinds of stories about things locally, that happen right here". *"It's my prayer that everyone in this room never go through such a thing. But if you know someone that does, the hardest thing for those people is the loss of being able to communicate with anyone else about it. Not being able to find anyone that can intelligently help them. It's not talked about, it's not understood.... and when it happens to you, you become an alien to everyone else"*.

What The Experts Say
The Amityville Horror (1979

Jason Karl, television presenter, actor and author. Jason is best known for being the Parapsychologist/ Co-Presenter for the first series of the UK television show 'Most Haunted' (2002-2003). He has authored nine books on the paranormal including the titles Illustrated History Of The Haunted World (2007) and 21st Century Ghosts (2007).

"The alarming tale of terror told by the Lutz's, of a terrifying journey into the unknown at 112 Ocean Avenue, Amityville, has long been a source of deep fascination for the paranormal community and indeed for myself. At the same time both frightening and strangely alluring, 'The Amityville Horror' is perhaps the world's most famous case of contemporary haunting. Whether sceptic or believer it is impossible to ignore the claims made by a family seemingly torn apart by an ancient force of evil; but whether these were the work of overactive imaginations, intentional fraud, or just maybe... the truth, will never be known.

As the alleged 'facts' of the case are explored there are some key salient points which I believe deserve closer contemplation. To begin with, why did Defeo Jnr. kill his entire family in cold blood? Was he simply a mad man? For such people exist throughout all corners of society, or was he, as he claims, possessed by a force which compelled him to commit second degree murder devoid of any apparent personal motive? Why did the sound of the gunshots not wake the other members of the household as he went, room to room, on his killing spree? Why did the neighbours not hear any sound as the grisly scene unfolded at 'High Hopes'? Could it be, as noted parapsychologist Hans Holzer has suggested, that during extreme psychic episodes, the boundaries of sound and the way it is perceived are temporarily altered? It is certainly true that sound can be manipulated by the spirit world, for I have witnessed this on a variety of occasions during my travels seeking ghosts around the world.

The case achieved notoriety immediately upon release of the first film version; a highly exaggerated drama allegedly based on the real life experiences of the Lutz family, and while the film undoubtedly escalated what might otherwise have been 'just another ghost story' to worldwide fame, was it really the motive of the Lutz's to 'cash in' with a preconceived falsehood based upon the fact that they had invested in a house they could not afford? This seems a risky business to me. Far easier, I would think, to sell up and move on, rather than imagine a fantastical account of haunting which would immediately brand you either insane or simply a liar, and certainly had no guarantee of financial reward?

The first film and its subsequent sequels, the book, written by Jay Anson, and the recent 2005 remake of the original prove that interest in The Amityville Horror is alive and well. With international media coverage the story finds itself well rooted in the cultural memory of both the USA and the UK. Interestingly, what scared audiences in 1979 is somewhat different to Hollywood's ideas in the new millennium. The original movie seems somewhat lacklustre in light of contemporary horror films, and the 2005 'Amityville Horror' remake reflects this. With a much stronger emphasis on 'Reverend Jeremiah Ketcham' as a central character, whose all pervading presence throughout the movie inflicts fear both into the onscreen family, and the watching audience, and with elaborate computer generated imagery, a ghost story gathering dust was brought colourfully back to life in true Hollywood style!

With the death of Kathy, and more recently George Lutz, the case will now perhaps begin to fade into the annals of psychic research; a case never fully explained and one which will perhaps rouse passions both for and against its validity well into the 21st century. The current inhabitants of 'High Hopes' say they have never seen the green slime, hooded figure or swarms of flies described by the Lutz's, Maybe that is because they were never there in the first place? Or maybe because this great ghost story has finally been laid to rest…"

The Entity (1982)

The Carla Moran Case

In 1982 The Entity became one of the most controversial horror movies ever released. Caused mainly by the subject matter, the story of a woman who is violently attacked and sexually assaulted by an unseen entity, there was even more controversy to come following the release. Many people doubt that the true story the movie was based on ever happened, or that the woman who the story was based on even existed herself.

The Entity tells the story of Carla Moran, played by Barbara Hershey. Carla is the victim of an unseen entity that repeatedly attacks her. It torments her in her bedroom, attacks her in her friend's home and even seizes control of her car whilst she is driving. Carla finally seeks help, unable to cope anymore with the attacks and fearing for her sanity and indeed her life. She looks to both sceptics and believers from scientific and paranormal professions to help rid her of the assailant and end her living nightmare.

Frank De Felitta claims to have interviewed the 'real' Carla Moran extensively for his novel and the screenplay of The Entity. He says of Carla's experiences:

'She was injured, so hurt by this thing, so emotionally destroyed by it'.

During the filming of *The Entity* some curtains on the set inexplicably tore from bottom to top. Also during filming the actor playing Carla's son broke his arm in a scene in which he tries to intervene during an attack on his mother. The 'real life' teenage son of Carla Moran had broken the same arm during the attack the scene was based on.

In 1980, two years before the release of the movie, Dr Kerry Gaynor and Dr Barry Taff brought out a book also titled 'The Entity'. The book recounts Gaynor and Taff's investigation into the Carla Moran case during the period of the attacks. Both

Gaynor and Taff would go on to work as technical advisors on the movie.

The 'real' Carla Moran was a single mother with four children living in Culver City, California USA in the mid 1970's. She had been the victim of repeated attacks by what she believed to be three entities. Two would hold her down whilst the third assaulted her. Carla reported attacks that even simulated penetrating rape in some instances. Over the course of almost a dozen incidents the number of entities involved decreased to just one. Carla sought help from counseling and books on the subject. It was whilst in a bookstore in 1974 that she met Dr Kerry Gaynor and Dr Barry Taff. Gaynor and Taff were two parapsychologists working under Dr Thelma Moss, who was a prominent parapsychologist at UCLA at the time. Gaynor and Taff specialised in haunting and poltergeist phenomena and after talking with Carla Moran at the bookstore, they arranged a meeting to discuss her case.

They visited Carla at her house where they conducted a two-hour interview. Gaynor thought she was holding something back so he kept pushing her for the information. Finally Carla said a ghost had beaten and raped her. Gaynor says:

'We laughed when we left her home, and I thought she was probably off her rocker'.

A few days later Carla Moran called Gaynor and told him several visitors to her home had seen an apparition. Due to the fact that they now had independent verification of phenomena, Gaynor and Taff volunteered to investigate Carla's case.

The second visit to the house, to start the investigation, saw the beginning of the activity that Gaynor and Taff were to witness throughout their study of the case. Gaynor reported seeing orbs of light almost immediately. Despite having both a 35mm and a Polaroid camera, the orbs were moving too quickly to be caught on film.

During the investigation Gaynor was standing in the kitchen talking to Carla's son. A cabinet door flew open and a pan shot out of it, landing three or four feet from the cabinet. Gaynor immediately tore the cabinet apart, examining it for any signs of a hoax or logical explanation. He found nothing.

Shortly afterwards Gaynor and the rest of the investigation team heard Carla Moran scream from the bedroom. She said the entity was in there. They rushed in to join her and as they saw nothing they asked her where it was. Carla told them it was in the corner of the room so they took a picture with the Polaroid camera. The picture came out blank. Carla shouted out again that the entity was in the corner of the room and the team took another picture with the Polaroid, again it came out blank. Gaynor wanted to make sure there wasn't a fault with the camera. When Carla told him the entity had gone he took a picture of the corner of the room with the same camera. The picture came out perfectly. A few seconds later, with the entity still gone, he took another photo. Once again the picture developed without a single fault.

The most interesting photographs were yet to come.

The entity came back and Carla claimed it was right in front of her face. The team took a photo of Carla. In the picture you could see everything from the curtains in the background to the buttons on Carla's dress, but where her face should have been was a blank. They took another photo when Carla once again claimed the entity was right in front of her face. Again her face came out blank in the picture, as if the entity was in between her and the lens, obscuring the camera. As before, when Carla told Gaynor the entity had gone he took another photo. The picture came out with no discrepancies and you could see Carla's face perfectly.

On the third night of the investigation the team decided to attempt a séance in Carla's bedroom. One of the photographers commented that the uneven and chipped paint on the walls caused discrepancies in his photographs. The investigators covered the walls entirely with black paperboards to avoid any misinterpretation of any findings. Gaynor also numbered the each board for use in the séance. As light anomalies began appearing Gaynor began asking questions, using the boards to obtain answers. He would say 'flash three times on board number two for yes' or 'flash twice on board number nine for no'. To the investigators astonishment the light would flash on the exact board it was asked to. Despite their excitement at apparently communicating with something intelligent Gaynor had his concerns. He wanted to make sure nobody was projecting a light onto the wall from within the room. He asked the light to move away from the wall, not really expecting anything to happen. The ball of light floated into the middle of the room. It began spinning, twisting and expanding in different directions simultaneously. As Gaynor explained this would have been very hard to hoax. Light has to be projected onto a flat surface; it cannot be projected into an empty space without the use of sophisticated equipment such as lasers.

The investigators had sealed off the bedroom during the séance and nine professional photographers had captured the orb from every angle of the room. The team described seeing three dimensional, greenish/yellow to white coloured balls of light, but the photos showed arcs of light. One such picture was a spectacular 35mm photo, showing reverse arcs of light over Carla Moran's head. The picture was published in Popular Photography Magazine; they had never published a 'ghost' photograph before and haven't published another one since.

Gaynor claims that during the investigation the team did witness the formation of a full figured apparition. They saw the head and shoulders take shape, then the greenish/white light extended to the ground to form a 'human' figure. The figure then just instantly vanished. Two men assisting the investigation passed out and had to be carried from the room after witnessing the apparition.

During the ten-week investigation Carla Moran was attacked around fifteen times. Despite Gaynor, Taff, psychics and professional photographers being on site for the investigation, Carla was never attacked in the presence of non-family members. Gaynor only observed bite marks on Carla's neck and bruises on her body.

Gaynor is convinced legitimate paranormal activity occurred in the house but stresses he found no evidence of anything paranormal about the attacks. This does not mean he totally rules out the possibility though. Talking of his examination of 900 cases over 25 years, Gaynor says:

> *'Sexual aspects to cases are not that unusual…it's far more a part of (paranormal) phenomena than is recognised. These may very well fall into the domain of psychological disturbances'.*

Gaynor believes as the investigation went on Carla became stronger. She realised something was really happening to her and she wasn't going insane. The investigation ended but the attacks continued. Carla moved five times and every time the entity followed. The phenomena diminished a little more after every move and about two years later the attacks stopped altogether. Gaynor and his team were not able to rid Carla of the assaulting entity; he believes through her own strength she outlasted it:

> *'I'm not an exorcist… I document the phenomena. I research the phenomena and I do a lot of counseling with these people'.*

Sceptics believe that Carla Moran is a fictional character created by Gaynor and Taff for their book. They believe that because Carla Moran is an alias and not the woman's' real name, that the woman never really existed. There is no way of finding out who or where the 'real' Carla Moran is and investigating the story further. This coupled with Gaynor and Taff's lack of evidence regarding the actual attacks, leads some paranormal experts to recommend *The Entity* to be treated as a complete work of fiction.

Others believe Gaynor and Taff have plenty of evidence from their investigation to prove that something paranormal happened to Carla Moran. The same people would also claim that Gaynor and Taff had created the name Carla Moran, and not the person, to protect the real victims' identity due to the violent and sexual nature of the attacks she suffered.

So what became of Carla Moran? If indeed there was a Carla Moran?

During the years after the release of *The Entity* various women have come out on American television claiming to be the 'real'

Carla Moran. The last person to do so was an elderly woman in 2004. The same woman had previously told newspapers in 2001 that she was Carla Moran and that she had been diagnosed with cancer.

As for the sceptics, those who don't believe Carla Moran was assaulted or that Carla Moran even existed. The people who demand proof that the story *The Entity* was based on really happened.

Well, Dr Kerry Gaynor has a final message for them:

'But what is proof? A ghost in a jar? Or at least that's what the scientific community would want. I want the public to know about it but I don't have an agenda. I'm not interested in standing on a pulpit and saying, "You must believe in ghosts". Something is going on that demands our attention. I'm much more interested in figuring it out".

What The Experts Say
The Entity (1982)

Lara Wells - Medium, Columnist and Speaker on the survival of the spirit after the physical death. Her many radio appearances include Kerrang Radio where she was deemed to be the 'Real Deal' and CFM and West Sound Radio stations for over 4 years where 'Live' meant 'Live'!

Lara was also the medium and criminal Face reader for UK publication Paranormal Magazine. She contributes to many weekly and monthly magazines and newspapers but still finds time to tour and see people on an individual basis.

Lara will soon be appearing in a television documentary about a spiritual family and their way of life and a program with her Psychic children. Lara was voted Most Popular National Female Medium at the UK's Spiritual ConneXtions Awards 2008.

"Most of us will remember the film *The Entity* as it sparked huge curiosity and intrigue into the woman it was based on. The woman concerned had allegedly declined for her name to be disclosed and this added to the mystery behind the making. The sceptics would reason that if the identity was secret then the person didn't exist. If this happened to you would you want to be known?

Many films have been produced on subject matters that we, as people, could easily find explanations for and the very idea that the horrific events actually did happen to a very ordinary woman (and bare in mind that she stood to gain nothing from reporting it) in circumstances that most of us could relate to brought home how it could be any one of us. This would be a lot to take on and digest for most of us. However, there were reports after the film was released, that various women stepped forward to claim that they were the 'real' Carla Moran. Could it be that the vicious attacks portrayed in the film brought recognition of similar goings on in these women's lives for the same reasons or that the very idea of an 'invisible' being was really the main cause of distress they had experienced in their own lives and would attempt to use this theory to pacify an already fully-fledged mental health condition?

The very existence of spirit survival after the physical death can be a difficult one to take on board. Up until now, it has evaded all scientific proof and, unfortunately, society is of the understanding that unless we have proof that we can see and record in a controlled (to their spec) environment, then they won't accept that the very theory exists. If we were to believe everything we could only see, would that limit our own experience?

There was documented evidence on this case by many, many professional people and if all the film did was to make you confront the possibility that an unseen world exists then maybe just maybe you could emotionally accept that what happened to the real Carla Moran could indeed happen to you."

The Haunted (1991)

The Smurl Haunting

The phrases 'Television movie', 'Made for TV' and 'Straight to video' can often deter a potential viewer. People seem to associate these movies with poor storylines, low budgets and bad acting. They are often 'based on a true story' and, to be honest, most of them do warrant a pressing of the 'off' button on the remote control.

If you look hard enough though there are some stories that have only ever graced the small screen that deserve to be told on the silver screen. Its not that these movies have any better production values then their counterparts, it's the fact that some of these stories are so intriguing that they deserve to be seen by a wider audience. One such case in point is the story of the Smurl haunting titled *'The Haunted'*. This TV movie was screened on American television in 1991 and tells the story of the Smurl family.

Jack and Janet Smurl move into their new home on Chase Street only to find that it is plagued by three separate entities and a demon. After suffering in silence from constant disturbances and even attacks from their ghostly tormentors, the Smurls seek help from the outside world. Can paranormal researchers and demonologists Ed and Lorraine Warren release the family from their living hell?

So just what was going on in the Smurl house? What is the 'true story' behind the movie?

Jack and Janet Smurl met in 1967. Jack served as a neuropsychiatric technician in the Navy and by 1968 the couple were married. They lived in Wilkes-Barre, Pennsylvania, USA but after hurricane Agnes had flooded most of the area in 1972 they were forced to relocate.

Jack's parents, John and Mary Smurl, bought a semi detached house in west Pittston, Pennsylvania in 1973. The house was built in 1896 and was situated in a quiet, middle class neighbourhood on Chase Street. Jack and his family moved with his parents and had no problems sharing the house with them. John and Mary Smurl lived in the right half of the duplex and Jack, Janet and their first two daughters, Dawn and Heather, moved into the left half. The Smurls spent a lot of time remodeling and decorating the house and the first 18 months on Chase Street went without incident.

However in January 1974 the first signs of paranormal activity began. The Smurls witnessed water pipes that would continually leak despite being repeatedly resoldered by a plumber. A television set literally 'burst into flames' for with no apparent cause and an unusual stain appeared from nowhere on a new carpet. Nobody in the house knew who or what had caused these strange occurrences. Most frightening of all for the family at this point were the marks found in the bathroom. A new sink and bathtub were found to be severely scratched, as was some freshly painted woodwork. It looked to all intents and purposes as if a wild animal had clawed at them.

As the months went by the activity in the house increased and by 1975 apparitions were being seen in the property. Jack and Janet's oldest daughter, Dawn, started witnessing 'people floating' around her bedroom. Footsteps were continuously heard on the stairs, drawers opened and closed of their own accord and empty rocking chairs rocked and creaked as if someone was actually sitting in them. The list of phenomena continued to grow.

By 1985, and with the arrival of twins Shannon and Carin, the family were growing tired and frustrated by the incidents. What had started as annoying disturbances was driving them to despair. The house was often freezing cold, vile smells lingered throughout the house and unplugged radios would suddenly turn themselves on and blare out music. John and Mary Smurl would hear loud and abusive language coming from Jack and Janet's side of the house even though the couple would not even be arguing at the time.

In February 1985 Janet was doing the laundry in the basement. She heard her name being called and after searching for whoever had shouted her, she realised she had been alone the entire time. Two days later an apparition appeared to Janet in the kitchen. The room went icy cold and a black, faceless human form appeared. The apparition walked through the wall and appeared to Mary Smurl on the opposite side of the house. The haunting activity became even more intense after these incidents. Rapping and scratching noises were constantly heard from within the walls of the house and several neighbours heard screams and strange noises coming from the Smurl property when nobody was even home and the building was empty. Most alarming of all was the physical attacks that now occurred. On the night of her 13 year old sister Heather's confirmation into the Catholic Church, a large ceiling fan crashed down to the floor landing inches away from Shannon Smurl, nearly killing her. On another occasion Shannon was tossed down the stairs. Jack and Janet began being levitated by an unknown source. Janet herself was violently pulled off her bed after making love to her husband. Jack was paralysed while this happened, gagging from a foul smell that filled the room. Even Simon, the family's pet dog, was subjected to attacks. He was repeatedly picked up and thrown by 'unseen hands'.

The Smurls were now at their wits end and desperate for help. Janet had heard about Ed and Lorraine Warren. The Warrens were psychical researchers and demonologists from Monroe, Connecticut. Despite Janet's scepticism, and due to the fact she had no one else to turn to, she called Ed and Lorraine. In January 1986, shortly after Janet had contacted them, the Warrens arrived at Chase Street.

They began their investigation by asking the Smurls about their family life, religious beliefs and other relevant factors. The Warrens, accompanied by Rosemary Frueh, a registered nurse and psychic, then began a tour of the house. They identified a bedroom closet as the crossover point between the two sides of the duplex and detected the presence of four evil entities in the building. One of which they believed was a demon. Without any evidence supporting family dysfunction, tragedy or any of involvement with the occult to invite the entities into their home the Warrens looked to another cause for the haunting. They concluded that the demon had probably been dormant for decades and had risen to draw on the energy of the girls entering into puberty and the family's strong religious beliefs. Both are common factors in poltergeist cases.

The Warrens then set out to expose the demon by provoking it, playing religious music and confronting it with prayer. Mirrors shook violently as did dresser drawers. On another occasion the demon reacted by spelling out 'you filthy b*****d, get out of this house'.

The situation escalated even further as Janet alleged to have been sexually assaulted by an incubus. Equally as terrifying were Jack's claims to have been raped by a succubus. He said the succubus took the form of an old woman with a young body. Her eyes were red and her gums were green. He also described her body as 'scaly'.

The Smurls had tried several times to obtain help from the church. Janet thought she was going to receive help from a priest called Father O'Leary but she later discovered no such priest existed. The Roman Catholic Diocese of Scranton said they would consult with experts on the Smurls case but thought it unlikely they would become involved.

With 'pig noises' now being heard coming from the walls Ed Warren was totally convinced that the Smurls had a case of serious demonic infestation. So with the church unwilling to come to their aid, Ed Warren brought a priest he knew to Chase Street. Father McKenna, later to become Bishop McKenna, was a traditionalist who refused to abide by the changes made by the second Vatican Council. He had performed more then 50 exorcisms for the Warrens in the past and was happy to help the troubled Smurls. Father McKenna performed the ancient rite at the Smurls home but it did nothing but serve to anger the demon even more.

The family were now in the second demonic stage, oppression, which according to Ed Warren followed the first stage which was infestation and would be followed by two further stages, those being possession and finally death.

As the attacks continued Janet and Mary Smurl had slash and bite marks on their arms and Carin Smurl fell seriously ill from a strange fever and nearly died. During an attack on Dawn Smurl by an entity she was almost raped. Father McKenna performed a second exorcism in the late spring but it seemed to have had as little effect as the first ritual he had performed.

The demon had now begun harassing Jack Smurl at work and even following the family on camping trips. After repeatedly being refused help from the church and knowing that it would be pointless moving home as the demon would just follow them, the Smurls decided to try another way to end their ordeal. Janet and Jack decided to appear on television, albeit anonymously. They were interviewed on the 'People Are Talking', show remaining behind a screen to protect their identity.

It would seem that the demon did not appreciate their appearance on the local Philadelphia television show as the attacks continued. Janet was levitated and thrown against the wall and in a separate instance a human hand came through the mattress of her bed and grabbed her by the neck. Jack was again raped by the succubus and the demon also appeared to him as a 'pig on legs' on another occasion.

In August 1986 the Smurls went public with their story. They gave an interview to the Wilkes-Barre Sunday Independent newspaper in the hope that somebody reading the article might be able to help them end their ordeal. The Smurl house became a tourist attraction to press, sceptics and curious members of the public. The press attention from such publications as the Pittsburgh Post Gazette, Buffalo News and Scranton Tribune finally pushed the Roman Catholic Diocese to take some action and they offered to take over the investigation. The Warrens had also planned a mass exorcism with several priests and prayer groups also visited the house.

Medium Mary Alice Rinkman examined the Smurls home and confirmed the Warren's findings. According to her there were indeed four spirits present. She identified a man named Peter who had murdered his wife and her lover and later been hung by a mob and also an old woman named Abigail .Rinkman

Identified another spirit as a powerful demon but was unable to give any details about the final spirit.

Bishop McKenna performed a third exorcism on the house and this time it had seemed to have been successful. There were no more disturbances. Three months later however it would appear that the ritual had not been such a success.

Just before Christmas 1986 Jack Smurl saw a black figure he believed was beckoning him into the third demonic stage…possession. He grabbed his rosary and prayed and the figure disappeared. Jack's hopes of it being an isolated incident were soon dashed. The banging, putrid smells and violent attacks started once again.

Tired, frustrated and beaten the Smurls moved to another town. The chance that the entities would not follow them was their last hope of ending their nightmare. In 1988, shortly after the move, the church performed a fourth exorcism which finally seemed to have freed the Smurls from their ordeal. In the same year, 1988, Jack Smurl's book telling the family's story titled '*The Haunted*' went to press. Three years later, in 1991, the television movie of the same name was released in the USA.

Many sceptics, amongst them some of the Smurl's neighbours, believe this only confirms their suspicions. That the family concocted the whole story in order to profit from book and film contracts.

The possibility of a financial motive being behind the reported haunting was one of many reasons for scepticism according to Paul Kurtz.

Paul Kurtz was the Chairman of the Committee for the Scientific Investigation of Claims of the Paranormal (CSICOP) at the time of the Smurl haunting. Kurtz and CSICOP became involved in the case once the story had broken to the media. With newspapers carrying daily reports on the Smurl's story at the time, members of the public and the media contacted CSICOP asking if they knew what was going on at the house. Kurtz dispatched two teams of investigators to West Pittston and also conducted an extensive 'over-the-phone' investigation. He contacted several members of the press who were working on the story and also members of the Smurl family themselves. In a report published in the Winter 1986/87 issue of The Skeptical Inquirer Kurtz concluded a number of explanations as to what really happened at Chase Street. None of the events, Kurtz says, were paranormal:

> 'Our investigation of the Smurl case thus far points to several possible alternative explanations for what has allegedly been happening without the need to invoke an occult or paranormal one.'

Kurtz's suspicions were also aroused by the fact that when one of his CSICOP teams arrived at the Smurl house they were denied entry by Ed and Lorraine Warren. The Warrens were now acting as spokesmen for the Smurls and said they alone had been given privileged access to the house. So the CSICOP team were not allowed to enter the building despite the fact that the Smurls had earlier given them permission to examine the house.

Kurtz also claims that when he asked the Warrens for permission to examine the video and audio tape evidence they claimed to have gathered he was given a number of conflicting answers as to why this would not be possible. Amongst these were that the tapes would only be released to the Roman Catholic Church and that Warren had lent the tapes to a television production company and could not remember their name. Kurtz says:

> 'For any demonological claims to be accepted they must be corroborated by independent observers. Thus far we only have the testimony of the Smurls and/or the Warrens, unsubstantiated by any kind of objective physical evidence...we are committed to the impartial examination of any such claims...But we were denied the opportunity to examine the site or freely question the claimants...'

Kurtz discovered, in conversation with neighbours of the Smurls, that they had been complaining to village officials for years about the foul odours coming from an inadequate sewer pipe near the Smurl home. This could explain the strange smells described in the haunting. He also discovered that many of the rapping noises had emanated from the walls adjacent to 17 year old Dawn Smurl's room. He wondered whether she could have been responsible for the noises herself. Kurtz noted that Dawn's statements fit the pattern of a teenager playing tricks to get attention. Kurtz requested that the Smurl family submit to a thorough psychological and physiological examination but they declined. Kurtz concluded his findings by outlying the possibility of the financial motives behind the alleged haunting:

'The fact that the Smurls have signed a book contract raises serious questions about their motives. No doubt however, a large segment of the public and of the media is far more fascinated by demons and ghosts than the possibility of a prank or hoax'.

So was the haunting of Chase Street really a terrifying reality of demonic infestation and evil spirits?

Or was it an elaborate hoax purported by the Smurls, with the help of the Warrens for financial gain? A story that fell just one step short of making it all the way to the silver screen?

What The Experts Say
The Haunted (1991)

Bill Bean – Survivor of a haunting, Public Speaker and Author of 'Dark Force' (MerionesPublishing.com 2007). Bill has turned his terrifying experience of living in a house occupied by evil entities as a child into a positive thing by bringing his families harrowing story to the world's attention. By doing this Bill intends to educate and bring the paranormal to people's attention along with helping support others who have been through the same traumatic experiences. Bill Bean has been interviewed on countless radio shows and has also featured on the Discovery Channel series, 'A Haunting'. The episode featuring the Bean family's story is titled 'House of the Dead' and aired on September 7, 2006 and is still being shown today. In 2007 Bill's book 'Dark Force' was published, documenting in his own words the terrifying and tragic story of the Bean family haunting.

"I remember seeing the movie at the time and immediately I made a connection based on my past experiences. I didn't know these people, all I knew is what I'd seen and then later read about the case, but it rang true to me. According to what I had read these were good, decent, Christian people and I don't know why or who it was but something evil manifested itself to them. Many a time I have wondered why these things occur. There's always a door that opens up. There always has to be something that happens to invite this in, to allow it to come in. Whether somebody had done something to encourage it, dabbled in the occult somehow to open a doorway, I don't know. That said, as the saying goes, 'If the devil leaves you alone then he's got you where he wants you'. What I'm saying is that these were Christian people and perhaps it is another possibility that Satan could and does attack those deep in faith. There's certainly something to that theory too.

There has to be a starting point to allow this evil to come in and whatever that may be it definitely happened in the Smurl case. If Jack Smurl was attacked during the haunting there's no doubt it was a demonic entity, I guess in this case you would define it as a Succubus and that's a very disturbing thing to experience. It's horrible. At the time of these events the Warrens were the people to go to. If you didn't go to the church for help, you went to the Warrens. They were the authorities in their field, in this type of situation. I have read many good things about them and I've also read negative things about them too. I would be more inclined to believe the good things about them as I've read far more good things about the Warrens than bad things. The point is regardless of what you may think of them or their investigation methods and techniques, the main thing to consider here is helping the victims of a haunting. The fact that the victim gets the help they need should be the main concern, not who gives it or how they get it and what your opinion of them is.

If my memory serves me correctly I think there were differences between the story and the movie. The content was altered, as happened with my story and many others. I know that 'Hollywood' have to cater for the mass audience and be as dramatic as possible but when it is your story that is being altered it does become frustrating.

I think the main positive we can take from the movie, regardless of whether it was absolutely true to the real case or not, is that it was made at all. The fact that these stories are getting out there to the public and people are now willing to talk about them is the main issue. Based on my opinion, on what I have read and seen regarding the Smurl haunting, it rings true to me. There were some similarities between this case and my own experiences, so I would have to lean towards saying that the Smurl's story is a true one. These things can and do absolutely happen to people."

Exorcism Of Emily Rose (2005)

The Possession Of Annelise Michel

The *Exorcism Of Emily Rose* was released in 2005 with the immortal words 'Based On a True Story' preceding its title on movie posters everywhere. Writer and Director of the movie Scott Derrickson came across the story after meeting a police officer in New York City USA. The officer specialised in researching demonic activity and the paranormal. He gave Derrickson a copy of a book about a real life case of demonic possession. After reading the book Derrickson felt so strongly about the story that he and co writer Paul Harris Boardman tracked down the author to discuss making the film into a movie. The author was a recently retired professor and the book had by now gone out of print, so the rights had reverted back to the author. Derrickson and Boardman struck a deal with the author and set about researching the subject of the paranormal.

They immersed themselves in books on demons, video and audio tapes of exorcisms and even interviewed priests who had performed exorcisms themselves. Derrickson found the whole subject matter very disturbing and said he would never do anything like that again.

Finally, after all their efforts the writers were ready to transfer the book to the big screen.

The film tells the story of Emily Rose (played by actress Jennifer Carpenter), an average teenage girl with ambitions of going to college, living in modern day America. She becomes the target and ultimately the victim of demonic forces. A sceptical attorney attempts to clear the name of the clergyman who exorcised Emily. Upon defending the priest the attorney must face her own 'demons' in the courtroom, and the question of whether powerful spiritual forces do really exist.

So what was the story held within the pages of the book that moved Scott Derrickson so much? What was the real story his movie was based on? Who was Emily Rose?

The real 'Emily Rose' was in fact a girl called Annelise Michel.

Annelise Michel was born on 21st September 1952 in the small town of Klinenberg in the heart of Germany. Michel was raised in a strict Catholic family in Bavaria with her 3 sisters by her parents Anna and Josef. The family enjoyed the normal life of a religious household until one day in 1968 when Anneliese began shaking uncontrollably and was unable to call out to her parents. After this attack her anxious parents took her to a Psychiatric Clinic in Wulzburg where a neurologist diagnosed Anneliese with Grand Mal epilepsy due to the strength of the epileptic fit she was admitted to the hospital for treatment.

More attacks were to follow and by the autumn of 1970 Anneliese was battling with the belief that she was possessed. She began seeing faces of demons on the people and things around her and voices were telling her that she was damned. Eventually Anneliese confided in the doctors, mentioning that the 'demons' had started giving her orders. The doctors seemed unable and unwilling to help. Aneliese lost all hope of medicine being able to cure her. She began suffering from depression and suicidal.

In the summer of 1973 her parents had become so alarmed by her behavior that they visited several priests to request an exorcism to be performed on their daughter. These requests were rejected on the grounds that, all the criteria the church needed to prove a possession could not be met in this case, and until these were met the church could not approve an exorcism. Some of these requirements include an aversion to religious objects, speaking in a language that the person has never learned and supernatural powers. Unwilling to perform the ritual, the church recommended that Anneliese continue with medication and treatment from the doctors.

Anneliese's behavior became more erratic and in 1974 Pastor Ernst Alt, who had been supervising her for some time, requested a permit to perform an exorcism. The Bishop of Wurzburg rejected the request and recommended Anneliese should live more of a religious lifestyle in order to find peace.

By now Anneliese was sleeping on a stone floor at her parent's house in Klingenberg. She refused to eat saying the demons would not allow her to, she ate only spiders, flies and coal and began drinking her own urine. She insulted members of her own family and even went as far as to beat and bite them. Anneliese would also be heard screaming throughout the house whilst breaking crucifixes, pulling apart rosaries and destroying other religious artifacts such as paintings of Christ. Under the influence of her demons, she would compulsively perform up to 400 squats a day and would regularly perform the act of tearing off her clothes and urinating on the floor.

On other occasions Anneliese bit the head off a dead bird and crawled under a table and barked like a dog for two days.

By 1975 the acts of self-mutilation that Anneliese had started committing were now commonplace and she was herself asking for an exorcism. In September of the same year Josef Stangl made an exact verification of possession and assigned Father Arnold Renz and Pastor Ernst Alt with the order to perform the exorcism. The 'Rituale Roman' would be the basis for the exorcism as at the time it was still a valid Cannon Law from the 17th Century.

Anneliese was believed to be possessed by several demons. Amongst those that identified themselves were- Cain, The Emperor Nero, Adolf Hitler, Judas Iscariot, Lucifer and a disgraced Frankish Priest from the 16th century named Fleischmann.

From September 1975 to July 1976 the rite was performed 67 times. One or two exorcism sessions were held each week and would take up to four hours per session. The attacks were so strong during these sessions that Anneliese would have to be held down by up to three men and sometimes even chained up; the demons would even answer the priest's questions through Anneliese in a growling inhuman voice. They explained such things as what they believed was wrong with the church or why they were in hell.

'People are stupid as pigs…they think it's all over after death…It goes on' says Hitler. Judas Iscariot describes Hitler as a *'Big Mouth'* and that Hitler has *'No real say'* in Hell.

Forty two of the exorcism sessions were recorded on audio tapes to preserve such details and sometimes family members and visitors were present during the prayers and incantations.

Amidst the period of the rituals Anneliese found that her life could return to a kind of normality. She went to church, went to school and even took her final examinations at the Pedagogic Academy in Wurzburg. The attacks continued however and the instances of being paralysed and falling unconscious increased. By now Anneliese had refused to eat for several weeks and though she had received treatment for epilepsy in the past, at her own request, doctors were no longer being consulted either. Anneliese, her parents and the exorcists decided to rely completely on exorcism.

June 30th 1976 was to be the last day of the Exorcism Rite. Anneliese was running a temperature, suffering from pneumonia and exhausted. Her knees had ruptured due to the 600 genuflections she performed during the daily exorcisms and unable to physically perform them herself, her parents helped carry her through them on this occasion.

'Beg for Absolution', Anneliese told the exorcists. She then said to her mother *'Mother, I'm afraid'*.

Anneliese Michel died that day, 30th June 1976. She was aged 23 and weighed only 68 pounds. Anna Michel recorded her daughter's death the following day and on the same day Pastor Ernst Alt informed the authorities in Aschaffenberg.

The investigation into the case began immediately. Prosecutors sorted through the facts of Anneliese's case and more then two years later they were ready to go to court.

The trial set reason against faith and questioned the existence of the Devil himself.

The 'Klinsberg Case' saw Anna Michel, Josef Michel, Father Arnold Renz and Pastor Ernst Alt accused of causing Anneliese Michel's death by neglect. The outcome would be decided by the answers to the questions: What caused Anneliese's death and who was responsible?

The cause, according to forensic evidence was starvation. The prosecutors claimed that the accused were responsible for the death of Anneliese Michel. She had refused to go to a mental institution where she would have been sedated and forced to eat. The specialists claimed that if the accused had force fed her as little as one week before death she would have been saved. Psychiatrists, who also testified for the prosecution, said that Anneliese's unsettled sexual development and diagnosed Temporal Lobe Epilepsy had influenced her psychosis. They also added that through the 'Doctrinaire Induction' the priests had provided the basis for her psychotic behavior. As a consequence, they claimed, Anneliese accepted her behavior as a form of demonic possession.

The exorcists, in their defence tried to prove the possession and the presence of the demons. They presented their evidence in the form of taped recordings of strange dialogues, such as that of two demons arguing which one of them would have to leave Anneliese's body first. None of the witnesses present during any of the exorcism sessions ever had a doubt over the authenticity of the presence of these demons.

The court was not convinced. Two years after Anneliese's death her parents, along with both exorcists were found guilty of negligent manslaughter and sentenced to six months in prison, suspended with three years probation. The verdict also included that it was the opinion of the court that the accused should have helped take care of the medical treatment Anneliese needed, but instead their use of naïve practices aggravated her already poor constitution.

A commission of the German Bishop Conference, formed after the trial, later declared that Anneliese Michel was not possessed. They decided the heart of the problem of the exorcism rite was the practice of speaking 'directly' to the Devil. Phrases such as 'I command thee...unclean spirit' caused the most damage during the ritual. It seemed to confirm to the 'patient' that he or she was possessed and the commission were keen not to be seen to be supporting the 'patient' in their 'delusion'. In 1984, with this in mind the commission petitioned Rome to review the exorcism rite and abolish the 'Rituale Romun'. After more then 10 years of editing the Pope approbated the new Exorcism Rite, more then 20 years after Anneliese Michel died. The new form of exorcism became available for worldwide use in 1999 but it did not include the changes the commission wanted.

Klemens Richter, professor for liturgical science in Munster, Germany said:

'We were astonished when Rome issued a changed exorcism formula in 1999 which left open the possibility of speaking to the Devil directly…but you can't know for certain that a patient is truly possessed by the Devil.'

Today, 30 years after Anneliese's death, with both exorcists and her father also dead, she is still revered by some Catholics who honour her as an unofficial saint. They believe she atoned for the sinful and wayward amongst their 'flock'.

'Buses, often from Holland, I think, still come to Anneliese's grave. The grave is a gathering point for religious outsiders. They write notes with requests and thanks for her help, and leave them on the grave. They pray, sing and travel on.'

Says Franz Barthel, the man who originally covered the story for the regional daily newspaper in Klingenberg.

So was Anneliese Michel, the real Emily Rose, the victim of demonic possession or the victim of neglect?

Norbert Baumert, chairman of the theological commission of the Catholic Charismatic Renewal in Germany and a Jesuit priest said of the findings of the trial:

'I personally believe that this case was handled in such a way as to play down the reality of the Devil.'

Whereas Franz Barthel, would seem to have another view on the case:

'The surprising thing was that the people connected to Michel were all completely convinced that she had really been possessed.'

It would seem that as ever there are always two sides to every story, the believers and the non-believers.

I think it only fitting that the last word be left for the man that brought Anneliese's story to the big screen and the attention of the world, Scott Derrickson, the director of *'The Exorcism Of Emily Rose'*:

'What made me want to make a film that was inspired by Anneliese Michel's story was the fact that no matter how you looked at her story it represented questions that were disturbing and somewhat unanswerable.'

What The Experts Say
Exorcism Of Emily Rose (2005)

John Zaffis – Paranormal Researcher, Investigator, Demonologist and Author of 'Shadows Of The Dark' (with Bryan McIntyre) (iUniverse.com Sept 2004).

John's research into the paranormal has taken him all over the United States, as well as Canada, England and Scotland. Television appearances include 'Unsolved Mysteries', 'Fox News Live' and the Discovery Channel documentaries 'Little Lost Souls' and 'A Haunting in Connecticut'. His radio work includes the 'Paranormal Nights Radio Show' with Brendan Keenan, appearances on 'Coast to Coast AM' and guest/co-host appearances on the 'Beyond Reality Radio' program hosted by The Atlantic Paranormal Society's Jason Hawes and Grant Wilson.

John also runs the 'Museum of the Paranormal' located in Stratford, Connecticut and regularly lectures at colleges, universities and libraries throughout the United States of America.

"The makers of *The Exorcism of Emily Rose* did their homework very well and conducted a tremendous amount of research into the case. I know a couple of people that were involved in the development of the movie. So having heard the actual audio tapes of the Annelise Michel case, from when she was going through the possession, and then comparing that to the scenes in the movie, the comparison is phenomenal. The portrayal of the clergy's involvement in the case was also very realistic and impressive to me. I was very intrigued with the movie and found it to be an excellent tool for people watching to use to comprehend some of the things that are involved when what I call a 'true possession' occurs.

Sometimes we don't know why a person ends up falling victim to a demonic possession but I believe that Annelise Michel was such a victim. Don't get me wrong, do I think there is a possibility that she may have had a mental illness, anorexia and other problems? Sure. In many cases these things go 'hand in hand' with possession.

When it comes to religion and the law there is a very big separation, even today. When you're trying to prove something on a paranormal level it is one of the most difficult things to do, especially in a court of law. Perhaps people are more open to understanding these things and realising what they are all about now more then they were at the time of the Annelise Michel case. I believe in keeping a very open mind when we are dealing with the paranormal. I mean, we are just scratching the surface of trying to understand the subject and delving into the many different perspectives of what it is all about. We know today that energy can manifest into different things but what I find intriguing is it has an intelligence to it. The energy seems to respond to certain things, it can cause things to happen. So I try and keep an open mind when it comes to dealing with anything when it comes to the subject of the paranormal, because you have to go 'outside your box' so to speak. You have to keep an open mind when studying this work and understand the different things that occur.

I'm a firm believer that people that are diagnosed with mental illness or similar problems, such as those that occurred in Annelise's case, can be helped by prayer. Does it cure their illnesses? No, I don't believe that, but I do believe that in my work I have seen the power of prayer help certain people in situations like Annelise Michel's where the same kind of thing was happening. There are people, who we call 'soul victims', that do fall victim to demonic possession and with the whole Annelise Michel case I feel that there is a strong possibility that she had fallen victim to something on a demonic level. I also think this was intertwined with what she was going through physically and mentally. This case was one of the most horrific things that Annelise Michel, her family and the clergy involved could have ever gone through. Thankfully these cases are a rarity."

An American Haunting (2006)

The Bell Witch Haunting

On May 5th 2006 a film about the Bell Witch legend was released in the cinemas. The movie, based on 'true events' is the most documented paranormal case in US history.

With more than 20 books written on the subject, many of the events surrounding the legend have been witnessed and documented by hundreds of people. It is also the only case in American history where an entity is believed to have caused the death of a man. That movie is *An American Haunting*.

The movie was filmed near the original location of the haunting the story is based on. Director Courtney Solomon claims to have encountered production difficulties, such as fires on the set, which were apparently unexplained.

The movie tells the story of the Bell family of Red River, Tennessee. Between 1818 and 1820 the Bells were haunted by an unknown presence that eventually led to the death of one of the family members. The haunting begins with a 'curse' put on the family by a local woman, as the result of a land dispute.

Starting with sounds around the farm and the sighting of a strange black wolf, the incidents soon escalate causing family members physical and psychological torment. None more so then Betsy Bell, the Bells' daughter, she is slapped, dragged and beaten by the entity. The Bells must search for a way to rid their home of the presence.

The spirit begins to communicate with them through sounds and eventually voices. It gives them no explanation for its actions, only the promise that one day it will kill one of the family.

In 1998 the manuscript of a local schoolteacher is found. The teacher lived on the property during the disturbances. John Bell had requested his assistance in investigating the haunting. It is only with the discovery of this manuscript that the shocking answer to what may have caused the haunting may finally be revealed.

The movie stars Donald Sutherland and Sissy Spacek, along with a brilliant performance from Rachel Hurd-Wood as Betsy, the Bells daughter and centre of the paranormal activity.

So what are the facts of the Bell Witch Haunting? What really happened?

John Bell and his family moved from North Carolina to Red River Tennessee in the early 19th Century. Bell bought some land and built a large log home for his family. Over the years the Bell family acquired more land and cleared fields in the area, gaining status and prominence in the community.

The nightmare began for the Bell family in 1817 with a seemingly innocuous event. John Bell was inspecting his cornfield when he saw an animal sitting in the corn. There have been various descriptions as to what the animal looked like. Amongst these are that the animal was a wolf, a black dog and even that the animal had the body of a dog and the head of a rabbit. Bell shot at the animal which became startled disappeared. He then returned home for dinner and thought nothing more of the incident.

That evening the Bells began hearing 'beating' sounds on the outside walls of their home Bell and his sons rushed outside to investigate only to realise the cause of the noises hap disappeared. The banging continued and became worse. The resulting investigations that followed continued to find no cause for the disturbances.

More was to follow; only now the phenomena had entered the Bell home. The children began waking in the night, complaining of noises at their bedposts, the bedcovers being pulled and their pillows being thrown to the floor. The noises continued but now there were whispering voices too. The voices were too weak to understand but sounded like an old woman crying or singing.

Betsy Bell, the youngest daughter of John Bell, became the focus of the entity. She began to be physically attacked by the invisible assailant. It pulled her hair, slapped her and would often leave visible marks on her face and body for days at a time.

After a year of disturbances John Bell became increasingly alarmed by the events. He confided in his closest friend and neighbour James Johnston. Johnston and his wife agreed to spend a night at the Bell house. It was a decision they would never forget. Upon retiring to bed they repeatedly had the bedclothes removed and were physically slapped. Having had enough of experiencing the activity first hand Johnston jumped out of bed and shouted:

'I ask you in the name of the Lord God, who are you and what do you want?'

There was no reply and the rest of his overnight stay was uneventful.

The Bell case was one of a few poltergeist cases where the entity could actually speak and over time the spirit's voice became stronger. It was able to quote scripture in the bible, sing hymns and carry intelligent conversation. Not all of the spirit's verbal communication was as seemingly innocent as these examples though. Guests at the Bell farm were often verbally attacked and had their secrets divulged to others who were present. The horrified guests would wonder how on earth the spirit could know such things about them. Another incredible example of the entity's ability is that it is that that it once quoted, word for word, two sermons that took place thirteen miles apart at the same time.

Word of the Bell disturbances spread and nobody knew who or what the spirit was or the reason for its torment of the family. The only thing that seemed certain was that the despite its little foray into the realms of upsetting guests of the Bell family, the spirit seemed intent on specifically terrorising the Bells themselves.

John Bell's sons John Jnr and Jesse had both fought under General Andrew Jackson at the Battle of New Orleans and in 1819 Jackson heard of the events at the Bell farm. Jackson decided to pay the Bells a visit, taking with him a large wagon and several men he travelled from Nashville to the Bell property.

As the wagon approached the house it suddenly stopped. Despite the horses trying to pull it, the wagon would not move. Jackson tried for several minutes to get the wagon to move but to no avail. Jackson said out loud that it must be the 'witch' preventing them from going any further, to which a female voice gave an unexpected reply. The voice said Jackson and his men may proceed and that 'she' would see them later. The party were then allowed to continue on to the house as the wagon once more moved on.

Inside Jackson and John Bell had a long talk and waited to see if the spirit would manifest itself. After several hours of waiting one of Jackson's men drew his pistol. He declared himself a 'witch hunter' and said he would kill the witch. The man then almost immediately screamed and began moving erratically around the room. He claimed he was being struck with pins and beaten and then ran out of the house.

The spirit announced there was another 'fraud' amongst Jackson's men and that 'she' would expose them the following night. Jackson's' men, who had fought in battles, were absolutely terrified. Despite them spending the night in tents in the field pleading with the General to leave, Jackson insisted on staying. He maintained he wanted to know who the other 'fraud' was. However, by midday the following day he and his men left, never knowing the answer.

Andrew Jackson later became the *President of The United States Of America.*

He is quoted as saying:

'I'd rather fight the entire British Army than deal with the Bell Witch.'

Meanwhile, Betsy Bell had become romantically interested in a young man named Joshua Gardner. The couple agreed to get engaged; despite this the spirit told Betsy Bell not to marry him. Wherever the two went the spirit taunted them. Whether it was the river, the cave or the field, the spirit persisted on tormenting the couple.

Eventually it became too much for them and on Easter Monday 1821, Betsy met Joshua by the river and broke off the engagement. Betsy and Joshua's schoolteacher, Richard Powell had showed an interest in Betsy. He wanted to marry her when she was older, although he had been secretly married to a woman in nearby Nashville. Powell was believed to have studied the occult. More significantly, the attacks on Betsy decreased after her engagement to Joshua was ended.

The spirit continued to show a dislike for John Bell. As his health deteriorated due to the stress of his ordeal the spirit would torture him even more. The spirit would show no mercy where John was involved, going as far as to slap his face while he was having seizures. It seemed the spirit was determined to see it's vow through to kill John Bell. Although it took great pleasure in tormenting John and Betsy Bell, the spirit seemed to be indifferent to other family members. It even appeared to have been fond of Mrs Bell, whom the spirit referred to as 'Luce'.

During the haunting Mrs Bell became very ill with pleurisy, the spirit decreased activity to allow Mrs Bell to rest more. It would offer to sing a song or a hymn for her in the hope of aiding her recovery.

The spirit often said to others that:

'Luce is a good woman.'

During her illness Mrs Bell stopped eating completely. The spirit pleaded for her to eat something fearing for her life. When Mrs Bell still would not eat the spirit offered to go and get her some walnuts from the forest. Minutes later the spirit asked Mrs Bell to hold out her hands.

When she did a shower of walnuts is reported to have fallen into her palms. The spirit asked Mrs Bell:

'Say Luce...why don't you eat the nuts?'

Mrs Bell answered she had no way of opening them. Seconds later witnesses reported hearing cracking sounds and seeing the shells crumbling. An unseen force was opening them. Although the spirit had relented in its activity somewhat during this period, even to the extent of appearing to show kindness, when

Mrs Bell recovered from her illness the phenomena increased again.

On the morning of December 20th 1820 John Bell died from a nervous system disorder. The family found a small vial of liquid John Bell had taken the night before. John Bell Jnr gave some of the contents to the family cat and the cat died almost instantly. This was followed by the spirit Remarking:

> 'I gave Ol Jack a big dose of that last night and that fixed him.'

John Jnr threw the vial into the fireplace and a bright blue flame shot up the chimney.

At John Bell's funeral the spirit was heard to laugh loudly. Mourners leaving the burial site reported hearing the spirit sing a song about a bottle of brandy. Following the death and burial of John Bell the spirit activity itself died down.

In April 1821 the spirit told Lucy Bell, the Bells other daughter that it would return in seven years time. In April 1828, seven years later, the spirit returned as promised. The visit involved the spirit discussing such profound topics as the origins of life and Christianity with John Bell Jnr. During the three week visit the spirit is said to have predicted the American Civil War, World War I, World War II and The Great Depression. Upon leaving the spirit again promised to return, this time in 107 years. The spirit said it would visit John Bell Jnr's closest descendent.

In 1935, 107 years later, John Bell Jnr's closest living descendent was Charles Bailey Bell. Charles was a doctor and lived in Nashville. He had written a book on the 'Bell Witch' that was published prior to 1935 and he died in 1945. Nothing was ever published as to whether he received the promised visit from the spirit.

The 'Bell Witch' is however believed to have returned in 1935 and taken up residence in Adams, Tennessee. This area was once a part of the Bell farm.

Today the cause of the Bell families haunting nearly 200 years ago is believed to be the source of many paranormal incidents in the area it made famous. On the land where the old Farm once stood is a cave, which has since become know as the Bell Witch Cave.

In the 1990's a picture was taken of a girl sat outside the cave entrance. When the photograph was developed, there appeared to be a man stood behind her. An expert analysis of the picture concluded this was not a double exposure. Faint sounds of people talking and children playing have been heard around the area. Unexplained lights have been witnessed too.

The cause of the Bell's torment and the ongoing activity witnessed regularly remains unexplained. Many theories for the haunting exist and vary from person to person. Some believe the spirit to be that of Kate Batts. Kate was an old neighbour of John Bell who believed he cheated her in a land purchase. Modern research has found that Mrs Batts actually outlived John Bell. It is recorded that the spirit once referred to itself as 'Kate Batts' Witch' however. With all of the witnesses and most of the evidence from the case no longer with us it would seem we will never get to the truth of what really happened to the Bell family.

One thing we can be sure of is regardless of the cause, something 'happened' on the Bell farm in the early 1800's and it is still reported to be 'happening' at the Old Bell farm nearly 200 years later.

What The Experts Say
An American Haunting (2006)

Phil Whyman – Paranormal Investigator, Researcher, Television and Author. Phil is best known for being the Parapsychologist/Co-Presenter for series two, three and four of the UK television show 'Most Haunted' (2003-2004). Phil was also a paranormal investigator on another UK television show, 'Scream Team' (2002), prior to his appearances on 'Most Haunted'. He is also the author of 'Dead Haunted' (New Holland Publishers Ltd 2007), a regular columnist for 'Chat It's Fate' magazine and has made numerous radio and television appearances. Phil has recently made a return to UK television screens and 'Most Haunted' for the Live episodes in 2009 and 2010.

"Almost everyone who has a sincere interest in the paranormal or ghost stories in general would have come across the classic story of the Bell Witch haunting, and I am no exception.

This story has fascinated me for many of my twenty years spent investigating the paranormal, and I was intrigued to hear that a new film – An American Haunting (2006) – was to be released, which was to be based on the 'true' events surrounding the incidents which occurred at the Bell Farm between 1818 and 1820 and that eventually led to John Bell's death.

Whenever I watch a film of this nature which is supposedly based on true accounts, I almost always come away from the viewing with a curiosity to find out more about the incidents that have just played out on the cinema screen – even more so if it is a subject that I am particularly interested in.

Whilst I did find the film entertaining with some very pleasing performances from the main protagonists, I was a little disappointed to see that it does seem to stray away from the original story of the Bell Witch and you feel that the ending is somewhat confusing.

At the beginning of An American Haunting we are led to believe that in 2006 documents written at the time of the incidents by eyewitness Richard Powell – later to become Betsy

Bell's husband – have recently been found in the attic of a house in Red River, Tennessee – the same place where the original story takes place. All very interesting, I am sure you will agree?

However, there have been no such documents ever found and it is believed that this was pure fiction on the part of another author, Brent Monahan, whose 1995 novel 'The Bell Witch: an American Haunting' is supposedly based around.
In the original accounts of the Bell Witch incidents, the Bell family are subjected to many traumatic experiences both mentally and physically, with a distinct divide as to which family members suffered mentally and which members suffered physical abuse at the hands of the entity. In the legend this entity was sometimes referred to as 'Kate', because at the time some people believed the incidents were the result of Kate Batts, who lived close by to the Bell family residence and who may or may not have taken a disliking to the family.

In the film the characters of Kate Batts and John Bell (played by Gaye Brown and Donald Sutherland respectively) have a fall out over land and she is seen to curse him and his daughter Betsy (Rachel Hurd-Wood) before leaving the hearing. This particular scene seems to form the basis of the entire film, in that it makes you think that Kate Batts has indeed cursed the Bell family and may be at the root of all their ghostly troubles.

However, this appears to be incorrect in that as far as information pertaining to events of the original Bell Witch haunting Kate Batts and John Bell never had a fall out over land or anything else for that matter, so this particular hearing never took place. Also worth noting is that to this day no documentation has been found which suggests that Kate Batts was involved in any of the supposed paranormal incidents which befell the Bell family.

In the original legend the entity 'Kate' takes a particular disliking to the head of the Bell family – John Bell – to the point of continual harassment both verbally and physically and may have even been held responsible for a mysterious condition that affected him. Betsy Bell was another of the household who suffered greatly at the hands of 'Kate' and she too was physically abused constantly. This aspect of the legend is maintained throughout the film and remains true to the original.

Things start to get a little confusing as the film enters its final quarter, and a rather strange twist develops that has no real grounding for ever having taken place. As the film progresses it becomes increasingly obvious that there is an underlying theme developing; a theme that tries to have the viewer believe that young Betsy Bell is the focus of abuse by her own father.

The film also seems to suggest – in the way that the ending is played out – that Betsy poisoned her father whilst her mother Lucy Bell (Sissy Spacek) watched on. While this may be an interesting theory it is also one which to date is unfounded, and again no documentation or reports exist to say that Betsy Bell was abused by anyone or that she in fact killed her own father by poisoning him; although this was his actual cause of death.

I can only assume that by including the possible abuse scenario the film's producers may be trying to give a reason for there being poltergeist activity at the Bell farm; in that somehow a physically and emotionally distressed Betsy Bell was herself responsible for manufacturing the goings-on via some form of psycho kinesis, similar to the main character in the horror film Carrie. Personally I think it is a shame that the film tries to impart the abuse theory on to those who watch it and I feel that this could possibly have been left out altogether.
Whether the incidents witnessed at the Bell farm was actually caused by paranormal means or not, there appears to have definitely been something going on during the years in question, and even to this day, in the vicinity of where the Bell farm once stood, there are incidents of strange phenomena still being reported.

If you are interested in the Bell Witch legend then by all means watch An American Haunting, but please do research the proper story afterwards – it's well worth the effort."

1408 (2007)

The Haunting Of The Hotel Del Coranado

Horror writer Stephen King is known worldwide for his fictional bestsellers such as *Carrie* and *The Shining*. These novels went on to become box office smashes on the big screen when they were adapted for cinema and turned King into a household name all around the globe. Over the years the books, and inevitable movies, have continued to flow from the pen of the 'master of horror'.

So it should have come as no surprise that in 2007 a movie based on the Stephen King short story *1408* was released by Dimension Studios. To many movie goers this was just another 'Stephen King' movie. The thing is…it wasn't. The *King* of horror fiction had in fact drawn the inspiration for this story from a very real source.

The movie *1408* tells the story of Mike Enslin, a sceptical paranormal investigator and author. Enslin has made his name evaluating paranormal phenomena in various locations alleged to be haunted and then debunking the claims in his books. Enslin receives an anonymous postcard of the Dolphin Hotel in New York that has the message *'Don't enter 1408'* written on it. Enslin finds out that the room is permanently unavailable to guests as more than fifty previous visitors to the hotel that had stayed in the room over the years, all met untimely deaths. After being informed that the Fair Housing Act requires hotels to rent unoccupied rooms the Dolphin reluctantly reserve room 1408 for him. Viewing an overnight stay at the hotel's most fabled room as a challenge and a chance to research some new material for his next book, Enslin travels from Los Angeles to New York.

Upon arrival Enslin is taken aside by the Dolphin's manager Gerald Olin. Olin offers Enslin an upgrade, an $800 bottle of cognac and access to documents regarding the deaths in room 1408 in a bid to deter Enslin from staying in the haunted room. Enslin accepts the cognac and the documents but insists on staying in the room. Olin warns him of the possible dangers to come, including the fact that nobody has ever lasted more than an hour in 1408, but Enslin is determined to spend the night in the room. Olin reluctantly agrees, giving Enslin the key and he finally checks into the room.

Once inside Enslin begins his investigation, commenting on the ordinariness of the room. As he dictates his lack of findings into his Dictaphone the clock radio in the room suddenly turns itself on. After turning it off and searching the room some more, the clock radio once again turns itself on, playing the same song. Enslin pulls the plug from the wall and the clock display flickers, changing from the time to '60:00'. The 60 minute countdown has begun. Will Enslin find out the secrets behind the haunting of room 1408? More importantly, will he survive to tell the tale?

It was a 'real life' Mike Enslin that inspired Stephen King to write the story 1408, although the story that went on to become the movie was almost never written at all. King originally created only a few pages of 1408 for his non-fiction book '*On Writing*'. These pages were to be used as an example of how to revise a first draft. He was so intrigued by the story that he ended up finishing a complete draft, adapted it for an audio book compilation of stories and it became a movie in 2007.

The real life story King was so inspired by was that of parapsychologist Christopher Chacon's investigation of a notoriously haunted room at the famous Hotel Del Coronado in California, USA. Chacon and his team's paranormal investigations were widely covered in the media and after coming across these reports, especially the Hotel Del Coronado investigation, King used this information as research and a background for 1408.

Christopher Chacon is a prominent figure in the paranormal community. He is an authority on paranormal phenomena, anomalies and the supernatural in general. Chacon began his career as a magician/illusionist before pursuing a career studying the unexplained.

In the early 1980's he joined up with Parapsychologist Lloyd Auerbach and formed a research team to investigate paranormal and psychic phenomena. Nine years later Chacon was recruited by The Office of Scientific Investigation and Research (O.S.I.R.), a scientific organization whose aim was to assess paranormal phenomena worldwide. It was with the O.S.I.R. that Chacon would develop the skills to explore the paranormal more thoroughly. Chacon has gone on to travel the world researching and investigating thousands of cases of alleged paranormal phenomena. These cases include alleged hauntings, poltergeist activity, UFO sightings, exorcisms, possessions and psychic phenomena. Chacon is also an author, writer, director and producer of television and film. His most notable creation being the award winning *PSI Factor: Chronicles Of The Paranormal* television show, which ran from 1996-2000 and starred Dan Aykroyd. Chacon continues to research and investigate the paranormal, and it was in this capacity that he caught the eye and imagination of Stephen King.

The Hotel Del Coronado in Coronado, San Diego, California, USA was built in 1888 and took only eleven months to construct. The Hotel is famous for many of its past guests; these include former American Presidents and movie stars. Yet the most famous previous guest of the Hotel did not attain her legendary status until after her death.

Kate Morgan's story is a tragic and mysterious one. Kate and her husband Thomas were con artists, she met him after being 'sold' to him as part of a poker bet that her father lost. Kate was a beautiful young woman and this attribute would play a key part in their unscrupulous activities. The couple's 'scam' would involve Kate and Thomas playing the parts of brother and sister. Kate would entice young men to court her and then inform them that they must seek the approval of her overprotective brother. She then told her 'would be suitor' that the best way to gain her brother's approval would be to play his favourite card game with him, which was poker. Once the trap was set Thomas would cheap the young man out of his money and then Kate would end the courtship. The couple would then make a hasty exit and move on to their next victim.

Kate and Thomas planned a stay at the Hotel Del Coronado for Thanksgiving 1892. They had booked reservations under the assumed names Lottie A. Bernard and DR. M.C. Anderson in order to hide their real identities and carry out their scam whilst at the hotel. The story goes that during the train journey to Coronado Kate told her husband that she was pregnant. Thomas went into a rage as this would surely put an end to their 'business' once his wife's condition became visually apparent. He was still furious as he left the train in Orange, California and Kate continued the journey to the Hotel Del Coronado alone.

So in November 1892 Kate Morgan checked into room 302 (which is now room 3312) and waited for Thomas to arrive. A few days later, and with no sign of her husband, Kate took the ferry to San Diego to check hotel registers to see if her husband had booked into any of them. Whilst in San Diego she is said to have purchased a .44 calibre gun and some bullets. Having found no sign of Thomas whilst in San Diego, Kate returned to the hotel.

The following morning, four days after arriving at the Hotel Del Coronado, Kate Morgan's body was found on the steps of the Veranda leading to the beach. The hotel reported the death and the coroner returned a verdict of suicide. Apparently a bottle of quinine was found in her room and she had all the symptoms of quinine poisoning. The suspicion was that Kate had tried to abort her pregnancy and it had gone terribly wrong. Some people suspected that Kate's death was not a suicide at all. It was alleged that forensic evidence had show that Kate had been shot in the right temple of her head. Further evidence showed no exit wound and no blood on the gun or Kate's hand. The gun was also found 'two steps above her head', all of which would point to the fact that she could not of shot herself if indeed there was a shooting. It is thought that the 'shooting' was covered up to protect the Hotel Del Coronado's good name.

A curious footnote to Kate Morgan's story is that the day after her funeral the maid who stayed in room 3502, and was said have become friends with Kate, disappeared. There was speculation that Thomas Morgan had killed the maid along with his wife. Another story is that the hotel staff found the maid's body then removed it, again in a bid to maintain the hotel's good name. Legend tells of room 3502 (the maid's old room) having had a 'murky' history of its own, a legend which echoes both Kate Morgan and the maid's stories. It is said that the mistress of Elisha Babcock (a previous owner of the hotel), like Kate Morgan, took her own life in the room shortly after finding out she was pregnant. It is said that, like the maid, her body just 'disappeared'. Perhaps again, as with Kate and the maid, it was a bid to maintain the hotel's reputation.

Whether it was poisoning or a shooting, suicide or murder, Kate Morgan's death and the disappearance of the maid still remain unsolved mysteries.

One thing became apparent shortly after the tragedies occurred, it would appear that both Kate Morgan and the maid were not quite ready to 'check out' of the Hotel Del Coronado just yet. Indeed it would seem that they were not the only two visitors from beyond the grave to check into the Hotel Del Coronado.

Staff and guests began reporting strange occurrences in the hotel. There were unexplained breezes and odd noises. There were also sightings of apparitions such as ghostly faces and the figure of a young woman in a black lace dress. Most of the reports of paranormal activity seemed to emanate from rooms 3502 and 3312.

Both rooms have reports of 'cold spots' and malfunctioning electrical appliances.

Electrician Alan May reported seeing a face on the television, which was turned off, whilst staying in one of the haunted rooms. The sighting is said to have been verified by one or two members of staff at the hotel. Hotel Del Coronado spokeswoman Lauren Ash Donohoe has stated that guests have reported the televisions turning themselves on and off and fans starting up on their own in both rooms although no electrical faults could be found.

The lights in room 3502 are reported to flicker and even turn on and off by themselves on occasion. There are also reports of objects moving around on their own in the room and cold breezes even though the windows are closed and there is nowhere for a draught to come from. Other phenomena guests staying in the room have encountered include an overwhelming feeling of oppression and sadness and hearing voices and murmuring even though there is nobody else in the room. Whilst investigating room 3502 Christopher Chacon used equipment to track fluctuations in the electro magnetic fields, humidity and temperature. Chacon recorded 37 abnormalities in one day and described the 'maid's room' as being a 'classic haunting'.

Similar paranormal phenomena were reported in room 3312 soon after Kate Morgan's death. Screens were reported to fall off the windows and the curtains would move despite the windows being closed. Witnesses have also reported seeing a strange glow coming from room 3312 despite there being nobody in the room at the time. Indeed Kate Morgan herself has been seen standing at the window in room 3312.

During the filming of the television show 'Dead Famous' in 2004 presenters Gail Porter and psychic Chris Fleming, along with guest Karin Lekas stayed in room 3312 at the Hotel Del Coronado in an attempt to contact the ghost of Kate Morgan. As the paranormal investigation began Chris almost immediately felt a presence behind him and chills on the back of his neck. Gail began to feel like something was 'very wrong'. Then the phone in the room rang. Gail picked up the receiver only to find that nobody was on the other end of the line. Gail then became overwhelmed with a feeling of sadness and her legs became heavy. She was inconsolable and visibly upset, crying uncontrollably. The television production crew became concerned about her well being. Chris believed the spirit of Kate Morgan was trying to channel herself through Gail and repeatedly asked the spirit to leave Gail and communicate through him. Eventually the experience was too overwhelming for Gail and she had to leave the room. Gail Said:

> "I felt dreadful, I felt absolutely dreadful…when I got up (from my seat) I felt my entire body was weak and I got pins and needles."

Gail, the shows confirmed sceptic, was asked by one of the production crew if she felt there was anything paranormal in room 3312 of the Hotel Del Coronado. Gail answered:

"Yes. For the first time in all of these shows we've done...I'm actually quite scared...Being the biggest sceptic around I can't explain why I felt like someone had broken my heart...I don't know what happened for however (many) minutes, I felt weird. For the first time I think I'm gonna have to say something paranormal happened in that room. Something very odd happened in that room."

Kate Morgan's ghost is not only restricted to haunting room 3312. According to various eyewitness accounts Kate has been seen walking down the Hotel's corridor too. Karin Lekas was a guest at the Hotel Del Coronado over 30 years ago where she claims to have witnessed a ghostly figure in the hallway. She believes her sighting was of Kate Morgan. Karin describes her encounter in her own words:

"We were walking back from dinner and as I approached the room, I was putting the key in the door, and I looked up over my right shoulder and I saw a beautiful woman putting a key in her door. As I'm turning the key she's looking at me and she's smiling, she's nodding and it's like we're saying goodnight to one another. So I open the door, go in and suddenly realise that I saw someone extraordinarily beautiful, transparent and in a Victorian gown. This was the 1970's; it wasn't the same kind of clothing we would wear in those days. So it occurred to me that this was a ghost. I jumped back out of the room as fast as I could to see if I could see her again, my husband was behind me but she had gone."

Shortly after the sighting Karin drew a picture of a woman in a Victorian gown, the woman she had seen and who she believes was the ghost of Kate Morgan.

Rooms 3312, 3502 and the hallway leading to them are not the only areas of the Hotel Del Coronado where paranormal activity has been reported. A woman in a Victorian dress has been seen gliding across the Hotel's dance floor and the ghosts of a little boy and a little girl have been seen and heard running down the corridors and playing on the stairs.

One of the most intriguing reports came from an electrician who worked at hotel. The electrician told Alan May, a former guest at the Hotel Del Coronado, that the light over the steps where Kate Morgan's body was found would not stay lit. The bulb in the light is constantly replaced, yet every time the new bulb is put in the light fuses out shortly afterwards. This is despite there being no sign of any electrical fault.

To try to combat the paranormal activity in rooms 3312 and 3502 the Hotel Del Coronado periodically change the room numbers to try and prevent some of the phenomena. Sceptics argue that some of the paranormal activity reported in the allegedly haunted rooms is not actually occurring in the correct rooms due to the number changes. An argument could be made to counter this of course. That being that as the hotel has such vast amounts of alleged paranormal activity reported throughout the building it may be that these rooms are paranormally active too.

Research has also revealed that room 3502, the 'maid's room', was at the time of her death occupied by a manservant. In fact some historians claim that in Victorian times the room would never have been assigned to a single woman. There was also no maid service on Kate Morgan's bill of $24, which some would say may question whether or not Kate knew the maid at all.

There are, it would seem, some inconsistencies in the story of Kate Morgan in both life and death. These inconsistencies may lead sceptics to call into question some of the evidence that supports the claims of a haunting at the Hotel Del Coronado. However, there are also an incredible amount of eyewitness reports and evidence to support the argument that the Hotel Del Coronado is very paranormally active.

Enough evidence to lead one of the paranormal's most renowned and respected investigators, Christopher Chacon, to investigate the hotel himself. The evidence was also convincing enough to catch the eye and mind of world famous author Stephen King and lead him to base his story *'1408'* on an actual paranormal investigation of the Hotel Del Coronado.

Has the legend of Kate Morgan and the Hotel Del Coronado become bigger than the reality of the story itself?

Do guests arrive at the 'haunted' hotel checking in their pre conceived expectations of seeing a ghost along with themselves?

Or do Kate Morgan and the other ghostly guests continue to reside at one of the most haunted hotels in America?

What The Experts Say
1408 (2007)

Mark Webb – Paranormal Investigator. Mark has been actively investigating the paranormal for the past 12 years and is best known for being the Paranormal Investigator/ Co-Presenter on various paranormal television shows in the UK. Mark has been the Paranormal Investigator on such TV shows as 'I'm Famous and Frightened' (2004), 'Haunted Homes' (2004-2006) and Living with the Dead (2007). Mark has also made numerous other appearances on radio and in the printed media.

"Stephen King would have to rank as one of my favourite writers. I also have to say that I have enjoyed the movie adaptations of his novels and 1408 is no exception. I have to admit that I was not aware that this novel was based on real events prior to being asked to complete my opinions on the movie.

The Hotel Del Coronado sounds like a truly fascinating location and one I would love to spend the night investigating. The fact this venue was investigated by Christopher Chacon and he found anomalies which led him to declare the hotel was a classic haunting just adds to its mystic. The stories associated with the hotel are authentic stories associated with reputedly haunted locations and you would have to say that these stories could be a reason for the occupants reporting paranormal activity.

In terms of the movie, it was a typical Hollywood adaptation of paranormal activity. The smallest of paranormal occurrences gets stretched into something a lot more theatrical. If you look beyond the explanation of the facts it was a very good movie and one I found most enjoyable."

History Or Legend?

Every culture has their myths and legends, stories of heroes and villains passed down from generation to generation.

There are also those historical figures and events that attain legendary status. There is no doubt, through documentation, that they existed, but their stories may have become embellished as they have been handed down through time. Over the years many of these people and historical events have had their stories transferred to the cinema screen. In some cases the stories have become even less factual, incorporating legend in place of reality to entertain the audiences.

To what extent have these movies replaced fact with fiction?

How do historical figures compare with on screen portrayals?

Is it possible to separate the myth and reality?

History or Legend?

Witchfinder General (1968)

Matthew Hopkins

In 1968 one of the silver screens most legendary actors, Vincent Price, portrayed one of English history's most infamous characters.

Witchfinder General tells the story of Matthew Hopkins a man who travels the country exploiting local superstitions and offering his services as a persecutor of witches. Whilst England is torn between the Royalists and Parliamentary Party battling for control. Hopkins gains power travelling from city to city extracting confessions from 'witches', lining his pockets with money and gaining sexual favours along the way. Hopkins persecutes a priest and incurs the fury of Richard Marshall, a soldier who is engaged to the priests' niece. Neglecting his military duties and risking treason, Marshall begins his relentless pursuit of the Witchfinder General seeking some justice of his own.

Claiming to be 'loosely based' on the 'true story' of Matthew Hopkins life, the movie left many a question unanswered about the life and crimes of the Witchfinder General. Research reveals there is indeed more to the life, death and even afterlife of one of history's most notorious men.

Matthew Hopkins was born in 1620 and was the youngest son of James Hopkins. James was a Puritan Minister and lived in Great Wenham in Suffolk, England. Little is known of Matthew Hopkins' childhood though it is thought that he would have been educated at a grammar school, and without a doubt he would have been instructed in the righteous preaching of the Puritan cause from his father. Matthew did not go onto University as his father and brothers had. The fact that his signature appears on a conveyance from 1641 suggests that he was an apprentice to, and himself became, a lawyer. By 1644 Hopkins had moved across the River Stour to Manningtree, Essex.

During this time England, and in particular Essex, was in the grip of 'witch fever'. Following the witchcraft laws of 1542, 1563 and 1604, the death penalty was liable for:

'Invoking evil spirits and using witchcraft, charms or sorcery whereby any person shall happen to be killed or destroyed.'

Hopkins began his career as the self-styled Witchfinder General in March 1645. He joined John Stearne, both having been authorised by the magistrates to investigate a suspected witch. The suspect, Elizabeth Clarke, was alleged to have brought about the cause of a convulsive illness and death of a local tailors' wife through witchcraft. Hopkins' primary tool in investigation was to use sleep deprivation. After three days and nights of this torture Elizabeth Clarke confessed. The one-legged widow admitted, in front of witnesses, to summoning beasts that were familiar spirits, which she used to harm others and that, the devil was their father. Elizabeth also divulged the names of other witches in Manningtree. Her confession led to the exposure of a coven that Hopkins claimed had sent a spirit to kill him. Hopkins and Stearne travelled the length and breadth of Essex in search of witches. They employed the help of Midwives and Witch Prickers in their efforts to gather evidence and persuade a jury. The Midwives, also known as search women, would identify the genital teats where imps were supposed to suckle on the alleged witch. Anne Leech, a widow from Mistley in Essex was examined by one of the search women. She admitted several offences after marks were found 'around the privie parts of her body'. 'Witch pricking' was the method of pricking a suspects 'witch mark' with a knife. If the witch mark did not bleed then this was said to prove the guilt of the accused.

In July 1645 twenty-nine women who had been held in a dungeon in Colchester, on suspicion of practicing witchcraft, were moved to Chelmsford to face trial. Hopkins had persuaded Rebecca Lawford, charged with causing a woman to miscarry, to turn crown evidence against several others to escape the noose. Hopkins and Stearne moved on to Suffolk to continue their witch finding crusade but returned to give evidence in the trials and were witnesses against many of the accused. The women were tried by the Earl of Warwick who was not a professional Judge but in fact a Puritan Soldier. At the end of the trials one woman was acquitted and another nine were reprieved due to insubstantial evidence. The nine women were remanded in gaol until their pardon applications were sent to parliament. At least one of them died waiting. The nineteen remaining women were to be hanged. English witches were not burned at the stake as they were in the continent. Death at the stake was reserved as punishment for traitors and heretics, under the Witchcraft Act of 1563, death by hanging was the sentence carried out on those found guilty of sorcery. Four of the women were hanged at Manningtree and the other fifteen were women met the same fate at Chelmsford. Margaret Moone collapsed and died on her way to the gallows. She had proclaimed on several occasions that the Devil often told her she would never be hanged. Elizabeth Clarke, the first woman accused of witchcraft by Matthew Hopkins, was helped to a height where the noose could be put around her neck (because of her disability) and then hanged.

Hopkins and Stearne went their separate ways once they had embarked on their 'cleansing' of Suffolk. Hopkins took the east side and Stearne took the west. By now Hopkins was enjoying the power and material trappings that went with being a Witchfinder. He employed two assistants, wore fashionable Puritan clothing and was earning fifteen to twenty three pounds per Town cleansed of witches. That being in a time when wages were as little as twelve and a half pence per week. Hopkins and Stearne had earlier faced a stand off with the townsfolk in Colchester during the witch trials in Essex, and now it would seem the people of Suffolk were growing concerned with both Hopkins' allegations and methods during his investigations in their County. Rumours were beginning to circulate that he was preying on confessions from elderly, defenceless women with pets. One example of this being:

'Faith Mills, of Fressingham, Suffolk, admitted that her three pet birds, Tom, Robert and John, were in reality familiars who had wrought havoc by magically making a cow jump over a sty and breaking a cart. She was hanged'.

Hopkins was also rumoured to be using a retractable blade during 'witch pricking'. That being the case, a guilty conclusion would be reached on the suspected witch every time during the test. Opposition to Hopkins' bloody persecutions had grown and the end was near for the Witchfinder General.

In 1646 a parishioner showed John Gaule, the Puritan Minister of Great Staughton, a letter written by Matthew Hopkins. The letter asked if he would be welcome in the parish. Gaule replied by preaching against Hopkins from the pulpit, and hinted that Hopkins himself was a witch. Gaule also published a book called 'Select Cases Of Conscience Touching Witches And Witchcraft', an expose of Hopkins' methods condemning him and Stearne. Gaule's preaching added to complaints already made against Hopkins and forced him to answer some awkward questions before Judges in Norwich. Hopkins protested he was the victim of rumours and conjecture. He was also by this time suffering from an illness, believed to be consumption.

Meanwhile, John Stearne had continued onto the Isle of Ely and Cambridgeshire but the damage was already done by John Gaule's campaign against the witchfinders. Public opinion was going against them and after the witch trials in Ely acquitted the accused witches, Stearne retired. He later wrote a memoir published in 1648 entitled ' A Conformation And Discovery Of Witchcraft' in which he exonerated both himself and Matthew Hopkins of any wrongdoing. By the end of the East-Anglian 'witch craze' as many as three hundred people are believed to have been accused and over one hundred were executed. In Suffolk alone Hopkins is believed to have had sixty-eight people executed.

So what became of the Witchfinder General?

There is a tradition that Hopkins was subjected to his own 'swimming' test: he floated and was therefore hanged for witchcraft himself by disgruntled villagers after returning from Suffolk to his home in Manningtree. Most historians believe that Matthew Hopkins died of tuberculosis in his bed shortly before the retirement of his partner John Stearne in the autumn of 1647. The parish records for Manningtree in Essex record Hopkins' burial in August 1647. He was buried at Mistley Heath, which is now an overgrown field. However, Mistley Heath does not seem to be the final resting place of Matthew Hopkins. For the reported sightings of his ghost in various locations in both Mistley and Mannningtree in Essex would suggest that Hopkins, and at least one of the women that he condemned to death, are not resting anywhere. Some of the Haunted locations associated with Matthew Hopkins are:

- Mistley Place, Mistley - A ghost reported to be the spirit of Matthew Hopkins has been seen around the 'Ducking Pond' by locals at what used to be Hopkins' headquarters.

- White Hart Inn, Manningtree - Matthew Hopkins is said to have frequented the establishment and it is reputed he can still be heard in the building to this day.

- 'Hopping Bridge', Mistley – A 'Phantom Jaywalker' seen wearing 17th century clothing is reported to be the ghost of Matthew Hopkins. He has been seen walking in the vicinity of the small hump-backed bridge known as 'Hopping Bridge'.

- Thorn Hotel, Mistley – The ghost of Matthew Hopkins has been reported here. A ghostly serving girl who used to work at the hotel is said to still walk along the corridors and a boy who was pushed under a cart and trampled to death during a fight is seen at the rear of the building.

- Red Lion, Manningtree – This public house is said to be haunted by a Victorian gentleman nicknamed George. Although many people claim the ghost is actually that of Matthew Hopkins.

- River Stour, Manningtree – The ghostly screams of a tormented witch being interrogated at the hands of Matthew Hopkins are said to be heard coming from the opposite shore.

- Seafield Bay, Manningtree – Elizabeth Clarke, executed on the orders of Matthew Hopkins is said to walk the shoreline of Seafield Bay. Sounds heard here on certain nights have been attributed to the screams of tortured witches and also the sound of Elizabeth Clarke's familiars looking for her.

The last English witch was executed in 1685, the last conviction for witchcraft occurred in 1712 and The Witchcraft Act itself was repealed in 1736.

Is the ghost of Matthew Hopkins still looking to rid the country of witches from beyond the grave? Unaware that times, and time itself has moved on? Or is the legacy of The Witchfinder General buried with him in a field in Mistley?

What The Experts Say
Witchfinder General (1968)

Dr Malcolm Gaskill, Reader in Early Modern History at the University of East Anglia, author of Crime and Mentalities in Early Modern England (Cambridge University Press, 2000) and Hellish Nell: Last of Britain's witches (4th Estate, 2001). His definitive study of the Witchfinder General story is Witchfinders: A 17th-century English tragedy (John Murray, 2005).

"There is much to be said in favour of Witchfinder General – but as a film, not as history. As ever with historical films, the problem lies in how far that emotional power derives from the premise that a true story is being told. The screenplay was based not on academic research, but on a novel by Ronald Bassett that self-consciously manipulated the known facts. The result: a travesty of historical truth.

The earliest scenes of the film attempt to establish its credentials as a reliable account. We open on an idyllic Suffolk hillside, the peace broken by the sound of a gallows being hammered together. Cut to a screaming woman being dragged through the streets by grim-faced peasants, led by a pious clergyman. As she is hanged, the camera pans away and refocuses on a mounted figure in the distance: Matthew Hopkins, Witchfinder General. During the Civil War, the administration of justice was disrupted, but it never collapsed, nor was Matthew Hopkins given an official mandate to hunt witches. Amid all its distortions and flights of fancy, one of the film's most striking errors is its total omission of court cases: witches are simply tortured, then hanged from the nearest tree.

What really happened in Suffolk was quite different. When news of gaols overflowing with witches reached London, a special legal commission was appointed, which then conducted a large number of trials at Bury St Edmunds. Hopkins himself never ordered anyone to be hanged, here or anywhere else. England was chaotic for a while in the 1640s, but never anarchic.

A quick word about John Stearne, Hopkins' associate in the witch-hunt. In the film, he is portrayed by Robert Russell as an ale-guzzling, wench-groping thug, in contrast to a more restrained, censorious and sanctimonious Hopkins. At one point, Stearne refers to Hopkins as 'a fancy boy', whatever that might imply. However, this is all made up and utterly unconvincing.

The film cannot be judged historically on its plot, which is almost wholly fictitious. Cornet Richard Marshall is in love with the ravishingly beautiful Sarah (Hilary Dwyer), niece of John Lowes (Rupert Davies), vicar of Brandeston. Marshall's quest for vengeance begins when Lowes is 'swum' as a witch (that is, put in water to sink or swim – if you did the latter, you were deemed a witch) and hanged, despite Sarah having slept with Hopkins to spare his life. It all adds interest and pace, and might be acceptable if it were seen as a fictional part of the story. But it isn't.

Nor is the film concerned with the complex and involving reasons why so many people believed that witches possessed the power to attack them through the use of diabolical magic.

Not unreasonably for a feature film, most screen time is a preparation for the climactic scene in the dungeon at Orford Castle. Hopkins and Stearne torture Richard and Sarah, then Richard breaks free and takes Hopkins to bits with a (very rubbery) axe. Bassett's novel stuck to the legend that Hopkins was hoist by his own petard – tried by the water ordeal, then hanged as a sorcerer. The reality was more bathetic: he withered away from consumption at his Essex home in 1647.

Unlike novelists and film-makers, historians observe the mundane as well as the sensational, and are obliged to let the facts get in the way of a good story. Chances are, however, that a different type of good story emerges when they do."

Countess Dracula (1970)

Elizabeth Bathory

In 1970 Hammer Film Studios, the legendary makers of Gothic horror, released *Countess Dracula*. Horror icon and 'Scream Queen' Ingrid Pitt played the embittered widow Countess Elizabeth Nadasy.

The ageing Countess inadvertently discovers that the application of blood to her skin can restore its youth and beauty. Enlisting the help of her devoted servant she kidnaps

and kills a maid, using the blood to make herself look 25 years younger. She embarks on a passionate romance with a young officer Imre Toth, whilst masquerading as her kidnapped daughter Ilona.

The Countess's happiness is short lived however as she discovers the restorative power of the blood is only temporary and must be the blood of a virgin. With the help of her servants she begins a campaign of horrific murders to keep her in a supply of blood and restore her beauty. Meanwhile, castle majordomo Captain Dobi, the Countess's former lover, schemes against both her and her new lover Toth. As the death toll rises the local people become more suspicious of activities behind the walls of the castle. Between the local's suspicions and Captain Dobi's scheme for revenge, will the murderous Countess be revealed?

So how does Hammer's version of history stand up to the documented life of the real 'Countess Dracula'?

Erzsebet Bathory, or as she is better known in the western world Elizabeth Bathory, was born in Hungary in 1560. The exact date is not known but it is commonly believed that she was born on 7th August. Elizabeth's parents, George and Anna Bathory belonged to one of the oldest and wealthiest families in Hungary. George and Anna were both Bathory's by birth; inbreeding amongst the aristocracy in the 16th century was not uncommon as the purity of the noble line was seen as the paramount objective. In 1546, fourteen years before Elizabeth was born, Prince Stephan Bathory was a commanding officer in the army who helped Vlad Dracula claim his throne back in Wallachia. Stephan, Elizabeth's uncle, later became the King of Poland. Her cousin was the Hungarian Prime Minister and another of her relatives was a Cardinal. Not all of Elizabeth's family were so prestigious though. Her brother Stephan was a noted lecher and drunkard and one of her uncles was a known devil worshipper. Other members of her family were mentally insane and perverted.

It is said that Elizabeth herself might have suffered from insanity from childhood. As a child she is believed to have had loss of control, fits of rage and seizures. These are believed to have been caused by epilepsy, possibly stemming from the inbreeding she was a product of.

In 1574, at the age of just fourteen, Elizabeth fell pregnant to a peasant lover. She was quietly hidden away until she gave birth. The child, a girl, was given to peasant foster parents to bring up.

A year later, in 1575, 15 year old Elizabeth Bathory married 25 year old Count Ferencz Nadasy. After the marriage the couple lived in Castle Sarvar, part of the Nadasy estate. It was within the castle walls that Elizabeth spent most of her married life, alone. Count Ferencz, later to become known as 'the Black Hero of Hungary', was often away fighting against the Turks. Whilst her brave and daring husband was pursuing his passion for battle, Elizabeth, described by her contemporaries as a beauty, became obsessed with preserving her youth. The exceedingly vain Countess spent many an hour admiring her own beauty in front of the mirror in Ferencz's absence. During this time she also took on young men as lovers, even going as far as to run away with one of them. The affair did not last long though and she soon returned home to the forgiving Count. Shortly after this incident Elizabeth began paying regular visits to her aunts' estate. Her aunt, Countess Klara Bathory, was an open bisexual and it is thought that her aunts' influence seems to have been a major factor in Elizabeth's sexual ambivalence and interest in the occult.

Ten years into her marriage Elizabeth bore Ferencz three daughters and a son. They were born in quick succession and Elizabeth was an excellent mother by all accounts.

With her husband still away for long periods of time Elizabeth became friendly with an old maid named Dorethea Szentes, who was known as Dorka. Dorka claimed to be a witch and besides practising witchcraft she also dabbled in black magic. Dorka became Elizabeth's helping hand and began instructing her in the ways of witchcraft and the black arts, whilst also encouraging her sadistic tendencies.

Dorka and Elizabeth began a reign of terror. They would find excuses to inflict punishment and torture upon the young servant girls in Elizabeth's service. They enlisted the help of Helena Jo, her children's wet-nurse and her man servant Johannes Ujvary. The four of them began disciplining female servants in an underground chamber in the castle.

Elizabeth would have a victim stripped naked and then whip the girl on the front of her nude body. She would do this as the damage incurred would be more severe to the front of the body rather then the back. Elizabeth also preferred to watch the victim's face contort as she metered out her punishment.

Another of Elizabeth's activities would be to have the girls dragged naked into the snow and doused with cold water where some of them even froze to death. Other servants suffered such punishments as beatings with a barbed lash or a heavy cudgel or even having pins stuck into sensitive parts of their bodies such as under the fingernails.

Elizabeth was now in her forties and, despite using cosmetics, could not cover the fact that she was losing her beauty. This fact was said to have bothered Elizabeth so much that she even developed an aversion to her beloved mirrors. Instead of spending her time in front of them, the pastime she had spent many an hour indulging in during her younger years, she now avoided them.

In 1604, Ferencz Nadasy, Elizabeth's husband, died of an infected wound. Elizabeth hurriedly sent her hated mother-in-law away and transferred herself to the royal court at Castle

Csejthe in Northwest Hungary. It is here that the horrific activities of Elizabeth and her trusted helpers increased, escalating from torture to murder. The group were now joined by Anna Darvula. Anna was alleged to be a witch, said to be Elizabeth's lover and also became the most active sadist of all the participants.

Elizabeth is said to have had stark naked girls laid on her bedroom floor that had been tortured so much, that you could scoop up blood by the bucketful. Servants were ordered to bring up cinders to cover the pools of blood. On one occasion Elizabeth was too sick to move from her bed so she had Dorka bring a girl up to her and hold her at her bedside. Elizabeth then opened her mouth and bit the girl on the cheek. She then ripped out a piece of the girl's shoulder before proceeding to bite the girl's breasts.

Although these instances are documented in testimony recorded at the trial of Elizabeth's accomplices, there is no supporting evidence of the most famous part of 'Countess Dracula's' legend. Around this time a young servant girl is said to have accidentally pulled Elizabeth's hair whilst combing it. The infuriated Elizabeth is said to have slapped the girl causing blood to spurt from her nose, splashing on Elizabeth's hand. Elizabeth is supposed to have thought the blood had reduced signs of aging on the skin where it had hit her hand. The popular version of this story, including the movie version, goes on to tell how Elizabeth bathed in the blood of virgins from here on to keep her skin youthful. There are various horrific eye-witness accounts of her crimes documented but none of them record this initial incident or any subsequent 'bloodbaths'.

Elizabeth's trusted helpers continued to provide her with girls, under the cover of hiring them as servants to the Countess, from neighbouring villages. In 1609 Anna Darvula died and Elizabeth took on a new accomplice/lover. Erszi Majorova was the widow of a tenant farmer and it was under her encouragement that Elizabeth turned her hand to the torture of girls from noble families. The carnage at Castle Csejthe continued, going on undetected. Although, in reality, Count Thurzo already probably had his suspicions about what was going on at the castle. Thurzo was Elizabeth's cousin, so in order to protect the family name he had chosen to turn a 'blind eye' to the disappearance of peasant girls. The murder of nobles however was much harder to ignore.

On 30th December 1610 Count Thurzo led soldiers in a night raid on Castle Csejthe. They found a dead girl in the hallway and many other victims dead, dying or awaiting torture in the cells in the dungeon. There were allegedly the bodies of 50 girls found within the castle's walls. Dorka, Helena and Johannes were arrested, as was Katrina Beneczky, the Countess's washerwoman. Erszi Majorova avoided capture during the raid but was arrested later. Elizabeth herself was held at the castle.

In January 1611 Elizabeth's associates were subjected to two 'show' trials, in which they gave evidence under torture or threat of torture. A servant of Countess Elizabeth Bathory gave evidence of the existence of a register in Elizabeth's own handwriting. The register apparently recorded over 650 victims names that had died at the hands of the Countess. The register was never actually produced though.

Helena Jo and Dorethea 'Dorka' Szentes were sentenced as witches. Their punishment was to have the fingers which had 'dipped in the blood of Christians' torn out with red hot pincers and then to be burned alive. Johannes Ujvary was decapitated and burned alongside Helena and Dorka. On 24th January 1611, Erszi Majorova was also sentenced and executed. Katrina Beneczky was exonerated by her fellow defendants and on the evidence of a servant was released without charge.

Countess Elizabeth Bathory appeared at neither of the trials and was never convicted of a single crime. Despite the King of Hungary demanding Elizabeth be tried her family refused. The King did have ulterior motives though. During his lifetime he had incurred a large debt against Elizabeth's husband. Her conviction would have meant the debt would have been written off and the King would have seized the Nadasy lands and all those of Elizabeth as a Bathory too. The Bathorys used all their influence to avoid any trial being brought against Elizabeth and instead declared her a menace to the family name. The family brought in stonemasons and the windows and door to Elizabeth's bedchamber in Castle Csejthe were walled up, with the Countess still inside. Only small slits for ventilation and the passing of food were left open.

After three years, on 21st August 1614, a guard looking through one of the slots saw 'The Blood Countess' lying face down on the floor of her bedchamber. She had died aged 54. Her estate was divided amongst her children and due to the local populace not wanting her buried at Csejthe; she was taken to her birthplace at Esced to be laid to rest, avoiding any desecration of her grave and further insult upon the Bathory name.

The real story of Countess Elizabeth Bathory may not match up to the legends of bloodbaths, vampirism and lycanthropy, but in many ways the 'true story' of the life and death of Elizabeth Bathory seems to have been far more of a horror story then any movie studio could ever have produced.

What The Experts Say
Countess Dracula (1970)

Lara Wells - Medium, Columnist and Speaker on the survival of the spirit after the physical death. Her many radio appearances include Kerrang radio where she was deemed to be the 'Real Deal' and CFM and West Sound radio stations for over 4 years where 'Live' meant 'Live'!

Lara was also the medium and criminal Face reader for Paranormal Magazine. She contributes to many weekly and monthly magazines and newspapers but still finds time to tour and see people on an individual basis. Lara has taken part in many TV programmes and will soon be appearing in a documentary about a spiritual family and their way of life with her Psychic children. Lara was voted Most Popular National Female Medium at the UK's Spiritual ConneXtions Awards 2008.

"Many of us are familiar with the legend of 'Dracula' and his exploits from horror to romance. Few of us are familiar with the female version of his namesake. It is written that 'Dracula' didn't exist as the blood-sucking vampire that he was. The story was in fact based on a female far more terrifying than the man himself- Countess Dracula or Elizabeth Bathory as she was formerly known.

It was alleged that Elizabeth discovered by chance that by applying blood to her skin, (then later by ingesting it) the ageing process was reversed and she could preserve her looks forever more. This led her to the years of ravaged killing of her servants who were especially sourced for her by her closest 'friends' who were later tried and deemed 'witches' which is a touch disrespectful of the witches in society today. The word witch means 'wise woman' and there is nothing wise about the bloodbath they embarked upon to please their royal friend.

Elizabeth's upbringing was less than conventional. Interbreeding was rife in the royal family in an attempt to keep the bloodline pure. However, faults in the bloodline gave rise to mental health issues and insecurities in Elizabeth and when she was forced to hand over her baby at the age of 15, these mental health issues became more prevalent and engulfed her very being. Her sanity was entirely compromised giving rise to the question of what would be the end result of one of histories most famous serial killers.

Transylvania embraces the legend of Dracula who 'feeds' the tourist industry. The very idea of blood giving life and youth to an individual when consumed, however could only be the idea of a woman, one who strived to remain youthful, couldn't it?"

The Curse Of King Tut's Tomb (2006)

King Tutankhamun

One of the most recognisable names in world history is that of Tutankhamun. Mystery surrounds his life, death and even the place where he was laid to rest. There have been many television and movie depictions of Tutankhamun, some of which focus on his life. More often than not though, these films concentrate on the discovery of his tomb and the mystery surrounding it. One of the most recent of these movies was the 2006 release *The Curse Of King Tut's Tomb*.

The film is set in 1922 in Cairo, Egypt and centres on the discovery of King Tut's tomb. Archaeologist Danny Freemont is searching for the tomb which is also said to contain the last of four pieces of an ancient emerald tablet. A tablet believed to possess great occult powers. Freemont is joined on his quest by Dr Azelia Barakat and eventually the two of them discover the legendary tomb. At the entrance to the tomb is an ancient rock of hieroglyphics which warn those who enter the tomb of Tutankamun will die. Freemont secures the entrance to the tomb and he and Dr Barakat return to camp. A spy learns of the tomb's discovery and alerts Morgan Sinclair. Sinclair is an academic rival of Freemont's and also the man who has in his possession the other three pieces of the ancient tablet. Sinclair had stolen the pieces on behalf of the Hellfire Council, a secret cabal of powerful men who plan to use the supernatural power of the tablet to maintain, and indeed extent, their domination of the world. Freemont and Dr Barakat return to the tomb not realizing they have been followed. What Freemont, Dr Barakat and Sinclair do not realise is that once all four pieces of the tablet will open the portal to Hell and unleash the demons of the underworld. As with most movie productions the real story is often a long way from the portrayal shown on the big screen. In some cases the thing a film and the real life character it involves have in common is a name. So who was the real Tutankhamun and what was the curse said to have come from his tomb?

Almost nothing was known of Tutankhamun prior to the finding of his tomb and even when the tomb was opened there was little in the way of any documentation found. Little is still known of his life but experts have managed to construct what they believe to be the facts as best they can from what is known about him.

His birth name was Tutankhaten meaning 'Living Image of the Aten'. He was crowned the 12th ruler of Egypt's 18th Dynasty in 1334BC in the old secular capital of Memphis upon the death of Akhenaten and Smenkhkare at the age of nine. His throne name was Neb-kheperu-re which means 'Lord of Manifestations is Re'. Also at the age of nine the new King was married to his half-sister. In the second year of his reign the King changed his name to Tutankhamun (Heqa-iunu-shema) which means 'Living Image of Amun, Ruler of Upper Egyptian Heliopolis). During his reign he is said to have married again to Ankhesenamun and believed to have had two daughters and no sons. He reinstalled the old religion of Amun and rebuilt and reopened the temples. This included extensive building work being carried out at the temples of Karnak and Luxor. Military campaigns are also believed to have occurred during Tutankhamun's reign. The campaign in Palestine/Syria is believed to have met with little success whilst the campaign in Nubia is thought to have faired much better. It is thought that Tutankhamun had little direct involvement in regard to them personally. His reign came to an end in 1325 BC as it is believed that he died no later than at the age of 18. This is by no means a certainty though as forensic analysis and clay seals dated with his death as being at the age of 17. The common belief is that Tutankhamun died as a result of an infection brought about by a broken leg. X-ray analysis of his remains later revealed a dense spot at the lower back of the skull. The x-rays, carried out by a group from the University of Liverpool in 1968, showed a subdural haematoma, which would have been caused by a blow. Such an injury could have been the result of an accident, but it may have been that the pharaoh was murdered. The theories began to surface that he may have been murdered by his immediate successor Ay, his wife or even his chariot driver. A group from the University of Michigan took further x-rays ten years later but it was a team of Egyptian scientists that caused a stir with their findings.

In 2005 the scientists, led by the Secretary General of the Egyptian Supreme Council of Antiquities, Dr Zahi Hawass, conducted a CT scan on Tutankhamun's mummy. The scan revealed a small sliver of bone within the upper cranial cavity, suggesting that his death was indeed the result of an injury. The interesting thing was though, that there seemed to be signs of calcification within the supposed injury, meaning Tutankhamun lived for an extensive period of time (estimated to be at least several months) after the injury occurred. This would appear to put paid to the murder theory. The same team also concluded that since Tutankhamun's brain had been removed post mortem during the mummification process and considerable quantities of resin had been introduced into the skull and hardened. They concluded from this that had the injury occurred whilst he was still alive the sliver almost certainly would not still be loose in the cranial cavity. Other scientists claim that the sliver of bone was loosened by embalmers during mummification but had been broken before then.

The cause of Tutankhamun's death is still the root of much speculation and still remains unknown. Had he been murdered? How old was he when he died? These questions remain unanswered, but there was even more mystery to come following the burial of the King, the discovery of his tomb and the curse surrounding it.

Lord Carnarvon was an amateur archaeologist who was introduced to Howard Carter in 1907. Carter had discovered the existence of a previously unknown King called Tutankhamun on some walls and, as he owned the rights to dig in the Valley of the King's on the West Bank in Cairo, he proceeded to try and locate the lost Pharaoh's tomb. By the Autumn of 1922 Carter had been searching for the tomb for 5 years. Carnarvon had been financing Carter's excavations for 15 years and was becoming disillusioned with the lack of return on his investment. Lord Carnarvon had spent the modern equivalent of half a million dollars backing Carter and was about to give up.

Carnarvon sought the advice of a psychic. The psychic told him to abandon the expedition as he saw danger ahead for him. With the excavation in jeopardy, Carter offered to finance the workforce. Carnarvon agreed and the dig continued.

On 4th November Carter discovered the steps leading to Tutankhamun's tomb. Carter sent an encoded telegram to Lord Carnarvon who was back in England at the time. The telegram read:

> 'At last we have made a wonderful discovery in the valley – a magnificent tomb with seals intact; recovered some for your arrival. Congratulations, Carter.'

Official records state that Howard Carter, Lord Carnarvon and Lady Evelyn Herbert (Carnarvon's daughter) saw the tomb at the moment of discovery. On 22nd November 1922 Carter made a tiny breach in the left-hand corner of the doorway and peered into the tomb using candlelight. Along with gold and ebony treasures Carter saw a promising sealed doorway between two statues. Carnarvon asked Carter if he saw anything and he replied:

> "Yes, wonderful things."

The tomb was said to have contained, amongst other things, 150 amulets. Carter's own papers suggest that he, Lord Carnarvon and Lady Herbert entered the tomb shortly after its discovery. Carter is believed to have said afterwards:

> "As my eyes grew accustomed to the light I was struck dumb with amusement."

Following the opening of the tomb, several weeks were spent cataloguing the contents of the ante-chamber. The first rumours of a curse surrounding the discovery of the tomb began in the days after the tomb was opened. A cobra attacked and killed Howard Carter's pet bird. As the cobra is the royal symbol of the Pharaohs the natives took this as a sign and proclaimed that before the winter was out somebody would die.

On 16th February 1923, Carter opened the sealed doorway that stood between the statues in the ante-chamber. He discovered that the doorway did indeed lead to a burial chamber. Carter had his first glimpse of the sarcophagus of Tutankhamun. When Carter and his team originally inspected Tutankhamun's mummy they were primarily interested in recovering jewellery and amulets from the body. Most of these objects were stuck to the mummified body by the embalming resins used during this process. As a means to remove the objects that were stuck fast Carter's team cut the mummy into various pieces; the head was removed, the torso was cut in half and the arms and legs were removed. The team also used hot knives to remove the golden mask from the head of the mummy which was also cemented by the resin.

The rumours of the curse appear to have erupted from a single incident on or around 6th march 1923. Lord Carnarvon was bitten by a mosquito on his left cheek and became ill. His condition worsened as the bite became infected and he developed a condition known as erysipelas. This resulted in septicaemia and pneumonia and on 5th April 1923 lord Carnarvon died in the Hotel Continental in Cairo.

Carnarvon's son reported that back on his estate in England his favourite dog howled and suddenly dropped dead. It was also claimed that all the lights in Cairo went out, plunging the City into darkness at the moment Carnarvon died.

During the time of Carnarvon's illness the press had fuelled the fire of the talk of a curse. Both London and New York newspapers published a letter written by novelist Marie Corelli which said:

'I cannot but think some risks are run by breaking into the last rest of a King in Egypt whose tomb is specially and solemnly guarded, and robbing him of his possessions. According to a rare book I posses...entitled' The Egyptian History of the Pyramids' (an ancient Arabic text), the most dire punishment follows any rash intruder into a sealed tomb. The book...names 'secret poisons enclosed in boxes in such wise that those who touch them shall not know how they come to suffer'. That is why I ask, was it a mosquito bite that has so seriously infected Lord Carnarvon".

According to Corelli the same Egyptian author also warned:

'Death comes on wings to he who enters the tomb of the Pharaoh.'

Variations of this warning began being reported in the press as actually being found on, around or within the tomb itself. A newspaper reported a story of a curse written in hieroglyphics in the tomb that read:

> 'They who enter this sacred tomb shall swiftly be visited by wings of death.'

Another rumour suggested that over the door to Tutankhamun's tomb was an inscription that read:

> 'Death shall come on swift wings to him that toucheth the tomb of the Pharaoh.'

Another variant of the warning was reported by John Vornholt who wrote:

> "In an outer chamber, they (Carter and Carnarvon) found a clay tablet that read: 'Death will slay with wings whoever disturbs the peace of the Pharaoh'."

None of these reported phrases actually appear amongst the hieroglyphics at the tomb, but the hysteria had already begun. Hundreds of tourists who had bought Egyptian antiques as souvenirs rushed to ship them back. This included, in one case, a mummy's severed arm. The United States Congress even debated passing a law banning Egyptian antiquities from American museums. To make matters worse, it would seem that Lord Carnarvon's death was just the beginning.

George Gould, a close friend of Lord Carnarvon, travelled to Egypt 'upon learning of his friend's demise'. During his trip to Cairo Gould visited Tutankhamun's tomb. Following his excursion he developed a high fever and collapsed whilst in the French Riviera. On 16th May 1923 George Gould died, less than a month after the tragic passing of Lord Carnarvon.

The next significant death said to be attributed to the curse did not occur until nearly five years later, but with it came a rapid succession of tragedies.

Arthur Mace, an archaeologist who had worked on the expedition, fell into a coma and died in April 1928. The team's radiologist, Archibald Reid, also died after returning to England.

Howard Carter's personal secretary, Richard Bethell and Bethell's father, Lord Westbury, were the next to come to an unfortunate end. Lord Westbury was killed when he fell from a window in his London flat on 21st February 1930. He left a note that read:

'I really cannot stand any more horrors and hardly see what good I am going to do here, so I am making my exit'.

His son, Richard Bethell, was found dead in his room nine months later in November 1930. He had died of heart failure. Advocates of the curse claimed Bethell's connection to the people involved with the discovery of Tutankhamun's tomb may have cost him and his father their lives.

In 1939 Howard Carter himself died. The man who brought King Tutankhamun to the world's attention finally succumbed to the cancer he had been suffering with. On 2nd March 1931, back in England, Carter died of Lymphoma. Sceptics would claim that, as unfortunate as Carter's death was, cancer is a common killer. Believers in the curse claim that the slow, agonising illness he suffered was an inevitable result of him entering the forbidden tomb seventeen years earlier. Over the two decades following the tomb's discovery over twenty deaths were attributed to the curse.

In 1966 the Egyptian authorities were planning to allow some of the tomb's relics to leave the country for an exhibition in Paris, France. Mohammed Ibrahim, Egypt's Director of Antiquities, vehemently objected to the relics leaving the country and argued against this happening with the authorities. In the same year Ibrahim was killed in a hit and run accident.

By 1969 Richard Adamson was the sole survivor of the original expedition team; he had been the security chief at the dig. Despite having had personal tragedies involving his family, such as the death of his wife and his son barely surviving an airplane crash, Adamson continually stated that any suggestion of a curse was superstitious nonsense. In 1969 Adamson appeared on British television once again restating his denial of any curse involving Tutankhamun's tomb. On his way home from the television studios he was involved in a car crash which was serious enough to leave him hospitalised. Following the accident Adamson is said to have proclaimed:

> *"Until now I refused to believe that my family's misfortunes had anything to do with the curse…but now I am not so sure."*

Three years later another chapter in the story of the curse was about to begin. Gamal Mehrez, Mohammed Ibrahim's successor as Egypt's Director of Antiquities, had always denied the existence of a curse. Since coming into the position he had publicly denounced the notion putting the deaths and misfortunes down to pure coincidence. In 1972 relics from the tomb in Cairo were loaded onto a Royal Air Force plane and flown to London, England for an exhibition. Mehrez, who was involved with the decision to allow the relics to travel to England, died before the aircraft took off.

Tragedy followed for members of the RAF flight crew too. Flight Lieutenant Rick Laurie suffered a heart-attack and died in 1976. Ken Parkinson, who was the flight engineer in 1972, suffered a series of heart-attacks until he had his final and fatal one in 1978. Other crew members admitted to having had partaken in a game of poker during the flight and to using the sarcophagus as a table. They believed this act of 'disrespect' may have contributed to the curse taking its toll on their colleagues including Lieutenant Jim Webb, who lost everything he owned in a house fire.

Tales of the curse continued to be reported, keeping the mystery alive long after the 'key players' themselves had died.

In 2005 the South African Independent online featured such a story. A South African woman owned an antique scabbard that she believed was stolen from the tomb of Tutankhamun. The scabbard was originally won at a gambling table by a South African sailor who was passing through Egypt. The sailor gave it to his daughter and shortly afterwards he was lost at sea. Days after his body was washed ashore his daughter died of leukaemia. The sailor's wife, believing it was the scabbard that had brought her family such bad luck, gave it to the woman who now had it. The current owner lost her own daughter to leukaemia shortly after receiving the artifact. She heard about the curse of Tutankhamun's tomb and the tragedies surrounding the people involved so she decided to get rid of the scabbard. The woman found a buyer for the artifact but the day before the transaction her husband suddenly died. The woman was now totally convinced that the scabbard carried the curse of Tutankhamun's tomb and as a result she contacted the ministry of culture in Egypt, offering them the artifact as a way of breaking the alleged curse she was now a victim of.

The following year Jim Ritter, the science reporter for the Chicago Sun-Times, wrote a story titled '*The Pharaoh's curse or coincidence*'. In the piece Ritter referred to some strange occurrences involving the scientists who x-rayed Tutankhamun's mummy.

On the journey to the site in Egypt the team encountered a very bad storm and one of their vehicles nearly hit a child en route. Once the team arrived and set up their equipment a usually reliable CT scanning machine wouldn't work. After eventually getting the equipment going they began the CT scan, immediately one of the scientists began coughing. The coughing attack was so violent that he had to leave the area. Cairo University radiologist Dr Ashraf Selim said:

"*It was a very interesting moment, and a very scary moment at the same time...I don't believe in the curse. I'm a scientific man.*"

There are many more cases of accidents, tragedy and death that have been attributed to the curse of King Tutankhamun's tomb. So many that you could write a book on them...and many people have.

The ideology behind the curse is based on the Arabs, who conquered Egypt in 641 AD and were the first people to express a fear of mummies. Arab writers warned people not to tamper with mummies or their tombs as they practised magic during funerals, not only that but paintings on the walls of the tombs seemed to suggest that mummies could return from the dead and seek revenge. With this ideology and an apparent abundance of evidence, in the form of reported 'victims', believers would say that the curse of Tutankhamun's tomb is a very disturbing reality.

Sceptics would present a very different case proving, in their opinion, that there is no such thing as a curse.

In 1986, Dr. Caroline Stenger-Phillip stated that as fruits and vegetables were found in the tomb, it was very likely that they grew mould. These would then form organic dust particles which may have allergic potency. There would be a possibility that archaeologists breathing these in could have an allergic reaction after breathing the particles in that could even lead to death. This may explain some of the deaths attributed to the curse.

A large amount of statistical research and analysis has been carried out over the years, much of which would also lend weight to the sceptical argument against the curse.

Egyptologist Herbert E. Winlock carried out one of the first of such studies just twelve years after the tomb was opened. He found that of the ten people who were present at the unwrapping of the mummy, none of them had died within the next ten years.

The organisation Great Pyramid of Giza Research published a slightly more detailed report that was even more revealing. They found that:

- 26 people were present at the opening of the tomb and only 6 died within 10 years.
- 22 people were present at the opening of the sarcophagus and only 2 died within 10 years.
- 10 people were present at the unwrapping of the mummy and none died within 10 years.

Another interesting report was made by CBC news on 31st December 2002. Mark Nelson from Monash University in Melbourne, Australia had conducted a study of Howard Carter's diaries. Monash discovered that 44 Westerners were in Egypt at the time of the discovery of the tomb and 25 of them were potentially exposed to the curse. The results of Monash's study indicated that the average life expectancy of those exposed to the curse was 70 years, compared to 75 years for those who were not exposed. He concluded, from an evidence basis, that the case for a curse was unsupported. Monash said:

> *"If you take into account the differences in age and in gender balance, then there was no statistical significant difference between the two groups."*

Another detailed study was carried out by world renowned researcher of claims of the paranormal and sceptic James Randi. In his book *Encyclopaedia of Claims, Frauds and Hoaxes of the Occult and Supernatural*, Randi lists the names of all the Europeans who were present when the tomb was opened and when they died. Randi enlisted the use of actuarial tables (which give your life expectancy based on where you live, how long your parents and grandparents lived, whether you drink or smoke etc.), to work out the life expectancy of all the people associated with Tutankhamun's tomb and who later died. Randi found that in reality those who were present at the opening of the tomb lived a year longer than they should have been expected to. Notable findings were that Howard Carter died at the reasonable age (for the times) of 66. Alfred Lucas, the chemist who analysed tissue from the mummy died at 79 and Dr. Douglas Derry, who actually dissected the mummy, died at 80 years of age.

In an article for the James Randi Educational Foundation in 2004, Randi also noted that Robert E. Fulton Junior, who was present at the tomb's opening in 1923 aged 14, died 81 years later at his home in New York, USA aged 95.

The main argument sceptics apply to their counter claims that there is no curse is that there is no scientific, mathematical or indeed logical evidence to support the claim. People were looking for answers that, at the time, science was not in a position to supply them with. Theorists were in their element and what they had published in the media was 'eaten up' by the public who believed it to be fact, thus 'fuelling the fire'.

Sir Henry Rider Haggard wrote at the time of Carnarvon's death that the curse was simply nonsense. He said the reporting of such a thing was:

> *'...dangerous because it goes to swell the rising tide of superstition which at present seems to be overflowing the world.'*

Speculation, rumour, superstition and coincidence, the sceptical view is that all of these things have made the curse of Tutankhamun's tomb the legend it has become. To those of a more 'spiritual' persuasion maybe, just maybe, the curse is a legendary reality that remains as much a mystery as the life of King Tutankhamun himself.

What The Experts Say
The Curse Of King Tut's Tomb (2006)

James Randi (stage name The Amazing Randi) - Investigator of Paranormal and Pseudoscientific claims, Magician, Escape Artist, Founder of the James Randi Educational Foundation and Author.

Today he is best known as the world's most tireless investigator of paranormal and pseudoscientific claims. He has received numerous awards and recognitions, including a Fellowship from the John D. and Catherine T. MacArthur Foundation in 1986.

Randi has made numerous television and radio appearances around the world. He is also the author of numerous books, including *'The Truth About Uri Geller'*, *'The Faith Healers'*, *'Flim-Flam!'*, and *'An Encyclopaedia of Claims, Frauds, and Hoaxes of the Occult and Supernatural'*.

In 1996 he founded the James Randi Educational Foundation (JREF). The JREF sponsors the famous million dollar challenge offering a prize of US $1,000,000 to anyone who can demonstrate evidence of any paranormal, supernatural or occult power or event, under test conditions agreed to by both parties. To date the prize remains unclaimed.

'It is very simple really, when somebody claims that there's some kind of mathematical effect, that people have died more because they were associated with a certain figure, or they had a certain letter in their name, or had some family background then there has to be some evidence of it. So what you do is you examine the mass of evidence that's presented and you find out whether or not it's true.

Now there is selective thinking going on here amongst people who believe in the curse because what they do is they look for causes of death that are unusual or unexpected but they don't look for perfectly ordinary causes of death. In other words if it can be shown that somebody who was intimately connected with the tomb had died at a very ripe old age, with no complications whatsoever and lived a rich full life, then that would be of no interest to the people who are trying to prove the curse. You cannot collect data in this way, only selecting what pleases you. You have to examine all the data. Data searching is not permitted in science, or indeed in life itself, if you are going to have a logical approach to life. Suppose if you had taken all the people who were in any way connected with Tutankhamun's tomb and died and you ran a computer program to find people, for example, a certain configuration or certain letter in their name. I'm sure you would find some that stood out statistically, but that doesn't mean that their death has anything to do with their involvement with Tutankhamun or the tomb. So what I did in my research on the curse is I took all the prominent characters who were known, of whom any records could be obtained, and I subjected them to a simple test using actuarial tables. Actuarial tables are used by insurance companies to set their rates and they need the correct data so they depend on them very heavily to work out permutations of the likelihood of various events such as premature death. They need to know what the likelihood is of these things happening by chance alone are so this is indeed a very good tool to use with claims such as the curse of Tutankhamun's tomb.

There were also other claims had to be researched in this case. Lord Carnarvon's dog was not barking at the time he died, this was an error that was made in the account of it. You will find that the dog was barking well before or well after he died if you check up on it. As for the lights going out in the city at the time of Carnarvon's death, remember most of Cairo was not served by electricity in those days. There were mostly private generators and people contracted out the use of electricity. There was no central municipal facility, so the power came from private suppliers and, hey, they run out of petrol every now and then. Power loss was common at the time.

With claims such as these, I think people are looking for some correlation so that they can get an article out of it or you've got nothing to write about. You cannot write an article saying there's nothing significant about the people who died who are connected with the King Tut's tomb, that's a very short article. Otherwise you could do a whole book on it, and books have been done on it, because people will find what they believe to be significant or they choose to consider being significant data and they'll write a book about it. Otherwise they haven't got a book. King Tutankhamun died a natural death or was assassinated is not an interesting book to a publisher. They will say take it someplace else.

People believe in curses as it is a very romantic notion and it gives people something to talk about. The curse is a very old idea that comes from before medieval times and I think we should move on from it. If there is evidence for it then I am all for it. I will support it and I will choose to believe it if there is evidence, but so far I don't see any evidence. That doesn't mean I won't see it tomorrow. I always say that I don't say there's no such thing as special powers or supernatural powers or qualities of this nature. I simply say that if you say there is such a thing, well then prove it and I will pay you the million dollar prize.'

Reality Or Myth?

Story tellers such as Hans Christian Anderson and the brothers Grimm knew all about using our worst nightmares and greatest dreams to incorporate terror or joy into their books, depending on which reaction they wanted to induce from their readers. This was a major reason why their work became a staple diet of bedtime stories. They knew the ability to dream can be both a blessing and a curse. We can dream about fairies and angels or have nightmares about goblins and monsters. The catch is we have no control over whether our dream will become a nightmare. Our imagination takes us wherever it likes once we doze off to sleep. So what happens when people start to see these 'fairytale' creatures while they are awake?

We have all heard stories we assume are urban legend or myths. He said, she said and 'a friend of a friend' told me. You know the kind of thing. They are the sort of stories that people dream up every day, except in modern times, long after the days of the storyteller, people are claiming to witness these mythical creatures for real.

Are there such things as fairies, goblins and monsters?

Do these creatures really exist, or are they just the figments of an overactive imagination?

What, if anything, do they want from us?

Are these stories just fairytales and urban legend?

Will we ever be able to separate the reality from the myth?

Fairy Tale: A True Story (1997)

The Cottingley Fairies

In 1997 Paramount Pictures released a movie that was based on an 80 year old mystery, and one of the most famous paranormal cases of all time.

Fairy Tale: A True Story tells the story of Elsie Wright and her cousin Frances Griffith. Whilst playing at a nearby Brook the girls capture two photographs of fairies and give them to Elsie's mother. Elsie's mother has the photographs analysed and they are pronounced to be genuine. The girls are suddenly thrust into the public eye and are visited by such famous celebrities as Sir Arthur Conan Doyle and even Harry Houdini. The girls capture more photos of the fairies in the Brook and Conan Doyle has them published in The Strand. The publicity causes such a stir that the village where the girls live is invaded by hundreds of people seeking a glimpse of the fairies for themselves. The fairies disappear, will they ever return?

So what is the real story behind this big screen fairy tale?

What did Elsie and Frances capture on camera at the bottom of their garden?

The real story behind the movie began in 1917, eighty years before the release of the film. In July 1917, 10 year old Frances Griffiths and her 16 year old cousin Elsie Wright had been playing at the Beck near the back of Frances' home in Cottingley, Bradford, England. When Frances came indoors she explained to her mother that she had slipped on some rocks whilst playing with fairies and gotten wet in the Beck. She was immediately sent to her room by her disbelieving mother. Elsie later persuaded Frances to ask her father if they could borrow his camera. That way they could take photographs of the fairies and convince the adults that they were telling the truth. Arthur, Frances' father, agreed to lend the girls his camera and they returned to the Beck to capture the evidence of the fairies existence.

The girls returned a couple of hours later and gave Frances' father his camera back. Arthur took the plate from the camera to his darkroom to develop it. Upon doing so he found the image contained some strange outlines around Frances which she maintained were the fairies they had been playing with. The story was 'forgotten' until the girls produced a second photograph a month later. This time the image showed Elsie playing with a solitary fairy. Arthur Wright once again quizzed the girls and they once again maintained the fairies were real. Frustrated that he could not prove the girls were playing a prank, despite extensive search for evidence, Arthur banned the girls from using the camera. The subject as far as Arthur was concerned was a closed matter.

It was around this time that both of the girl's mothers had been attending Theosophy meetings (theosophy being a type of Spiritualism). They were attending one such meeting in Bradford, discussing 'fairy life', when Polly Wright mentioned the photographs the girls had taken. The lecturer asked to see them and so at a later meeting they took the photos along. The lecturer was astonished and when the photographs were shown at the Theosophical Society in Harrogate the audience were convinced that they were seeing physical evidence that fairies existed.

Word spread of the pictures and soon Arthur Conan Doyle, himself a famous Theosophist, heard about the photos. Conan Doyle had been studying the existence of fairies and wanted to further examine them. In May 1920 he sent a letter, enclosing prints of the images to his friend Edward Gardener who in turn requested the original plates. Upon receipt of the plates Gardener forwarded them onto photographic expert Harold Snelling. Snelling was a specialist in fake photography and Gardner hoped he would be able to shed some light on the pictures after examining them. Snelling produced two new negatives from the original plates, but used higher quality stock, thus making the images sharper and clearer. He deduced from these pictures that they were a single exposure, the fairies were not made of fabric or paper and that they were not painted onto a photographed background. He also ascertained that the images had moved during exposure. Once these results were gathered an appointment was made with the manager of Kodak to examine the photos, to give a second opinion. Three photographic experts were given the task of studying the pictures and after doing so refused to issue a certificate of authenticity. They agreed with Snelling that the negatives were single exposure and that the pictures showed no sign of being faked. However, they said that these facts could not be taken as conclusive proof of their authenticity. The experts at Kodak went on to say that the photographs might have been made by using the Beck and the girl as a background, enlarging the pictures and painting in the fairies before taking images on half and quarter-plate photographs of those images. Though the experts agreed this would have been time consuming and have taken great skill to achieve, photography lent itself to a multitude of processes and the girls might have made these pictures artificial. One telling statement overheard from one of the experts may explain their real attitude toward the photographs. The expert was heard to say:

'...after all, as fairies couldn't be true, the photographs must have been faked somehow'

Undeterred by this and still fascinated by the photographs Conan Doyle wrote a letter to Elsie Wright. He explained that he had seen the photographs and he would like to talk to her and Frances before he left on a trip to Australia. Conan Doyle also wrote to Elsie's father regarding the photographs. He explained he was writing an article for *The Strand Magazine* and would like to use the pictures in the piece. He also asked if he could come and have a 'half hour chat' with the girls. Wright replied to Conan Doyle, explaining that Edward Gardner had already written to him regarding the matter and arranged to visit them in July. Gardner arrived at Cottingley as arranged and after talking to the girls, believed them to be honest and genuine. He certainly thought they were telling the truth. Gardner met up with Conan Doyle following his return to London and both men agreed they must try and get more proof from the girls. Gardner once again ventured up to Cottingley, this time he took with him a tripod, two cameras and twenty four stock plates. Each of the plates had been secretly marked to avoid them being tampered with. He asked Elsie and Frances to take more photos of the fairies and returned to London to await the results. Following two weeks of bad weather in Cottingley Gardner received a letter from Polly Wright. She explained that following a dull morning the girls had managed to get two more pictures of fairies. Polly had discovered this when she returned from having tea with her sister. Arthur Wright then sent the plates to Gardner in London. Gardner sent an urgent telegram to Conan Doyle, who was by now touring in Australia. Conan Doyle was overjoyed at the news that the girls had managed to capture further evidence of the fairies existence. Upon his return Conan Doyle discovered that Elsie and Frances had in fact taken three further photographs (not two as Polly Wright had said) bringing the total to five. Conan Doyle decided that this was sufficient evidence to release what he believed to be authentic proof of the existence of fairies to the public.

In November 1920, *The Strand Magazine* published the first two pictures the girls had captured along with an article describing how and where they were taken written by Conan Doyle. He also wrote about the general subject of fairies in the article. Within days the magazine was sold out and the controversy began. Opinion was split between believers and sceptics. Conan Doyle was berated by the sceptics who could not believe that the creator of *Sherlock Holmes* had been taken in by such a blatant forgery. Conan Doyle retaliated with a follow up article in the next issue of *The Strand Magazine* in which he published the following three fairy photographs. He accompanied these with an article reiterating his belief in the authenticity of all the pictures and the existence of fairies themselves.

The debate raged on, staying in the news and the public eye. As 1921 came around Edward Gardner sent Geoffrey Hodson to Cottingley. Hodson was an associate of Gardener's and also a psychic. Gardner sent him to Cottingley to further investigate the phenomena. Hodson remained there for some time investigating the case with cameras and his 'psychic tools'. Following his time there he claimed to have seen many fairies and spirits but failed to capture any photographic evidence as proof of his claims. Undeterred by this Conan Doyle published *'The Coming Of The Fairies'* in 1922. Many sceptics continued to openly scoff at his belief and mocked his credibility further. Conan Doyle died in 1930, still believing in Elsie and Frances and that fairies existed.

Fifteen years later Edward Gardner rekindled interest in the case with the release of his book about the events. In 1945 the book, entitled *'A Book of Real Fairies; The Cottingley Photographs And Their Sequel'*, once again brought the case into the news and debate amongst the public. Interest eventually waned once more and it was not until twenty years later that the case would make the news again.

In 1965 the *Daily Express* newspaper interviewed Elsie Wright. They had tracked her down in a bid to get to the bottom of the story. In the interview she admitted she might have photographed:

'Fragments of my imagination'

Yet she refused to say whether she had somehow managed to photograph her beliefs or invented the whole thing. With the profile of the case raised again Edward Gardner released another book entitled *'Pictures Of Fairies: The Cottingley Fairies'* in 1966. The book was a success and debate raged again as to whether the pictures were real or not. Edward Gardner died in 1970 and the following year the sceptics decided to 'step up' the hunt for the truth regarding the Cottingley fairies.

In 1971 BBC Television's *'Nationwide'* team aired a televised study of the photographs using one of Kodak's laboratories. The reports from these tests proved the photographs to be faked but Elsie Wright remained evasive during the interview with her in the same program.

Five years later, in 1976, Yorkshire Television's *'Calendar'* program drew the same conclusion regarding the photographs authenticity. Once more Elsie and Frances refused to openly admit as to whether the images were fakes.

Two years later paranormal sceptic and 'debunker' James Randi became involved in the debate. After further analysing the photographs Randi claimed he could identify strings in the pictures clearly holding the fairies up. Randi then wrote to Elsie Wright asking her to admit that the photographs were faked. Elsie replied to Randi's allegations, asking him where she would have hung the strings from. Further annoyed at her refusal to admit he was right, Randi included a whole section in his 1982 book *'Flim Flam'* to the case, where he openly claimed the whole Cottingley Fairies episode was a hoax.

Later the same year what many expected was inevitable came to light. Toward the end of 1982 and in mid 1983 Elsie and Frances admitted that the Cottingley fairy photographs were indeed fakes. They explained that they had drawn the fairies themselves, tracing the pictures from a book and after mounting the pictures on cardboard they held them in place with hat pins. In one of the photos (showing a fairy leaping into the air next to Frances), sceptics had in the past claimed to have spotted what appeared to be a hat pin poking through the midriff of the fairy. It would seem they had been right. Elsie and Frances claimed that once the story had 'gotten so out of hand' they felt that they could not go back on their claims. After Conan Doyle got involved they dare not confess as he was so famous they did not want to make him look foolish. By the time Conan Doyle had died Frances had a daughter of her own who believed the story too. Frances and Elsie didn't want to shatter a little girl's beliefs in fairies so they continued their pretence.

Ironically, as if to add insult to injury, the drawings of the fairies in the photographs were traced from a book published in 1914 called *'Princess Mary's Gift'*. One of the short stories contained in the book was written by Arthur Conan Doyle himself.

So with the admissions in the 1980's it would appear that this true story is in fact not true at all. The admission of a hoax by those who perpetrated it makes *'cut and dry'*. Case closed, right? Well…maybe not.

Elsie Wright admitted that all five fairy photographs were faked but Frances maintained that the fifth image was genuine. The one thing that both Frances and Elsie upheld, even after their admission, was that they had both regularly seen fairies at

Cottingley Beck in fact it was the continual dismissal of their claims that they had seen fairies by adults that spurred them on to take the photographs. To show what they had seen. There was also another witness that claimed to have seen the fairies who came forward.

During the 1960's Ronnie Bennett had worked as a forester in Cottingley woods. Whilst working there he claimed to have seen three ten inch tall figures amongst the trees. Although he did not claim they were fairies, the 'gnome-like' description he gave of the figures did seem to resemble the creature in the second faked Cottingley fairy photograph.

There were also the claims, albeit unsubstantiated, by Geoffrey Hodson that he too had seen the fairies whilst undertaking his investigation in Cottingley for Edward Gardner.

So what conclusions, if any, can we draw from all of this?

Certainly at least four, if not all five, of the photographs were hoaxes. The verdict based solely on this evidence would suggest that the case of the Cottingley fairies was indeed a fairytale.

On the other hand Elsie Wright, Frances Griffith, Geoffrey Hodson and Ronnie Bennett all claimed to have seen fairies on Cottingley Beck on several different occasions. Indeed Frances maintained that the fifth Cottingley fairy photograph was indeed genuine. Proving, (if this is the truth) that the case of the Cottingley fairies is a tale of real fairies.

Whilst the Cottingley fairy photographs, Elsie Wright, Frances Griffith and indeed the whole incident itself have been investigated extensively, maybe there is cause for the Beck itself to be further investigated? Perhaps the location of the sightings may reveal some of its secrets to a modern day investigation. Who knows, a present day vigil by an investigator with enough belief in them may just give the fairies confidence enough to 'come out and play'. Maybe then we might just get the real photographic evidence Conan Doyle went to the grave believing we already had.

What The Experts Say
Fairy Tale: A True Story (1997)

James Randi (stage name The Amazing Randi) - Investigator of Paranormal and Pseudoscientific claims, Magician, Escape Artist, Founder of the James Randi Educational Foundation and Author.

Today he is best known as the world's most tireless investigator of paranormal and pseudoscientific claims. He has received numerous awards and recognitions, including a Fellowship from the John D. and Catherine T. MacArthur Foundation in 1986.

Randi has made numerous television and radio appearances around the world. He is also the author of numerous books, including *'The Truth About Uri Geller'*, *'The Faith Healers'*, *'Flim-Flam!'*, and *'An Encyclopaedia of Claims, Frauds, and Hoaxes of the Occult and Supernatural'*.

In 1996 he founded the James Randi Educational Foundation (JREF). The JREF sponsors the famous million dollar challenge offering a prize of US $1,000,000 to anyone who can demonstrate evidence of any paranormal, supernatural or occult power or event, under test conditions agreed to by both parties. To date the prize remains unclaimed.

"I got to know Elsie Wright very well. Elsie and I exchanged a lot of correspondence. Most of the correspondence I received from her was to the effect of *'you awful man you, you are trying to spoil everybody's fun'*. What she was saying was it was all a fake of course, but she wasn't too disturbed about saying that and she eventually did say it to the BBC. Elsie was never at loggerheads with me in any way, in fact we became quite friendly although I never met her in person unfortunately. When she corresponded with me she was always calling me a rascal and saying *'aren't you the cunning one Mr Randi'*. It was all said in a very, very light-hearted vein. She and I would have hugged right away had we met. As for Frances, I never contacted her as she didn't want anything to do with me, she wouldn't respond to any questions about the case.

Regarding the case, I have a full set of slides in my possession that were owned by Edward Gardner. Gardner toured all over the world with a set of slides talking to theosophical groups in every country you can imagine showing these slides. The slides I have are not the ones that have previously been published. The ones Gardner toured around with contained several slides that he simply disregarded or didn't even notice. Now Gardner was either very dense, not very observant or had poor eyesight because in some of the slides I have you can actually see the cut out fairy figures lying on their sides on the ground. Gardner didn't even notice this. The figures are rather obscured by plants and things but these are obviously cut outs that the girls disregarded.

Mr Wright, Elsie's father, made a handsome amount of money out of his participation in this whole thing. They paid him handsomely to be involved in the book and the Strand Magazine story. I have a lot of correspondence between Conan Doyle and Mr Wright in which he makes no bones about the fact that he wants to make some money out of this thing. He was getting paid £50 at a time, now in 1917 £50 was a lot of money. That's an interesting angle, he's in it for the money and he's making sure he gets paid. I'm sure Mr Wright knew that this was a hoax. I don't think Mrs Wright knew because she was a dedicated theosophist and she wanted to believe in fairies. Indeed she needed to believe in fairies, so I think she certainly did believe in them and the photographs.

To me the movie based on the case both pleased and annoyed me in parts. I have been to the home in Cottingley and the current owners at the time were kind enough to let me in and take photographs and have a look around. I was also at the Beck at the back which is immediately adjacent to the back of the house. It essentially looks just as it did way back in 1917, which is how the movie captured the location which I was very pleased with.

There are a couple of points in the movie that did not stay true to actual events. These are the things that annoyed me about the film. As they got toward the end of the film it looked to me as if they decided to romanticise it a little more. The part I'm referring to in particular is the scene where you see the fairies flipping around and the parents actually see them. Now the parents always said that they never actually saw the fairies in the real case. The father I'm sure was just trying to protect himself but the mother on the other hand was, in my opinion being scrupulously honest and never saw anything. Mrs Wright believed that the girls were pure of heart and that's why they could see the fairies and she couldn't. So the poor dear probably went to her grave believing that she probably would have seen them if she'd have been pure. So when they said they hadn't seen the fairies in real life, and the movie showed the fairies silently going by as if to say *'oh my god they're real'*, I think that may have been added to fluff up the end of the movie somewhat. They probably didn't think they had enough believers stuff in there to make it attractive. I think that's probably what they did, but that's only my opinion.

The other difference between the case and the movie is a big one and the most glaring discrepancy of all. If you remember this one thing about the movie and think it over you will see it's true. It's a thing I noticed straight away and thought it rather peculiar.

In the movie the girls are never together when they see the fairies. Elsie goes away and comes back rapidly to report to Frances that she has seen fairies. Frances then runs off and comes back breathlessly to tell Elsie that she saw the fairies too, but the two of them never saw the fairies at the same time in the movie. Now this is interesting because the photographs, if the photographs are of a real event, are of Elsie photographing Frances with fairies. It seems unusual to say the least that one of the main elements of the actual case should be portrayed so differently in the movie."

The Brotherhood Of The Wolf (2001)

The Beast Of Gevaudan

The year 2001 saw the release of a French movie titled *Le Pacte des loups* which literally translates into 'the pact of wolves'. Universal Pictures acquired the American rights to the film for a few hundred thousand dollars and, under it's English title *The Brotherhood Of The Wolf*, it became the highest grossing French movie ever. The film grossed $10.9 million in the USA (even with a limited theatrical release) and $70 million worldwide.

The film is set in the 1760's when a mysterious beast is terrorising the province of Gevaudan in France. Gregoire de Fronsac, the royal taxidermist, is sent by King Louis XV to capture the animal. Fronsac is assisted along the way in his quest and after studying the bite size of a victim, he deduces that the creature that carried out the attack must way in excess of 500 lbs. After finding a fang made of steel whilst examining another victim, Fronsac's initial scepticism of the beast's existence grows stronger. To add to the mystery, another witness tells him that the animal has a human master. As the investigation seems to be getting nowhere, the King sends his weapons master, Lord de Beauterne to put an end to the mystery. Beauterne kills an ordinary wolf and orders Fornsac to alter the body to resemble the eyewitnesses' accounts. Fronsac does as he is instructed to and the animal's body is sent to Paris.

The body of the 'fake' beast is put on display by the King for all to see that the creature has been slain. Whilst in Paris, Fronsac is shown a copy of a book entitled *L'Edifonte* (The Edifying) by one of the King's advisors. The book explains that the beast has come to punish the King for embracing science and theorists whilst abandoning religion. Fornsac quickly realises that the beast is an instrument of a secret society. *The Brotherhood Of The Wolf* is using the beast to undermine the King in the eyes of the public so that they can take over the country.

In order to keep him quiet, Fronsac is given an appointment in Senegal. He is also warned to 'keep his mouth shut' and go along with the 'official line' that the beast has been killed. Meanwhile the attacks continue in Gevaudan, proving that the real beast is very much alive. Fronsac decides to return to Gevaudan and ignore his orders, determined to put an end to the beast's mysterious reign.

The movie is based on the real life legend of the Beast of Gevaudan. The beast is a creature that is said to have been responsible for a series of unsolved attacks and murders in France in the 18th century.

Gevaudan is situated in the Margeride Mountains in the south of France. Today it is known as the Lozere department. The legend of the beast of Gevaudan began in 1764, when the first reported sighting to give a description of the creature occurred. On the 1st June 1764 a woman from Langogne saw a large wolf-like creature in the trees around the farm where she was working at the time. As she attested, the creature charged directly toward her but was driven away by the bulls on the farm.

Thirty days later the first official victim of the beast was reported not far from Langogne, near the village of Les Hubacs. The unfortunate woman to be attributed as the first person to be killed by the beast was Jean Boulet on the 1st July 1764. The sightings and attacks continued throughout 1764 and a more thorough description of the beast began to unfold.

The creature was described as being wolf-like in appearance yet much larger; in fact witnesses reported the beast to be more like the size of a cow then a wolf. The creature had a 'greyhound-like' head and large fangs protruding from its jaw. It had a wide chest and was covered in red fur, except for a distinctive black stripe that ran down the length of its back. Witnesses also described the beast as having a long sinuous tail that had a 'lion-like' tuft of fur on the end of it.

In January of the following year an incident occurred that brought the attention of the beast to the King of France himself. On the 12th January 1765, a group of men were attacked by the creature. Jacques Portefaix and six of his friends managed to fend off an attack by the beast by grouping together. King Louis XV heard of their fight for survival and awarded the brave boys 300 Livres.

With his personal interest in the case stirred, the King enlisted the services of two professional wolf hunters. Jean-Charles-Marc-Antoine Vaumesle d'Enneval and his son Jean Francois were sent to find and slay the beast. The men arrived in Clermont-Ferrand on the 17th February 1765 and began their search. They spent several months hunting wolves, along with eight bloodhounds they had taken with them which had been trained with the specific task at hand in mind. Unfortunately Jean-Charles-Marc-Antoine and Jean Francois were unsuccessful in their quest and the King relieved them of their duties.

In June 1765 the men were replaced by Francois Antoine who arrived in le Malzieu on the 22nd June 1765. Francois Antoine (wrongly referred to as Antoine de Beauterne by some sources) was the King's harquebus bearer and Lieutenant of the Hunt. Three months later Antoine appeared to have put paid to the Beast of Gevaudan's murderous spree. On the 20th September 1765, he killed a large grey wolf that measured 80 centimetres in height, was 1.7 meters long and weighed 60 kilograms. He named the beast Le Loup de Chazes, after the nearby Abbaye des Chezes where the creature was killed. Antoine said:

"We declare by the present report signed from our hand, we never saw a big wolf that could be compared to this one. Which is why we estimate this could be the fearsome beast that has caused so much damage."

The local villagers agreed that this was probably the Beast of Gevaudan and it had been a wolf that had been responsible for the killings. The wolf was stuffed and sent to Versailles. Upon his return, Antoine received a hero's welcome and was rewarded with awards, titles and a large sum of money. However, the relief and jubilation of the people of Gevaudan was short lived.

On the 2nd December 1765 the beast struck again. Two children were severely injured in la Besseyre saint Mary by a creature fitting the creature's description. The attacks and reports continued to come in, some of which claimed that the beast was accompanied by another such animal or even with young. It was not until eighteen months later that the attacks would cease. The killing of what was believed to be the Beast of Gevaudan is surrounded by as much controversy as the legend of the beast itself.

The slaying of the creature is said to have happened on 19th June 1767. Jean Chastel claimed to have killed the animal at the Sogne d'Auvers but his account of events is looked upon with some scepticism. Chastel was part of a large hunting party that was in Sogne d'Auvers on 19th June 1767. The local farmer and inn keeper said that during the hunt he took a moment to sit down and read from the bible and pray. Whilst he was praying the beast is said to have come into view and stared at him. Chastel claimed he finished his prayer and then shot the beast twice with silver bullets. Afterwards he is said to have made the comment:

"Beast thy shall kill no more."

The fact that this event is mentioned in several novels about the case and that the sightings and attacks by the creature ceased after Chastel claimed to have slain the Beast of Gevaudan, seem to be the only evidence that lend weight to this version of the creature's demise.

It is extremely difficult to establish the exact number of victims the Beast of Gevaudan claimed during its reign of terror. Given the basis of many different sources and reports the figures come in at over 306 attacks, which include 51 wounded and 123 killed. A more accurate estimate can be based on official documents which put the figures at 198 attacks and 88 killed. The generally accepted figure is that the beast killed between 60 and 100 people.

So what was the creature that terrorised the province of Gevaudan between 1764 and 1767?

Reports stated that the creature's method of killing was somewhat unusual for a predator to say the least. The creature targeted victim's heads, often crushing or removing them. This is unusual for a predator as they more often than not target the legs and the throat. Another strange trait of the creature was that it seemed to target people over cattle. A normal predator would rather attack livestock then a man. The Beast of Gevaudan reportedly would even attack people whilst cattle were in the same field and leave the cattle unharmed. It was also reported that the creature was able to leap up to thirty feet into the air, but this most probably results from an error in the measuring of its tracks. The beast also attacked more women and children than men, as if it was targeting them specifically. This fact would seem to have a normal explanation rather than a paranormal one. In the 1700's women working on countryside farms tended to work alone or in pairs, making themselves an easy target. Men, on the other hand, often worked in large groups and tended to use implements that could also have been used to defend themselves against an attack, such as sickles and scythes. Another trait of the beast's method of attack was that it would usually attack on sight. This would suggest the story of Jean Chastel's killing of the beast may have been embellished at best. The fact that Chastel claimed to have finished his prayer while the beast looked on does not coincide with the creatures' normal *'modus operandi'*. The story of the prayer was most likely added for religious or dramatic purposes.

With all the data collated from witnesses and research into the attacks theories were made as to what the Beast of Gevaudan actually was. One of the more incredible explanations offered for the beast's identity at the time was that he was a creature sent by God as some form of punishment for people's sins. Another theory was that it was an unholy creature summoned by a sorcerer who lived in the area. At the time of the attacks some of the people even believed the beast was a *loup-garou* or 'werewolf' as it is known in the English language.

Almost 250 years after the reign of the Beast of Gevaudan it is possible to make a much more 'educated guess' as to what was responsible for the attacks in the province between 1764 and 1767:

The Wolf Theory

Many of the witnesses believed the beast to be a large wolf. As was stated earlier, the beast is said to have attacked humans whilst ignoring livestock in the vicinity. This seems to be totally out of character with the animal. Wild wolves will usually avoid humans and attack cattle when their natural supply of prey is depleted.

However, some experts believe that the wolves of the 18th Century were a far different breed then the animals they have become today. The wild wolves in the Beast of Gevaudan's day were far more aggressive then the wolves of today. Experts believe that the more 'cautious' animal the wolf has become today is a result of natural selection, and are less prone to attacking humans who are far more capable of protecting themselves with weapons such as firearms. Even so there are still wolf attacks today, some of which are commonplace in areas of abject poverty where there is a lack of predator control and weaponry, lending further weight to the theory that wolves will attack humans when they 'think the odds are in their favour'. Perhaps the Beast of Gevaudan could have been a wolf.

The Wolf-dog Theory

The wolf-dog theory has many supporters, amongst those is naturalist Michel Louis. Louis is the author of the book *'La bete du Gevaudan: L'innocence des loups'* (The Beast of Gevaudan: The Innocence of Wolves). Michel believes that the creature was some form of wolf-dog 'hybrid'. The wolf-dog hybrid is noted as not sharing their wolf parent's fear of man, and also as being trainable like their dog parent. Another notable follower of the wolf-dog theory is the television show *'Animal X'*. This theory lends credence to a few eyewitness reports that claim the beast was accompanied by a human master. It also suggests that the creature could be trained and would have no fear of attacking humans as it would take the traits of both the wolf and the dog. Could the Beast of Gevaudan have been a wolf-dog? Even more interestingly, could the creature have been an animal that was trained by a man to kill?

The Hyena Theory

This theory suggests that the beast may have been a captured exotic animal that has escaped, more specifically a hyena. Both the African striped and African spotted species of hyena have been known to attack humans. Even more interesting is the fact that hyenas are known to primarily bite the facial areas when attacking humans. The same method used by the Beast of Gevaudan. Conversely, hyenas are not very good jumpers and do not have a smooth running gait, two traits that were attributed to the beast by eyewitness accounts. In Loren Coleman and Jerome Clark's 2001 publication *'Cryptozoology A-Z'* there may be even more evidence to suggest the beast was a hyena. In the book there are claims that Franz Jullien, a taxidermist at the National Museum of Natural History in Paris, France made an interesting discovery. Jullien found an animal, similar in the description to that of the beast, that had been stuffed and on display between in the museum between 1766 and 1819. The most astonishing discovery he made was that this creature had been listed as being shot by Jean Chastel. The animal had been identified as definitely being an African striped hyena.

Was this definite proof as to the identity of the Beast of Gevaudan?

The fact is that between 1764 and 1767 something or someone attacked between 60 and 100 people in the Gevaudan province in France. I think we can safely say that statement is beyond doubt. As to what the Beast of Gevaudan was, well that's not as easy to establish. As we have seen, the theories range from werewolves to hyenas, and even to God himself.

The real story of the beast is one that is still cause for debate amongst crytozoologists and conspiracy theorists today. It would appear the answer to finding out what the Beast of Gevaudan really was may have disappeared with the creature itself in 1767.

What The Experts Say
The Brotherhood Of The Wolf (2001)

Neil Arnold – Cryptozoologist, Paranormal Researcher and Author. Neil is the author of *Monster! The A-Z Of Zooform Phenomena* (CFZ Press 2007), the world's first ever reference guide to the monsters that cryptozoology fails to investigate, Mystery Animals of the British Isles: Kent (CFZ Press 2009) and has two more books due for release in 2010. Neil also runs Kent Big Cat Research in the UK. He contributes articles for Animals & Men magazine and has appeared in the press, on radio and television worldwide.

"The 'beast' of Gevaudan is a great monster story, it's up there with the other classic monsters such as the Abominable Snowman and the Loch Ness monster although it is a very much ignored, yet cult offering from the dark gods that had substance to its hideous existence, whether in the form of spectral predator or mere escaped exotic pet, but whatever it was, it had all the drippings of a chilling werewolf story, as well as being, especially now, a precursor to the modern big cat mystery or could have been something else entirely, but let's take a quick stroll into the abyss, the black lair of bones, blood and beating hearts. The movie 'Brotherhood Of The Wolf' was certainly a much needed commentary of this classic case, albeit one dramatised, but thankfully not bogged down by awful effects. In fact, 'Brotherhood' remains one of the finest crypto-related films ever released, even if its fiction clouds the facts of the original ghastly story.

Wolves caused much terror in France during the earlier centuries, but during the 1700's many believed that a creature roamed the wild mountain districts of Lozere that was more frightening than any wolf, more terrifying than any rabid wolf, and stronger than any wolf pack, so much so that those who inhabited the district of Gevaudan believed the creature to be of superpower, with a thirst for human blood that could never be quenched. Whilst some of the attacks attributed to the unknown beast may have been merely the work of wolves, what the locals were describing in the forests was not wolf-like at all, but a marauding mauler the size of a bull, reddish in colour and extremely powerful, able to carry off a child and vile enough to eat a flailing woman.

Was the so-called beast of Gevaudan a mere wolf on the rampage ? If so, then it must have been a rabid animal to act so furiously, however, many that described the animal believed it may have been some weird hybrid, or maybe not a wolf at all. Possibly an alien, out of place creature or something supernatural, but whatever the case, humans were the only food on the menu of this marauder, and with so many wolves living in the area, why were attacks not as frequent in the years before the mass human slaughter ? Did the killings really cease after the shooting of a strange looking creature that seemed to be more hyena-like than wolf-like ? Were the beast killings a mere sinister cover-up for even more bizarre crimes ? We will never really know and so we can confuse ourselves with constant theories and suggestions, in fact some have even concluded that the 'beast' was a large cat, possibly a puma, that may well have escaped from a collection, but if so, would it prey on humans all the time when there would have been so much other fodder in those dark forests ? Whilst leopards and the likes are perceived as man-eaters in their countries of origin, out of place exotic cats that roam the bush of Australia, or lesser dense areas of Britain, are not attacking humans. Even the cougars that inhabit America do not kill so frequently, and although they do apply a throat bite, have a long tail, and a fawn hue, why didn't anyone recognise the dead beast as a large cat ? It seems apparent that those who saw the beast thought it wolf-like but far too big to be a wolf, and yet the animal that was eventually killed by Jean Chastel weighed just over one-hundred pounds.

In 1960, reports written out by surgeons who examined the body from the 1700's, were studied, and experts revealed that the animal was most likely to have been a wolf. However, during the late 1990's, a French taxidermist, Franz Jullien, who worked at the National Museum of Natural History in Paris, determined that the creature that was shot was a hyena, and that its body had been kept in museum from 1766 until 1819.

According to cryptozoologists Loren Coleman and Jerome Clark in their 1999 book, Cryptozoology A – Z, "Novelist Henri Pourrat and Gerard Menatory had already proposed the hyena hypothesis, based on historical accounts, since Antoine Chastel (Jean's son) reportedly possessed such an animal in his menagerie, a hypothesis now supported by a zoologist's identification. While Jullien's rediscovery must be congratulated, questions remain about the role of the Chastels as creators of a false story involving an escaped hyena in order to cover the rumours of one of the Chastels being a serial killer."

Let us look at the hyena possibility, and the possibility of other similar creatures before we delve into the murky waters of the supernatural, a line which creatures such as the Chupacabras straddle.

Members of the Hyaenidae family resemble dogs but are more closely related to the cats and civets of this world. There are four species, the Aardwolf, as well as the Brown (Parahyaena brunnea), Striped (Hyaena hyaena) and Spotted Hyena (Crocuta crocuta). These animals have large heads and large ears, long front legs and shorter back legs, a mane on the back of the neck, except in the spotted variety, as well as a bushy tail, and short, blunt retractable claws. The coat is spotted or striped, although the brown hyena only has stripes on the legs. These animals have powerful jaws with which to kill, and the spotted hyena is the most ravenous of the hunters and they can take down very large, horse-sized prey, and they are well equipped scavengers too. The spotted hyenas have been known to fend off lions, whereas the brown and striped variety tend to kill smaller prey and eat left-overs from what other animals, such as leopards may kill.

Hyenas can swallow flesh and bone, powerful teeth are capable of crushing what they digest, and they regurgitate what they cannot swallow, although the Aardwolf tends to feed off smaller prey still such as insects. The striped and brown hyenas live I pairs and small groups, whilst the spotted hyena lives in a much larger clan. More importantly, and with regards to the Gevaudan killer, the spotted hyena can weigh up to one-hundred and fifty pounds, the brown hyena just over one-hundred pounds and the striped hyena twenty or so pounds less. However, one thing we must remember about these animals is that they inhabit warm areas such as Africa and Asia, so for any one of these to be the Gevaudan suspect, we must look towards an escapee from a private collection, or something let go on purpose.

The female spotted hyena is slightly larger than the male, the clans they are part of can inhabit a territory of up to three-hundred and fifty square miles, and if they hunt alone they can gorge themselves on up to one-third of its body weight.

The striped hyena prefers the open woodlands of Africa and Asia, it is grey to pale brown in colour with up to six vertical bars on its flank, it is generally a solitary hunter with a black and white tail, whereas the brown hyena has a dark, shaggy coat with stripes on its legs, a pale coloured mane and grey face. All of these hyenas can reach up to four-feet in length but none of them have tails that measure over ten inches in length.

The Grey Wolf (Canis lupus), can grow up to five-feet in length and weigh up to one-hundred and thirty pounds, it is the largest member of the canid family and an ancestor of the domestic dog, it was once the world's most wide ranging carnivore, found in Europe, Greenland, North America and Asia. These animals have a tail that can measure over a foot in length and they are able to take down prey as large as a moose, they have large feet and claws, powerful legs, the Red Wolf (Canis rufus),which inhabits North Carolina in the United States, can reach up to four-feet in length, weigh ninety-pounds and their coat can appear tawny-greyish-black, but it is unlikely such an animal, which is now considered endangered, was the beast of Gevaudan, and from here, any other unusual and out of place suspects tend to get smaller in size, from the Maned Wolf (Chrysocyon brachyurus), a fox-related animal confined to Central and East America, which has distinct stilted legs, thick reddish fur but, interestingly, a central back stripe. They, however, hunt small prey such as rabbits and mice, and although they can reach over four-feet in length, they only weigh up to fifty-pounds, whilst the Jackal (Side-striped, Golden and Black-backed), which inhabits parts of Africa, is lighter still, as is the Coyote which inhabits North and Central America, and none of these animals, except for the Grey Wolf or the Hyena would attack a human, and certainly not with the brutal frequency of the Gevaudan beast.

Large felids can also be dismissed due to the descriptions from the time, although a large cat, judging by many historical accounts, would seem the most likely to be around, as many documented cases from Britain have been found where cats, mainly Leopard, Puma and Lynx, have escaped from collections.

The film exaggerates the story of the Gevaudan mauler even more, in its fantasy the portrayal is of an armoured lion-like beast summoned and instructed by a dark magician. It is unlikely that anyone who watches 'Brotherhood' will see the reality or realise that once upon a time an even fiercer creature roamed the French region. However, for those not interested in cryptozoology, such films still remain vital in informing the public that not all monsters are merely celluloid nightmares, but representations of creatures that once prowled reality, proof that it's not just a movie after all."

The Mothman Prophecies (2002)
The Legend Of The Mothman

In 2002 a movie was released in cinemas that asked the question 'What Do You See?'

The chilling tag line was from a film which also claimed to be 'Based On True Events'. That film was *The Mothman Prophecies*.

The film tells the story of a man driven to investigate the mysterious circumstances surrounding his wife's death. Whilst doing so the journalist, John Klein (Richard Gere) uncovers the terrifying secrets behind the Mothman, a timeless, nameless beast whose appearance is a portent of doom for all those who have witnessed it.

Klein discovers there is a connection between the creature and the small town of Point Pleasant, West Virginia, where he finds the community are paralysed by fear. The townsfolk are plagued by strange visions, chilling premonitions and a feeling that something is watching them and waiting for disaster to strike. As events unfold a disturbing and horrific phenomenon is revealed and the town of Point Pleasant would never be the same again.

Another tag line from the movie asks 'If you see it, are you safe? If you don't…are you next?'

So what is it? Who is the Mothman? Who saw it? And what really happened in Point Pleasant that left witnesses terrified and scarred the small town forever?

The Mothman was a name given to the creature that was seen by over one hundred witnesses in the Charleston and Point Pleasant areas of West Virginia, USA between November 1966 and December 1967. It is also claimed that the creature has been seen in the area as recently as 2005. Most witnesses describe the creature as being the size of a man, having wings and most strikingly, having terrifying, glowing red eyes.

The Mothman was first sighted on November 12th 1966 in Clendenin, West Virginia. Five men preparing a grave described seeing a 'brown human shape' lifting off from behind nearby trees and flying over their heads. This sighting was not made public until after stories of the Mothman had began being reported to the media. The first of which occurred three days later.

On November 15th 1966 two young couples from Point Pleasant, Roger and Linda Scarberry and Steve and Mary Mallette, were driving in Scarberry's car. They were passing an old World War II TNT factory about seven miles from Point Pleasant in the late evening when they noticed two red lights in the shadows near the gate of the factory, by an old generator. They stopped the car and were terrified to see the lights appeared to be the glowing red eyes of an animal in the car headlights. The animal was like nothing they had ever seen before according to Roger Scarberry the beast was:

> *'..Shaped like a man, but bigger, maybe six and a half or seven feet tall. With big wings folded against its back.'*

Roger's wife and fellow eyewitness Linda Scarberry added:

> *'…we couldn't believe what we really saw, this thing was standing there, it had a body like a real man you could see (the) muscles in its legs. We sat there for a minute and looked at each other and then we took off.'*

The couples drove off in the car and headed for route 62. As they went down the exit road they saw the creature again standing on a ridge near the road. The creature spread its wings and took off, following the car to the city limits before disappearing.

The couples went to the Mason County Courthouse and relayed their story to Deputy Millard Halstead. He followed Scarberry's car back to the TNT factory but found no sign of the creature Halstead said:

> *'I've known these kids all their lives. They'd never been in trouble and they were really scared that night. I took them seriously.'*

The following day the Sheriff's Office had a press conference at the County Courthouse to discuss the sightings and it was after this that the press dubbed the creature 'The Mothman' after a character in the Batman television series.

That night, November 16th 1966 Raymond Wamsley, his wife, Marcella Bennett and her baby daughter Teena were visiting friends close to the TNT plant. As they left to get into their parked car a figure appeared from behind it. Startled, Marcella Bennett fell over and landed on baby Teena. She said the creature seemed like it had been lying down and slowly rose from the ground and had large feathered wings. After a few seconds Marcella got to her feet, picked Teena up and ran back to the house, as she did so she thought she heard the creature fly away as she heard the sound of wings flapping. Marcella reached the house and the family locked themselves indoors. They heard the creature shuffling around on the porch of the house and as Raymond Wamsley phoned the police it even peered in through the window at them. By the time the police arrived the creature had disappeared. Marcella Bennett recalled:

'(It) was all very frightening. It was one of the worst experiences of my life...and (I) hope it's the last. It still bothers me to talk about the creature'.

Marcella Bennett relived the event for months afterwards and had medical treatment to deal with the anxiety she suffered. She still has dreams and visions of her encounter to this day.

Author John Keel was researching UFO sightings in the area at the time the stories broke so he decided to head to Point Pleasant and investigate for himself. Keel's visit to the town turned from weeks to months as the reported sightings of the Mothman increased. He became convinced something very terrifying and real was happening in the town.

Connie Carpenter was driving home when she saw something unusual at the side of the road. What she thought was a shadow caught her attention so she slowed down to see what it was. To her horror she discovered the shadow was in fact the Mothman. The creatures wings came out from its back and it flew up into the air. Connie then claimed the creature swooped straight for her car. All she could see was its glowing red eyes. Connie fled back home as quickly as she could and after losing the creature on the way, locked herself indoors for days.

Keel began gathering the stories of the Point Pleasant sightings and was getting even more incredible information. Some witnesses were now suffering physical symptoms such as strange burns to the skin and enflamed, swollen eyes following sightings of the Mothman. Keel began to connect the sightings with UFO reports that were coming in from Point Pleasant at the same time.

Doris Deweese who lived on Madison Avenue in Point Pleasant at the time reported seeing UFO's going over her house every night at the time of the Mothman sightings.

Bob Elliott saw what he believed was an alien craft from his kitchen window around the same time too. Bob saw rotating lights in the sky that were about four feet high and six to eight feet wide and the multicoloured lights disappeared as quickly as they had appeared and made no noise.

Another sighting of the time was made by Dottie Campbell, another Point Pleasant resident who saw a cigar shaped object in the sky. Dottie stood transfixed as she watched the craft, according to Dottie it had lights on the side and was completely silent.

Keel himself saw hovering lights in the area which he said would respond to flashing torchlight at them. He said as he did this they would flash back. Keel claims he saw so many of these lights that he lost count of how many he had seen. The National Guard and State Police had now become involved in the search for the Mothman and local residents had begun locking their doors at night. Something the small community had never done in the past. Keel continued to travel to and from his New York home following phone calls about more sightings in Point Pleasant to investigate the case more closely. It would seem there were other people beginning to take an interest in the events that were going on in Point Pleasant too. Strange visitors began to show up in the town, dressed from head to toe in black. It appears they didn't want the towns' stories to be told and threatened those who spoke. Dottie Campbell, who had witnessed UFO phenomenon in Point Pleasant, received a visit to her home from a man dressed in black who gave her a chilling warning. Dottie recalled:

> *'He said we don't wanna hear any more about this and he left. So after he had said what he did we didn't say any more about it.'*

Connie Carpenter's husband Keith returned home one night to find himself locked out of the house. He let himself in and discovered Connie cowering in the bedroom. He slowly managed to coax out of her what had happened. She told him she had gone out to get into the car that morning and a car pulled up. A man dressed in black called over and asked her for directions. Connie walked over to the man to give him the directions and as she did he tried pulling her into his car. Connie managed to escape and ran back into the house. Not long after the incident Connie, who had previously reported seeing the Mothman, found a threatening note left on her porch. It read:

> *'BE CAREFUL GIRL I CAN GET YOU'*

Local Point Pleasant newspaper columnist Mary Hyre was helping John Keel with his investigations. Unfortunately she died soon after the events in Point Pleasant, before she could discover what was going on there. Local residents who knew Mary said she was the kind of person who would hunt for the truth until she found it. Maybe this could have contributed to Mary's downfall. For Mary had told friends that she had been visited by the men in black several times, she noticed one thing about the threatening visitors above all else, they never once blinked their eyes. They had asked her questions about the Mothman and acted in such a way towards her that she also told her friends that she feared for her life. Despite feeling truly threatened by the men in black Mary was determined to continue investigating the story of the Mothman. John Keel said he had worked with many press writers and Mary was one of the most trustworthy, he had no reason to doubt her regarding the matter. Despite theorists claiming this could be the CIA trying to silence witnesses by intimidation the American Government has denied any involvement with the men in black incidents in Point Pleasant. John Keel contacted the USAF in Columbus, Ohio and they also denied any involvement.

The sightings continued in Point Pleasant. On November 24th 1966 four people saw the Mothman flying through the air over the TNT area. At 7:15am on November 25th 1966 Thomas Ury was driving along route 62, north of the TNT area when he saw something from the corner of his eye at the riverbank. It came over the trees and as he drove along he realised it was a huge bird. Thomas said the bird had an estimated wingspan of ten to twelve feet. He had never seen anything like it and was scared but not terrified:

> 'It's a strange feeling...I've never seen anything like it before and I hope I never do again. It's unbelievable.'

On November 26th 1966 Ruth foster of Charleston, West Virginia saw the Mothman standing on her front law, but when her brother-in-law went out to look it had vanished.

In the morning of November 27th 1966 the Mothman chased a woman near Mason in West Virginia and on the same night two children reported seeing the creature in St Albans.

Still more reports kept coming in. Five pilots were standing on a local airstrip when what they described as a giant, dark coloured bird hovered above them. Amongst the witnesses was one of Point Pleasant's most upstanding and respected residents, Everett Wedge. He claimed the creature he saw was big enough to lift a man and that he had never seen a bird that big. Wedge said:

> 'I might not quite have 20/20 vision now but I did then.'

In February 1967 a Red Cross ambulance was chased by the Mothman. The drivers looked out of the window as they drove along and saw a huge creature hovering over them. They said they saw what they described as 'huge claws' descending as if it was about to grab the ambulance. They managed to escape its clutches and lost their pursuer. There were other cases involving blood. Curiously, Keel found from his research that many of the female witnesses who claimed to have seen the Mothman were having their menstrual cycles at the time of their encounter. Was there any relevance to the case regarding these findings?

Other strange phenomena were being reported in Point Pleasant, even animals were not safe now it would seem. Dogs began going missing and cases of cattle mutilation were being reported. These included the anus of the cow being removed completely.

Eyewitnesses now complained of nightmares and dark premonitions. Even reporter Mary Myre told friends she had had a disturbing dream about Christmas presents in the water.

By December 1967 John Keel was back in New York planning another return to Point Pleasant to further his investigations. Strangely, he had received several anonymous phone calls warning him not to go back to the town. Main Street in Point Pleasant leads directly onto Silver Bridge which spanned the Ohio River, connecting Point Pleasant, West Virginia and Gallipolis. Silver Bridge was an eye-bar chain suspension bridge built in 1928 which was used by local residents several times a day.

At 5:05 pm on December 15th 1967 the bridge was full of traffic. Many of which were Christmas shoppers. Suddenly the bridge began to shake. As Charlene Wood got to the traffic lights just before joining the bridge she saw the bridge shaking. She thought a boat had hit the bridge from underneath so she put her car into reverse and backed up hastily. Just as she did this the bridge incline raised up. Charlene's car stopped with her tyres right on the edge of the incline as the bridge broke off and crashed into the water. Charlene climbed from her car as other vehicles entered the icy water and disaster unfolded in front of her eyes. Silver Bridge collapsed catastrophically and disappeared beneath the water. Forty Six people died making it the worst American Bridge disaster at the time. It took days to recover the bodies and vehicles from the river.
A Department Of Transportation inquiry concluded that the bridge had collapsed due to the failure of a single eye-bar in a suspension chain that had a slight flaw when manufactured. The bridge was nearly forty years old, poorly maintained and has been carrying more traffic then it had been designed for. The report also said it was a miracle the bridge had stood for as long as it did. Another bizarre coincidence was that the bridge had collapsed 13 months from the first sighting of the Mothman and

the eye-bar pin responsible for the disaster was pin number 13. There was also a sighting of the creature on the bridge at the time of the disaster which was reported to the Sheriff. Curiously, some people who claimed to have encountered the Mothman previously found themselves unexpectedly way laid when they tried to cross the bridge that afternoon. Witnesses also claimed to have seen the mysterious men in black climbing around the bridge in the days before the collapse. After the disaster the anomalous activity at Point Pleasant seemed to abate and eventually disappear. As if the Mothman had done his job and tried to warn the residents of the in suing disaster. The UFO sightings, cattle mutilations and the men in black encounters disappeared too, as if it had all been connected to the disaster.

John Keel went on to publish his collection of first-hand experiences in his book *The Mothman Prophecies* in 1975. There have also been books published about the Point Pleasant phenomenon such as A.B. Colvin's *The Mothman's Photographer* and Jeff Wamsley's *Mothman: The Facts Behind The Legend* and *Mothman: Behind The Red Eyes.* There are many views as to what happened in Point Pleasant both explainable and unexplainable.

Sceptics claim the scientific explanation for the Mothman phenomena was a mass hallucination that was cleared up by the shock of the bridge tragedy. Others blamed the tragedy on a curse placed on the town by Chief Cornstalk, a Native American Chieftain over 200 years ago. Local ornithologists claimed the Mothman was really just a big bird all along. A Sandhill Crane. The species superficially matched the descriptions of the Mothman and has two patches of flesh that could be mistaken for red eyes. Eyewitnesses such as Thomas Ury disagreed, claiming the Sandhill Crane is the *wrong colour* and *too skinny* to be the creature he saw. It is also claimed that the local ponds of the TNT area had been left to become polluted by waste from the old munitions factory and some wondered if the Mothman could have been a mutant bird caused by the horrible effects of toxic waste.

Others believe the Mothman is synonymous with the Garuda of the Far East and the Thunderbird of Native America. They believe that the Mothman was fulfilling a pre ordained role that involves stopping heinous crimes and disasters by sending messages and visions to ordinary human beings. They believe the Mothman was trying to warn the people of Point Pleasant about the bridge collapse to try and overt the disaster.

This may not be as far fetched as it initially appears for the Mothman has risen again it would seem. Sightings have been reported around the world since Point Pleasant and always before major disasters occur:

- 1985 Mexico City, Mexico: Sightings of a huge, strange bird were reported in the weeks before a major earthquake devastated the City.

- 1986 Chernobyl, Ukraine (formerly U.S.S.R): Locals reported encounters with a 'bird-like' man over several months before a horrific accident at a nuclear power plant.

It has been seen before and no doubt it will be seen again, whatever the explanation, the Mothman terrified all who saw it. Real or not it would seem the legend of the Mothman lives on.

What The Experts Say
The Mothman Prophecies (2002)

Jeff Wamsley – Director of the Mothman Museum, Paranormal researcher and author. Jeff is the Director of the Mothman Museum in Point Pleasant, West Virginia and also a resident there. He is the co-author of 'Mothman: The Facts Behind The Legend', (with Donnie Sergent Jr.) (Mark S. Phillips Publishing 2001) and author of 'Mothman: Behind The Red Eyes' (Mothman Press 2005). Jeff has also made countless press, radio and television appearances and is considered one of the world's leading experts on the Mothman phenomena.

"It has been over 40 years since my hometown was thrust into the spotlight. People in Point Pleasant, West Virginia were reporting sightings of a mysterious giant bird or creature of some sort in the nearby TNT area which is located about seven miles north of the small, close knit town. Reporters and investigators began to ascend on my hometown like bees to honey with believers and debunkers alike hoping to get a glimpse of the "Mothman". The Mothman saga is no doubt one of the most interesting and unexplained phenomena that has peaked the world's attention, what did they see? Is it still out there?

I grew up with the Mothman legend along with many of the people who encountered it. Knowing many of the key eyewitnesses has provided me with a different perspective and has enabled me to uncover vital information and possible clues that may help others to understand this unsolved mystery. To this day there are still a handful of those original witnesses that refuse interviews and will not speak to anyone, including myself, about what they saw over 40 years ago. Several of these witnesses have made it clear in claiming "I know what I saw and that is all I am saying about it". My personal opinion is that if the Point Pleasant Mothman sightings were a well organized hoax, as some believe, then why haven't any of these silent witnesses came forth to break their silence and put an end to all the speculation? Maybe that question can be answered this way. In a thirteen month period spanning from November 1966 to December 1967 there were over 100 reported sightings(who knows how many other people were afraid to report what they saw) to law enforcement authorities in Point Pleasant. All of these people described what they saw as seven feet tall, shaped like a man but with a 10 foot wingspan and prominent glowing, red eyes. It is highly unlikely that all of these people knew each other let alone being able to pull off this sort of massive hoax. The large number of witnesses and very similar descriptions has given the Mothman story credibility and at the same time presented the ultimate question: what did they see?

Since the release of my books (Mothman:The Facts Behind the Legend 2001 and Mothman: Behind the Red Eyes 2005) I have had the opportunity to do many interviews, answer questions and ultimately represent the accounts of those witnesses who were there when it happened. Most interviews contain many of the questions that those who are curious about the Mothman story want to know. What did it look like? Did it make any noises? Did it ever harm anyone? Usually the last question is one that I always expect and to this day I cannot really answer unless more clues and archives are discovered. That question is what do you think they saw?

The theories and explanations for what the Mothman was and possibly still is are vast and colourful. Some think that what people were seeing was simply a large Sand hill Crane or a bird of some sort. I can say that most of the original witnesses do not agree with this theory and are adamant about what they encountered. These witnesses stumbled across a creature or animal that was definitely not of the norm or anything they had ever seen before. Many of them have expressed frustration because they cannot come to any reasonable explanation as to what they saw. This may explain why many of them refuse interviews and simply prefer to remain quiet about their chilling experiences.

People are curious as to whether any physical evidence exists to substantiate the Mothman sightings. Are there any photographs or film to confirm or prove the Mothman story? I do not know of any of this type of evidence but through more research and interviews who knows what may be discovered. I can honestly say that these people encountered something that changed their lives in many ways. Just their hesitation and reluctance in talking about their experience makes me wonder what exactly is preventing them from sharing their accounts, why are they still terrified 40 years later?. The Mothman story remains an open book with more clues and eyewitness accounts forthcoming. The witnesses hold the key to solving this incredible mystery with their descriptions, experiences and evidence.

I have spent the last 3 years compiling and archiving many of the existing clues and Mothman related items here at the world's only Mothman Museum in downtown Point Pleasant, West Virginia. People from all over the world have visited the museum to research the Mothman story firsthand. Is the Mothman real? Come and see for yourself, read the eyewitness accounts…you decide."

The Untold (2002)

The Search For Bigfoot

Mythological creatures and fabled beasts have been a long time favourite of film makers. Sometimes the plot of the movie can seem as fantastical as the creature at the heart of the story and some would say that was the case with the 2002 movie 'The Untold', which was released in the USA under the title 'Sasquatch'.

The film tells the story of Harlan Knowles, billionaire and President of Bio-Comp Industries. A Bio-Comp company plane goes missing over the remote forests of the Pacific Northwest. Amongst the passengers is Knowles' daughter. When the search and rescue mission is finally called off Knowles assembles a team of experts in a bid to locate the missing aircraft and his daughter. The team eventually find the wreckage and it becomes apparent that the carnage that was once the plane and crew could not have been caused by a plane crash alone. As the team try and find out what happened, something starts watching and following them in the woods. The team begin to realise what started out as a rescue mission has brought them face to face with one of the world's most legendary creatures and the only people left to rescue may be themselves.

Like another fictional movie, 'The Blair Witch Project', *The Untold* claims to be based on actual accounts, a claim that was made to increase box office appeal. Unlike 'Blair Witch' though, the legend that *The Untold* is based on may very well be a reality. The legend I am referring to is that of the existence of the fabled Sasquatch.

The Sasquatch is described as being a man/ape creature that is between seven and eight feet tall and is native to North America. Long before settlers came to the country from Europe the Native Americans knew of the creature's existence and named it Sasquatch, which means 'hairy giant'. Tribes such as the Lumme believe that if you look Sasquatch in the eye he can steal your spirit. The belief amongst Native Americans in the existence of such a beast is still very real to this day as Naturalist James Swan explains:

"Modern Western culture jokes at Bigfoot but in the Indian culture Bigfoot is serious. This is a real being, a real creature with spiritual powers that lives in wild places. It's a guardian of sacred places and it's not a joke at all."

One of the earliest recorded sightings of Sasquatch was made by a man near what is now known as Jasper, Alberta, Canada in 1811. The man who claimed to have seen the beast was a fur trader named David Thompson. Since then there have been numerous sightings of Sasquatch in Western Canada and in several American States. The creature has been sighted in the Pacific Northwest, Ohio and as far south as Florida.

Sasquatch first came to the general public's attention when, throughout 1958 and 1959, numerous footprints attributed to the beast were found in the forest in Bluff Creek, Northern California, USA. Bob Titmus was one of the men who found footprints that measured an average length of 15.6 inches and had an average width of 7.2 inches. The press reported the findings and in 1958 the term 'Bigfoot' was first coined by a news reporter, giving Sasquatch another name to be known by.

Nine years later the most famous, or infamous depending on your point of view, sighting of Bigfoot occurred.

In 1967, Roger Patterson and Bob Gimlin were on an expedition to Bluff Creek looking for the elusive creature. Patterson and Gimlin were riding on horseback through the forest when they unexpectedly found what they were looking for. Bob Gimlin explained:

"We came around a bend in the creek where there was a downfallen tree. At that point, as we came around the bend and the creek there, this creature was standing beside the creek. When we came upon the creature it was standing still by the creek. It immediately turned around and started to walk away."

Patterson's horse was startled by the creature and threw him off. Fortunately he was able to get to his feet and grab the 16mm camera he had in his saddlebag. Bob Gimlin described what happened next:

"Roger Patterson turned on his movie camera ran after it (Bigfoot) as far as he could and finally he stopped and it walked away. Its appearance was just a large, large humanoid creature walking like a human being."

The footage Patterson filmed that day is still the most famous footage of an alleged Bigfoot to date.

Not all encounters with the creature have been sightings. In 1984 Bruce Hoffman was gold prospecting near Clackamas River, in Oregon, USA, when he claimed to have heard the 'call' of a Bigfoot. Hoffman described his experience to investigator Greg Long:

"I had to park a couple of hundred feet from the River, and I had to walk a little ways back towards the small stream that was running into the River. Just before I got to the small tributary, I would say from one-eighth of a mile to a quarter of a mile away, down in the woods, I started hearing this yell, or a call. The sound had a base tone, a muscular sound to it, and the sound got loud. You could hear how it went up through the trees and up into the sky. The sound travelled about three to four miles to the ridge of the mountains. You could hear the sound hit the mountain."

Outdoorsman Bill Monroe also witnessed what he claims was the howl of a Bigfoot. Monroe was elk hunting one afternoon when he heard the chilling cry. He recounted his experience in an article for the Portland Oregonian; the newspaper he wrote for at the time:

"The deafening screaming, choking, belching moan from the ridge was chilling. The kind of scream that sends mothers scurrying to find their children. The kind of scream no cougar or bear could ever squeeze from their throat…unless it was their last. Piercing, echoing, guttural: a single, horrible, high-pitched-yet-throaty, inhuman, unnatural creation of Steven Spielberg that makes your skin crawl."

It was another Bigfoot sighting that started a chain of events that would lead to what is claimed to be an actual Bigfoot call being recorded. Warren James of the Native American Lumme tribe reported a sighting to the tribe's Police Chief. James said:

"I went duck hunting in the evening about six fifteen, six thirty. I looked up, this thing got out of the ditch and I froze. My knees started shaking…It was Bigfoot. After that I sold my guns and I never did go hunting again."

At the time of Warren James' encounter Lumme Police Chief Chas Das Ska Dum Which La Lum was receiving a flood of Bigfoot reports. Cha recalls:

"I answered so many calls on him that people were making fun, saying we (the Lumme tribe) were seeing things, smoking dope, that we're drinking or something, saying there's no such thing. The more they taunted about it the more I wanted to prove there was such a thing without killing him. I did not want to kill this animal. I wanted to prove he existed."

It wasn't long before Cha was given the chance to try and do just that, as he was about to have an encounter of his own with the creature.

"I received a call from Scott Road, I was driving north on Chief Martin Road which is just off from Scott Road. I could hear this screaming, I could see this thing running right toward my car as it came into my bright light. I could see it was a Sasquatch. He had his mouth wide open showing me all his teeth. He was coming at me in an aggressive manner."

As the creature bore his teeth to Cha it let out a loud piercing call, the sound of which was picked up on Cha's police radio. Cha remembered:

"It was a very high-pitched screaming. Blood curdling, make your hair stand on end scream."

Back at the Lumme Police Headquarters they were able to record what Cha claimed to be the call of a Sasquatch. The recording was then taken for analysis which was carried out by Michael Dee, a zoologist and mammal expert. Dee concluded:

"I've heard it and it's like nothing I've ever heard before. It's not a noise but whether or not an actual creature made that noise, I can't

determine that. It doesn't sound like anything that I'm familiar with and I'm certainly familiar with almost all the mammals that are in North America and their calls."

Cha, on the other hand, was in no doubt as to what he heard and saw during his encounter:

"He looks so human, the facial features are so much like our own that it's almost like he's saying 'Where did you come from? What are you? I wanna talk to you, I wanna communicate'. There's not a doubt in my mind that Sasquatch exists."

In 1988 wildlife biologist John Bindernagel was hiking in Strathcona Provincial Park, British Columbia, Canada when he heard a 'whoo-whoo whoop' call in the woods. Bindernagel also found sixteen inch, 'human-like' footprints whilst on the hike. He also heard an 'ape-like' call at a friend's cabin in 1992 near Comox Lake, also in British Columbia, Canada. Bindernagel says he knows of no other creature in North America or Canada that makes such a call, and he believes what he heard was a Sasquatch trying to communicate with it's own kind.

In June of 1988, the same year as Binderangel found 'Bigfoot footprints', Sean Fries reported an unusual experience whilst camping on the North Fork of Feather River in California:

"I made camp and cooked a few trout that I caught earlier. I was getting a little tired so I decided to turn in. I climbed into my tent and lay down on my bedroll. I let my dogs run around because they always stay close to camp. I started to dose off to the crickets chirping when suddenly I woke up, it was as if I had one of those dreams where you are falling. I could tell there was something very wrong. It was dead quiet, no crickets, nothing, and my dogs came running into my tent shaking. These dogs were very aggressive. I grabbed my rifle and pistol along with a flashlight and stepped outside the tent. I couldn't see anything, but I had that sensation of being watched. I grabbed some firewood and threw it on the embers left from the dinner fire. Then I heard some very heavy footsteps behind me in the trees. There was also a very strange odour, almost like a cross between a skunk and something dead. This thing circled my camp site all night long."

The following summer Elmer Frombach Jnr took his family on an outing to the Canadian Border. Elmer was an electrician and prospector from Seattle. On the 15th July 1989 Elmer went to stake a claim in the woods near his family's campsite. Elmer recalled:

"I had a four by four cedar post that I was using to stake the claim and of course I had all of the normal things like surveyor's ribbon and a compass and different items which would be used to lay out the claim boundaries. As I travelled up into the upper areas I was now about 1500 feet and I noticed the trails in the area were somewhat isolated with trees being snapped off and laid over the trail in certain spots which looked as though they were strategically placed to block the trail off. So I laid the cedar post down on the ground and went up the hillside to where I could walk on the trails easily again."

Elmer had just started to take ore samples when he realised he was not alone. As he chipped away at the rock he heard a sound that seemed to be mimicking the noise he was making. Elmer put down his pick and investigated:

"As I walked around the hillside the pounding seemed to cease for a short period of time and then it resumed again and I thought maybe the boys are up here playing a trick on me."

Elmer shouted up to whoever was making the noise up on the hill and suddenly something came rolling down the hillside:

"I thought at first I had triggered an avalanche of some type until I saw a big black hairy mass right behind all of those rocks and twigs and then I began to wonder is this a bear I'm seeing? Or is it something else?"

As the creature stood up Elmer drew his gun:

"...At the time I remember thinking 'I've got to try and find a way to scare it' and I fired a shot above it's head and it turned, just slightly, and then proceeded to walk down the trail as though I wasn't even there. As it walked away from me it took perfect human-like strides down the trail only like a giant man. At that point in time I thought the thing was probably gone, but this thing had crouched down at the end of the trail and it picked up a rock the size of a basketball and was using it to bang against the other rocks. Yet again it made a slight sideways turn, just enough to see me out of the corner of its eye. I was scared and I wanted to get out of there and I kept running down the hillside and

the thing was in hot pursuit the whole way. I was absolutely terrified. I had a hard time figuring out how that thing could cover so much area or if there were actually more than one of them. I've never been more scared in all my life. The creature could very easily have caught me had it wanted to, why it didn't is still a mystery to me. I still can't understand it."

Perhaps the creature was protecting its territory and had given chase to Elmer and then stopped as a kind of a 'territory charge'.

Another experienced outdoorsman, Clayton Mack, saw an odd looking creature whilst fishing at the Kwatna Inlet on the British Columbia Coast. Mack, a Native American of the Nuxalk Nation was also a grizzly bear hunter for 53 years and knew the area as well as any man when he had his encounter:

"I had a 30 foot boat with a single cylinder engine. I got to Jacobson Bay about 15 miles from Bella Coola, when I saw something on the edge of the water. It was kneeling down like and I could see his back humping up on the beach. It looked like he was lifting up rocks or maybe digging clams. But there were no clams there. I turned the boat right in toward him. I wanted to find out what it was. For a while there, I thought it was a grizzly bear, kind of light-colour fur on the back of his neck like a light brown. I nosed right in toward him to almost 75 yards to get a good look at it. He stood up on his hind feet, straight up like a man and I looked at it. He was looking at me. Gee, it don't look like a bear, it has arms like a human being, and it got a head like us. I keep on going in toward him. He started to walk away from me like a man on two legs. He was about eight feet high. He got some drift-logs, stopped and looked back at me. He looked over his shoulder to see me. Grizzly bear don't do that, I never see a grizz run on its hind legs like that and I never see a grizzly bear look over his shoulder like that. I was right close to the beach now. He stepped up on those drift logs and walked in to the timber. Stepped on them logs like a man do. I watched as he went a little higher up the hill. The wind blew me in toward the beach, so I backed up the boat and keep on going to Kwanta Bay."

Bigfoot sightings continued into the 1990's and more and more detailed accounts began being reported from very credible witnesses. Todd Neiss was a sergeant in the United States Army

Guard. Whilst on manoeuvres in the Oregon Coastal Range in 1993 he had an unusual sighting:

"Across the ravine I could distinctly see three large black figures. I would estimate the largest one to be between eight and nine feet (tall). The two that flanked it were a full head shorter. I tried to think whether they were bear or elk and then when I saw them shuffling back and forth I could very plainly see they were upright on two legs, during that entire time all three of them were standing on two legs. I was approached by another sergeant who walked up to me and said 'Sergeant Neiss did you see what I saw down at that second rock quarry?' Not to be made a fool of I said,' Well I don't know what did you see?' He followed with, 'Well for lack of a better word what I saw were three large, hair-covered Bigfeet'."

One month later two women were driving on a remote country road 100 miles away late at night. The driver, who wished to remain anonymous, reported that a creature had been sat by the side of the road in the darkness. As her car came to a halt it stood up and walked across the road in front of the headlights, before disappearing into the trees on the other side of the road:

"We had just come around a bend in the road when I saw movement and I slowed down for the anticipation of something crossing in front of me. That's when it stood up and moved across the road without once looking at us and disappeared. We couldn't make any sense of it. It was very close to a human yet it wasn't. There was no physical signs of clothing, shoes, jacket, hat. There was no neck. The arms were very long and swinging with the momentum."

Two years later, 1995, veteran Bigfoot hunter Paul Freeman and former game warden Bill Laughery, were following the sounds of 'odd screams' that had been heard in the Blue Mountains of southeast Washington State. Local resident Wes Summerlin joined them and the three men went to an area where Bigfoot tracks had been found. In a clearing there were several small broken and twisted trees that were dripping sap. Caught on the trees were large clumps of long black and brown hair. They also found droppings that were two to five inches long and full of half-eaten carpenter ants, from which they deduced the fallen trees had been pulled apart for the ants that could be found inside them. During their search the men observed an ape-like creature at a distance of ninety feet through binoculars. They claimed the creature was eating yellow wood violets.

The hair samples gathered by Laughery, Summerlin and Freeman were sent to Ohio State University for DNA analysis. The tests were inconclusive. Dr. W.Henner Fahrenbach 'determined microscopically that the hair appeared to have come from two individuals of the same species, that it differed in colour, length and hair growth cycle between the two sets, had not been cut and was indistinguishable from human hair by any criterion'. Researchers at the University said that the hair DNA extracted from both hair shaft and root was too fragmented to permit gene sequencing.

Also in 1995 Terry Endres and two other men were researching an area known for Bigfoot sightings for a local cable television show. They came across a large dome shaped structure made of brush and branches. It was large enough for three fully-grown men to sit in and was obviously not a natural occurrence.

Dallas Gilbert has also claimed to have found similar constructions. The most controversial of his claims are that he has discovered a possible Bigfoot community and burial site. His story is however weakened by the fact that he is very reluctant to disclose the exact location of the site. Gilbert told the Daily Times of Portsmouth, Ohio, USA:

"There are places where you can see territorial markings and snaps that the creature has made in the trees. There are even canopies and bows made of trees for him to sleep under."

Gilbert also described the burial site which he claimed was marked by a stone:

"It looks like a tombstone almost, you can see the outlines of the creature's eyes, head and his teeth."

No remains have ever been found nor has any other evidence been recovered in the area. To date the only evidence for this site is Gilbert's own testimony.

In September 1998 Dave Shealy managed to take 27 photographs of a seven foot tall creature in the Florida Everglades. Shealy said:

"I had been sitting up in the tree for about two hours every night for the past eight months. I dozed off for a little while, and when I woke up I saw it coming straight at me. At first I thought it was a man, but then I realised it was the skunk ape."

Shealy followed the tracks of the animal and made what he claims is an amazing discovery; small footprints he says appear to have been made by a baby skunk ape. Shealy believes there are an estimated nine to twelve skunk apes roaming the Florida Everglades at present. Most witnesses of a sighting report seeing them in groups of three or four.

Some Sasquatch reports are very strange indeed, even going as far as to involve interaction with the creature. Stan Johnson claims to be one such 'contactee'. Johnson says he first met the creature when he was a small boy. He described him as a seven foot tall 'wild man' and encountered him near his home in the Ozark Mountain region of the USA. Following his first contact with the Sasquatch Johnson would meet him in the woods every day after school and talk. Johnson says he has had several other encounters since then and believes the creature comes from another dimension. This is certainly one of the most bizarre explanations offered as to where the creatures come from.

With personal accounts and sightings seeming to be plentiful, surely the weight of evidence deserves to be examined more thoroughly as to what these creatures are.

For nearly two hundred years now, these beasts have been sighted in several States of the USA, especially the Pacific Northwest, Ohio and even as far south as Florida. There have also been numerous sightings in Western Canada. Many of these sightings have been reported by experienced 'outdoors people' and 'adventurers' which lends credence to their authenticity. To add to the testimony of witnesses there have also been more than 700 footprints attributed to Bigfoot that have been collected over the years. These have an average length of 15.6 inches and an average width of 7.2 inches. By comparison the foot of a seven foot three inch tall basketball player is 16.5 inches long but only 5.5 inches wide.

Tufts and strands of hair have also been collected and analysed, but as most of them have proven to be that of bears or other non-primates it has not added to the weight of evidence for the existence of the creature to date.

Photo's, film footage and video of the creature are extremely rare. At worst they are fuzzy, hard to see and inconclusive. At best when you can view them clearly, they are highly controversial and often suspected of being hoaxed. The Patterson/Gimlin film is by far the most famous and scrutinised footage ever taken of the creature. Debate amongst experts over the authenticity of the footage has raged for over thirty years. Recently some people have come forward to claim that they participated in the hoaxing of the film, but even their testimony has been called into question itself.

The even rarer claims of the discovery of Bigfoot dwellings and burial sites have never been verified or authenticated. The few cases of close contact that have been reported are very suspect too.

Sasquatch, Bigfoot, Yeti or Skunk Ape, whatever name you know him by, if such a creature does exist what is it and where did it come from?

The Hidden Species Theory

There are many animals that exist today that were once thought to be mythical creatures. The people of Kwanda, for example had long known of a huge, dark, man-like beast that swung through the tree tops emitting a fearful cry; scientists first tagged this creature in 1901. The creature in question was the mountain gorilla.

Other animals that were regarded as folklore include the snow leopard, the pigmy hippo and the giant panda which was not discovered until 1936 in China. Nobody believed these creatures existed until they were discovered in the far corners of the world by explorers.

There are also creatures that exist today that man may have never thought possible in the past. One of which is a mix of goat and antelope found in the remote forests of Northern Vietnam called the saola. Another example is a strange mix of duck and beaver found in Tasmania called the ornithorinx.

The point being, there are new species and mixtures of existing species being discovered all the time.

The reason Bigfoot may as yet have gone 'undiscovered' could be because the areas in which he supposedly lives are mostly inaccessible or covered with dense vegetation, leaving him hidden from sight. In fact in the Pacific Northwest area, a 'Bigfoot hotspot', there are seventy three aircraft that were lost between Northern California and Alaska since World War II that still remain missing according to FAA figures. Surely, if anything, this proves that the area is indeed easy to remain hidden in for large amounts of time. Other areas in which 'Sasquatch-like' creatures have been sighted in include the Himalayan Mountains, the Borneo jungle, the Amazon forest and the Pamir-Altai. All of which are equally inaccessible and hostile to man. Creatures living in small groups could easily remain hidden in these areas. All the previously hidden or lost species are primitive animals, as Sasquatch appears to be a more evolved creature it would make sense that he would find it easier to hide from man.

The Gigantopithecus Theory

This theory suggests that the creature is a descendant of a race of giant apes, the Gigantopithecus Blacki. This species are an extinct primate that lived in Asia and retreated into the Himalayas five hundred thousand years ago. Palaeontologists have described Gigantopithecus Blacki as a large, ground-feeding, ape-like genus about the size of a modern gorilla, with molar teeth well adapted to crushing tough material and flattened canines. One theory says that Gigantopithecus walked upright. By the size of the animal it is most likely it did not. In fact none of its descendants evolved to walk upright, nor has any other ape evolved to walk upright naturally.

The first Gigantopithecus tooth was found in 1932 by a Dutch Palaeontologist, G.H.R. Von Koeingswa in a Hong Kong apothecary shop. Since that time thousands of teeth and only a few jawbones have been found in China and India. Worldwide only a handful of teeth and jawbones have ever been discovered. It is more plausible that the Saquatch is a descendant rather than an actual living representation of Gigantopithecus. Even though the species is supposed to have died out half a million years ago, his descendants could possibly still survive, however, there is no significant evidence to support the theory that this is the case. However, there is that slight possibility that the Gigantopithecus Theory could one day solve the mystery of the Sasquatch.

The Missing Link Theory

The late populations of Homo Neanderthal lived in Western Europe and Central Asia at least up until 30,000 BC. During the same period a similar humanoid (Cro-Magnon) also lived in Central Asia. After the late Homo Neanderthals hybridised with modern Homo sapiens in Europe, he quickly became the dominant specie and the other species disappeared. This left Homo sapiens to become our ancestors.

So what is known is that the extinction of the ancient European populations occurred more recently than 30,000 years ago at various intervals from Western to Eastern Europe. What is not known is what happened in Central Asia. Probably the evolution of the Cro-Magnon's deviated from the older populations which became extinct, but it is not known when the last groups of these older populations disappeared.

It may be possible that Saquatch could be the descendant of one of these populations and indeed be 'the missing link'.

The Giant Ape Theory

Many scientists believe that these creatures that have been witnessed across the world are giant apes such as the orang-utan and gorilla.

The relationship between Sasquatch and Homo sapiens has not been proven to be any closer than that between our species and the other great apes, except in shared posture and means of locomotion. With the exception of his upright posture and loss of hair, man's differences from other primates are mainly his brain and the departure from the normal primitive lifestyle. Whilst all the other species have relied on physical abilities and instincts to survive, man has shifted this reliance to his brain.

In the case of the ape-man (Sasquatch, Bigfoot, Yeti, etc.) verses ape, it would appear that the locomotion contrast is very similar to that which separated the first australopithecine from the ancestral African ape.

Given this theory, if upright posture is what makes an animal a human, then the reports of Sasquatch describe a human. Alternatively, if it is the brain that distinguishes Homo sapiens from their animal relatives, then the Sasquatch is an animal, an upright ape and nothing more.

The Giant Ape Theory also lends its weight to the sceptical view that witnesses are either mistaken, perhaps imagined their encounters or even, in some instances, faked the whole thing.

Many sceptics dismiss outright the sightings, footprints, photographic and video evidence brought before them. They also claim that the lack of any kind of remains of these creatures ever being found is also proof that they do not exist. To coin a phrase 'that's the nature of the beast'.

Strip away the hair from the beast in question and the bipedal Sasquatch expresses many more human features than ape traits. On the other hand, humans also display many ape-like qualities without resorting to walking on all fours.

Man will never know for sure what these creatures are, or if they even exist, until one is captured. No doubt until one is captured man will continue his search for this conclusive evidence. Only then will we find out for sure if Sasquatch is a mere legend or a remarkably elusive reality.

What The Experts Say
The Untold (2002)

Mike Hallowell – Cryptozoologist, Paranormal Investigator, Journalist and Author. Mike is a freelance writer and specialises in penning books, newspaper columns and articles about the paranormal. He also writes extensively about Native American culture and spirituality, and has Indian heritage in his family. His first book 'Herbal Healing' was published in 1985. Since then he has penned a number of other books including 'Ales & Spirits', 'Invizikids' and 'The South Shields Poltergeist' which he co-authored Darren W. Ritson.

Mike contributes regularly to a number of journals and newspapers. He has penned his 'WraithScape' column for The Shields Gazette for over a decade, and it is the longest-running paranormal column in a provincial newspaper in the UK. He is also a regular columnist with Vision magazine, and contributes to other periodicals such as 'Beyond', 'Paranormal' and 'Magnolia'.

Mike has starred in as number of documentaries about the paranormal, including The Ghost Detectives with Tom Baker, filmmaker Gary Wilkinson's Anatomy of a Haunting and G. P. Taylor's Uninvited Guests. He regularly appears on the BBC and other channels both in the UK and abroad.

During his decades of investigation into the paranormal and alternative spirituality, Mike has interviewed most of the main players in the field including Colin Fry, Uri Geller, Tony Stockwell, Cliff Crook, Larry Warren, Richard Freeman, Stephen Holbrook, Jonathan Downes, Derek Acorah, Billy Roberts and Nick Redfern.

Mike was the founder of the Twilight Worlds Paranormal Research Society, but left the organisation after a number of years due to disagreements regarding how it was being run. He is currently the patron of the North East Ghost Research Team and a UK regional representative of the Centre For Fortean Zoology.

"Sasquatch, perhaps like no other cryptozoological creature, has caught the imaginations of investigators worldwide. There is no mystery about this; the legendary Bigfoot has certain qualities which set it apart from many other "monsters". It is anthropomorphic, for starters; and anything that looks human, even if only vaguely, will engender feelings of kinship. When we look at Sasquatch, we are looking in part at ourselves.

Another quality that Sasquatch seems to possess is a personality chillingly close to our own. Sasquatch can steal, but it can also give. It can fly into a rage, but sometimes display kindness. It can attack without warning, but also show fear. Sasquatch, whatever it may be, surely possesses a place on the taxonomical tree uncomfortably close to the one that we inhabit. Sasquatch is our cousin.

And yet, for all the similarities, the Hairy Man of the Woods is essentially an enigma. Some witnesses say it possesses glowing red eyes similar to the legendary Black Dogs of British folklore. It can seemingly appear and disappear at will, and has – up to now – eluded everyone who has set out to verify its existence. Sasquatch is like the reclusive neighbour we never see; we know he's there, but we only detect faint, sporadic signs of his existence.

Some years ago I was travelling down the Dorcheat Bayou in Louisiana with a Native American friend when we spotted something hiding behind a tree. I assumed it was a bear, but my friend knew better. Wraith-like, it flitted from one hiding place to another. And yet, I knew that it was watching. Don't ask me how, but I knew. I tried to film the creature, but as it was dusk the results were insubstantial. They certainly wouldn't convince a sceptic or a cynical academic. But that's the strange thing about paranormal investigation - the longer you spend in this wacky profession the more diluted becomes the need to find out the answers to things. There was a time when I wanted to know everything; now I just savour the moment and enjoy the experience. Finding out "the truth" about things takes second place. I know that Sasquatch exists, and I don't really care whether anyone else agrees.

There are certain common denominators with Sasquatch sightings that lend themselves heavily towards the notion that the creature is real. A large number of witnesses report that the creature possesses the most wretched body odour. Further, Sasquatch sightings are also often accompanied by the unmistakeable smell of sulphur. Why? I don't know. That's just the way it is. If we ever capture one we may find out. Sasquatch also has a habit of making "tipis" out of tree branches. Whether the purpose behind this is practical, cultural or spiritual I can't say, but Sasquatch just loves to tie tree branches together in bizarre but recognisable ways. A few years ago, I had the privilege of joining members of the Centre for Fortean Zoology when they tried to track down a Bigfoot-like creature that had been seen by numerous witnesses – not in the USA, but in the heart of rural Northumbria. The extraordinary thing was that this creature, too, made Sasquatch-like "tipis" exactly the same as those fashioned by his North American counterpart. It is small but significant parallels like this that should demonstrate to those of an open mind that something truly extraordinary is roaming around in the wilderness – and not just in the good ol' US of A.

The hot money, it is safe to say, banks on Sasquatch being a hitherto undiscovered primate of some kind. This may well be the case, but we can't be absolutely sure. There are aspects of Sasquatch behavior that bear no similarity whatsoever to that of any other living thing on the planet. Witnesses sometimes say that they experience an intense "mental bonding" with the creature, as if it can not only read their mind but also manipulate their thoughts. Some have even attempted to shoot the beast, only to report that the bullets seem to bounce off with a metallic clanking sound, or that the creature simply disappears in a flash of light. These (and other) peculiarities suggest that Sasquatch may not be a conventional flesh-and-blood creature at all, but something far, far stranger.

Those who deny the existence of Sasquatch often point to these enigmas as proof-positive that witnesses must simply be imagining things. However, I learnt a long time ago "never to say never" in the world of paranormal research. Just because things don't behave the way that we both expect and want them to do does not mean that they don't exist. The problem is not that the existence of such bizarre animals is impossible, but simply that the arrogance of the human species prevents us from coping well with things we don't understand.

I also learnt a long time ago that the dichotomy between one paranormal phenomenon and another is not always as clearly defined as we'd like it to be. Human nature is such that we much prefer to be able to wrap things up in neat parcels. We like to cubby-hole things so that we can grasp their essence better. Unfortunately, the world of Forteana doesn't allow us to do that. Seasoned researchers know that poltergeist phenomena are often accompanied by apparitions or "ghosts", and that – this is true – sightings of Sasquatch often seem to precipitate a sharp rise in UFO sightings. Some have suggested that Sasquatch may not be a creature of our planet at all, but something from a distant niche in the universe brought here by "flying saucers" for reasons beyond our ken.

Personally, I tend towards the notion that Sasquatch is not from another planet, but perhaps from another dimension. If Sasquatch hails from a world parallel to our own, but one in which the laws of physics are radically different, then this may explain why it seems to engage in such bizarre behavior when it visits our own abode. Of course, the question that naturally follows on from this proposition is why, when Sasquatch is here, it isn't forced to obey the physical laws that govern our own plane of existence. One answer may be that Sasquatch isn't really "here" at all; perhaps we are simply allowed, from time-to-time, to catch a glimpse of the beast in its own world. Maybe we are allowed the briefest peek through a portal into another vista that is *like* our own, but different. So many questions, and so few answers.

It seems to me that Sasquatch fulfils a need in us humans. *Homo sapiens* are built in such a way that we always need something to engender a sense of wonder in our souls. We cannot be satisfied with knowing everything, because this effectively kills off our need to strive. When there is nothing left to discover, we will become the most pitiable of creatures. A Biblical prophet once said, "When there is no vision, the people perish". Sasquatch, then, keeps us alive – for it provides us with a reason to keep on searching.

Do I know what Sasquatch is? No. I do not fully understand my liver, heart and kidneys, either, but my lack of understanding does not diminish the necessity for me to possess them. One day – just perhaps – we will reach across the metaphysical divide and touch the Hairy Man of the Woods. Until then, I'll rest content in the knowledge that he's out there somewhere and that the enigma of his existence feeds my spirit. I've a lot to thank him for, really."

Mee-Shee: The Water Giant (2005)

The Quest For The Ogopogo

Lake and sea monsters are the stuff folk lore and legends are made of. Over the years many sightings of these creatures have been reported from all over the world, and it was one of these creatures that the 2005 movie *Mee-Shee: The Water Giant* was based on.

The movie begins with an American oil company losing a drill whilst flying over a Canadian lake. An employee, Sean Cambell is sent to Canada to recover the equipment. Whilst using an underwater submarine to investigate the bottom of the lake he discovers deep giant rivers. The legend is that these rivers are used by the sea monster Mee-Shee. Sean has taken his son Mac along with him on this trip and eventually Mac sees the creature in a cave that leads to these rivers. Meanwhile agents from a rival company sabotage Sean's equipment and search for the drill themselves. Whilst searching for the drill underwater the saboteurs see Mee-Shee and shoot the creature with a harpoon. When Mac finds the injured Mee-Shee in the cave he removes the harpoon and tells Laura, an environmental ranger about the creature. The events that follow lead to conflicts with the saboteurs and the search for the missing lake monster.

The movie cost $40 million to produce and was filmed on Lake Wakapitu, Queenstown, New Zealand in 2002 and in England with a water tank and C.G.I in 2003 and 2004. *Mee-Shee: The Water Giant* premiered in London, England on 28th June 2005, to some critical praise although there were mixed evaluations of the special effects.

The 'real-life' legendary creature that Mee-Shee was based on was that of the Canadian lake monster known as Ogopogo. The legend of Ogopogo began with the Aboriginal population in Canada, and while the movie was in production complaints from one Aboriginal chief caused the film and its title character to be renamed. According to the director of 'Mee-Shee', Barry

Authors, most of the Aboriginal leaders supported the use of the name Ogopogo for the movie and the character. The one man who vehemently opposed the use of the name was a Penticton chief named Stewart Phillip. He did not want the names 'Ogopogo' and 'Okanagan' used because:

> *"It's an international concern among indigenous people about the exploration of spiritual entities and beings and what not for commercial purposes. This is not an isolated incident."*

The Maori people owned the land on which the movie was shot and they supported the views of Phillip. As a consequence, Barry Authors and the production company relented and used the name Mee-Shee for the project.

Who is the creature whose name had caused so much controversy and so many problems to the makers of the film?

The existence of a belief in Ogopogo in the local area of Lake Okanagan, British Columbia, Canada pre-dates western settlement in the area. Petroglyphs found near Powers Creek depicting a serpent-like creature may represent the earliest evidence of the existence of the legend of the beast. Lake Okanagan is 130 miles long and 800 feet deep and somewhere within its depths a creature described as being between 6-20 meters in length, tan to black in colour and having a 'snake-like' body is said to dwell. Native folklore places the lair of the monster at a cave beneath the lake under Squally Point near Rattlesnake Island. Tribes in Okanagan carried animals with them that could be sacrificed in the event of them sighting the creature. This was because they believed that when a storm came the monster would rise from the water to claim a life. The tribes people named the creature 'N'ha-a-itk' which means Lake Demon. Belief in N'ha-a-itk became a part of the Aboriginal's culture in Okanagan and it is documented in the history of Okanagan Mission that the local populace were unwilling to fish near Squally Point. Although the tribes people had been claiming to see N'ha-a-itk long before this, the first recorded sighting of the monster was made by Mrs Susan Allison in 1872. Mrs Allison was a pioneer and author from British Columbia.

By 1926 a non-Aboriginal board of trade renamed the creature Ogopogo. The Name came from a comical song of the time:

'I'm looking for the Ogopogo,
His mother was a mutton (or sometimes earwig),
His father was a whale (or sometimes snail),
I'm going to put a bit of salt on his tail.'

In the same year, 1926, the first clear sighting witnessed by a large number of people occurred. Thirty cars along an Okanagan Mission Beach all had occupants who claimed to have witnessed the same event. They all reported seeing Ogopogo. Bobby Carter, editor of the Vancouver Sun at the time wrote:

'Too many reputable people have seen (the monster) to ignore the seriousness of actual facts.'

Another 'mass sighting' would happen 21 years later, only this time it would be on the water. In 1947 a number of boaters on Lake Okanagan all reported seeing Ogopogo at the same time. Mr Kray, a witness, described what he had seen at the time:

"(It had) A long sinuous body, 30 feet in length, consisting of about five undulations. Apparently separated from each other by about a two feet space, in which part of the undulations would have been underwater. There appeared to be a forked tail of which only one half came above the water. From time to time the whole thing submerged and came up again."

Sightings continued into the 1950's and in 1959 another interesting report was made by witnesses on the lake. Two couples, the Millers and the Martens, saw what they described as a 'tremendous creature' whilst in their motor boat on Lake Okanagan. The couples described the animal as having a snake-like head and a blunt nose. The creature was swimming 250 feet behind their boat for over three minutes before it submerged and they lost sight of it.

Arguably the most famous sighting of the Ogopogo was to take place nine years later. In 1968 Art Folden and his wife were returning home from a trip. As their car neared the Peach Mount area of Okanagan, Art spotted something in the lake. Art said to his wife:

"Look, there's Ogopogo."

Art's wife mocked him, but undeterred he stopped the car, got out and began filming the creature. The footage Art captured was the most compelling evidence of Ogopogo caught on camera at the time and became known as 'The Folden Footage'. Folden filmed the creature from a hill above the shore. The film shows a large, dark, animate object propelling itself through shallow water. The object is seen surfacing and submerging at various speeds and various intervals. An interesting aspect of the footage is that the object is seen 'taking off' at very high speeds producing a mass of waves as it does. The film was analysed and enhanced and showed a solid 'reptilian' 3D object.

Following the Folden sighting the volume of eyewitness reports increased in the 1970's. This began with Ed Fletcher of North Vancouver capturing what he claimed was a photograph of Ogopogo in 1976. Around the same time Paul Pugliese had an encounter with the creature too:

"I had a taxi and I took a passenger to the hospital. I was coming down Abbots Street when I looked at the lake. I was surprised. I seen this thing come out of the water, it was like a horses head with kind of horns on it. Well he was huge, like a big serpent. Then a fella comes up behind me and he says, 'What you looking at?' I said, 'I seen Ogopogo over there'. He says, 'Where? Where?', 'Over there', I said. I had the door of the car open and I stepped out just a little bit. The creature slipped back into the water and the fella said, 'Gee look at the big waves there', and all we could see were these big waves going to the boat place. Then they disappeared. I got back into the car and I pulled into Willow End. I went in where all the people were having breakfast and I told them, 'I just seen Ogopogo', and they said, 'What the heck, have you been drinking?'"

In October of 1978 Bill Steciuk was crossing the bridge from the west side of the Okanagan Lake towards Kelowna. Bill caught sight of a movement in the lake and stopped his car, going to the rail of the bridge for a closer look. All the traffic behind him stopped and he was joined by approximately 20 other people.

All the witnesses reported seeing what appeared to be a head with three black humps protruding out of the water behind it. The creature was seen to swim for about a minute until it submerged beneath the water and disappeared.

Toward the end of the 1970's another witness came forward who claimed to have seen Ogopogo. The woman, who wished to remain anonymous, gave a detailed account of her experience:

"We were up on the beach having a picnic and my daughter was on the swings when I saw this creature underneath the wharf. When I turned around and saw it I realised it was the legendary Ogopogo, I just freaked out. I ran, I grabbed the baby and ran down to the beach and I yelled over and over it's him. It was fishing or whatever it was doing. It was there for quite some time then it straightened out and it went along the poles near the beach. As it travelled along just the three humps were showing. They were from one end of the poles in the water to the other, in the space the three humps were. It travelled along the beach 'til about where the beach goes around the corner and then it turned and went straight across the lake. Now I would hesitate to go on the lake 'cos I think it's such a huge thing that it could turn a boat over and not being a swimmer, I would drown so I don't. I haven't been on the lake since."

As a new decade rolled in there were eight sightings of Ogopogo alone in 1980. One of which was reported by the Rieger family who were out on their boat on the Okanagan Lake. Frank Reiger recounted:

"It was a beautiful day, the water was as calm as glass and I just took a look across and I could see a big wave coming. At that time I just didn't take much notice of it. It just kept coming closer and I just thought to myself why would there be a wave coming if there's no wind or anything? So I called my son, I said, 'Come on back here and take a look and see if you think what the hell's coming down the lake here'. So he took a look at it and he said, 'Gee I don't know'. He had his son, my grandson, along with him and he said, 'Hey grandpa, that's the Ogopogo'. It would have run right into us but we had to veer the boat off alongside and then we followed it alongside for about 15 to 20 minutes. I'd say the monster was possibly 14 to 16 feet long which was sticking above the water about 3 feet. It had quite a hump on the shoulders and a hump on the tail. I'd say the tail was approximately 30,

40, 50 feet. You couldn't see the end of it but it did have a long tail. It had four legs and I'd say the monster weighed maybe 30 tonnes."

Frank's son, Jim Reiger added:

"His head was moving from side to side, it seemed like he was looking for fish or feeding or something like that. He was stirring up a tremendous amount of water."

Frank Rieger concluded:

"If I hadn't have seen it I would never have believed it, and actually I don't care if anybody believes me or not. I saw this thing, I know it's here."

Author Arlene Gaal documented literally hundreds of Ogopogo sightings and in 1981 she took her third photograph of the monster in four years. In the same year a member of the Wachlin family also captured Ogopogo on camera:

"It was right around Regatta time, July 24th, 1981 around 1pm. We were in a rented ski boat and were running on the west side of the lake in the vicinity of Peachland, just a bit northwest of the tip of Rattlesnake Island. A water-skier had just passed us going fast in the opposite direction to us when suddenly a creature surfaced directly in front of us facing a north-easterly direction. We saw no head, just a body, my thoughts being that the head might be laying flat just below the surface. At first I thought it was the wake of the other boat, but then I realised that the boat's wake was going in the other direction. As we came closer, the creature broke into a fast-paced undulating motion. I pointed our boat directly at it but as we neared it, the creature dove, causing a large frothy whirlpool. I turned the boat around and could see the creature two or three feet below in the water. It moved at great speed at least half way across the lake before it dove deeper and out of sight. The creature was at least 50 feet long and seemed to be either very dark green or black."

Three years later, 1984, Ogopogo was once again captured on camera as a member of the Svensson family claimed to have taken a photo of the creature in the lake.

As the 1990's approached two more sightings took place in 1989. The first was made by Ernie Giroux and his wife. They claimed to have seen an animal with a round head that looked 'like a football'. Hunting guide Ernie told the press:

> *"It was about 15 feet long and swam real gracefully and fast."*

The Giroux's also reported that at one point the creature's neck and body came out of the water. The second sighting of Ogopogo in 1989 was made by a used car salesman, Ken Chaplin. Unlike the Giroux's, Chaplin managed to capture the creature on film. Chaplin had seen Ogopogo before and was revisiting the location where he had previously seen the monster. As he chatted to his father Clem, who had accompanied him on the trip, a snake-like animal suddenly emerged in the lake. The Chaplins observed as the animal turned and flicked its tail, creating a splash in the water. Fortunately Ken Chaplin managed to capture the event on camera. Some people claimed that what the Chaplins had seen was simply a beaver as the tail splashing is a common characteristic of the animal. Ken Chaplin refuted this claim as beavers are approximately 4 feet long and Chaplin alleged the animal he saw was 15 feet long. On a visit to the location a few weeks later Chaplin, accompanied by his father and his daughter, saw the creature again and managed to capture more footage of the monster.

As the new millennium began a spate of sightings occurred within the space of a year.

In 2000 a businessman and his wife were boating off Rattlesnake Island near Peachland. The couple watched what they claimed was the head and neck of a large creature swimming through the water for several minutes. One of the strangest reports happened in the same year. It was reported that at around midnight, on a Monday, six adults, four of whom were security guards, saw a strange looking creature on Bernard Avenue. According to the witnesses the animal was 12 feet long and had four flippers (two at each end). The eyewitnesses claimed that it 'thrust forward like a caterpillar'.

Also in 2000 a minister and his wife hiking in Kalamoir Park on the west side of Okanagan Lake spotted a creature swimming on the surface of the lake. The couple managed to capture a photograph of what they believed was Ogopogo.

The same year some tourists from Prince George, British Columbia were taking a stroll in Bertram Creek. They suddenly noticed a disturbance approximately 300 feet out in Lake Okanagan. What looked like a log was moving parallel to the shore against the waves. The witnesses estimated the object to be 40 feet long and they observed it for around 45 seconds before it disappeared.

The most compelling encounter with Ogopogo also occurred in 2000. Daryl Ellis, a marathon swimmer, reported being accompanied by two creatures during a swim on Lake Okanagan. As he passed Rattlesnake Island Ellis was joined by the two animals that followed him for a while before disappearing. Ellis described one of the beasts as being 20 to 30 feet long and the other as being smaller. As he neared the Okanagan Lake floating bridge in Kelowna a creature came within 9 meters of Ellis. He claimed this creature had a large eye the size of a grapefruit.

The year 2000 saw the first expedition to establish what people were seeing on and around the Okanagan Lake. Bill Steciuk had himself seen the Ogopogo back in 1978 and in 1999 he began to assemble a team of researchers for his expedition. The team searched Lake Okanagan in august 2000, but found no sign of the creature. A second expedition was mounted in 2001 and unfortunately once again no concrete proof of the existence of the Lake monster was found.

On 19th July 2001 Dan Basaraba captured a photo of something unusual on the lake. Incredibly on 19th July 2002, exactly a year later, Basaraba made another sighting which he also managed to capture on camera.

Bill Stecuik and his team planned a third expedition for August 2003 but due to the Okanagan Mountain Park fires in that year, they had to postpone their quest for the time being.

There are several theories as to what the Ogopogo is, if indeed the creature does exist at all. These can be put into three categories.

Lake Monster Theory

Lake and sea monsters are said to be descendants of long thought to be extinct or yet to be discovered species. With the Okanagan Lake being 10 miles long and 800 feet deep there would be plenty of room for such an animal to exist and also remain elusive in. Sightings suggest that Ogopogo is a 'many humped' variety of lake monster and, as suggested by British Zoologist Dr Karl Shuker, could be a primitive serpentine whale such as Basilosaurus. With sightings occurring over a span of more than 150 years, and with more than one monster being seen at one time on at least one occasion, it would seem that there may in fact be more than one Ogopogo.

Mistaken Identity Theory

It has been suggested that many of the sightings of Ogopogo can be dismissed as mistaken identity. Amongst the causes of this are such things as logs, otters and even a suggestion that the lake monster may even be nothing more than a lake sturgeon.

Myth, Legend and Hoax

With much of its history based in myth and legend some people suggest that this is indeed all there is to the 'Ogopogo' story. With little to no 'hard-evidence' of the creature's existence the stories that have been passed down from generation to generation form most of the case history of the monster. These stories are commonly known in the Lake Okanagan area and this knowledge, coupled with an overactive imagination may hold the key to some of the purported 'sightings' of Ogopogo.

What The Experts Say
Mee-Shee: The Water Giant (2005)

Neil Arnold – Cryptozoologist, Paranormal Researcher and Author. Neil is the author of *Monster! The A-Z Of Zooform Phenomena* (CFZ Press 2007), the world's first ever reference guide to the monsters that cryptozoology fails to investigate, *Mystery Animals of the British Isles: Kent* (CFZ Press 2009) and has two more books due for release in 2010. Neil also runs Kent Big Cat Research in the UK. He contributes articles for Animals & Men magazine and has appeared in the press, on radio and television worldwide.

"With the only physical evidence for Ogopogo being limited to unclear photographs and film debate will rage on as to what the creature is.

For those witnesses who have testified to seeing Ogopogo, no more proof is needed. For those sceptics who doubt the witnesses and evidence presented so far it seems no amount of eyewitnesses or photographs will ever be enough. Like many of the crypto zoological mysteries of the world, it would seem that the only way to prove the Ogopogo's existence beyond a shadow of a doubt will be to capture the beast. Until then the real answer to the mystery may well remain hidden deep beneath the waters of the Okanagan Lake.

I have often considered myself an expert on cryptozoological-related movies. Since childhood I have collected literally thousands of commercials, documentaries, TV shows, cartoons and movies, from blockbusters to obscure b-movies, which have had connections to sea monsters, Bigfoot, lake creatures, extinct species, rediscovered beasts etc, so to be asked to write something on *Mee-Shee: The Water Giant* and relations to the famous Okanagan serpent named Ogopogo is an honour. However, I would like to put a different angle on this section, as Jason has already given you, dear reader, a slant on the movie and also a history of the alleged real beast.

For me, cryptozoology has been given a hard time in reference to movie adaptations. Facts are usually cast aside in favour of fantasy, when usually the facts are far stranger than the fiction created, some cases are literally ruined by glossy effects and big name actors, whilst more obscure versions make no money at all, rely on trashy production and are swept under the carpet in no time. Of all the cryptids given screen coverage, lake and sea monsters are probably the most popular, goodness knows how many dire horror films have revolved around a rampant Loch Ness monster. As if the continued repetition of inaccurate documentaries and news features is not enough to send cryptozoologists round the twist, we have this appalling films which depict such water leviathans in only two restrictive ways. As mentioned, most serpents and lake monsters are portrayed as demonic, or simply very angry creatures, usually disturbed in their murky lair, as is the case with *Mee Shee: The Water Giant*, and this unfortunate plot line is in fact one of the most common when directors decide to use a water monster as their chosen subject. Of course, the likes of Nessie, and now the second most famous lake beastie, Ogopogo have become symbolic of the crypto-field with the Yeti and Bigfoot by their side. Programs such as *The X Files* have brought such shaky legends to life in the modern day, but of course, I recall them as far hazier and scarier legends in the '70s when such mysteries were really taking off and hitting the bookshelves.

Crypto-related movies are actually quite common. Lists I have compiled are in the thousands now. The first real lake monster movie was *The Secret Of The Loch* filmed in 1934, and little has changed since that title regarding plot. In the modern era, to make such movies appeal to a wider audience director's cannot resist the temptation of turning such myths into child-related fantasies, where the creatures we so often fear in the unknown depths, become the symbol of true friendship as man continues to destroy the land and pollute the waters around him. There is, in many mind the possibility that large, undiscovered beasts still lurk in the inky waters across the world, and of course, even in the smallest ponds, rivers and streams. Everyone loves a mystery, and not every mystery is confined to the darkest corners. The only way to being in the money however, is to feature a loving monster on the end of the hook, and in the case of *Mee Shee* and so many others this theme has never altered in the slightest. Whilst such films continue to pull in the cash, is it really what we want from directors ? Of course, this isn't to say that we want *The Water Giant* to be a marauding, face-ripping, blood-drinking creature, but surely a middle ground can be found, because as I've already said, the friendly monster and killer on the loose have been done to death, why not a factual film ? And this is why, despite collecting thousands of such films, it is a rare commodity to find any movies that find a middle ground, where the audience and creature are treated with equal respect. We either get *Jaws* or *Cloverfield,* two successful movies which have seen things come from the sea but strike fear into our hearts, or we get *The Water Giant* alongside *Magic In The Water, Loch Ness,* or the incredibly bizarre German film *Nessie, Das Verruckteste Monster Der Welt!* And an American spoof called *Amazon Women On The Moon* which connected Nessie with Jack The Ripper!

The disappointing theme of *The Water Giant* originated with movies such as *Beast From 20,000 Fathoms (1953)* concerning an atomic explosion in New York which upsets a resident dinosaur, something echoed in many of the Japanese *Godzilla* films, whilst a friendship with monsters began in the obscure 1955 film *Voyage To History,* which concerns four young boys who find an underground river and a land of prehistoric monsters. In 1957 *The Monster That Challenged The World* saw a sea beast, or should that be, giant sea snail disturbed after an underwater earthquake shakes its dirty domain and another atomic explosion occurs in *Behemoth The Sea Monster(1959)* causing a dinosaur to attack London. Strangely, this theme has never altered, even to the present day, so I can see why *Mee Shee* and others have gone for the more 'watery' façade. However, serious monster hunters amongst us have always searched for that certain riveting film, something akin to when, as a nine-year old boy I watched *The Legend Of Boggy Creek,* without doubt the finest crypto-related movie of all time concerning a hairy humanoid said to haunt the Arkansas river bottoms. Sure, the film had its scary moments when the monster finally got agitated by the intrusion of man, but the way it was filmed has only since been echoed by the sinister majesty of *The Blair Witch Project* and this is the kind of feel that is all too rare in cinema nowadays, and especially when bringing cryptozoology to the big screen.

Us humans have always had a love affair with monsters but only when the beasts are on the rampage and then destroyed at the bloody climax, or they are eating fruit from our children's hands, and this mushy love interest and bond has always come to the fore meaning the true cryptozoological aspects of a movie are all too obscured and never able to reach the audience who may in fact want to explore the mystery after they leave the cinema. In the 1985 movie *Baby – Secret Of The Lost Legend* a population of Brontosaurus are discovered in African swamps, and of course killed until a group of scientists build a friendship with a baby dinosaur. Such bonds were broken in the *Jurassic Park* series but in 1996 Ted Danson starred in the big-budget *Loch Ness* which in reality is merely a British version of *The Water Giant*. As mentioned, a year previous *Magic In The Water* emerged with the same theme, a fantastic lake creature named Orky in British Columbia harassed by journalists, mean businessmen and toxic waste which develops a friendship with youngsters. To be honest, it's sickly stuff yet it remains a constant theme in crypto-related movies, the final nail in the coffin being *The Water Horse: Legend Of The Deep (2007)*, a blockbuster of a movie based on the children's novel by Dick King Smith set in the 1940s in which another agitated but friendly creature, once again in Scotland, is hatched after a boy finds a giant egg whilst the army decide to converge upon the waterway in defence of their land during wartime. Again, it's all very predictable stuff echoed in many previous big-budget renditions and obscure, straight-to-dvd/vhs versions. *Stanley's Dragon* in 1994 was a British TV movie with a similar theme revolving around a mysterious egg and a little boy, in 1988 a sea dwelling monster croc' turns nasty in *Dark Age*, even the *Scooby Doo* gang have, on several occasions upset lake monsters and gill-men. A serpent is befriended in the 1973 children's series *Sigmund & The Sea Monsters*, *Doctor Who* encountered the Loch Ness monster and in 1944's serial *Haunted Harbour* a sea serpent legend is manufactured to keep tourists away…whilst in many other movies such watery forms are created to bring the tourists in.

So, is *Mee Shee: The Water Giant* just another dated monster movie of watery proportions, bereft of originality and idea, and lacking any kind of intelligence to make its mark on a crypto-shy audience ? Of course it is, but what's new ? It seems that the theme of such movies reflects the reality in a sense, because if such serpents and leviathans were to surface as a scientific fact, then I'm sure they would become endangered very quickly, but possibly loved by children. So, like all monsters the world over it's probably best that the middle ground we seek is in fact never found and that's likely to be the case because as such beasts remain elusive to our eyes, so do genuinely interesting crypto-related films."

Sources

Rebel Without a Cause (1955) (Warner Bros) (Movie)

Witchfinder General (1968) (Tigon British Film Productions Ltd) (Movie)

Countess Dracula (1971) (Hammer Film Productions Ltd) (Movie)

The Exorcist (1973) (Warner Bros) (Movie)

The Omen (1976) (20th Century Fox) (Movie)

The Bermuda Triangle (1979) (Movie)

The Amityville Horror (1979) (MGM) (Movie)

The Entity (1981) (20th Century Fox) (Movie)

Poltergeist (1982) (Warner Bros) (Movie)

Poltergeist II: The Other Side (1986) (MGM) (Movie)

Poltergeist III (1988) (MGM) (Movie)

The Haunted (1991) (TV Movie)

Fire In The Sky (1993) (Movie)

Fairy Tale: A True Story (1997) (Movie)

Brotherhood Of The Wolf (2001) (Movie)

The Untold (2002) (Movie)

The Mothman Prophecies (2002) (Movie)

The Exorcism Of Emily Rose (2005) (Sony Pictures) (Movie)

Mee-Shee: The Water Giant (2005) (Screen Media Ventures) (Movie)

An American Haunting (2006) (Movie)

Alien Autopsy (2006) (Warner Bros) (Movie)

The Curse Of King Tut's Tomb (2006) (Movie)

1408 (2007) (Dimension Films) (Movie)

Alexandra Holzer

Barrie John

Bill Bean

Brad Steiger

Darren Ritson

Dr Malcolm Gaskill

James Randi

Jason Karl

Jeff Wamsley

John Zaffis

Lara Wells

Mark Webb

Mike Hallowell

Neil Arnold

Nick Redfern

Philip Mantle

Phil Whyman

Steve Younis

'In Search Of The Mothman' (Documentary)

666: The Omen Revealed – (Documentary)

Fear Of God – (Documentary)

'The Exorcism Of Emily Rose - Genesis Of the Story' (Documentary)

Unexplained Mysteries: The Monster Show (Television)

Unsolved Mysteries: Bigfoot In Oregon (Television)

Unsolved Mysteries: Mummy's Curse (Television)

Arthur C Clarke's Mysterious World – Monsters Of The Lake Episode (Documentary) (ITV, 8pm, 7th October 1980)

Dead Famous – Series 1: James Dean Episode (Living TV 6th July 2004)

Dead Famous – Series 1: Lucille Ball Episode (Living TV 20th July 2004)

Eamonn Investigates: Alien Autopsy (Documentary) (Sky One, 8pm, 4th April 2006)

'Audio Martini' Paranormal Talk Radio Show – Host Rick Wood with guest Rick Moran – July 2007

Murder In Amityville – Hans Holzer (1979) (Book)

Flim-Flam: The Truth About Unicorns, Parapsychology and Other Delusions – James Randi (1994)

The Encyclopaedia Of The World's Greatest Unsolved Mysteries – John And Anne Spencer (1995) (Book)

An Encyclopedia of Claims, Frauds, and Hoaxes of the Occult and Supernatural – James Randi (1997)

Vanished! Mysterious Disappearances – David Clark (1998) (Book)

Cryptozoology A to Z – Loren Coleman & Jerome Clark (2001) (Book)

Alien Autopsy Inquest – Philip Mantle (2007) (Book)

The Skeptical Inquirer 11, Winter 1986-1987

When Ghosts Attack (FATE November 1998) (Article)

Seattle Post Intelligencer - Friday, September 9, 2005

What In God's Name?! - Eric T. Hansen (The Washington Post, 4th September 2005) (Article)

The Curse Of Superman - Polly Dunbar (Daily Express, 13th July 2006) (Article)

Curse! What Curse? - Nadine Ling (Daily Star, 13th July 2006) (Article)

Max Headroom Creator Claims He Made Roswell Alien Autopsy Film – Marc Horne (The Sunday Times, April 16th 2006)

Alien Autopsy – Game Over – Philip Mantle (Article)

http://www.bbc.co.uk

http://www.bellwitch.org

http://www.bermuda-triangle.org
http://www.channel4.com
http://www.crimemagazine.com
http://www.ghosts.org
http://www.history.navy.mil
http://www.livescience.com
http://www.jamesdean.com
http://www.northernlightsparanormalsociety.com
http://www.ogopogoquest.com
http://www.paranormal.about.com
http://www.paranormaldatabase.com
http://www.randi.org
http://www.salmineo.com
http://www.skepdic.com
http://www.theexorcist.com
http://www.unmuseum.com
http://www.uk.imdb.com
http://www.wikipedia.org

About The Author

Writer and broadcaster Jason Day was born and raised in Scunthorpe, England where he lived for nearly thirty years until moving to Essex. Jason was the longest serving feature writer for 'Paranormal' magazine (March 2006 – January 2008), the largest monthly paranormal publication of its kind in the UK at the time, writing over twenty articles during that period. He has also been a regular contributor to paranormal publications such as 'FATE' magazine in the USA (the longest running paranormal magazine in the world) and 'Ghost Voices' magazine in the UK. He is also the author of the paranormal books 'Haunted Scunthorpe' (The History Press, September 2010) and Paranormal Essex (The History Press, 2011 release). Jason also works with others in the written media, including some very prominent names in the paranormal community.

His interest in the paranormal was sparked by his love of film and passion for reading. Jason grew up on a staple diet of 'Hammer Horror' movies and the written works of Peter Underwood, Dr Hans Holzer and Harry Price. With the advent of television shows such as 'Arthur C Clarke's Mysterious World' and 'Strange But True' Jason was hooked. He decided to begin researching and investigating cases of the paranormal for himself and the fuse was lit.

Jason's experience working in the paranormal field has been varied, ranging from being a regular co-host on the 'Friday Night Paranormal Show' on Pulse Talk Radio to being the featured article writer for the paranormal reference website ghostdatabase.co.uk. Jason is also the chief consultant for the Famously Haunted Awards organisation on MySpace. He has been a guest on several radio shows, appeared at various paranormal events and given lectures about his work within the paranormal field and the subject of the paranormal in general.

Jason currently hosts 'The White Noise Paranormal Radio Show' on Blog Talk Radio and has interviewed such figures in the paranormal community as James Randi, Dr Ciaran O'Keeffe, Derek Acorah, Lorraine Warren, Nick Pope, Stanton Friedman, Richard Wiseman, Ian Lawman, Jason Karl Katrina Weidman and Richard Felix. Now in it's Third Series and well on it's way to a hundred episodes, The show can be found live online every Friday night from 10pm-Midnight on the Blog Talk Radio website at http://www.blogtalkradio.com/famously-haunted or alternatively at the Official White Noise Radio Show Website (http://www.whitenoiseparanormalradio.co.uk). Jason and the show recently won two awards at the International Paranormal Acknowledgment Awards 2009. Jason was named Best International Paranormal Radio Show Host and The White Noise Paranormal Radio Show was voted Best International Paranormal Radio Program.

One of three founding members of a small not for profit based in Essex, paranormal investigation team by the name of S.P.I.R.I.T (Society for Paranormal Investigation, Research, Information & Truth - established March 2006), Jason's commitment to researching, investigating and the search to explain the paranormal continues. In early 2010 Jason became managing director of Phantom Encounters Ltd, an events company offering a variety of paranormal experiences to the public ranging from ghost hunts to UFO sky watches and monster hunts. You can find out more about Phantom Encounters events at www.phantomencounters.co.uk and more about Jason himself at his Official website (http://jasonday.webs.com).

PHANTOM ENCOUNTERS

OVERNIGHT GHOST HUNTING EVENTS
PARANORMAL INVESTIGATIVE EXPERIENCES™
UFO 'SKYWATCH' EVENTS
MONSTER HUNTS

To book an event, or for more information - please see our website:

WWW.PHANTOMENCOUNTERS.CO.UK

Or call 07795 494 807 or 01223911675

WHITE NOISE
PARANORMAL RADIO

FRIDAY NIGHT 10PM

HTTP://WHITENOISERADIO.WEBS.COM